Alice's Boys

Alice's Boys

K. W. Newens

Alice's Boys
First Edition
DeerVale Publishing™ May, 2021

Author contact information at www.DeerValePublishing.com

ISBN 978-1-7365689-0-3
eBook ISBN 978-1-7365689-1-0

Cover by Images In Ink
Graphic Credits: Jody Courtney; Ashley Weaver;
Lisa Yesh & Ren Barbaree; Gina & Jim at
The Owl and the Crow Shop

Dedication

My father, Roy Newens, was a veteran of the United States Navy, serving through both World War Two and the Korean War. He was aboard USS *Tennessee* when Pearl Harbor was attacked. This book is dedicated to his memory.

To all the men who served on the ships and other duty stations mentioned and who actually held the positions my characters hold in the book, I give you my apologies for removing you from the storyline. It is in no way intended to slight your service to the armed forces or the United States. Your service and sacrifice, from the humblest Apprentice Seaman to Presidents Roosevelt and Truman, saved our country for me to grow up in. As an American, I will be forever in your debt.

Prologue

We blaze our trail through life, as individuals and families, trying to be in charge, but we all collide with events that will only later be called "history." The Stevens, Roberts, and Jenkins families learned this well, and sometimes painfully. History overtakes us while we are not watching, and not nearly ready. It sometimes must also be hidden, another fact these families knew all too well.

A key piece of their history was one ship, a naval marvel of its time hidden from the world, on which Alice Jenkins' two sons would one day find themselves.

Because of the "Five-Power Treaty" adopted in 1922, by which the major nations that had won World War One sought to limit the size and power of battleships, battle cruisers, and aircraft carriers, construction of the new *South Dakota*-class battleships begun by the U.S. in 1920 was abruptly halted. The unfinished hulls were all scrapped, and their armor used to modernize older ships.

Or so the official history read.

One vessel, intended to be the lead ship in her class and the most heavily armed and armored ship in the world, survived. As her five sisters were scrapped, she was spared, and secretly redesignated.

The crew nicknamed her "Soda," and she would never be listed in *Jane's Fighting Ships*. Instead of sailing as the pride of the fleet, she became the navy's clandestine, floating proving ground for technological improvements on American warships of her time, and long into the future.

Every major improvement, from gunnery and radar down to baking ovens and toilets, was first tested on her.

Listed in a classified file as "BX-1," Battleship, Experimental, Number One, she bore no hull number and was neither christened nor commissioned. For the most part, her career on the seas was unremarkable. The exception was seven days in 1944, and involved Alice Jenkins' two boys, whose story was remarkable indeed.

But like the ship, their story was written into the files of history with invisible ink, and remains unknown to millions.

PART ONE

Poverty To Plenty

One

April 17, 1897
Sunnyside, New Mexico Territory

The sun was nearly up, turning the clouds on the eastern horizon a brilliant orange and pink. The air was crisp, reminding those who lived on the plains that even though the day promised to be pleasant, a snowstorm the next day was still possible. A cow in the pasture nearest the barn at the Nelson Ranch watched her new calf take his first wobbly steps as a meadowlark trilled from a fence post and a rooster in the barnyard crowed his announcement of the new day.

Alice Jane Roberts lay in bed, propped up with pillows, gazing at her newborn son. She was as fit as any athlete and stronger than some men from working on the ranch, but after twenty hours of labor was barely able to hold the nine pounds of new life. The baby slept, also exhausted from the ordeal of entering the world. Her husband Delbert had ridden his horse eight miles like a madman through the darkness to summon the doctor, leaving her with Hannah, the wife of their employer James Nelson, and Maria Salas, a servant girl no older than Alice, to serve as midwives. The doctor arrived at ten o'clock, in her twelfth hour of labor, and then fought through the rest of the night to save her and the child. He took no credit, saying it was simply a miracle from God that the two survived. Knowing the pay of a cowhand on a small ranch, he also asked no fee of Delbert. The rancher's wife discretely gave him two twenty-dollar coins, almost a month's pay for the cowboy, as he sat at the table drinking a cup of coffee before heading back to town. He smiled in silent thanks. Finishing his coffee, he rose and put on his coat to face the early morning chill. Delbert shook the doctor's hand.

"Thank you, sir. I watered and fed your horse around four-thirty. It got too loud in here for me to stay," he said with a sheepish smile. "He should be fine to get back to town."

"That was very kind of you, son," the doctor replied as he patted the young man's shoulder. "Congratulations. He looks like a fine boy."

The doctor closed the door, on his way to another day at the office. As he turned onto the road back into town, he noticed that the morning star seemed much brighter than usual, and very high in the sky. His up-all-night fatigue made him lose interest quickly. He barely noticed as the star brightened more, then shot off to the east at an impossible speed. *That's what tired eyes will get you,* he convinced himself.

"Have you decided on a name?" Mrs. Nelson asked Delbert.

"Well, ma'am, we figured as kind as you and Mr. Nelson have been to us, we'd name the baby after one of you. So, since he's a boy, I reckon he's going to be James," Delbert said quietly.

"James Delbert," Alice whispered from the bed.

"Mrs. Nelson, is that alright with you?"

"Yes, Delbert," she smiled as a tear streamed down her worry-creased cheek, "that is most certainly alright."

The depression resulting from the stock market crash the previous spring had been hard on the Nelson Ranch. In the autumn of 1896, James Nelson delivered two hundred fifty steers and one hundred cows with their spring calves to the Livestock Exchange in Las Vegas, the closest railhead in New Mexico, for sale. The proceeds from the sale of the cattle plus a portion of the ranch land allowed Nelson to stay in business. When Nelson and his four hired hands returned home from the sale, he informed two of the cowboys, Oliver Sinclair and Jessie Martinez, that they were no longer needed and that they were to collect their things and move on. Nelson gave each of them an extra fifty dollars in addition to their normal pay.

Delbert and Alice were allowed to stay, together working for a little more than what one top hand would make. Martinez took exception to the situation and declared he and Sinclair should stay instead of Delbert. Words led to fisticuffs, and when Martinez produced a knife, Mr. Nelson shot him. Martinez died two days later.

The sheriff ruled the shooting justified and Sinclair went on his way, but the incident ignited a hatred for Nelson in Oliver Sinclair that would never wane. He really liked Jessie and felt cheated by Delbert and Alice working cheaper as a couple. He silently vowed revenge someday.

Over the next three years the Nelsons, with Delbert and Alice by their side, fought seven days a week for the survival of the ranch. They teamed with a neighboring ranch to gather the herds, brand the cattle, and trail them to market. Maria was left alone for days at a time to care for baby James, who was already being called JD so as not to confuse him with the boss. They barely noticed when the United States declared war on Spain in 1898. "Remember the Maine" didn't resonate deeply with people trying to save their livelihoods. There was far more concern for home and hearth than for a foreign war.

On a particularly hot July day in 1899, Alice looked at

Delbert from her horse as they rode home. Both of their faces were crusted in dust from moving cattle to new pasture. Her dark brown hair, braided in pigtails on each side, looked gray where the dust had clung and made her attractive face look years older. Delbert's ruddy complexion appeared ashen, despite his good health. Only the tracks where the sweat had run down their faces showed somewhat clean skin.

"Do you think we'll ever get more help on this place?" she asked with a hint of desperation in her voice.

"I don't know Alice. Maybe someday," Delbert answered wistfully.

Delbert proved to be not only hard working and loyal to the Nelsons but quick to learn every aspect of running the ranch. He and Alice together were as capable as any two men, a fact not lost on Mr. Nelson. In time he was able to reward them financially, paying both of them forty-five dollars a month, top hand wages.

Oliver Sinclair had found work in Sunnyside at the general store and rented a small, musty room above the local stable. He squirreled away every extra dime until he had enough money to buy two cows and lease a small pasture along the Pecos River east of town. He did so for only one reason. He wanted a registered brand. He petitioned the Livestock Board and was granted a brand consisting of the letters O and N with a long line, or bar, running under the letters. He branded his cows the day the Board's letter arrived, but in doing so he first applied the letter J, then branded over it with the narrow "0" iron he'd had made, to see if the J would blend in. It did, much to Sinclair's approval. James Nelson's brand was the JN. Sinclair planned to steal calves and yearlings from Nelson, alter their brands, and claim them as his own.

It wasn't hard to find accomplices. Every ranch in the

area had been forced to cut back so there was a fair-sized pool of men needing money. Sinclair assembled a band of four, all good on a horse and with a rope. No one seemed to miss a single calf or derelict cowboy. Later, he became braver and the group began taking a few calves and yearlings from other ranches as well, but Sinclair still took particular pleasure in branding over the J on James Nelson's cattle.

The plan worked well for more than two years. Sinclair was slowly accumulating a nest egg hidden in his room. He only had to pay his accomplices enough to keep them in whisky for a few days. He had even added two more cows to his herd to nurse the calves he stole, along with a handful he bought legally to have some semblance of legitimacy. The brush in his pasture offered concealment from prying eyes, so an accurate count of his herd by an outsider was impossible.

By the start of 1900, the financial condition of the Nelson Ranch had recovered to the point that Mr. Nelson purchased more cows and began looking for more help. Late one cold February morning, Oliver Sinclair looked up from the shelf he was dusting to see James Nelson outside the general store. Sinclair stood frozen, fearing he'd been found out. He had waited on Maria and Mrs. Nelson many times, but hadn't seen Mr. Nelson since he left the ranch. Nelson brushed the snowflakes off his shoulders and wiped his feet as he removed his gloves, then came inside.

"Hello, Oliver," Nelson smiled as he approached the counter and extended his hand. "My wife told me you were working here. I was wondering if you'd consider coming back to the ranch. Things are looking up again and I'd like to see you back."

"I might, Mr. Nelson. What are you thinkin'?" Sinclair's hatred for Nelson helped mask his relief at not being accused of rustling cattle. A plan began to form in his mind as he forced himself to shake Nelson's hand.

"Thirty-five dollars a month, every other Sunday off."

"That kid and his woman still with you?"

"Yes, Delbert and Alice are still with me."

"What're you payin' *them*?" The plan was becoming clearer to Sinclair.

"That's my business, Oliver. Are you interested, or should I look for somebody else?"

"Well, it's better pay than this, but damn sure harder work." *Cheap bastard*, he thought. Sinclair knew he was worth all of forty dollars a month. The plan had come together in Sinclair's mind. He forced a grin.

"Guess punchin' cows is in my blood, Mr. Nelson. When do you want me?"

"As soon as possible," Nelson smiled back, "I have some yearling steers to brand and take to town in April."

"Goin' to Las Vegas?"

"That's right. We'll join up with a drive from the OY and the Flatiron at Santa Rosa."

"I can be there by noon, boss."

"Thank you, Oliver. I'll see you tomorrow."

Sinclair waited until Nelson got on his buckboard and headed down the street before taking off the apron he was wearing. He walked into the store office, tossed the apron to the owner, and quit on the spot. He next went and signed ownership of his cows over to the pasture owner to cover the past due pasture bill. He also paid his stable board and rent, and then went to the saloon on the edge of town where he knew he would find at least one of the people he needed to see.

One of his men was there and sober enough to understand what he was being told. As the man rode off in the light snow to find the others, Sinclair returned to the stable. He spent the rest of the day in his room, deep in thought, fleshing out his plan.

That night, huddled around a bottle at a corner table of the saloon, he shared his plan with his four henchmen. The next morning, he gathered his belongings, saddled his horse, and quietly rode out of town.

Over the next six weeks, he saw two members of his gang get hired for the upcoming drive. Sinclair made himself the valuable ranch hand he could be, working with Mr. Nelson, Delbert and Alice every day gathering, sorting, and branding steers to make a uniform group to take to market. Their work was interrupted once by a snow storm in March, forcing them to work harder on the pleasant days, but by the end of the month they were ready to move the cattle.

Two

April 6, 1900
Sunnyside, New Mexico Territory

James Nelson, Delbert Roberts, and Oliver Sinclair, along with Billy Fergeson, a cowboy borrowed from a neighboring ranch, set out with their ninety freshly gathered and branded yearling steers to join the larger drive of six hundred head bound for the Livestock Exchange in Las Vegas, some one hundred miles away. After meeting the drive, Nelson planned on sending Delbert and Billy back home while he and Sinclair continued on to Las Vegas.

Sinclair smiled and waved at Mrs. Nelson and Alice Roberts as they rode off. He regretted that Alice wasn't coming with them. He would have loved to orphan that miserable little kid of theirs. He took comfort, though, in knowing that Alice would have to spend her life wondering where he was and grieving for her stupid, dead husband.

The next night, the two accomplices not hired for the drive slipped into the big herd while their colleagues rode night watch and the four cut out about fifty steers, heading west to a prearranged rendezvous point with the Nelson cattle and Sinclair. In the morning, the two Sinclair men reported the strayed cattle and volunteered to make amends by tracking them down and bringing them back to the drive. After breakfast, they rode off in pursuit of the "strays." The ruse was necessary as all five members of

Sinclair's gang would be needed to re-brand the Nelson cattle before joining the drive.

Just before dawn of their third day on the trail, James Nelson awoke to a sound in the sagebrush. The moon had set and the eastern horizon was barely visible. The stars provided just enough light to allow the shadows to blend into each other. He assumed a horse had come loose from the picket line they had strung up when they made camp the previous afternoon, but the horses were well broken and this one would not stray from the others. Sinclair was riding night watch and would be coming in soon anyway. He could tie the horse up. Delbert and Billy were asleep a few feet away, Delbert having been relieved by Sinclair at midnight.

Nelson rolled onto his side and hoped for a few more minutes sleep before the light required him to start his day. He heard the sound again, closer this time, and sat up to look around.

The brass plate of the rifle butt struck Nelson squarely in the back of his head, fracturing his skull. An involuntary grunt escaped his mouth as he collapsed, startling Delbert awake. As he flailed against his bedroll to get up, Delbert felt the weight of a man land on his legs. An arm wrapped around his neck from behind as a knife thrust repeatedly into his chest and belly. Next to him, he could hear Billy's ragged breathing as he struggled with two other men. The grip around Delbert's neck never slackened and his last sight as his vision faded was a shadowy figure kneeling next to Mr. Nelson, cutting his throat.

Oliver Sinclair wiped the bloody knife on James Nelson's bedroll as he stood and looked at the four men that joined him during the night.

"Alright, boys," he said as he put the knife in its sheath, "let's get to work."

Three

April 9, 1900

It was a grueling day roping all the Nelson steers and altering the JN brand on the Nelson cattle to Sinclair's <u>ON</u>. By late afternoon, the five men were tired and filthy but finished. There was neither time nor desire to tend to the bodies of their victims, save for dragging the dead into the brush away from the fire before they turned in for the night.

At daybreak, they set out with the stolen cattle and the fifty or so head that had "strayed" from the main drive. They trailed the cattle north, hoping to catch the main herd south of Santa Rosa just after dark. They pushed the cattle harder than normal. The steers would lose some weight, but since every pound was free it didn't matter to Sinclair. The two men not hired for the drive split off, taking the extra horses with them so as not to arouse suspicion prior to meeting the drive. They agreed to meet south of Las Vegas to divide their shares of the pay, then go their own ways.

The plan went off without a hitch and they entered the camp after mixing their cattle into the herd. Sinclair and the two men he planted on the drive approached the trail boss.

Leroy McDonald had spent more than forty years trailing cattle in Texas and New Mexico, working for some of the most legendary ranches in the west, starting at age ten helping the cook on a chuck wagon. He advanced through the ranks of the cowboys, trailing herds of two thousand steers up the Chisholm and Goodnight–Loving trails. He was thankful that the railheads had moved closer to the herds as he advanced in age. A rattlesnake bite ten years earlier had left him with a weakened heart, but he had proven his worth as the manager for the OY Ranch and could still make a "short" drive, as he referred to the two hundred miles to Las Vegas. He looked up from his supper as his two men led a stranger to the chuck wagon fire.

"Where you boys been?" he asked, "You would've been back yesterday if you were worth anything."

"They surely would have too, sir, but they found me in a pinch and helped me out," Sinclair said. He wanted to make sure neither of the other two would slip up and say something stupid. "I had two men quit on me with my cattle and these men helped me gather. I was hopin' to join you and go on to Las Vegas. I'll do all I can to help, sir."

McDonald's eyes narrowed. "I don't know about that," he said. "We're supposed to meet up with James Nelson and his cattle later tomorrow. I'm not sure the agent in Las Vegas will want any extra cattle. And I'm not about to turn around and bring any of mine home on account of you."

"Well sir, that's where I got lucky," Sinclair replied. "My men and I passed by the Nelson place the other day and he said he had quite a few sick cattle. He said he didn't want to risk losin' none or making any of your cattle sick on the trail, so he's stayin' home to let 'em heal up and get some weight back on."

"What's your name, mister?" McDonald's eyes pierced Sinclair, looking for any sign of deception.

"Walter Schmidt, sir. I have a little place way south of Fort Sumner. Please let me come with you, sir. I had no business ever thinkin' I was a stockman. I had to sell my mother cows last fall to the bank, and these steers are all I have to get me and my family back to Ohio. Please, sir, I just have to get them to Las Vegas."

McDonald stared at the man for a good minute. Sinclair even managed to conjure a tear out of each eye. McDonald relented.

"I don't want one peep of trouble out of you, understand? When we get to Las Vegas, we sort your cattle off and you wait until we settle with the broker before you set foot in that office. You'll ride drag the whole way."

Sinclair actually sobbed a little as he took McDonald's hand and pumped it madly. "God bless you, sir! You have saved my children's lives. I mean that. Thank you, sir! Oh, thank you so much! I'll repay your kindness somehow, someday, I swear."

McDonald pulled his hand from Sinclair's. He didn't take to such outbursts of emotion. "Yeah, well, get some supper," he said as he walked away.

Obeying McDonald's order, Sinclair rode drag, the man bringing up the rear of the herd and choking on the dust the cattle raised, all the way to Las Vegas. To cement "Walter Schmidt's" incompetence as a stockman, he even let a few steers cut back on him along the way, prompting much swearing and berating from the other cowboys who had to turn back and help him get the cattle back in the herd.

At the Livestock Exchange corrals in Las Vegas, he helped sort his cattle off the main herd and waited patiently as the others were sorted, tallied and paid for. McDonald even wished Sinclair well as he left the office to begin his journey home. The two Sinclair men that rode with McDonald collected their pay and headed out to find their other two accomplices southwest of town.

Alone with the broker, Sinclair was free to use his real name to match the brand on "his" cattle. No one saw his deception in the brands and he received his cash from the broker.

He left the Livestock Exchange and ate an early dinner at the Castaneda Hotel. He wouldn't have time to eat a full meal again for a day or two, he thought. After leaving the hotel he stopped at the general store to buy a few provisions for the trail and then asked the clerk if the store had any rat poison, knowing full well there would be some. Paying for the two packets of strychnine crystals and his other supplies, he then went to a small saloon on the outskirts of town and purchased two quart bottles of whisky. Once out of town, he poured out part of one bottle and carefully mixed the strychnine into the full one, then slowly rode on until he found his men, camped at a gap in the hills southwest of town, just before sundown.

"Hey boys, let's celebrate!" Sinclair called out as he rocked back and forth in the saddle, waving the part empty bottle. His men quickly surrounded him, slapping him on the back and taking the bottle from him as he half dismounted, half fell off the horse. They led him to a small campfire they had built, where they proceeded to dig out cups and finish off the bottle.

Sinclair let the liquor take effect as he divided the cash among the five of them and then announced he had a surprise. Weaving back to his saddlebags, he produced the second bottle and filled their cups to the brim. It only took a few minutes before one of the men began to complain of a sudden backache.

"You're just stiff from riding. Have another drink and relax," the very sober Sinclair laughed.

Before long, all four men were writhing in seizures. Sinclair calmly shot each one in the head and retrieved the cash from their bodies. He shot the two Nelson Ranch horses as well, partly for spite, but also because they carried the JN brand. Then, tying the others together in a string, he mounted his own horse and led them away in the twilight.

A FRANTIC Alice Roberts and Hannah Nelson notified the sheriff when Delbert and Billy failed to return home as planned. Sinclair was in Las Vegas before they knew anything could be wrong. It took two more days for the search party to find the bodies of the three men, and by the time they reached Sunnyside their corpses were in no condition for viewing by anyone except the mortician.

Mrs. Nelson paid for the men's funerals. Delbert and Mr. Nelson were buried on the ranch near a small grove of cottonwood trees not far from the houses and barns. Billy was buried in Fort Sumner as decomposition had made it simply impossible to transport his body back home to his family in Texas.

The sheriff's posse intercepted Leroy McDonald and his men as they were returning home, where they learned of Sinclair's deception, including his use of the alias Walter Schmidt. The posse rode quickly for Las Vegas, but Sinclair's head start was enough to evade them.

The bodies of Sinclair's men were found south of town. Telegrams were sent to the sheriffs in surrounding counties and even to the Texas Rangers, but no early leads came. A man matching Sinclair's description was seen in Trinidad, Colorado, trying to sell some horses three weeks later, but the trail ended there.

Four

April 24, 1900
Sunnyside, New Mexico Territory

Alice Roberts stood over her husband's grave as the sun began to set. She wasn't allowed to see him, to touch him, to kiss him good-bye when they brought him home. Her thoughts returned to how they had met almost four years before. Delbert had found her crying in front of the little hotel in Sunnyside, a rebellious sixteen-year-old with nowhere to go and no idea how to get there.

He hid her in a camp he made on the Nelson Ranch for two days, sneaking food to her until he found the nerve to introduce her to the Nelsons as his wife. A month later, on one of his rare days off, Delbert had the priest in Fort Sumner marry them. The Nelsons learned of their deception later, but forgave them, having become quite fond of the couple. The Nelsons were childless, but began to look at Delbert and Alice as if they were their own.

Now there were no tears left, but still Alice cried. She cried for the loss of her protector, her friend, her lover, and the father of her son. She cried for fear of the future. Ever since the funeral, she had started and ended each day at this spot, the downy seeds from the cottonwoods clinging to her hair and dress. The remaining hours were spent in the ranch manager's house she had shared with Delbert, attending to little JD's bare necessities and unable to do anything else.

The sun was nearly gone, now, when a long shadow crossed Delbert's grave. Alice looked up to see Hannah Nelson approaching, stopping next to James' headstone. The two stood together in their shared grief. As the light faded and twilight grew, Hanna looked at Alice.

"I'm thinking of hiring a new man to help around the ranch. He'll be here tomorrow. Could you take him around the place with me? It would do you good to get out. Maria can watch JD. She misses seeing him."

"I don't think I can, Mrs. Nelson. There's just too much of Delbert everywhere I look." Alice paused for a moment before she continued. "In fact, I've thought about it a lot, and I think it would just be best if I leave."

"But where will you go, dear? You have a child to care for. You know you're welcome to stay, and I know you're as good as any man for working."

"I know, and I'm very grateful to you for everything you've done. But I fear if I stay, I'll simply die. I have to try to start over again, and I just can't when I see his face everywhere on this ranch. Maybe if I go home my folks will take me back. Besides, no other man would work with a woman on a ranch. Only someone as kind as Mr. Nelson would. You know that."

"Well, you stay another day. If this new man works out, you and I will take a trip and visit your parents. I'm sure they'll take you back."

"Thank you, Mrs. Nelson."

"Would you like to join me for dinner? Maria made extra and she'd love to see JD. So would I."

"That would be very nice. Thank you," Alice said as the two walked back to the house. She paused and looked at Hannah. "Do you think they'll ever catch Oliver, Mrs. Nelson?"

"I don't know, dear. Maybe someday," Hannah said

with hope.

The applicant for the new hired hand was an amiable and very capable man of thirty. A husband and father of two, he had worked for other ranches and had a spotless reputation. He was accompanied by his younger brother who was well known for being a skilled horseman. Mrs. Nelson hired both on the spot.

The following day, she helped Alice load her few possessions along with a fussy, three-year-old JD into the buckboard. The three set off for Sunnyside, where they spent the night, then on to Alice's old home twenty miles further east. They left early, but it was still nearly noon before they could see the ranch a mile away. As they came closer, the women noticed a single rider coming towards them from the ranch at a trot. At first, his features were hidden in shadow by the brim of his hat, but Alice smiled for the first time in two weeks when she recognized her brother, William Stevens. Soon he recognized her as well, spurring the horse to a gallop and screeching her name in glee.

"Allie! Allieeee!" For a man of twenty-four, he acted like a boy at Christmas. He slid his horse to a stop and bounded to the buckboard, pulling a startled Alice out and spinning as he hugged her. "I never thought I'd see you again! Oh Lord—look at you!" He held her at arm's length, then bursting into tears pulled her to him again. Alice's joy and grief came out together, holding her brother fast to her as the tears flowed.

"Who's that, Momma?" a confused JD asked from the bed of the buckboard.

"Son, this is your Uncle Will," Alice explained, wiping her face with her hands. "He lives here with your grandma and grandpa and Uncle Matthew."

William became suddenly serious. He eased his bear

hug and looked at Hanna. "Ma'am, forgive me, but my sister and I need a minute," he said with a look of concern on his face.

"Of course," Hanna replied, as she eased the buckboard several yards up the track.

William took Alice by the arm and walked the other way a few more steps as he collected his thoughts before looking her in the eye. "What made you come back?"

As quickly as she could, Alice explained her situation, then asked, "Now what made you get so serious all of a sudden?"

William took a deep breath. He hated what he had to say next. "Allie, Ma died six months after you left. We wanted to tell you but Pa wouldn't let anybody try to find you."

Alice had grieved too much already. She couldn't grieve any more for the moment. "What happened?"

"It was Pa. You remember how he started to act oddly before you left? He got worse after that. He blamed everybody for you leaving, but Ma got the worst of it. He got mean and accused her of all sorts of horrible things. Then he started drinking. Bad. One night he beat her up pretty bad and just rode off. I found him passed out in Fort Sumner and brought him home. But she got pneumonia right after that, and she died a few days later. I sent Matt off to Las Vegas to school. He only comes home every now and then. I haven't seen him since Christmas."

Alice stood silent for a long moment, letting the news settle in. "What about Daddy?" she finally asked.

"He doesn't say two words anymore. He barely eats. He gets up in the morning and just sits and drinks and stares off into nothing. He's not mean to anyone anymore. He's not anything. He's just there."

"Maybe it's good I came back then. Maybe I can help

take care of him."

"Don't Allie, please don't. He's lost his mind. It's no place for your boy. I'm worried he'd do something bad if he saw you. The last time I mentioned you, I thought he was going to kill me. I had to knock him down hard to make him stop."

"But I don't have anywhere else to go, Will. My grief won't let me stay with Mrs. Nelson. And I don't have anything except for what's in that buckboard."

"I've got an idea if you'll trust me," he said. Taking her hand, he led her back to the buckboard. "Ma'am," he said to Hanna, "I'm grateful to you for bringing my sister home, but I'm sorry to say she can't stay for her own safety. I'm afraid you'll have to leave. But if you'll take her to Sunnyside and wait for me until tomorrow, I'm pretty sure I can make this work out. Would you do me this favor?"

Hannah Nelson smiled kindly at William. She had heard rumors about Mr. Stevens. "I'm very sorry to hear that, young man. Yes. We'll wait for you in Sunnyside."

"I can't thank you enough, ma'am. You've been very kind to my sister in every way. If you'll come to the barn with me, I'll get you some lunch to eat on the way back to town."

They rode to within a few hundred feet of the buildings when William split off and continued on to the house as Mrs. Nelson took the buckboard behind the barn. He slipped quietly through the back door and soon reappeared with a cloth-wrapped bundle under one arm and a jug of water in the other hand. Running to the buckboard, he passed the bundle to Alice.

"It's just dried apples and cornbread, but it will hold you till supper," he said. "I have to get back. I think I woke Pa up when I left. You better get going. I'll see you tomorrow." He turned and trotted back to the house. Mrs. Nelson took a wide turn around the corrals to avoid the house as they left.

That night, William made sure his father got blind drunk. After he was certain his father was passed out, he entered his father's office. Just before the Panic of 1896, his father, not trusting the local bank in his growing insanity, had withdrawn every cent and kept the ranch's money in a safe in his office. For the past four years the ranch had operated out of this safe.

William knelt in front of the safe and opened it. There wasn't a great deal of cash left, but they would sell some cattle in June and he knew what he had to do. Taking ten fifty-dollar bills and placing them in an envelope, and another five in his wallet to cover his expenses, he retired for the night. The next morning, he was up before daybreak and had a horse fed and hitched to the buggy before breakfast. Returning to the barn, he met the ranch foreman coming out to start his chores.

"I have to be gone for a few days, Charlie. I have to help Alice. Don't say a word to the old man and keep him drunk." He was off before the foreman could reply, but didn't need to worry. Charlie loved Alice as much as her brothers did. He had even toyed with the notion of killing Mr. Stevens a couple of times just to get the girl back home. Had he known she was only thirty miles away he probably would have. The horse was fit and the trip to Sunnyside took William just a little more than three hours. Normally, the fresh green of the buffalo grass and the budding blossoms on the yucca would have caught William's eye, but his thoughts were on his sister and her predicament. Arriving in Sunnyside, he stopped first at the stable and arranged for the care of the horse and buggy, then to the combined postal/telegraph office, and finally on to the hotel. He found Alice and Hanna in the cramped dining room. Their lunch had just been served.

"May I buy your lunch, ladies?"

"Why thank you, kind sir," Hannah demurred. Alice blushed at the older woman's faux flirtation. William had always been chivalrous in her eyes. He pulled out a chair, removed his hat, and patted JD on the head in one smooth movement as he sat down and ordered his lunch.

"I think I know of a way to help you Allie," William said, "I have a friend in California. He came into some money drilling oil. He loves horses and he's built a fancy stable with a little brood mare herd and needs someone to run it. I just sent him a telegram and if he's willing, you could work for him. I told him how good you are with horses and that you needed some help."

"California?" Alice caught herself being too loud for a lady. "Will, that's like going to the moon! How am I supposed to get to California?"

"I have that planned. And don't get carried away until we hear back," Will said as his meal was served. "But would you be willing to go? He's a good man. I can vouch for him."

"Will, I don't know. This is all so sudden." Tears welled in her eyes for a moment. "But, I don't know what else to do. I guess I'll go. I have to."

"I'll write you every week. I pick up the mail for the ranch so you can write, too. Pa won't know. I really don't think he'll last much longer the way he's going. Maybe someday, after he's gone, you can come home."

"Maybe someday," Alice replied glumly.

Mrs. Nelson listened politely before she put down her fork and dabbed her mouth with a napkin. "Pardon my interruption, but just how do you know this man, William?"

"We met at college, ma'am," William explained, "in

Albuquerque. Ma thought I should have more formal schooling. Anyway, we became great friends and have stayed in touch, even though I had to quit school and come back here. He really is a good man. He grew up around Santa Fe and moved to Los Angeles after college. He's been very successful with his oil business, from what he tells me."

"What is your friend's name in California? I grew up near Santa Fe as well and may know the family."

"His name is Phillip Jenkins, ma'am. His father owned interest in several mines in Colorado and New Mexico."

"My, it is a small world. I know his parents well," Hanna smiled as she turned to Alice. "If he is half the man his parents wanted, you'll be well cared for, dear. They are wonderful people. If it's agreeable to you, I would say it's a good opportunity. It's certainly better than around here." She returned her attention to William, "When do you expect to hear back?"

"His company's office isn't all that far from the telegraph office in the train station, ma'am. If the lines are good, I would expect to hear back no later than tomorrow morning."

Mrs. Nelson turned again to Alice. "Would you like to come back to the ranch with me and wait there, dear?"

Alice thought for a moment then shook her head. "No, Mrs. Nelson, I don't think so. There's just sadness there for me and all the good parts of Delbert are still with me wherever I go. Whatever happens next will start from here."

"Then I think I'd better go back today," she said as she rose from the table. She hugged Alice a very long time before she stepped away. "I'll miss you terribly, dear," she said as she wiped a tear from her cheek. She bent down to face JD, gently cupping his face in her hands. "And you be a good boy for your mother, young man," she said as she kissed his forehead. "I'll miss you, too."

JD smiled at Mrs. Nelson. He didn't quite understand everything that was happening, but he knew everything would be alright. "I'll be good," he said.

"I'll go get your buckboard ready for you ma'am," William said as they entered the hotel lobby.

Hanna Nelson collected her things in her room while William went to the stable and harnessed her horse. She and Alice were waiting outside the hotel with JD when William drew the buckboard to a stop. As he stepped down, she took his hand.

"I can see how very much you love your sister. I know you'll do your best for her." She hugged Alice and JD one last time before William helped her in the buckboard. "Good-bye dear. Please don't forget to write."

"I won't," Alice smiled through tears of hope and sadness as the buckboard eased away and down the dirt street, the horse's hooves raising small puffs of dust with each footfall. She and her brother stood and watched Mrs. Nelson until she turned the corner two blocks away and headed out of town. "What now Will?" Alice asked.

"Well, I suppose I'd better ask for Mrs. Nelson's room so I have a bed tonight. Then I'd imagine it will take at least until supper for us to catch up. Then we'll see."

"You don't seem to be too worried."

"You don't know how much I've prayed for you, Allie. Don't worry."

Five

There wasn't much to do in Sunnyside. Over the past few years, businesses and residents from Fort Sumner had been moving the few miles to the outskirts of Sunnyside, forming essentially two adjoining towns. The Army had shut down the actual fort almost thirty years before and the town dwindled to a few more than one hundred people. Other than the fort's dubious fame for a failed attempt at ensuring the internment of the Navajo and Mescalero Apache on a reservation, the shrinking town had only the grave of one Henry McCarty to boast. McCarty's headstone bore not his birth name, but his two aliases: "William H. Bonney" and "Billy the Kid." The lack of distraction provided the perfect setting for William and Alice to become fully reacquainted, as well as allowing William to become completely captivated by his nephew.

JD had been heartbroken by his father's death, but the curiosity and rambunctiousness of the three year old could not be held in check by sadness forever. He remained subdued because of his mother's grief, but meeting his uncle had allowed him to be more of himself, and the two quickly became pals. They spent the morning looking through the entire general store and watching the black-smith shoe a horse and repair a cracked rim from a wagon wheel. Alice spent her morning reading in the parlor of the hotel, patiently waiting to hear from William's friend Phillip Jenkins in California, and trying to develop some form of an alternate plan.

Shortly before noon, William and JD entered the hotel, giggling at a private joke. William allowed JD to give his mother an account of their morning's adventure. William then took up the story, relaying the news of their last, and for JD, least interesting stop, the postal/telegraph office. He passed a folded piece of paper to his sister. She was shaking as she unfolded the telegram and read the body of the message:

Will, Sad to hear your news. Your sister is welcome here and will do fine I know. Advise when we can meet her train. Regards, Phil.

Alice read the message twice before looking up at William. "What now?" she asked.

"Well, we need to get you to the train. The stage to Las Vegas comes through tomorrow. I got you two tickets. Then you can take the train from Las Vegas all the way to Los Angeles."

"Las Vegas," Alice said flatly, her eyes downcast. "I can't go there, Will. Delbert died going to Las Vegas. I just can't."

"Sure, you can. You have to." He paused for a moment, thinking. A look of resolve came over his face. "I'll go on the stage with you. I'll get word to the ranch that I'll be gone a while. It'll be fine."

"It won't be fine!" Alice's eyes flashed with anger. "You don't know how much it hurts. You don't know what it will be like wondering every inch of the way if this is the spot where he died, wondering how much pain he felt, wondering how hard he fought to get away. You don't know what it's like to be alone in your grief and hating the person who caused it and knowing he got away with it."

"You're wrong there, baby sister. I've been grieving for Ma the last two and a half years. You don't know what it's like wanting to have your own father arrested for killing your mother and sitting in the same house with him, wishing for him to die. You don't know what you can do until you try. You've helped hold a ranch together. You've taken care of a family. You've done more than a lot of people. We both know you can't stay here, but you're going to a safe place with people who will care for you just like I would. You can do this. You just have to try."

"If you'll come with me to Las Vegas, I think I can do it."

"Of course, I'll go with you. That way we can both drop in on Matt."

"Why, that's the best thought I've had for a long time!" Alice's eye sparkled at the thought of seeing her younger brother. "Would you really do that for me?"

"Absolutely. In fact, I'll accompany you to Santa Fe. I'll need to find a fellow I know here in town to take the buggy back to the ranch and let Charlie know what I'm up to. It'll take me a while to get back, but it will be well worth it."

"Then I'll do it. We are going to get on that stage and we will go to Las Vegas and see our baby brother! I can make it to California after that." Alice's strength was coming back in spades. "I love you, Will. You've always been my hero."

"We're family, Allie. No matter where we are, we're going to stick together." Will was blushing, until he reached over to tousle JD's hair. "Isn't that right, partner?"

"Right!" JD beamed.

"Well, I'd better get moving," William said as he

adjusted his hat. "You stay here with your ma, partner. I'll be back before long."

William crossed the dusty street and once again entered the post office, which also served as the office for the stage coach company that delivered Sunnyside's mail, and purchased a ticket for himself to Las Vegas. His next stop was the bank where, unbeknownst to his father, he kept a modest personal account. One of clerks at the bank, Jacob Gray, was also a friend from college. William offered Jacob ten dollars to take the buggy back to the ranch, then ride a ranch horse back to town and board at the stable until his return. Gray was happy to help, but refused William's offer of payment. He promised he would deliver the buggy on Saturday. William scribbled a note to his ranch foreman explaining the situation and left it with his friend. He was a very happy man when he arrived back at the hotel for lunch.

The stage arrived late that night and was ready to depart the next morning at 8:00. JD was jumping with excitement to ride in a coach, much to the amusement of his uncle and mother. William kept JD distracted as the coach drove past the road leading to the Nelson Ranch. Alice sat silently, not allowing herself to cry, as she stared at the grove of cottonwoods where Delbert lay until the road turned away from the river. An early start the next day saw them in Las Vegas late that afternoon. Alice got the family rooms at the Castaneda Hotel while William bought tickets to Santa Fe at the train station. They could catch the next train to Santa Fe on the first. Washing up and dinner were chores enough for the tired travelers after bouncing on the stage for two days and soon all were asleep.

The next morning, they walked to the dormitory at New Mexico Normal School and asked the hall director for Matt. They were escorted to a small parlor to wait. Before long, a young man of nineteen, six feet tall and broad shouldered, walked through the door. It took Alice a moment to realize she was looking at her baby brother. He was shorter than her five feet six and a skinny fifteen year old the last time she saw him. She gasped when it finally sank in that this was Matthew, causing the young man to break out in laughter as he swept her off the floor in a bear hug. As the joy of the reunion tempered and JD was introduced to his other uncle, Alice was shocked when Matthew turned to William and asked expectantly, "Is he dead?"

"Matthew!" she exclaimed. She caught herself from continuing.

"No!" William interjected quickly. "Matt, Allie lost her husband a couple of weeks ago. She tried to come home."

"Oh, my. Oh, Allie, I am so, so sorry," Matthew said, chagrined. He idolized his sister and was proud of her for leaving home. He bore a scar above his left eye from the beating his father gave him for defending her actions. "I just figured it was the only way I would get to see you again."

"It's alright, Matt. You couldn't have known." Alice took Matthew's hand in hers. "Is he really that bad?"

"He really is, Allie. Maybe someday we'll talk about it. But not today. Today we'll celebrate!" Matthew enthusiastically announced. "Let me show you around before lunch."

A slow, meandering walk of the campus followed, the four stopping frequently to visit, play with JD, and meet classmates. The campus was small, but the grass was turning green and the trees were putting out new leaves under the spring sunshine, giving the siblings a sense of hope for better days. After walking the campus, the family walked back to the Castaneda for lunch and visited in the lobby until dinner and into the evening. Finally, Matt departed for his dormitory.

"I'll meet you for breakfast before you leave tomorrow," Matt promised.

"We'll see you then, Matt," Alice smiled. William and Alice were quiet as they walked upstairs to their rooms with Will carrying a sleeping JD. He paused before taking JD into Alice's room.

"I know you don't ever want to talk about it, but I know why you left. Charlie told me about it finally. He said he saw what happened with you and Ma before you ran away."

"I know. He told me he saw them too," she replied, "and no, we will never talk about it." She took JD from Will's arms to put him to bed.

"They came back again and took Ma one more time before she passed. It was the first time I had ever seen them."

"And they didn't do anything to help her, did they?" Alice's voice was acrid with hate. "I know they could have if they had wanted to."

"No. But I don't know if anyone could have helped, Allie." Will quietly closed the door.

Matthew was waiting at a table in the Castaneda's dining room when his family came down from their rooms the next morning. He also had a small bag next to his chair and announced that he was going to accompany them to Santa Fe to send Alice off. They walked to the Santa Fe Railroad station and the train pulled in shortly thereafter. After arriving in Santa Fe, they spent the remainder of the day exploring the old city.

They were up early the following morning, and ate breakfast together at the café in the train station. As they ate their meal, William slipped Alice the envelope he filled at the ranch office before he left. She glanced at the contents and looked at William with raised eyebrows and wide eyes. William smiled and held his index finger against pursed lips. "Just in case," was all he said.

Matthew grinned knowingly, happy to see the old man's precious money going to his sister. The westbound train was late, arriving at 8:30 instead of the usual 7:45, giving them more time to visit. As they stood on the platform saying their good-byes, JD began to cry.

"What's wrong, partner?" William asked as he knelt in front of the boy.

"I want you to come, Unca Will," JD sniffled.

"Don't you worry, JD. You'll come back to see me and Uncle Matt a lot. We're partners, right? So, you have to come back to make sure Matt and I are doing a good job. Now you have to be a big boy and take care of your Momma, alright?"

"Alright," he said, wiping his eyes.

"Alright, partner," William hugged the boy to hide his own tears. He stood and looked at Alice. "I'll send a telegram to Phil letting him know you're on your way. You should be in Los Angeles early Wednesday morning."

"Take good care of each other," Alice said as she took her brothers into her arms. "I'll write you both every week. I promise."

"As will we, Allie," Matt promised, as she turned to board the train. The brothers followed her up the steps and down the aisle until she and JD were seated. On the way out, William handed the conductor a twenty-dollar bill. Pointing to Alice, he quietly said, "Make sure those two are taken care of, please."

"It will be my great pleasure, sir," the conductor smiled as he folded the bill into his vest pocket.

The brothers stepped on to the platform just before the

porter swept up the step and swung onto the car, waving to the engineer and crying "All aboard!" A few seconds later the locomotive's bell rang out. The train began to creep forward and William and Matthew waved at Alice and JD one last time as their window disappeared into the steam cloud. They stood a few moments longer before they walked into the station. "What now, big brother?" Matthew asked.

"Well, first thing, I need to send Phil that telegram. Then I need a beer."

"Kind of early, isn't it?"

"It's been a hell of a week."

"And you still have to get home."

"Yup."

"Then let's get that telegram sent. I'm thirsty too."

THE TRIP to California was tiring but uneventful for Alice and JD. The conductor did his best to keep them comfortable. He allowed them off the car ahead of the others, who were either single men or men with their wives. At every meal stop, and made sure they had enough time to wash and eat. He also used some of his tip from William to buy the cooperation of two rather irascible gentlemen in the lounge car, paying for their first drink every night in exchange for their false chivalry at meal stops. JD was also the beneficiary of peppermint sticks that magically appeared from the conductor's coat pocket at opportune times. Alice was thankful it was May. She couldn't imagine how hot the car would have been if they were crossing the desert in summer.

Six

May 3, 1900
Los Angeles, California

The train pulled into the Santa Fe's La Grande Station in Los Angeles at 8:30 Thursday morning, just a few minutes behind schedule. Alice coaxed a sleeping JD awake, and after thanking the conductor for all his courtesy, stepped off onto the platform. She stood for a moment on the platform, stretching and gawking at the strange, Moorish architecture of the building, before walking towards the baggage car to collect her things.

She suddenly became aware of someone walking alongside her. She turned her head to find a man not many years older than her smiling at her. He wore the nicest suit she had ever seen, with a diamond stick pin in his necktie and bowler hat that was spotless.

"You must be Alice," the man said through a broad smile beneath a blonde moustache, "Will said to look for the prettiest girl with the handsome little boy."

Alice blushed and self-consciously began trying to make her hair look more presentable, saying, "I wish Will had told me to look for the dashing fellow in the bowler. I must look a fright." She extended her hand, "Pleased to meet you, Mr. Jenkins, I'm Alice Roberts and this is my son, James."

"My pleasure, Mrs. Roberts," Jenkins replied, matching her formality. "Forgive my familiarity when I stopped you, but I didn't want you to have an incorrect impression of the stranger at your side. And don't fret about your appearance. I'm sure I would look much worse if it were me stepping off the train in Santa Fe." He turned his attention to JD, bending low and patting his head. "And how are you today, young man?"

"Tired," JD replied.

"I bet you are," Jenkins laughed. "Would some breakfast make things better?"

"Yes sir!" JD was suddenly much more awake at the mention of food.

"Well, let's get your things and then we'll eat." Jenkins' happy mood was infectious. Alice was perking up along with JD, despite her fatigue. They walked to the baggage car, accompanied by a Mexican man of about forty, obviously an employee of Mr. Jenkins. Soon Alice had her belongings collected on the platform.

"Everything there?" Jenkins asked.

"There isn't much, but it's all there," Alice answered.

"Very good. Jorge, would you take Mrs. Roberts' things to the surrey, please?"

"Si, Senor Phillip," Jorge replied.

"Thank you. Please feel free to join us for breakfast when you're finished."

"Oh, gracias, Senor Phillip," Jorge smiled. He hefted the trunk over his shoulder and headed off through the station. He returned a short time later for the remaining bags. Phillip Jenkins would not leave until the luggage was off the platform.

As Jorge trudged through the station, Phillip gestured toward the building. "And now, if you'll follow me to the Harvey House, we'll get some breakfast."

He led them through the still-new-looking station, now

almost six years old, and out the front doors on Santa Fe Avenue. They turned and walked the short distance to the Harvey House next door, along with a fair number of the other people who had been on the train. Seated at their table, coffee and fresh orange juice was served, but Phillip waited until Jorge had joined them to allow him to order with them. The waiter cast a sideways glance at Jorge when he returned to take their orders. Phillip noticed.

"Is there something wrong?" Phillip asked the waiter.

"No, Mr. Jenkins. Nothing at all," the waiter replied. "How may I be of service to you?"

Orders were placed and the waiter retreated to the kitchen.

"I just can't abide with people who act like him," Jenkins said to Alice. "They feel so superior to the Mexican people and I'll bet his great-great grandfather was some indentured servant from England. Jorge's great-great grandfather sure wasn't."

Breakfast was served shortly and Phillip's good mood quickly returned, sharing stories of escapades in college with William, where he studied geology and engineering, and then how he came to explore for oil in California. His father had made a fair-sized fortune in mining but remembered well his hardscrabble beginnings as a prospector in Colorado and how he had escaped financial calamity more than once by pure chance. He passed that attitude of humility and gratitude to Phillip, loaning him three thousand dollars for his prospecting and reminding him that he expected to be paid back.

"I got very lucky," Phillip reminisced, "I struck oil on the first parcel of land I bought, and then used that money to buy as much of the surrounding land as I possibly could. Before long I had several very productive wells."

Phillip hedged his bet in exploration by selling his

mineral rights to a larger oil company while maintaining ownership of the land and leasing the surface rights to the company. He then purchased and reorganized a drilling supply company. Profits from this new venture were much more consistent and Phillip used this money to purchase a six-hundred-forty-acre farm near the town of Glendale, north of Los Angeles.

"These days I take the train into Los Angeles and stay in an apartment I built into my office three days a week. I let my managers run the business, except for opening major accounts and contract negotiations," he explained, "and in time I'd like to sell the business." At only twenty-five years of age, he had a bright future.

The meal had been over for some time and JD was beginning to fidget in his chair when Phillip ended his story. Producing a watch from a vest pocket, he rolled his eyes when he saw the time.

"Good Lord, it's nearly ten," he said. "Why on Earth didn't one of you shut me up?" Jorge only smiled. He had endured many a meal like this.

"I don't mind, Mr. Jenkins. It's a fascinating story," Alice assured him.

"Well, I need to get to work and you need to get settled. Jorge will take you to the farm and show you around. I'll be by to check on you on Friday."

"Before you go, I want you to know how very grateful I am to you for giving me this chance. I was at my wit's end when Will sent you that telegram."

"Well, you'll have to prove yourself, but by the way Will described how you work with horses, I'm sure I made the right choice. I don't like how some of these so-called caballeros treat a horse. It's sure not like I remember how we did it in New Mexico."

"I think I understand. I've seen some pretty rough

cowboys. I'll do my best for you, Mr. Jenkins."

"I know you will. And you have six colts waiting for you to prove it. You're welcome to start on them whenever you're ready," Phillip smiled as he rose from the table, "but for now I have to say good-bye."

"Good-bye, sir."

Jorge led Alice and JD across the street from the Harvey House to a beautiful dark green surrey. A boy of about twelve sat in the front seat minding the horse. Alice saw her belongings securely tied to the tailgate. Jorge helped her into the back seat then lifted JD in before stepping up onto the front seat and taking the reins from the boy, whom he introduced to Alice as his son Emilio. He released the brake and flipped the reins lightly across the bay gelding's back. The horse leaned into the harness and walked from the curb into the now busy horse and trolley traffic of the city.

They headed north through Los Angeles and eight miles later turned down a long drive lined by newly planted oak trees. A grove of orange trees occupied the area to the right of the drive and olive trees were on the other. A large two-story, Spanish-inspired house sat at the end of the drive.

Jorge took the surrey around the residence to the carriage house and stable. Alice had never seen anything so fancy that was designed for horses. Some people in Sunnyside lived in more humble conditions. Whitewashed corral fences connected to the barn on both sides and at least a dozen horses occupied the corrals. The carriage house was located next to the corral on the side of the barn. Behind the barn was a large round pen and training arena, and beyond it another ten mares and foals grazed a pasture. A frame cottage stood next to the carriage house, its stucco walls painted white, with a little flower bed in front of the porch. Beyond the cottage was another, larger house, but nothing to rival the main residence.

A vegetable garden an acre in size filled the space between this house and the main residence. A woman and girl of about ten were working in the garden. Beyond this house were more corrals with sheep, hogs, a few cows, and a smaller, more modest barn. A large water tank similar to those along the rail line rose in the center of the farmstead. The surrey stopped at the cottage.

"This will be your house, Senora Alice," Jorge said as he set the brake. "I will put your things inside for you." He and Emilio helped Alice and JD out then led them to the door, which he unlocked, handing the key to Alice. "You won't need it, but Senor Phillip says it is important for a lady to feel safe."

"Thank you, Jorge. I doubt that I will need it as well."

Jorge smiled. "I will get your things."

Alice and JD stepped inside the front room of their new home. The room was modestly furnished, but the furniture was of very good quality and the room was spotless. There were two bedrooms, similarly furnished, and a fully stocked kitchen with a good wood stove and, to Alice's surprise, a sink with a faucet. She knew now why there was a water tower in the center of the yards. She walked to the sink and hesitantly turned the faucet, then let out a surprised yelp when water actually flowed from it.

"It's good water to drink," Jorge said as he came in with her trunk. "There is an artesian well on the hill in back. Senor Phillip ran water to all the houses. He is very smart."

"He certainly is," Alice agreed, "and very thoughtful of his employees."

"Si. He has been very good to me and my family," Jorge smiled as Emilio came in with more of Alice's belongings. "We are very happy here. Maybe you will be too, I think."

"I hope so, Jorge. Thank you so much for helping bring in our things."

"Do you need anything else, Senora Alice?"

"No, and thank you again. I'd better start putting things away. Could you show me around the barn and horses later, Jorge?"

"I will be there all afternoon, Senora Alice. Come when you are ready."

Alice thanked Jorge and Emilio again then began unpacking. Both bedrooms had more wardrobe and dresser space than she and JD had clothes and her few personal items, mementos, and toys for JD easily found a place. By the time she was finished it was lunch time. She made a small meal for herself and JD, who was so tired from his travels he nearly nodded off at the table. Alice sent him to bed as she washed their dishes. He was sound asleep in a few minutes. The thought of a nap crossed her mind as well but her curiosity about her new job was stronger than her fatigue. She changed from her dress to a set of work pants, shirt, and boots. She braided her hair in pigtails, donned her work hat, and headed out the door toward the barn.

She found Jorge whitewashing a new board that he had replaced in the corral fence. He seemed shocked to see a woman wearing pants, but made no comment as he laid down his brush and proudly showed Alice around. The barn looked as if it were built the previous week. The walls were made of thick adobe blocks and stucco was applied to the walls both inside and out. Jorge explained that the stucco was almost all new, having been repaired after an earthquake the previous year. Eight roomy wooden stalls with Dutch doors ran down each side of a wide central passageway, or alley, that was floored with oak railroad ties. The tack room at the end of the barn was the size of two stalls and filled with saddles of almost every kind and size along with dozens of bridles and halters lining two walls, each on its own hook. Across the alley from the tack room was a well-stocked farrier's room with anvils, steel for shoe blanks and all the tools needed for proper equine hoof care, including a small forge.

The carriage house was equally impressive. As large as the barn, it housed the surrey that had carried them from town along with a buckboard, a two-seat buggy and a single-axle cart. Harnesses and horse collars lined the walls.

After showing Alice the other outbuildings, Jorge returned to the barn to introduce Alice to the horses. The pens on one side of the barn housed eight yearlings. The other side held six two-year-olds: two colts, and four fillies, each with their own pens that opened from the stalls in the barn. Jorge gave each animal's life story. They finished at the gate to the pasture, where Jorge pointed out each mare by name and matched her to the yearlings and two-year-olds. Finally, he pointed out the herd stallion, a tall but muscular liver chestnut, grazing with the mares. Jorge explained that Phillip had purchased the stud two springs ago. The yearlings at the barn were his first foal crop.

An adjoining pasture kept the saddle and carriage horses and Jorge introduced them to Alice as well. Alice noted that there was not a plain looking horse in sight, and while she didn't know the bloodlines of some of the mares, it was obvious that Phillip Jenkins knew his horses.

Returning to the two-year-olds, Alice slowly walked along the end of the pens, or runs as she called them, outside the barn. She paused at each gate, observing each horse's reaction to the stranger staring at them. Two of the fillies and one of the colts slowly approached her. She stood motionless, letting them explore her scent and actions. One filly allowed her to slowly reach out a hand and gently touch her face. The remaining filly stood near the barn, seemingly uninterested with the new human. The other colt, a copper-colored sorrel, behaved far differently than his cohorts. He raced into his stall only to bolt back out, charging halfway down the run, his neck bowed and nostrils flared. With his eyes wide, he shook his head defiantly. He was thickly muscled and they rippled in the sunlight under his shiny coat.

"He should be gelded," Jorge said as he returned to his paint brush. "Senor Phillip thinks we should wait a year, but this one is a *diablo*."

"Maybe someday," Alice said. She never looked away from the colt, but continued the stare down. "Maybe he just needs to stop being afraid of everything. We'll see."

She spoke just loud enough for Jorge to hear, but not enough to spook the colt further. The colt broke his stare with a snort, crow hopping in a circle before resuming the stare down. Alice never moved. The colt again spun and trotted into his stall. Alice remained as she was. A few minutes later, unable to resist his curiosity, the colt stuck his head out the stall door. He walked out of the stall, his head still high, but the bow was out of his neck. His nostrils were normal and his eyes were less wide. The two looked at each other for another minute. This time, the colt walked away to the water trough. He took a drink, keeping an ear cocked at Alice, then walked back into his stall. She smiled and continued around the runs to the barn door. Walking toward the tack room, she noticed the colt remained in his stall to continue his study of her. She continued to ignore him and entered the tack room where she selected a halter and lead. She walked to the stall next to the colt. It held the filly that allowed Alice to touch her and walked in. She continued out into the run and sat on the ground next to the water trough.

The filly walked slowly towards her, stopping to watch her and taking small sniffs of her. Alice never moved. As she sat, she glanced at the colt in the adjacent run who was keenly watching the scene unfold. The filly finally touched the brim of Alice's hat with her muzzle, then down her arms to the halter and hands. Palm down, Alice slowly extended her hand to the filly to explore. Satisfied that there was neither threat nor feed value in Alice, the filly walked away.

Alice slowly rose and crossed the run to the fence separating the filly and colt and leaned against the fence, keeping her eyes on the filly and ignoring the snort behind her. She stood there for the better part of an hour, never acknowledging the colt. She was able to gently pet the filly on her second approach. Finally, she heard the colt slowly approach her. She crossed her arms and stepped a few inches away from the fence. A few minutes later she felt a muzzle touch her back. Alice spent the rest of the afternoon in the pen until she had a halter on the filly, then left.

Jorge had finished his work on the fence and moved on to other chores, but kept an eye on Alice and what she was doing.

"You're smart to start on the gentlest one first, Senora Alice," he said as she came out of the barn.

"I didn't start on the filly, Jorge," she smiled, "I started on the colt."

Over the next few days, Alice continued to work with the filly, allowing the colt to watch and become familiar with her. Late in the afternoon of the third day, she walked into the colt's run. She simply stood, allowing the colt to approach her on his own terms. She never touched the colt for two more days, until he was at ease with her. Finally, she was able to pet the colt's head and neck and began letting him get used to the feel of the lead, then the halter, around his head. She was beginning to slip the halter over the colt's nose when she noticed someone watching her from the shade of a nearby tree. It was Phillip Jenkins. She continued to concentrate on the colt until she had the halter on and off a few times. The next time she looked up Jenkins was gone. Alice put the halter away and walked to her house to make supper. JD had been watching from the porch.

"Mr. Phillip was watching you, Momma," he said. "He was smiling."

"I'm glad to know that, son." Alice smiled as well. "What would you like for supper?"

"Pancakes!" JD exclaimed.

"You always want pancakes," Alice laughed.

Seven

September 9, 1900
Glendale, California

The spring and summer had been eventful for Alice. The two-year-olds were all now being trained under saddle. She and Phillip Jenkins had many conversations regarding the horses and Alice was surprised by his remarkable knowledge, from pedigrees to training. He was perfectly capable of training the two-years-olds himself but simply didn't have the time. Alice's abilities with the horses were his equal, though, and he knew it as well as she did. The two had become quite comfortable with each other discussing training strategies with the horses.

All the two-year-olds had presented challenges, but the skittish stallion they had named Diablo was by far the hardest. It seemed that for every gain Alice made in calming the colt, he found two ways to frustrate her, including a kick in that nearly broke her leg. Jenkins was at work in Los Angeles when the incident occurred but Jorge stepped in and summoned the doctor from Glendale. Jorge's wife Carmen had been caring for JD during the days so Alice could concentrate on the horses. She immediately began cooking for two families, taking Alice's meals to her and helping with her care. Jenkins found out two days later when he returned from Los Angeles for the weekend. He wanted to check on her the evening he returned but, seeing no light on in her cottage, waited until morning. He knocked on Alice's door the next morning shortly after breakfast.

"Come in, Carmen," Alice called from her bedroom.

"It's not Carmen, its Phillip," Jenkins called through the door.

"Oh my!" Alice was completely flustered. "Oh, Mr. Jenkins, please wait a moment! I'm not decent!"

"I'm sorry to intrude, Alice." It was his turn to be flustered. "I just wanted to see how you were doing. I can come back later."

"Would you mind terribly doing that? I still need some help from Carmen to get dressed."

"Of course. Please have Carmen come to the house and let me know when I can visit."

"Thank you so much, Mr. Jenkins. She should be here any minute."

Phillip retired to the main residence. Twenty minutes later Carmen knocked timidly at the door to let Jenkins know Alice was able to see him. He quickly walked across the yard and Carmen let him in the cottage. Alice was sitting in a chair in the little front room. She had one of her work shirts on, but her lower body was firmly wrapped in a large quilt and her legs propped up on a chair from the dining table. "I hope you don't think I was rude when you came. I was wrapping my leg in hot towels when you arrived."

"You were the farthest thing from rude," Phillip said, "I was just so taken aback to hear you'd been hurt I wanted to check on you immediately. Tell me what happened."

"Well, I'm a little embarrassed to say," Alice said, "I had finished riding Fancy and put her up, then caught Diablo and took him to the hitch rail. I brushed him down to saddle him and somehow the brush flipped out of my hand and went up in the air. Like a fool I reached up too fast to grab it, and it spooked the colt. I guess he thought I was going to hit him or something, and the next thing I knew I was across the alley. I must have been knocked out for a few minutes, because the next thing I could remember was Jorge helping me into the house. He said he heard the ruckus and found me in the barn, then after getting me in bed and calling Carmen to watch me, he rode into town to get the doctor."

"But the doctor is sure the leg isn't broken?"

"He's sure. He bent it every way you could think. I nearly passed out before he quit. Then he showed me how to soak towels in hot water and wrap my thigh to get the swelling down. He gave me some awful tasting stuff to help with the pain and said to stay off my feet for two weeks. I haven't ever been off my feet for two weeks. I may go crazy before that. I have work to do with the horses and I feel so badly for Carmen, too. She's so good just to watch JD and now she's taking care of me on top of all her other chores. I just feel awful."

"Well, we are going to have to do something to make you more comfortable. And ease Carmen's burden. I'll make arrangements for a nurse to help you out so Carmen doesn't have to. She can stay in the house and we'll put you and JD up there as well so she can properly keep an eye on you."

"Mr. Jenkins, that's very kind of you but it's an awful lot of trouble! I feel even worse for causing all this! I'm so, so sorry. I'll help pay for the nurse."

"Alice, I care for anyone who works for me like I want to care for you right now. It's my policy from the oil field to the office to here to take care of my people. And on top of that, you're my friend's sister and . . . ." He stopped himself and for a moment seemed unable to speak. He quickly recovered and continued, "You're not about to pay anything. You need to get better and get back on those horses. And while you're healing up, I'm going to have that colt gelded."

"No! Mr. Jenkins, please don't do that. Diablo has his problems, but if we cut him now, I'll lose all the trust I've built up with him. He needs to be, I agree, but let's wait until he's better trained before you do it."

"All right. We'll wait on that. But we'll get you in the house today. Margaret and Theresa can help you until the nurse arrives."

"Oh my. I hope they won't mind."

"They won't mind at all, I'm sure. They're very impressed by you. They say you never seem to sit down—always doing something with one of the horses or playing with JD. They don't know where you get the energy. Frankly, I wonder sometimes myself."

"Well, I just do my job, Mr. Jenkins. I enjoy working with the horses. To me it doesn't feel like work."

"It shows. It's a joy to watch how you can get along with them. Now, what do we need to do to get you into the house?"

Alice giggled. "I guess I better put something on besides my drawers before we do too much else."

"Oh. Yes . . . well . . . I suppose I'd better uh . . . let Margaret and Theresa know so they can make up your room." Phillip was blushing and he knew it. "I'll get Carmen to give you a hand."

"Thank you, Mr. Jenkins. You're very kind."

"You can call me Phillip if you want," Jenkins muttered, still blushing.

"Thank you, Phillip," Alice said quietly.

Jenkins felt relieved to be out of what was becoming an awkward conversation. He found Jorge and sent him to get the bay gelding from the pasture and hitch him to the buggy. He then headed to the house and sipped at a cup of coffee while he waited.

It took some time for Alice to get dressed. She had to wear a dress as her leg was too swollen and painful to fit into her pants. Jenkins and Carmen steadied Alice for the walk across the yard to the main house. She had some difficulty making it up the steps, and just made it to a divan in the sitting room. Carmen and Theresa, Jenkins' maid, helped lift her legs onto the cushion. She was pale from the pain and asked Carmen to fetch her medicine from the cottage. Carmen quickly reappeared with the dark amber bottle the doctor had left, and Theresa brought a spoon and glass of water from the kitchen. Alice retched slightly as she forced the medicine down then greedily drank the water to get the foul taste out of her mouth. Phillip took the bottle from Carmen and sniffed the open top, grimacing at the smell.

"Laudanum," he said. "No wonder you don't like it."

"Oh, it's just horrid," Alice said, "but it does help." Her color began to return as the pain subsided.

"Well, unless I can help you all, I'd better get into Glendale and arrange for a nurse," Phillip said as he handed the Laudanum to Theresa. She took the bottle and walked towards a hall.

"I'll get Alice's room ready while you're gone, sir."

"Thank you, Theresa," Phillip replied, "I'll be on my way, then."

"Thank you again, Mr. Jenkins." Alice's speech was slightly slurred from the Laudanum.

"Just rest. I'll be back soon," Jenkins smiled as he turned the doorknob and walked out, heading with a purpose to the carriage house. A few minutes later he was headed down the road to Glendale with the horse at a brisk trot.

Theresa quickly moved a comfortable chair and ottoman from the parlor into the largest guest room, along with a commode. Carmen had told her that Alice fell trying to get to the outhouse the previous night and had laid in the yard for some time before JD found her and came to Carmen for help. Theresa wasn't going to have that happen again. She also made sure the smaller bedroom across the hall was properly cleaned for JD. She returned to the sitting room to find Alice nodding in and out of a drug-induced nap on the divan. She refilled the water glass and left her to rest.

Crossing the yard to Carmen and Jorge's house, she checked to see if Carmen wanted to send JD to the main residence. Carmen said that JD was "helping" in the garden and she would send him to the main house before dinner time. Theresa returned to the house to let Margaret, the cook, know that the boy would not be having lunch with them.

Glendale was not that big of a town. It was still unincorporated and Phillip knew the local physician well enough to walk into his office in the middle of the day and get five minutes to visit. The doctor asked about Alice, and agreed a nurse would be helpful for at least a week. He knew of a retired nurse in town and referred Jenkins to her with a quick note of introduction.

Two hours and a cup of tea later, Jenkins was headed home with Edith Simmons, Alice's new nurse. They arrived back at the farm around six. Phillip introduced Edith to Alice and Theresa, who collected her things and showed her to her room next to Alice's. Margaret appeared from the kitchen to learn that there would be six for dinner.

Edith was a very knowledgeable woman of sixty-five

who had served in field hospitals during the Civil War. The horrific wounds requiring amputation deservedly received the bulk of attention during the war, but horse-related casualties were also common. She became very adept at rehabilitating crushing injuries to legs and arms suffered from a horse being shot out from under its rider. At nearly six feet tall and stoutly built, with steel gray hair pulled back tightly into a bun, she was a commanding presence. She helped Alice to her bedroom and lent Alice a hand as she undressed. She chuckled to see that Alice in her modesty had cut off the leg of her bloomers so that she could wrap the leg with hot towels without completely disrobing. Edith gently examined the swollen and dis-colored left thigh. It was nearly twice the size of the normal leg and the trauma left a large, purplish-black area from above her hip to below her knee, with a tight, fluctuant swelling over the outside half of the thigh where the hoof had impacted.

"Well, there certainly wasn't any fat to help absorb the blow," she said as she compared the size of the two legs. Alice was as fit as could be from her hours in the saddle. "Let me guess. The doctor was too modest to actually look at your leg, wasn't he?"

"He was," Alice confirmed.

"I thought so," Edith said, shaking her head. Why some doctors considered it improper to examine a woman's body closely always baffled her. "How many times a day do you hot-wrap your leg, dear?"

"Morning and evening, just like the doctor told me," Alice answered.

"That's good. It helps to keep the blood from clotting in your veins and made that fluid come to the surface. But we've got to relieve the pressure under your skin or it may die and slough off. We don't want that."

"So, what do we do?"

"After dinner, I need to clean your leg very thoroughly with soap and water. Then I'll lance that area where the fluid has accumulated," Edith explained. She paused, taking Alice's hand, "It won't be pleasant, I fear."

"Worse than twenty hours of labor?" Alice smiled.

Edith burst out laughing, "No, it won't be that bad! But we will have to keep the leg bandaged and very clean so it won't get infected. I brought some bandages with me but we'll need to change the dressing frequently for a few days. I'm afraid I'll have to ask someone to get some material for bandages from Los Angeles. I know the material I need can't be found in Glendale. I'll discuss it with Mr. Jenkins. How often do you need the laudanum?"

"Only two or three times a day, generally when I have to go to the outhouse. I take some when I come back inside. I tried to take it before I went out, but it made me too woozy and I fell. I had to have some this morning after walking over here from my house."

"That's good. You can actually get addicted to it, as bad as it tastes. If we get enough fluid out of your leg the pain will diminish a fair bit so you won't need as much. That and the commode will make things easier."

"Then I'm all for getting the fluid out."

Edith helped Alice get back in her dress. "Good," she smiled, "I'll go tell Mr. Jenkins what we'll need. Now listen, I'm here to help you in any way. If you need anything from a drink of water to help using the commode or cleaning up, you call for me, understand?"

"Yes, ma'am," Alice smiled back, "You're the boss!"

Edith shook again in laughter, saying, "You pick up on things pretty fast, girly." She helped Alice get back in her dress and back to the sitting room, then walked to the kitchen to find Phillip. Margaret informed her that he was changing for dinner, which was nearly ready. As she was speaking, Carmen knocked on the back door with a washed and hungry JD. Carmen introduced JD to Margaret, who in turn introduced Edith. JD was a little confused, but he was polite to the two women, and wanted to see his mother. Edith led him to the sitting room, where Alice explained their new temporary living situation. Happy-go-lucky as ever, JD accepted the news with, "Alright, Momma," and went to see his new room.

Dinner was spent with the adults getting to know each other and JD obediently quiet, listening. When asked by Jenkins what he did during the day, he happily told how he had helped pull weeds in the garden, then helped Carmen and Jorge feed the lambs, cows, and pigs, while Emilio milked the cows. He smiled when Jenkins thanked him for all the help he was providing. Alice excused him to his room to get ready for bed.

The conversation turned to Alice's leg and Edith explained her plan to remove the fluid from Alice's leg. Jenkins informed Edith that there was a supply of bandage material, but that he would bring more from Los Angeles. He planned to go into town on Monday and return with the supplies then go back on Tuesday as normal for work, provided he wasn't needed for anything at the farm. Margaret collected the dishes, with Edith helping. In the kitchen, Edith asked Margaret if it would be a great effort to heat some more water. Margaret placed two sticks of wood in the stove and opened the tap to fill a large pot with water. Edith was surprised to see running water, but was very thankful, as she was for the house having actual bathrooms with tubs. She would be able to be very clean with her procedure this way.

As the water heated, Theresa brought soap, wash cloths and towels to the bathroom while Edith collected her bandage material and a small instrument bag from her room. The instruments, including a scalpel, were a gift from a Union surgeon at the end of the Civil War. She returned to the kitchen and asked Margaret for a small pan, which she filled with water and placed on the stove to boil the scalpel. After the scalpel had boiled several minutes, she removed it from the stove and took it to the bathroom, along with the large pot of water which was now steaming vigorously.

Finally, Edith and Theresa helped Alice walk from the dining room to the bathroom, where she gave Alice a dose of laudanum. They steadied Alice as she disrobed from the waist down and painfully stepped into the tub. Edith knelt at the side of the tub and gently cleaned the swollen leg, washing first with soap then rinsing with water. She repeated these steps several times. Theresa stood by, ready to catch Alice if she lost her balance for any reason.

Taking the scalpel, Edith looked up at Alice. "Alice, I want you to take Theresa's hand. I'm hoping I can make one quick little poke with this and that's all I'll need to do. Are you ready?"

"As ready as I'll ever be," Alice smiled. The laudanum was kicking in. She took Theresa's hand in hers and stared straight ahead. Edith's hand barely moved as the blade quickly flicked through the skin, opening a half inch long incision. Alice flinched in pain, then looked at Edith. She giggled a little when she asked, "That's it?"

"That's it," Edith answered.

"I've done worse than that fixing a barbed wire fence," she grinned as the giggle returned.

Theresa interrupted. "So, you're alright to stand?" She was ghostly pale.

Edith glanced up and immediately ordered Theresa to sit on the floor to avoid fainting. She barely made it down before slumping onto her side.

Edith looked up at Alice. "Are you steady enough to keep standing or would you rather sit on the edge of the tub?"

"Just to be safe, maybe I'd better sit."

"That's fine," Edith replied as she helped Alice down. "Now I need to work some more of that fluid out. It may hurt a bit."

"It actually feels much better already. Go right ahead."

The small incision had produced a steady stream of straw-colored fluid. Edith was thankful to notice that there was no odor, indicating that no infection was present. Using gentle pressure, she massaged as much fluid from the swelling as she could, then washed the entire area again before applying a dressing over the thigh to place even pressure over the swollen muscles. By the time she had finished drying Alice off and completed the pressure dressing on the leg, Theresa had come around and was able to help Alice step out of the tub.

Between relieving the pressure under her skin and the laudanum, Alice was surprisingly more mobile. She could almost dress herself. Wrapped again in the quilt, she hobbled across the hall to her bedroom, where Edith helped her into her nightgown and then into bed. Theresa apologized for not being more help, but Edith cut her short.

"Not one word of apology, dear. I should have told you what to expect. I feel like a fool. I'm the one to apologize. I'm very sorry."

"Well, I still feel a little foolish. I've helped deliver foals and calves and didn't give this a thought."

"It's different when people are involved sometimes. You're not the first."

"Well, all's well that ends well," she smiled. Turning her attention to Alice, she said, "I almost forgot. I found a cane for you to use if you wish. It's right by your night stand."

Alice looked to her side. "Indeed, it is," she smiled. "Thank you so much for everything, both of you. I'll never be able to repay your kindness."

Theresa took her hand. "Get well and get back on those horses and you've paid me more than enough. It's such a thrill to see how you've changed them."

"Alright, girls," Edith interrupted, "you both need to get some rest after your ordeals. Off to sleep for both of you!"

"Yes, ma'am," Alice and Theresa replied together.

Edith turned down the lamp so that it barely shown. "Don't forget. If you need me, you call me, young lady," she admonished Alice as she closed the door.

"Yes, ma'am," Alice whispered. She fell asleep almost immediately, despite a mild headache she blamed on the laudanum. She slept soundly for several hours for the first time since the accident.

Sometime in the middle of the night, she was awakened by a voice speaking her name. Looking out the window, she noticed that the yard seemed dimly lit. This struck her as odd, as she knew it was the new moon. She was immediately gripped by the fear and anger that came with the realization of what was going on. She closed her eyes.

"Damn you," she whispered, "why can't you just leave me in peace?"

"*I'm sorry to upset you Alice. I was hoping we could help,*" the voice spoke in her mind.

"Well, you can't." She thought she was only speaking in her thoughts, but the laudanum betrayed her and she mumbled her words aloud.

"*I would like to examine your leg. I believe I can help*

you," the voice insisted. The large window in the bedroom opened on its own and Alice lifted off the bed and floated gently out the window.

"No," Alice moaned, unable to move as she left the room. The window closed behind her.

Alice woke again, but now the sun was peeking over the horizon. She convinced herself that it was all a dream, aided by laudanum. Edith was in the room a few minutes later to change the dressing. After removing the bandages, she froze, staring in astonishment at Alice's leg. The swelling was completely gone. Only some slight discoloration of the skin remained and the stab incision made to drain the fluid was all but healed.

"What on Earth is this?" Edith looked at Alice in bewilderment. "This simply can't be."

"I'm sure I don't know," Alice feigned the same confusion as Edith, but she now knew all too well she had not been dreaming during the night.

"How does it feel?" Edith asked as she squeezed the muscles in Alice's thigh. "Any tenderness?"

"None."

"Well, let's get you up and put some weight on it."

Alice swung her legs over the edge of the bed. Where the day before the swelling prevented her knee from bending, it now bent ninety degrees. She gently put her feet on the floor then stood, gingerly shifting her weight from one foot to another, and finally lifting her uninjured foot completely off the floor and bearing her full weight on the bad leg. Edith could do nothing but gawk.

"It's a miracle . . . a miracle," she kept whispering. Finally, she pulled her eyes away from the leg to look Alice in the eye. "Do you need help dressing?"

"I don't think so, but don't leave, just in case." Alice was able to dress herself with no problem. Edith watched and walked out of the room with her, staying at her side until she was seated for breakfast. As the two women sipped their coffee, JD bounded into the room. Hugging Alice, he asked who she was talking to during the night.

"I didn't talk to anyone, son," she lied, not knowing quite what he had heard. "I must have been dreaming."

"But I heard you. I did."

"Maybe *you* were dreaming, then," she said as she pulled him close, fighting back a tear, "but I didn't talk to anyone all night."

"But Momma . . ."

"But nothing, young man. That's enough." Her tone was too stern. Edith noticed.

"Yes, ma'am." JD sat down at the table as Phillip strode into the room.

"And how is our patient, nurse?" Phillip asked as Margaret poured his coffee. He was in his usual good mood.

"Markedly improved, I think." Edith cast a look at Alice that said, "I won't say anything if you won't."

"Bully! That's marvelous. I can't wait to see you up and about again."

"She still has a way to go, but getting that fluid out helped quite a bit."

"I'll be sure to get those extra bandages today. Is there anything else you may need?"

"If the store has some tincture of iodine, could you get some please? I doubt I'll need it, but if I do, I won't have time to wait."

"I'll make sure I get it. Alice, is there anything the horses require?"

"Yes, actually," Alice replied, "Could you ask Jorge to cut the grain ration back to about one third of what they've been eating? I don't want them too hot when I get back on them, especially Diablo."

"I'd rather cut his throat than his grain, but I'll let Jorge know," Jenkins said with a twinkle in his eye.

The conversation lulled as Margaret served breakfast. The laudanum had killed Alice's appetite, but she forced herself to eat. The meal had no flavor to her. *One more reason to stop taking that awful stuff,* she thought.

"Well, I know that it's poor form to eat and run, but I have a train to catch," Phillip said as he slid his chair back. "If you will excuse me, I'll see you this evening."

"Thank you, Mr. Jenkins," Edith said.

"Both of you make yourselves at home," he replied before closing the door.

The women sat silently until they saw Phillip head down the driveway. Alice sent JD off to Carmen to start his morning. Margaret cleared the table and soon the clatter of dishwashing could be heard from the kitchen. Edith finally broke the silence.

"Alice, I need to say something. I've seen a lot in my time, but I've never seen an injury like yours improve overnight like this. It physically can't happen. And your little boy wasn't the only one that heard you last night. I heard you too, and got up to check on you. I thought perhaps you were delirious from the laudanum—or worse, had developed blood poisoning. But when I walked into your room, you were nowhere to be found. I was looking throughout the first floor of the house for you when I noticed that it was light outside, but by the time I got to the front door it was dark, and you were back in bed when I returned to your room. Now mind you, I'm just horribly confused and not implying anything, but do you have any idea what happened last night?"

For a moment, Alice considered telling the truth but couldn't. Not to a stranger. "I assure you, Edith, I have no idea how my leg got so much better and I have absolutely no recollection of speaking, or getting out of bed, all night. In fact, it was the best sleep I've had since the accident. I don't recall dreaming or anything."

Edith studied her for a moment. "Well, since neither of us can explain this I think it would be wise to treat this injury like we have been. I want to keep a support bandage on it so fluid won't begin to build up again. We'll keep applying the hot towels as well."

"I think that makes good sense."

"And," Edith added with a sly smile, "I think you better lean on that cane a lot when you're out of your room, at least for a few more days. I don't think either of us wants to have to explain a miracle to Mr. Jenkins or anyone else."

"And that makes even more sense." There was relief in Alice's voice. "And I really would feel better having you keep an eye on me a few more days."

"Well, since I can't explain the improvement, I have no idea if you'll relapse just as quickly."

Phillip returned that evening with the supplies Edith had requested the night before. Edith assured him that he could return to Los Angeles the next morning for the remainder of his work week. Alice didn't suffer a relapse. The biggest challenge she and Edith faced for the next several days was to maintain the charade of slow but steady improvement in Alice's leg.

After a week, Alice began walking with only a slight limp, but still used her cane "just in case." When Phillip returned Thursday evening, he was delighted with the "improvement" Alice had made during the week. That night at dinner, Edith informed Phillip that, so long as Alice stayed off her feet another week and off a horse a week more, her services would no longer be needed. The next morning, handsomely paid, Edith was driven back to

Glendale by Jorge.

Over the weekend, Phillip doted on Alice to her mild annoyance. At Monday dinner, after JD had been excused, Phillip asked Alice if she required him to stay home from work for the week.

"Oh, Phillip, I hardly think that would be necessary," Alice replied as diplomatically as possible.

"It would be no bother," Phillip replied.

"It's very kind of you, but really all I require is sitting down. In all honesty, I feel very badly still having to stay in the house and have someone cook and pick up after me. And frankly, it's quite awkward having you helping as much as you are."

"Think nothing of that! You have medical orders and they need to be followed to make sure you completely recover," Phillip replied firmly but gently. There was a long pause before he continued, "Besides, I have to confess something. Alice, I've wanted to find a way to talk to you about this for some time, but haven't been able to, so I suppose this is the best way. I just want you to know how much I admire you and the way you care for your son and the horses. I think you are a remarkable woman, and my confession is that I'm beginning to care for you quite a lot."

Alice was silent, staring at her plate and sorting out the emotions assaulting her. Over the previous few weeks, she had come to the realization that what she thought was an undying love for her late husband had been, in hard reality, a girl's infatuation fueled by her anger at her father. She also found herself having to come to grips with the feelings for Phillip that had been growing. Just as the two-year-olds in the barn were maturing and learning, so was she. She realized that she was developing many feelings for Phillip that she had felt for Delbert, and these emotions ran deeper and were more complex than what she felt for the boy she had married. But he was a wealthy businessman and she was a simple cowgirl. How on Earth could they get along? She finally looked up at Phillip. He was also looking at his plate.

"Phillip," she said, looking back at her plate and trying to steady the trembling in her voice, "I really don't know how to respond." She finally looked at him. Their eyes met and both seemed near tears as she continued. "What I mean is there is so much going on in my head and my heart right now, I can't put words to them. But I want you to know that many, many of the things in my heart are good." Another short silence ensued before Philip replied.

"Then perhaps it is best for me to go to work in the morning and we can have a few days to think."

"I think that would be a good idea. I would like a few days to sort this out." She suddenly giggled, "Lord knows I need something to occupy me while I can't ride."

Phillip's shoulders shook with silent laughter, relieved the tension had been broken. "Well, with that, I think I'll retire, unless I can help you in any way."

Alice smiled widely, also relieved. "No thank you, kind sir," she replied, as she took her cane in hand. She was thankful that she remembered to limp a little as she headed for the hall to her room. Once the door was closed, she leaned her cane against the night stand and paced for the next twenty minutes, trying to mentally digest all the things that had happened the past two weeks. Her mind then wandered further to how drastically her life had changed in four short years. She lay awake in bed half the night.

Breakfast the following morning was eaten in silence, Phillip bolting his food before abruptly excusing himself. As he opened the door, Alice stopped him. Rising from the table, she nearly forgot to take her cane in hand as she walked to meet him at the door. She extended her hand, which he eagerly took with both of his own.

"We'll work this out," she said, searching his eyes for a sign of his true feelings. "I want to work this out. We just need some time."

"I know we will," he said as he lifted her hand to his lips. "I'll see you Thursday."

The next three days passed at a snail's pace for Alice. She obediently stayed off her feet all day Tuesday and Wednesday, although she stopped using her cane by Tuesday night. When she could read no more, she would sit on the veranda of the house, staring for hours at the San Rafael Hills that rose beyond the orange and olive groves, listening to the songs of birds and the breeze sighing through the trees. She ached to get back to work every time a whinny snuck around the corner from the barn. All the while, she thought of Phillip and what life could be like if she were to allow herself the folly of being involved with the man who now was her employer, but seemed to desire more.

By Thursday afternoon she was in a thoroughly bad mood and even had a spat with Theresa as to her level of activity, having been caught walking in the front yard. She apologized quickly, blaming her boredom, and Theresa was as quick to accept the apology. Theresa knew the lack of work had to be maddening for Alice. She had no idea of the additional emotional struggle. Alice returned to the veranda and propped her left leg on a stool, although by now there was not a hint of trauma visible on or in her leg. She waited patiently after that, watching a small band of laborers that had begun picking the early ripening olives. She surprised herself when she felt a little thrill at the sight of the buggy turning into the driveway. She suddenly felt like she should hurry inside, so as not appear to be waiting for Phillip, then chided herself for being silly and calmly picked up the book she had brought out with her. Finding her place, she began reading. When the horse's hoof beats were audible, she glanced up, smiled demurely, and returned to her book. She didn't rise when Phillip got off the buggy, although she felt like she should. Phillip and Jorge exchanged a few words before Phillip mounted the two steps to the porch.

"Well, good evening, Alice. It's good to see you outdoors again. I take it you're feeling better." Phillip's words lacked their usual enthusiasm and fatigue showed on his face.

"Much better, thank you," Alice said, matching Phillips subdued mood. "At least physically. I fear I have a bad case of cabin fever. I simply can't wait to be able to move about tomorrow, and I really don't know if anyone can keep me off a horse for another week."

"We can visit about that after dinner, perhaps. Forgive me for being out of sorts, but I've had a rather rough week in town."

"Is everything alright?"

"As far as business, very much so. I signed a contract with a new oil company today for supplies. But the negotiations were tricky and I burned a fair bit of midnight oil to pull it off. I fell asleep on the train coming back today, I do believe for the first time since I moved out here."

"Well, you certainly are as somber as I've ever seen you. Perhaps you can take a short nap before dinner."

"No, I fear if I lie down, I won't wake up until morning."

"And what's the sin in that?"

"No sin, but I'm not sure I'm brave enough to skip a meal that Margaret has prepared," he said with a wry smile.

"I hadn't considered that danger," she smiled as well. "Perhaps a good wash-up with cold water will get you through."

"Good thinking. If you'll excuse me, I'll do that. See you at dinner."

"I suppose I'd better clean up myself," Alice said as she rose to follow Phillip inside. "I'm sure I got dusty sitting around all day."

Phillip began to giggle, the kind of giggle that comes from someone who is tired and punchy and hasn't had a laugh for a while. Alice couldn't help joining in. She hadn't laughed all week, either. It took several attempts for them to regain their composure before entering the house. Phillip continued to chuckle as he ascended the stairs.

Phillip's normal good humor had returned when he came down for dinner. He provided more details of the deal he had worked out with his newest customer. The new oil company was owned by a brash and arrogant man from San Francisco whose experience and knowledge were in shipping. While well-heeled financially, Phillip could see how this company could and probably would fail. Phillip insisted on having a local bank act as the financial agent for the oil company, paying him cash. The client was terribly offended and stormed out of the room. He returned Wednesday, hat in hand, having discovered the only drilling supply company in the area was Phillip's.

"And on that happy note, young man, you had better get ready for bed," Alice said to JD. There were things she needed to discuss with Phillip. "I'll be by soon to tuck you in."

"Alright, Momma. Good night, Mr. Phillip," JD said as he climbed down from his chair.

"Good night, JD," Phillip smiled as he watched the boy head for his room. His smile then focused on Alice. "I can't tell you how impressed I am with that little boy. You're doing such a fine job raising him."

"Thank you, Phillip," Alice blushed, "I just try to do what my mother did with my brothers and me. And Carmen is just as important as I am these days. She's taught me so much about how to be a good mother."

"There's no denying that. She keeps her little brood very well in line."

"Phillip, forgive me for changing the subject, and I know you're tired, but I need to speak to you about some things tonight, if you don't mind."

"Of course," Phillip became more serious, maybe even a little apprehensive. "What's on your mind?"

"Well, first of all, I feel like I can care for myself and JD with no problem now. My leg feels perfectly normal and I have bothered Theresa and Margaret more than enough. I think I'd like to move back into the cottage tomorrow."

"I see. I suppose you're well enough to care for yourself. I can't see any sign of a limp when you walk. So long as you promise to stay off the horses for another week. I don't want you to reinjure that leg. It could be very serious if you do." Phillip's tone, while soft, was also very serious.

"I promise. I can't say I won't walk down to the barn to visit them, but I won't get in the pens for another week. I may go mad, but I promise."

Phillip chuckled, "I don't think I'd like to see you out of your mind, but I doubt that will happen. Would you care for a little brandy? I was thinking maybe we could visit on the veranda for a bit."

"I'm not sure, Phillip," Alice replied. Then seeing the disappointment in his face, quickly added, "I mean about the brandy, not the visit! If it makes me feel as stupid as the laudanum did, I want no part of it. But I'd love to visit. And feel free to have a drink if you care to. I certainly don't mind."

Phillip was thankful for the clarification. "Thank you. I'm not sure if you know, but your brother and I have written occasionally ever since we left college. I've known about your father's drinking problem for some time. I don't want you to think I might have a one as well."

"Oh. No . . . not at all," she replied, taken aback. She suddenly felt defensive. While Will had told her that he and Phillip had written each other, she never considered what Phillip knew about her family, and her, before they met. She was thankful Phillip had his back turned to her as he poured a small snifter of brandy at the cabinet across the dining room from her. She was able to compose her face before he turned back to her.

"Shall we?" Phillip gestured toward the front door. Alice nodded and the two walked to the front door. Phillip opened the door for her and waited for her to sit down before he closed the door. The veranda was dark, shaded from the moonlight and only illuminated by the light from the lamps in the front parlor that filtered through the windows. Phillip pulled a chair closer to Alice and sat as well. He took a sip of brandy before he spoke. "Alice, I have . . ."

"Phillip, forgive me for interrupting, but I just have to know before we discuss anything else. Just how much do you know about my family? About me? It's really none of my business what all you and Will write each other about, but I need to know things that pertain to me. Especially now." She was thankful the dim light didn't show her trembling chin.

"I completely understand, Alice. That is what I want to discuss. In all honesty, all Will ever said about you before April of this year is that you were a marvelous horsewoman even as a girl, and how much you made him laugh. I know that you and your father had a huge falling out. Over what, he never said. I know you ran away from home and that Will and Matt wanted to try to find you, but your father forbade it. I know your father started drinking and that he became a cruel man to everyone. And now I know he's ill and doesn't have much time left, in Will's opinion. That is the simple and plain truth."

"Thank you, Phillip," Alice said. She hoped her voice didn't betray her relief that Will had not divulged any more details. "And in all honesty, I never knew you even existed until Will and I reconnected after my husband died. The last thing I ever considered was leaving New Mexico and coming to work for a perfect stranger. I didn't want to come here, but I was desperate and both Will and Mrs. Nelson vouched for you and your family."

"And now?" Philip finished his brandy in a gulp, bracing for what Alice might say.

"And now, I realize that I've grown up a lot since I left home. I've learned many important things. Maybe not in the correct order, but they've been learned, nonetheless. I've learned that I didn't really love my husband. I was infatuated. I loved having a home again but I've also learned it wasn't the kind of home I wanted forever. I've learned I can make my own home for my son and me, but I've also learned that you need to have people who care about you to give you the courage to push through your self-doubt and fear. Will and Mrs. Nelson taught me that, and you and everyone here have convinced me of that. I've learned that I really am a pretty darn good horse trainer. I've learned I have a very good friend in my employer. But I've also learned that things can get complicated, especially when it comes to family and matters of the heart."

"That's quite an education, Alice. Some people live

their entire lives and don't learn what you know. I have to tell you I've learned a lot the past five months myself. I learned that a good family can suddenly be torn apart for no apparent reason. Will's letters taught me that. I've learned that making money isn't the most important thing in life and if you don't do what you really like for a living the money doesn't make it better. I've learned that being invited to parties and dinners by so-called friends every week is sometimes just a way for self-important socialites to market their vacuous little girls to a well-off suitor. I've learned that a strong, confident and soft-spoken woman is as rare as a four-leaf clover. And I've learned that more joy can be found in watching a little boy make mud pies than in signing a fifty-thousand-dollar contract. I've had a week of short nights, Alice, but not because of this new deal I made. I lost the sleep thinking about you and what your thoughts were."

"That's the complicated part for me right now, Phillip. We are certainly good together as employer and employee. We're very good together figuring out horses and I truly enjoy your company. I think we'll continue to become closer and I think someday very soon I'm going to wake up and know I'm in love with you, but not yet. It's like breaking a horse. You see what could be in a colt, and you really like what you have to start with, but you know that if you rush, the colt won't turn out the way he could have if you'd been more patient with him. Does that even make sense?"

"It makes more sense than anything I've heard in years, Alice. I couldn't have said it any better. I don't want to do anything that will jeopardize what we've begun here. But I do want to clarify something right now, and I'm serious about this. As far as everyone on the farm is concerned, I'm still your boss and you're the horse trainer, but as far as I'm concerned, you are not my employee. I want you to be completely free to do as you choose with the horses. I just can't think of you as an employee anymore. Does *that* make any sense?"

Alice laughed softly. "Not a bit. But I know what you mean." She stood, leaned over and kissed Phillip on the top of his head. "Go to bed, boss, you need to rest." She went into the house before he could respond and walked to JD's room to put him to bed.

Phillip stayed on the veranda a few more minutes, watching the stars, hoping that he might yet find a way to win this wonderful girl's heart.

"Maybe someday," he said to the stars as he stood and went inside.

Eight

October 16, 1900
Glendale, CA

"Senora Alice, you have a letter," Jorge called from the buckboard as he pulled the horse up in front of the carriage house. "Your brothers are very good to write you like they do!"

"They certainly are, Jorge," Alice agreed as she pulled the saddle off Diablo. She couldn't believe the change in the colt in the two weeks since she had returned to riding. His total demeanor had turned on a dime. She was making good strides with every horse, and was giving each a half-day's ride in the countryside a week as well as daily work in the arena. She carried the saddle into the tack room and led the colt to his stall as Jorge unloaded the supplies he had brought from town. When they had both finished, Jorge fished her letter from a packet of envelopes.

"Thank you, Jorge," Alice said as she retired to the tack room. She made sure the wet saddle blankets were hung to dry properly before she sat down on a stool and opened the letter. It was from Will.

Oct. 3, 1900
Dear Allie,

I'm not sure why I feel so odd telling you this, but Pa passed last night. Since I wrote last, he had gotten weaker and weaker. He stopped eating altogether, only drinking a little water from time to time. He even quit the whisky. It's odd, but day before yesterday he talked more than I could remember in more than a year. He seemed to be in his right mind and was kind and quiet when he spoke. He and I just talked most of the day and into the evening. Somehow, he even made me chuckle a time or two. He also wanted me to tell you that he was sorry for everything that happened with you and Ma and that he misses you and loves you, and hopes that someday you'll forgive him.

The doctor told me that we have to wait for the Justice of the Peace to come to Sunnyside before we can read the will. Why, I'm not sure, but it will give Matt time to get here. He just left for school last week. I'm told that the Justice of the Peace should be here next week. I'll let you know what the will has to say as I have no idea when Pa wrote it. It's been in the safe for years.

Matt asked me to send his apologies for not writing. He and Charlie have been doing the work of three with me staying at home to care for Pa, and he worked right up to the day he left for school.

I don't know if I should even tell you this, but I think you need to know. Not long before he died, Pa finally told me that he had "company" while I was with you and Matt on our trip to Santa Fe. He said they took him for a ride and he felt better when he got back. Then they came again last night, just like they did the night Ma died three years ago. But Pa never knew they took him. He seemed to have slept through the whole thing, and he passed not long after they put him back in bed. I don't know what this means for sure, but thought you ought to know.

It sounds like you have your horses lining out nicely and I'm relieved to know your leg is healed. Now that you are able to, maybe Phillip would consider letting you come out for a visit. It's a good time to give those young horses some time off and we would love to see you and JD. I bet he's growing like a weed. Take care of yourself and I'll write again next week after we read the will and figure out what all it means. Hug JD and tell him 'Unca Will' said hello.

All my love,
Will

Alice sat for a long time, trying to sort through all the emotions that the letter evoked. She grieved her father's death despite their falling out and wished she could have been home to comfort him in his last days, to hear him say, "I'm sorry," and "I love you," and to say to him, "I forgive you and I love you." She was thankful she never knew the man he had become. She was determined that the memories of her father would be those of a happy young girl learning to ride from a loving father. Her running away was neither her fault nor her father's, she had concluded. It was *them*, and they didn't intend what happened, either. Things happen sometimes, she had learned, some bad, some good. All she could do was control how she responded to things beyond her control, and work the response for the good as best as she could. A teardrop fell on the letter, bringing her thoughts back to the barn.

Wiping her face on her cuffs, she folded the letter neatly and placed it in the envelope, then in her hip pocket. It was Tuesday. She had two days to wait until she could discuss her news with Phillip, and more to wait for Will's letter regarding her father's estate.

She found herself loving Thursdays, because she knew

Phillip would be coming home and they could share news of the business, work with the horses, and play with JD. While he had always been pleasant and jovial, there had been a change in Phillip over the last month. He had peace of mind, Alice thought. She realized that she did as well. They still kept up appearances. They ate their meals in their respective homes and most certainly slept in their own beds, but were often seen riding together or spending their evenings visiting, either on the veranda of the main house or on Alice's little porch. She had never mentioned in letters to her brothers that she and Phillip were growing close. She was still deep in thought when she looked up to see Jorge watching her from the alley.

"Is everything well, Senora Alice? You've been sitting so long I thought you were hurt."

Alice smiled at Jorge. He was always so kind to everyone, and especially to her. "My heart hurts amigo. My daddy died."

"Oh, Senora, I'm so sorry. You should go to your brothers. They will need a woman's love at a time like this."

"I think so, too. I hope Mr. Jenkins will allow me some time off."

Jorge walked over to Alice and gently patted her shoulder. "Senora, we all have eyes. Senor Phillip will let you do anything you choose. He cares very much for you."

Alice blushed, saying, "I guess then since you have eyes, you know I care for him very much as well."

"Si. We are all happy to see this. Senor Phillip is a good man, but he was lonely before you came. He didn't think so because he kept himself busy working and going to his parties, but I could tell. A lonely man has a look about him, even when he is happy. He doesn't have that look anymore."

Alice studied Jorge for a moment. "You're a very wise man, Jorge. Very wise, and a true friend. Thank you for being both for me."

Jorge's blush was visible despite his dark complexion. "You have seen much sadness, Senora Alice. You are also a good friend for me and my family. We are here for you any time you should ever need us."

"Thanks, my friend," Alice placed her hand on Jorge's shoulder as she spoke. "Well, we had better call it a day. You need to get to Carmen and I need my little man home."

"Don't be afraid to love him, Senora. It is meant to be." Jorge patted her shoulder one more time before he turned and walked out of the barn. Alice followed a few paces behind. As they approached Jorge and Carmen's house, JD came running.

"Momma! Momma! Come see!" Jorge also followed the pair to the garden where three large pumpkin vines snaked out of the garden fence; the big, green pumpkins were just beginning to show a hint of orange. Alice was appropriately thrilled in her reaction to please JD. As they turned to head home, Jorge spoke again.

"All beautiful things mature with time and love."

Two days later, Alice and Phillip were drinking coffee on Alice's porch after dinner when he received the news about Alice's father. Like Alice, he had mixed emotions about the news. Alice had filled in gaps about her father that Will had omitted, which did nothing to endear the man to Phillip, but he sympathized with Alice and was amazed at her willingness to forgive. When Alice finished telling him her plans, he was nodding his head in agreement.

"I totally agree that you and JD need to go back. You and the boys need to be together for many reasons. When did you say the Justice of the Peace was due to come?"

"Will said 'next week' when he me wrote on the third,

so last week sometime," Alice explained. "The boys should know the details of the estate by now."

"I don't like that you're two weeks out of touch with them. Why don't you and I visit the telegraph office in Glendale in the morning?"

"I don't follow you. What good would a telegram do? It still needs to be delivered to the ranch, and then we have to wait for Will or Matt to reply. That's two more days at least. Probably three or four."

"I don't plan on waiting for a reply. I intend to inform Will that we'll be in Las Vegas on Monday."

"Well, I'm not sure if they would . . ." Alice froze midsentence, her eyes wide, piercing Phillip with her gaze. As she lifted her coffee cup to her lips, she asked, "I beg your pardon, sir, but did I just hear you say '*we*' would be in Las Vegas Monday?"

Phillip's face was beet red with embarrassment. He sat frozen for a moment, then managed a sheepish grin, "Slip of the tongue?" he squeaked.

Alice was just about to swallow when the answer came. She nearly choked but managed to spew the coffee out into the yard before collapsing in laughter. Phillip's hasty apologies and attempted explanations only fueled her paroxysms. He had no choice but to join in, and they leaned against each other for support until their mirth had subsided. Wiping her eyes, she wrapped her arms around Phillip's neck. "I love you, Phillip Jenkins. Would you be so gallant as to accompany me to New Mexico so as to confirm to my brothers that I've lost my mind?"

Phillip's arms wrapped around her waist. "It would be my greatest honor to confirm your insanity to your dear brothers." He kissed her softly on the lips. "I love you, too, Alice. But I know I am perfectly sane." Her playful cuff to the back of his head sent them into another round of giggling. Phillip retired to the main house and Alice to her modest bedroom. Neither fell asleep quickly. Neither stopped smiling.

Despite their short night, both Phillip and Alice were up well before the sun. Alice fed the horses and had half the stalls mucked out when Jorge entered the barn, thoroughly confused. After learning the day's plan from Alice, he immediately went to catch the bay gelding and harness him to the buggy. When he returned to the barn, he shooed Alice off to change into a dress.

She had just finished washing the breakfast dishes when Phillip knocked at her door. She put the dishes away and soon the two were off for the Southern Pacific station in Glendale. On the way, they discussed how to phrase the telegram to Will and Matt. Phillip decided the easiest way to accomplish all they needed to do was to go into Los Angeles, so he could let his office staff know he would be gone for a while, as well as purchasing their train tickets to New Mexico.

The livery stable took the gelding for the day and the couple walked from there. They entered the Glendale station of the Southern Pacific a little after eight o'clock. The ticket agent was surprised to see Phillip on a Friday, casually dressed, and even more so to see him in the company of a woman.

"Good morning, Mr. Jenkins," he said as they neared his cage, "this is a pleasant surprise. How can I help you?"

"Good morning, Mr. Blake," Phillip replied, "I need two tickets for the 8:45 to Los Angeles, please."

"Very good, sir," Blake replied. Taking Phillip's cash, he quickly prepared two tickets and passed them to Phillip. "Have a good day."

Thanking the agent, Phillip and Alice took a seat near the platform door. At 8:30, the whistle of a locomotive sounded and the train eased to a stop a few minutes later. Phillip and Alice found seats and, at 8:45 precisely, the car lurched forward as the train headed to Los Angeles. They stepped off the train at the Southern Pacific's Arcade Station half an hour later and walked the two blocks north to Phillip's office. Phillip's manager was in a meeting at the company warehouse across town, but his secretary assured him they would hold the fort until his return.

From the office, they only had to walk a few more blocks east to the Santa Fe La Grande Station. The dome of the huge building loomed over them as they entered. At the ticket counter, they were able to purchase three tickets to Las Vegas. Their train was a limited-stop service to Albuquerque, with an overnight layover. Alice was relieved to find out they would have sleeping berths for the trip. She might actually be rested when she arrived. The train was scheduled to leave at 2:45 p.m. the next day, Saturday, and they would arrive in Las Vegas at 6:30 Monday evening.

They crossed the large open area of the station to the Western Union desk, where Phillip sent a telegram to Will, in care of Jacob Gray at the bank. Phillip remembered Jacob from college as well, and knew he would get the message to Will.

Their chores finished, Phillip and Alice left the La Grande Station. They sauntered, arm in arm, back up Second Street towards Phillip's office. Crossing Alameda, they continued another block west to Central, and Phillip led Alice to his favorite café for lunch.

As they were finishing their meal, Alice asked Phillip, "I hope this doesn't strike you as selfish, but would it be possible for me to look for a couple of new dresses before we go back today? I really only have two and it would be nice to have another one or two that won't be dirty when we get to the ranch." Phillip sat for a moment, looking thoughtful. "I have my own money, Phillip, if that is a concern," Alice added.

Phillip chuckled, "I'm sorry, dear. Money wasn't my concern in any way. I was thinking of where we could go. We'll have to take the trolley, but there's a nice shop not all that far from here. I'm sure they'll have something to your liking."

Two hours later, Alice was looking at three new dresses and a hat she had selected at one of downtown Los Angeles' finer shops. The clerk gave the total and Alice reached into her handbag.

"Allow me, Alice," Phillip already had his wallet out.

"No, Phillip, I'd like to do this myself," she replied gently, but her eyes were firm.

"As you wish, m'lady," he smiled.

"Thank you, kind sir," she said, batting her eyes in jest, then paying for the items.

She did allow Phillip the gallantry of carrying the packages. Back on the trolley, they made their way to the Arcade Station and boarded the next train for Glendale. Once settled on the train, they fell into a comfortable silence, holding hands and looking out the window.

They were back at the farm in time for dinner. Alice prepared a light meal for JD and herself. When she surprised him during dinner with the news that they were going to visit his uncles, he was beside himself with glee. Alice quickly packed her new dresses and some work clothes, along with JD's clothes, in her small trunk.

Nine

October 20, 1900

The next morning, they were both up early, although they didn't need to leave until 10:00. Alice prepared breakfast for JD and nibbled on a biscuit with her coffee, too excited to eat. Making sure JD was properly scrubbed, and threatening him with staying home if he got dirty, she went to the barn and fed the horses with Jorge, informing him she had decided to turn the two-year-olds out to pasture for a while to let them absorb all they had learned, and to make room for the weanlings when she returned. She also asked him to arrange to have Diablo and the other colt she named Buddy gelded. For a moment she thought Jorge was going to kiss her he was so happy.

Returning to her cottage, Alice changed clothes and cleaned up for the trip. She decided on wearing her new hat, despite the fact that they would take the surrey all the way into Los Angeles. Jorge knocked on her door a few minutes before 10:00. He loaded Alice's luggage on the carriage and they found Phillip waiting on the front porch of the main house with his bags as they rounded the corner. He tossed his bags in the back and hopped into the back seat next to Alice. Complimenting Alice's new hat, they set off.

They pulled up to the La Grande Station at quarter to twelve. Phillip and Jorge carried the luggage into the station and checked them in for the 2:45 train. Phillip then sent a telegram to Albuquerque arranging lodging for their layover. The limited would not stop in Las Vegas and they would have to take another train out of Albuquerque on Monday.

Jorge politely refused joining them for lunch, saying that Carmen had sent him with food to eat on the way home. Phillip sent Jorge on his way and he, Alice, and JD enjoyed lunch at the Harvey House. They took their time, preferring the relative quiet of the restaurant to the bustle inside the station.

Finally, at 2:20, Phillip paid their check and the three went back into the station. Phillip purchased a copy of the *Los Angeles Times* and they made their way to the platform where their train waited. Unlike the car Alice rode from New Mexico in April, they entered a car near the front of the train and were shown to two compartments, each with two, fold-out bunks and a cushioned bench seat. The porter informed them they were welcome in the lounge car to the rear, and that they would be stopping in Barstow for dinner.

Alice hung her new dresses in the small closet in the compartment. JD sat on the bench seat and stared out the window as the train pulled out, waving at the people on the platform. It wasn't long before JD was nodding, and Alice laid him in the lower bunk for a nap. She was just about to lie down herself when a soft knock came at the door. Making sure JD was secure, she stepped into the hallway, where Phillip was waiting. They walked back to the lounge car, where they had coffee and attempted to get through the newspaper. It wasn't long before they were chuckling at their vain attempts to stay awake, and retired to their berths for a nap. They all slept until they heard the porter announcing that the train was approaching Barstow, and they quickly got ready for dinner. Back on the train, they finally read the paper before retiring. The desert night allowed for comfortable sleeping and the limited made good time.

The next morning, an early fall storm settled on Arizona. As the train pulled against the grade and a light snow on the way to Flagstaff, JD kept his face glued to the window watching the flakes fly past as Phillip and Alice talked.

"I have to ask you something, Alice," Phillip's voice seemed strained. "I have to confess that I'm afraid of something."

Alice took his hand. "What's wrong, Phillip?" she asked, genuine concern in her eyes.

"I am absolutely petrified that you'll stay with your brothers and not come back to California with me. I believe you when you say you love me and you know I love you, but I'm still afraid."

"You shouldn't be," she replied calmly. "I'm not going to change things on a whim. We'll learn what's in the will and make plans with Will and Matt after we know. Then you and JD and I will go back to California and make our plans together. I love that ranch and I love my brothers, but I love you more. It doesn't matter what happens in New Mexico. I want to be with you."

"No matter what?"

"No matter what."

"Then I suppose I should ask you something."

"Yes?"

Phillip glanced around the lounge car at the other passengers as he took a small box from his pocket. He opened it, revealing a stunning diamond ring before he leaned over and whispered, "Will you marry me?"

Alice fought the urge to jump up and down in delight and scream. Instead, she squeezed Phillip's hand like she was trying to stay on a bucking colt. She couldn't stop the tears of joy from streaming down her cheeks, though. "Yes," she whispered back. "Yes, yes, yes, yes!"

"Why are you crying, Momma?" JD asked, "Why are you sad?"

"I'm not sad, little man. I'm very happy."

"Then why are you crying?"

Phillip lifted the boy onto his lap as Alice removed her glove to try on and admire her engagement ring. "JD," he said, "sometimes ladies, and men too, get leaky eyes when they get really happy. Now, I have a question for you. Could I be your daddy? I love you an awful lot and I promise I'll take good care of you and your mother."

"I guess so," the little boy said, "Like Unca Will?"

"Even better," Phillip said as he hugged JD tight.

The early fall storm made for cool weather the remainder of the trip and they arrived in Albuquerque that evening. They walked quickly to the hotel in the chilly air for a late dinner. They were underway by 11:00 the next morning. The train stopped for lunch in Santa Fe, then made several other stops before it finally pulled into the station in Las Vegas at quarter to seven. Alice smiled widely, and then snickered as the train came to a stop and JD recognized his Uncle Will standing on the platform.

"Unca Will! Unca Will!" he cried out. Alice had to shush him with a tap on the top of his head. He barely contained himself waiting to get off the train, then raced to Will, jumping into a bear hug from his smiling uncle.

"Hello, partner!" Will exclaimed as he hoisted JD above his head. "Look how big you've gotten! Can I set you down for a bit and hug your momma?" He didn't wait for a reply, but gently lowered the child to the platform and took Alice in his arms, then held her at arm's length, "My, oh my. What a proper lady you've become," he said, admiring his sister.

"Oh hush," Alice scolded playfully, "Can't a girl buy a new hat?"

"That's the first hat you've ever owned that wasn't made of felt and you know it," Will retorted, "and it's high time. You look lovely."

"Thank you, Will. That's very sweet of you."

Will kissed her cheek before extending his hand to Phillip. "And how are you, old friend? It was very gallant of you to escort my sister all the way home."

"My absolute honor, friend," Phillip replied, "I frankly couldn't think of anything I'd rather do. We'll fill you in on the details later."

Will looked at his sister with raised eyebrows. She was blushing.

"I can't wait," Will replied, smiling. "Well, let's get your bags and head to the hotel for dinner. Matt's holding the cook at gunpoint until you get fed."

"I'd hate to start our visit with bloodshed," Phillip laughed, "we'd better get moving!"

Their bags were quickly retrieved and soon they were in the lobby of the Castaneda Hotel. Matt was waiting for them in the lobby. After checking in, dinner was spent with Will and Phillip catching up. As dessert was served, Will cleared his throat, suddenly more serious.

"Alice, I suppose we ought to talk about why you all came," he said. "The Justice of the Peace came last Thursday and Pa's will was read. He wrote it ten years ago when everything was going well for the ranch and for us. It was very straightforward. He left everything to Ma. And if she died before him, everything was to go to the three of us, either as a trust until we all turned eighteen, or as equal partners if we were over eighteen to do with as we see fit."

"So, the ranch is ours," Alice replied after a pause.

"Lock, stock, and barrel, but there's more," Will replied. "It appears that Pa was more of a businessman than we knew. He also owned interest in four other ranches, three in New Mexico and one in Colorado. He also was a partner in the Livestock Exchange here in Las Vegas. And there are bank accounts in Las Vegas, Springer, Raton, and Trinidad. We have no idea what all this involves yet. When he cleaned out the account in Sunnyside, I don't know if he did the same at the other banks."

"I'm assuming you're going to have a lawyer work through all this?" Phillip interjected.

"Absolutely," Will confirmed, "but at the moment I don't quite know who we should retain. Any ideas?"

"Actually, yes." Phillip took a sip of coffee before he continued, "Oscar Templeton in Santa Fe. He did very well for my family when my father sold most of his mining interests. Just let him know what your wishes are and he'll take it from there."

"Excellent. I'll write him tonight if you have his address."

"I do, actually," Phillip took his wallet from his jacket pocket and fished out a calling card. "Here you are."

"Thanks, Phil. You always were prepared."

"I have a sad dependence on lawyers in business," Phillip chuckled, "Be sure to let him know you were referred by me. We might even be able to visit him when we head back to California."

"Speaking of that, and whatever you say is fine, how long will you be with us?"

"Until I get tired of cooking for you savages," Alice giggled.

"Who said we'd eat it?" Matt retorted, then winced as Alice delivered a discreet but hard kick to his shin.

Phillip and Will both had to cover their mouths with

their napkins to keep from disrupting the entire room with laughter. After they had regained their composure, Alice looked at her brothers.

"Well, we also have some news you two need to know. Phillip?"

Phillip put his napkin back in his lap and took another sip of coffee before he spoke. "Will, I suppose I wasn't completely forthcoming when I would mention Alice in my letters. While she's proven herself to be a master horsewoman, I didn't mention that she has also stolen my heart. I have proposed to her and she has accepted, and with your blessings I'd like to marry her."

Will sat silently for a moment before looking at Phillip and Alice. "Remind me to never play poker with you two," he said smiling broadly, "Neither one of you ever even hinted at something like this. Did you know anything like this was going on Matt?"

"Not an inkling," Matt replied, also beaming.

"Well, if Alice has said yes, I won't say no. You've been like a second brother to me, Phil, and I'll welcome you as a brother-in-law with pride. But know this. If you hurt my sister, I will defend her honor with a fury you can't imagine."

"And he won't be alone," Matt added.

Phillip smiled and looked the brothers in the eye as he raised his glass. "Then I propose a toast to the honor of the woman we love. To Alice Roberts."

"To Alice," Will and Matt replied in unison.

"Well, I'm too tired for such gallantry right now," Alice blushed as she folded her napkin. "If you gentlemen will excuse me, I think JD and I will retire to bed."

The men rose and Phillip helped Alice with her chair. A brief but humorous argument arose with JD wanting to stay with "the rest of the men," in his words.

"Maybe someday, my little man, but not tonight," Alice said as she kissed his forehead. She and JD headed for their room and the men to the bar for a brandy.

After they were served and cigars were lit, Phillip returned the conversation to business. "I'm assuming you two know Alice well enough to know she'll expect a full say in how this estate is handled?"

"Oh, yes," Matt replied, "We're not fools enough to think we can boss her around."

"Absolutely," Will agreed, "she may be more entitled than we are, considering all she's been through."

"I'm happy to know that," Phillip said, "she's sure had a whirlwind of a life the past four years."

"I'm just glad the whirlwind set her down with you, buddy," Will said. "So, what is our plan from here?"

"I've been thinking about that," Phillip said, "Instead of you writing that letter to Oscar tonight, why don't you and I jump on the train back to Santa Fe tomorrow and meet with him? I'd be happy to introduce you, and we can get the ball rolling faster that way. Regardless of what you three decide, you'll have to notify all the partnership ranches and the banks of your father's death as soon as possible, and Oscar can start on that immediately."

"And baby brother stays behind to take care of Alice?" Matt didn't seem angry, but confused.

"Sorry, Matt," Will said, chagrined. "Would you rather go? I have no problem with that."

"I have no objection, Will. I really would like to get to know Matt better," Phillip assured.

"I really don't care, either," Matt replied, "I was making a joke, but I kind of like Phillip's suggestion. I'd like to get to know him as well."

"Well, let's plan on that, pending the boss lady's opinion at breakfast," Will grinned.

"To the boss lady," Matt laughed, raising his glass.

"To the boss lady," Phillip laughed as well.

They finished their cigars, then stood to head for their rooms. As they crossed the lobby, Phillip stopped, looking at the front desk.

"Hold up, boys, I just remembered something I read." Approaching the night clerk, he asked if telephone service had reached Las Vegas. The clerk replied that the Southwestern Telephone Company had finished their long-distance line from Santa Fe in May and that calls could be made from the train station between 8:00 a.m. and 4:00 p.m. daily. Thanking the clerk, he turned to Will and Matt. "Well, I'm glad I thought of that. I'll try to reach Oscar by telephone in the morning. I'd almost bet he has one. That will save us all some time."

"And now you see how he got rich, little brother," Will said to Matt as he wrapped his arm over Phillip's shoulder. "The man just thinks faster than everybody else."

At breakfast the next morning, Phillip told Alice of his plans to reach Oscar Templeton and, if possible, meet him in Santa Fe with Matt. Alice agreed that it was a good idea to try to contact Templeton by telephone if possible. As to the other interests, they agreed they didn't want to maintain the partnerships in the other ranches, and would seek to sell their interest in them. They all seemed to have a desire to hold their interest in the Las Vegas Livestock Exchange, however.

Their business concluded, they finished their meal and headed to the Santa Fe station for the telephone call. After a long session with the operator in Santa Fe, Phillip was connected to Templeton's office. Unfortunately, he was in court, but could see them later that day. Matt and Phillip agreed to take the train back to Santa Fe and the others wait in Las Vegas. Will was thankful he had thought to bring all the papers regarding the estate. He and Matt made sure all the documents were in the satchel at the hotel before Matt and Phillip headed back to the train station.

The train ride to Santa Fe allowed Phillip and Matt to get well acquainted. Although seven years his senior, Phillip was impressed with Matt's maturity and level head. By the time the train pulled into Santa Fe, the future brothers-in-law were becoming friends. As they got off the train, Phillip smiled and waved to someone further down the platform. Matt's eyes widened as a mountain of a man in a gray suit and black hat strode down the platform.

Oscar Templeton stood six feet, six inches tall and weighed nearly three hundred pounds. With a dark complexion, jet black hair and a massive moustache, he was as intimidating a figure as one could imagine. He was well aware of this fact and employed it frequently in the courtroom.

Phillip's hand was completely engulfed when the two greeted each other. Matt prepared to have his own hand crushed by this giant, but Templeton knew his own strength and gripped Matt's hand firmly, but with great control.

"Phillip, it's been a long time," Templeton said as he led them through the station and down the street to his office. "How have you been?"

Phillip gave a thumbnail sketch of his life in California and how he came to meet the Stevens family. They entered a bustling office, with several clerks and secretaries scuttling about. Templeton employed two associate attorneys as well. As they sat at Templeton's desk, Phillip turned the story over to Matt, who explained the reason for their visit. Producing the documents from the satchel, he handed them to Templeton. The lawyer read the will very carefully before scanning the other documents. Phillip and Matt waited patiently. Templeton finally looked up.

"Well, most of this will be fairly straightforward," he began. "I see you already have several copies of the death certificate, which will expedite most of the transfers. In fact, you could handle all the bank account transfers without me."

"We think it would be best to have representation with out-of-town banks, and especially the one in Trinidad," Phillip said.

"Thank you, Phillip, I appreciate that, and it won't take much for my office staff to do, with one exception. I'm afraid I represent one of the banks mentioned in the will. The one in Las Vegas actually. I can't appear to have a conflict of interest in the matter. However, I'll send a note with you to the bank president attesting to the will being legal and you can transfer ownership of the account yourselves. It's simply a matter of enquiring with the bank for the account information, giving them a copy of the death certificate, and transferring the account to the three of you. As far as the home ranch is concerned, you simply have to transfer ownership with the County Clerk in Santa Rosa. No need for my services on that. Now, as to your ownership interests in the ranches and the Livestock Exchange, what do you three want to do?"

"We would like to sell our interest in all of them, except for the Livestock Exchange." Matt replied.

"I'll have to research how the partnerships were filed in each county, but under territorial law in New Mexico you should still have standing to sell your interests, or sue for them if need be, based on the partnership agreements you have. I'll have to check on Colorado law as to the ranch there, but it should be similar, except for negotiating the worth of the ranches. But I can be persuasive in that department when I have to be."

"As I can attest," Phillip grinned.

"You wouldn't be thinking of Mr. Stratford, would you?" Phillip just smiled wider. Matt was dying to ask, but kept his tongue. He knew, however, that his family had the right man for the job. "Will you boys be staying the night?"

"Actually, if we hurry, we can get back on the train and be back in Las Vegas tonight. We really need to get to the ranch and further discuss our plans."

"I understand. I'd be happy to treat you to dinner, though, if you'd like."

"That's very kind of you, Oscar, but we really should head back."

"Say no more. I'll be in touch soon."

"Thank you. I'll try to stop by when Alice and I return to California. We plan on visiting mother and father before we leave."

"Give them my best when you do." Templeton smiled as he stood to escort Matt and Phillip to the door, thanking them for the business.

Matt and Phillip hustled back to the train station. The eastbound train arrived late, giving them a chance to get aboard. Matt purchased tickets to Las Vegas while Phillip bought box lunches, and they just made the train. Once on the train, Matt couldn't hold his curiosity any more.

"Phillip, I hate to pry, but I'm curious as heck about that Stratford you were smiling about with Mr. Templeton. What was that about?"

Phillip smiled as he remembered. "Buford Stratford is the son of a wealthy man from Illinois who found himself in Colorado Springs working for six dollars a week, and got gold fever. He started prospecting around Cripple Creek, worked up one mine, and then sold it to finance another one that produced big. Unfortunately for him, one of his tunnels accidentally went through a small claim my father had. Father tried to negotiate a settlement with him unsuccessfully for over four years. Well, Stratford put the mine up for sale last year and Mr. Templeton filed an injunction to block the sale pending the settlement of this claim dispute. Stratford is this little, scrawny, sickly alcoholic and he called Templeton into his office in Colorado to tell him how the cow ate the cabbage. Templeton told Stratford what father wanted to settle the injunction and was refused—until Templeton picked him up, tucked him under an arm and carried him to the courthouse in Cripple Creek, where Stratford found it in his heart to buy my father's claim for a considerable sum."

"I would consider that pretty persuasive," Matt laughed.

"Well, father was also holding up a seven-million-dollar sale with the injunction, so Templeton did what he did as much for show as business," Phillip chuckled. "But it goes to show he's not a man to trifle with."

They arrived back in Las Vegas too late to visit with Will and Alice that night. At breakfast the next morning, Matt recounted the meeting with Templeton and his optimism for settling the estate. As Templeton predicted, the banking in Las Vegas was finished before they boarded the stage. The account was used for the deposit of annual dividends from the Livestock Exchange. While the railroad owned the land and stockyards, the actual trading of livestock was managed by a group of investors, Mr. Stevens among them, who hired a broker to manage the actual buying and selling of the livestock that passed through the Exchange. The account had a balance of just over nine thousand dollars and the Stevenses decided to leave the account open for the time being. As they bounced along in the coach headed home, the group was surprisingly quiet. They had all communicated so well by mail that there was little catching up to do. Long, comfortable periods of silence marked the trip.

Arriving in Sunnyside, the family retrieved their buck-board and saddle horses from the stable. The final leg of their trip from Sunnyside out to the ranch became more animated, with the siblings reminiscing as they drew closer to home.

As they approached the ranch house, they saw their old dog, Dan, trotting toward them. Alice wept with joy at the sight of her old friend, hopping from the buckboard and taking the old dog in her arms. JD was not far behind, waiting to make a new friend.

Will smiled from his saddle and leaned over to whisper to Phillip, "Wait until she finds out her old mare is still around."

Ten

October 28, 1900
Fort Sumner, New Mexico Territory

Almost before they realized, a week had passed. Phillip and Alice made wedding plans for December, with Matt and Will agreeing to come to California for the wedding and staying through Christmas. Financial planning took up much of their time. Phillip, always thinking ahead, suggested investing in real estate and the developing telephone and electricity companies, knowing how they were making strides in expanding in Los Angeles and the surrounding areas. The Stevens trio agreed, and charged Phillip with exploring these options, although they all agreed to wait until the sales of their shares in the other ranches were completed to make final decisions.

Their planning completed, Matt, Phillip, Alice, and JD took the stage back to Las Vegas. Matt and Alice concluded the family's business with the Livestock Exchange, and the four then took the train to Santa Fe. Phillip introduced Alice and JD to his parents, who were cold in their reception, but warmed slightly after learning of her connection to the Nelsons. Matt met again with Oscar Templeton. He was happy to learn that the bank accounts in Springer, Trinidad, and Raton were still open, holding balances in excess of fifty thousand dollars combined, and that ownership would soon be transferred to him, Alice, and Will. Templeton had enlisted the services of a land speculator of some repute to enquire of the partnership ranches and other neighboring properties as to their willingness to sell and asked them for a price that would satisfy them. He would report the prices to Templeton when he received word from the ranches to use in negotiating the amount to demand for his clients.

Meeting back at the hotel, Matt relayed his finding to Alice and Phillip over dinner. At one point during the meal, JD asked to go to the restroom. Phillip took him, excusing himself from the table. Alice watched him as they walked away then looked at Matt.

"I need to tell you something," she began, "I wanted to mention it to both you and Will but I just couldn't get you two alone without being obvious. Phillip doesn't know about the 'visitors' that come for me. They showed up again after I got hurt, and I hated them for coming back again, but took me into their ship and healed my leg. The nurse called it a miracle and I told her I had no idea what happened. We didn't tell Phillip either, because we weren't sure if my leg was really healed. We just kept it to ourselves. I faked a limp for two weeks so no one became suspicious."

"Wait a minute. You're saying that those . . . *things* fixed your leg?"

"I don't know what else to tell you. My leg was bigger than yours that night at dinner, and almost normal when I woke up the next morning. All I can remember is that I knew they were outside and I was cussing them for being there, then I was lifted out of bed. When I woke up the next morning my leg was nearly normal."

"Well, you'd better say something soon," Matt cautioned, "you know they'll probably come back. They always seem to."

"I know, but I'm so afraid it will harm our relationship. Anybody would think I'm crazy. But at least now I'm convinced they really don't mean me any harm."

"We'll back up your story. You know that."

"Thank you, Matthew. You've both always been so considerate of my feelings on this. And let Will know I wish I could have told him myself. The last time they were brought up I told Will we'd never speak of it, but that was before this last visit when they helped me."

"Here they come," Matt said as he saw Phillip and JD returning, "Time to change the subject." Dessert was spent talking of the wedding and Phillip's family.

The next morning, Matt began his trip home, including a side trip to the courthouse in Santa Rosa to transfer the deed for the ranch, supplied with the proper documents provided by Templeton's staff. Phillip, Alice, and JD boarded the train at noon to begin their trip home. They had a short layover in Albuquerque, then boarded the limited to Los Angeles.

Late that night, Alice awoke to a soft but persistent knock. Putting on her robe, she opened the door and Phillip rushed in. He pulled up the shade on the window, and pointed excitedly. "Alice, look at that!" he whispered.

Alice gasped as she sat down and looked. There in the night sky, less than a mile away, the familiar triangular shape flew alongside the train, matching its speed.

"Don't be alarmed, Alice. We don't need to examine you," the voice said.

"Then why are you here?" she asked.

"We were hoping we could contact your future husband. Sadly, he cannot hear us."

Not knowing how to react or what to say, she looked at Phillip. He seemed completely unaware of the conversation.

"You won't believe it, Alice, but I've seen that thing before," Phillip whispered, "I saw it, or something just like it, once when I was a boy. My parents said I was imagining it, but there it is!" The craft followed a few more seconds, then shot into the night sky

No better time than the present, Alice thought.

"Phillip, let's go to your compartment so we don't wake JD," she said. They made sure JD was still sound asleep, and then slipped out of Alice's compartment and up to Phillip's just forward.

"Did you see it? Did you see it, Alice?" Phillip was almost giddy with excitement. "I can't believe I got to see something like that twice! Oh, I'm so happy you were here to see it too! Anybody besides you would call me drunk or crazy!"

"You're neither drunk nor crazy, love," Alice said, "Now just calm down. You need to know something. I've seen that thing before, too. In fact, I've seen it several other times. Now you have to trust me that I'm not crazy."

"I absolutely trust you, dear."

Alice collected herself and took a deep breath. "That thing is a ship from another planet. The . . . I don't know what to call them . . . creatures, I guess, they told me they are scientists that have been studying Earth for a long time. They study everything about Earth, including people. They have several dozen people around the world that they study in depth."

"How . . . how do you know all this?" Phillip was thunderstruck. There was a long pause.

"Because when I was four years old, they took me onto their ship. They took my mother and me and examined us from head to toe then put us back. My mother explained that they have been studying her family for three generations. She said they mean no harm, but I was so scared I couldn't believe her. They examined us three more times. The last time they examined us together, Daddy saw their ship and watched as they took us inside. That's what started all the trouble. Daddy's mind was starting to go by then and he accused Mother of 'conjuring' the ship like she wanted it to happen. Before long he started accusing Mother and me of being witches and every little thing that went wrong was our fault. That's what forced me to leave home. They examined me after I ran away as well. They told me I was pregnant with JD before I even suspected. I've hated them from day one until now."

"What's different now?"

"Will you forgive me a white lie if I tell you?"

"It depends on how white, but I'm sure I will," he smiled reassuringly.

"When Diablo kicked me, they showed up the night Edith lanced my leg. They took me into their ship and healed it. I don't really remember going on the ship, but I know they were there, and when I woke up the next morning my leg was almost normal. Edith said it was a miracle, but I wanted her to stay in case whatever they did to me didn't work. I didn't tell you because I wanted to be closer to you and I'm still thankful how it all worked out."

"Well, I can't say I'm sorry you did what you did," Phillip said as he kissed her, "If they played a part in us being where we are today, I'm grateful. I'm very sorry it affected your father the way it did, though."

She laid her head on his shoulder. "That's one of the oddest things about this. Will told me in a letter once that on the day he took me to the train to come to California, they visited Daddy. They came again just before he died. Somehow, I think he made peace with them and himself before he passed. If they helped heal his mind enough to be right with the Lord and with the boys and me, I'm grateful.

And the fact that it all led me to you is the best thing that ever happened to me."

They sat quietly for several minutes before Phillip spoke again. "Do you believe in God, Alice?"

"Of course. My earliest memories are of Daddy reading the Bible to us. We lived so far from Sunnyside that it was hard to go to church, but we had a Christian home."

"So, what does God have to do with these creatures?"

"I'm not sure, Phillip. But if God created everything that means he must have created them, too."

Phillip sat silently, digesting this thought before he spoke. "We always went to church after we settled in Santa Fe. Will and I even went sometimes when we were in college. I stopped when I moved to Los Angeles, but I think I . . . we . . . should start. Don't you?"

"I think that would be very good for us, and especially for JD."

"There's a little Methodist church in Glendale. I know some folks who attend."

"That sounds fine to me, dear," Alice said.

"We better check on JD."

They left Phillip's compartment and Alice slipped into hers, smiling at the sleeping child. Phillip blew her a kiss from the door before he closed it. He ruminated for over an hour on all of what he had learned in the past few minutes before he turned to prayer. What he had seen had muddled his concept of faith, but had not destroyed it. He prayed simply for wisdom to sort out the mystery. *Maybe someday,* he thought.

Eleven

December 18, 1900
Glendale, CA

Alice touched up her makeup for the umpteenth time before
Theresa gently pinned her veil into her hair and draped it
over her face. Alice's meticulous planning had paid off. All
the details of her wedding were falling into place perfectly.
Phillip's parents and sister arrived on the fourteenth, still
not thrilled at Phillip's decision to marry Alice. Matt and
Will, accompanied by his new lady friend, Peggy
Osterhaus, arrived the next day. These six, along with Jorge
and Carmen, plus six friends from the Glendale Methodist
Church and its pastor, made up the wedding party, much to
the dismay and offense of Angelino socialites and the
society press, who were salivating for a story of the
marriage of one of Los Angeles' most eligible bachelors to
a woman unknown to them. Both Phillip and Alice agreed
that this should be an intimate, very private affair for only
the people they were closest to. They were now gathered in
the small ballroom on the first floor of the house.

Theresa carried the train of Alice's dress as they
walked downstairs, where Will was waiting to walk her
down the aisle. Teresa opened the double door at one end
the room, and the church organist began Wagner's
"Wedding March" on the piano near the door. Phillip and
the pastor waited, smiling, at the opposite corner of the

room. There wasn't an aisle, per se, as the family and guests were seated in individual chairs arranged in a semicircle, with a walkway open in the center. JD sat between his uncles and served as ring bearer. The ceremony was brief but meaningful. JD was as serious as anyone could ever recall and fulfilled his duty without flaw. A kiss and a loud "amen" from the assembled party sealed the marriage of Alice and Phillip Jenkins.

The photographer Phillip hired took two photographs of the couple, one indoors and one outdoors, as well as one of the assembled families. He would not be paid until he delivered the prints and the photographic plates to Phillip, and then only after he was convinced the press had not received any copies. A gourmet dinner featuring home–raised beef and lamb, Margaret's magnum opus, completed the celebration. Three days later, Alice mailed a brief wedding notice to the *Times.*

Alice and Phillip didn't leave on their honeymoon for another two weeks, deciding the company of family through Christmas was superior to an immediate vacation. The family enjoyed a relaxing week that included a proud Alice leading a trail ride for the family on her two-year-olds with her and Diablo leading the way. Phillip's sister Juanita took an immediate liking to Alice and JD which helped blunt the continued chilly attitude of her parents about the whole affair. Alice remained respectful and cordial with her new in-laws, trying very hard to gain their approval without demeaning herself in the process. Will was beginning to lose patience with Phillip's parents but kept a civil tongue.

Christmas revolved around JD, who received more gifts than he had ever seen before—so many that he cried, overwhelmed by the avalanche of affection and attention. When all the presents were opened, Phillip sat JD on his lap and asked what his favorite present was. The tears welled up in the little boy's eyes again as he buried his face in Phillip's chest.

"You, Daddy," he said.

Twelve

March 22, 1901
Glendale, California

Alice and Phillip were busier than they had ever been, beginning more advanced training on the now three-year-olds, starting the two-year-olds, and with spring progressing, foaling out the mares. They also had never been happier. After their honeymoon in San Francisco, Phillip legally adopted JD, but Alice asked that they not change JD's last name in honor of Delbert, and would let him decide when he was older if he chose to change.

In February, Phillip sold his drilling supply company for over half a million dollars. The estate of Alice's father had netted her just over eighty thousand dollars in cash, thanks to the efforts of Oscar Templeton. The real estate speculator Templeton hired had received the predictable inflated valuations from the ranches to a prospective buyer. Templeton then used those offers against the ranches for the Stevens' shares and negotiated fairer but still lucrative sums. Alice and Phillip invested much of this money in real estate, in local telephone, electric, and natural gas companies supplying the rapidly growing Los Angeles metropolitan area, as well as purchasing stock in other major national companies. Will and Matt invested a fair portion of their inheritances in a similar manner, allowing Phillip to manage the funds. Phillip had structured the surface rights leases on his oil field properties to rise and fall with the production of the wells, which were now at peak production. He and Alice lived very comfortably on these payments.

Phillip stayed at home fulltime, spending much more time on the horses. Telephone service had expanded in the Glendale area, and Phillip paid to install service to the farm, along with electricity to all the buildings, and had completely updated the plumbing. Most of the business he conducted now was by telephone. He went into Los Angeles only on occasion to meet with realtors, stock brokers, accountants, and his attorney. Family outings into Los Angeles and the surrounding area were common, even trips to San Francisco and San Diego. It was on these trips that JD became fascinated with the sea and ships, especially the great ships of the U.S. Navy anchored off Long Beach and in San Diego.

They were on their way home from church on a sunny but breezy Sunday morning, discussing the topic of the sermon and making plans for the week, when Alice casually asked Phillip if they could hire someone to help with the horses.

"Well, I suppose we could, although I think we're keeping up pretty well right now," Philip said with a slight smile. "Are you considering firing me?"

Alice chuckled, "No, I'm not considering firing you, silly," then, after a pause, added, "I may have to fire me for a while, though. I think I might be pregnant."

A sheepish grin and a slight blush crept across his sharp features. "My. That didn't take long. Are you sure?"

"Not completely," she replied through her own blush, "I'll go to the doctor this week and see what he thinks, but I'm pretty sure."

"We'll give him a call tomorrow first thing."

"I don't think we should tell anyone else until we're sure, though."

"I agree, and you're right about finding someone to help. I won't be able to ride all fourteen colts and do a good job. I'll reach out to some folks we know. I'm sure we'll find someone."

JD had been sitting silently between them. His curiosity finally got the better of him. "What's 'pregnant,' Momma?"

"Well, it means that you might be getting a new baby brother or sister. Would that be alright with you?"

"I guess," JD said. "Will I have to feed and water him like I do the lambs and pigs?"

"No, honey, I'll take care of that," Alice replied as seriously as JD had asked. Phillip kept his eyes forward, biting his cheek to keep from laughing.

On Tuesday, Alice saw the doctor in Glendale, who agreed she was most likely pregnant. With no reliable test available, a "wait and see" attitude was the usual course of action. The doctor did allow Alice to keep riding for the next month, but wanted her to stop after that. She mentioned that she had ridden while pregnant with JD until she couldn't fit in a saddle, but the doctor was unmoved, as was Phillip.

Two weeks later, a letter of introduction arrived from the ranch Phillip and Alice had purchased their stallion from for a young man named Randall Burke, giving him high recommendations for the job of assisting Phillip training the horses. After consulting with Alice, Phillip replied that Mr. Burke sounded like the man he needed.

Burke arrived at the farm for his temporary job exactly one year after Alice had arrived. Quiet and unassuming, he quickly fit into the routine of the farm. His style of training matched Phillip's and Alice's very well and soon he was working all the two-year-olds. Phillip continued training the three-year-olds. To his and Alice's happy amazement, Diablo had become the quietest and most easily handled of all the horses. He spooked only once with Phillip when they flushed a covey of quail from some tall grass on the hillside behind the pastures, but immediately quieted down and continued on his way, much to Phillip's satisfaction.

By the end of May, Alice was comfortable to simply watch and advise. Her pregnancy was becoming obvious now, and she was quite happy to feel free of the need to keep working simply to survive, as she had to do while carrying JD. She still did a little ground work with the two-year-olds when Randall was riding the others. She also was very happy to start teaching JD to ride a pony they had purchased for him.

The rest of the spring and summer passed quickly for the Jenkins family. A trip back to New Mexico in June saw the wedding of Will Stevens to Peggy Osterhaus in Las Vegas. Alice was thankful they didn't have to take the stage to Sunnyside. She wasn't sure she would have been able to attend if that had been the case.

The three-year-olds all were turning into solid working horses and interested buyers frequently visited. By August, all were spoken for, to be picked up in September, except for Diablo. Alice insisted that he stay for her personal use after the baby was born. Unable to ride but wanting to stay active, Alice busied herself helping Carmen in the large garden and, as the vegetables ripened, helping Margaret in the kitchen. She had only a basic knowledge of canning and preserving food and Margaret was happy to teach her. She also walked the long driveway from the house to the main road twice daily.

As Alice's due date approached, Phillip became more and more nervous and, despite Alice's perfectly normal health, checked her into California Hospital in Los Angeles. Phillip was an acquaintance of the hospital's founder, Dr. Walter Lindley, as well as several other physician-owners of the hospital and it was there, on November second, that Robert Phillip Jenkins was born. Alice had a far easier labor and delivery than she had experienced with JD, much to Phillip's relief. JD was introduced to his baby brother a few days later when his parents returned home. While happy to meet Bobby, he was disappointed that the new member of the family wasn't very entertaining. Phillip told JD to just be patient and he would be playing with his little brother before he knew it.

Thirteen

April 19, 1906
Glendale, California

Nerves were frayed at the Jenkins farm. Everyone had all but forgotten the fun of JD's ninth birthday party held just two days before. Early news from the previous day's earthquake in San Francisco was so bad as to not be believed. Over the past five years, as Phillip's business interests had become more diversified, he and Alice had made friends all around California, and more than a few in San Francisco. Phillip had stopped trying to contact any of them by telephone; the operators all assured him there were no intact lines into the city.

The quake was large enough to have shaken the family from their beds a little after 5:00 a.m. and sent them and all the employees running out of the houses to the safety of the open space between the houses and the barn, but no appreciable damage was seen at the farm, save for some cracking of stucco on the outbuildings. JD and Bobby were terrified, as was Alice. She had never experienced a quake of this size. Later learning how far away they were from the epicenter frightened her even more for friends and acquaintances in San Francisco.

Phillip was a calming influence for the family although internally he was horribly concerned for his friends, not to mention his investments in the bay area. He was thankful he had spread his still growing fortune among many interests in many areas of the state. His father's serendipitous ability to avoid financial ruin in only one industry convinced him to avoid putting all his eggs in one basket years before. But today he worried much more for the people than the businesses. Neither he nor anyone else on the farm did much work other than feed the livestock and milk the cows, and he and Jorge made sure the pipeline from the artesian well was intact. To their relief it was, with the water remaining clear as it ran into the tank. School in Glendale was cancelled for the day, allowing JD to stay at home.

After lunch, everyone was surprised to see a horse and rider coming down the driveway and even more surprised to learn it was a Western Union courier with an urgent telegram for Phillip and Alice. Fearing the worst in light of the news, Phillip read the telegram, then sighed and smiled in relief as he passed the telegram to Alice. The message was from Matt announcing the birth of twin girls to Will and Peggy named Frances and Sylvia. Phillip drafted a quick reply of congratulations along with an assurance of their safety, assuming news of the earthquake would reach New Mexico soon.

Things were beginning to approach normal by dinner. The boys, still nervous, asked if they could "camp" in the front yard instead of sleep inside. The weather was pleasant enough, so Phillip and Alice saw no harm. They set up a pup tent in the grass some twenty feet from the veranda and left the light on. Alice was thankful she had to step outside at one point and tell the boys to settle down and go to sleep. It meant they had stopped being nervous about the earthquake and had begun acting like her ornery boys again.

Alice didn't sleep well. A little, nagging headache

wouldn't leave her and she constantly awoke at the slightest disturbance, including a mild aftershock that got the boys nervous again. The eastern horizon was beginning to lighten when she finally gave up and walked out onto the veranda to check on the boys. Looking up at the sky, she sighed as she noticed a particularly bright star continue to get larger. She stepped off the veranda and onto the lawn. A little more than a minute later the ship hovered over her. The boys bolted from their tent and cowered behind their mother, despite her assurances that they were safe.

"*Hello Alice,*" the voice spoke in her mind "*Are you well?*"

"Hello," she replied silently, "I am well, thank you. And thank you for helping me on your last visit. I wasn't very friendly that time."

"*I understand. I was not supposed to interfere, but we hoped helping you would be seen as a token of our goodwill.*"

"It was. So was your visit when you flew by the train. My husband was very excited to see you."

"*It's unfortunate he is unable to communicate with us.*"

"Can you hear *me*?" Alice looked down to see JD now standing silently beside her, with Bobby next to him, both looking at the craft.

"And me?" Bobby echoed.

"*Yes, James and Robert, I can hear you,*" the voice replied. "*It seems you have your mother's ability. Alice, we would like to include your sons in our study.*"

"You won't harm them?" Alice still didn't trust them completely.

"*No, you have my promise not to harm them. We will only examine them from time to time, as we have you.*"

"It's alright, Momma," JD said, taking her right hand, "We're not afraid. Are we, Bobby?"

"Nope," Bobby said, as confidently as a five-year-old could.

"Alright, then." Alice smiled and reached her other hand out to Bobby, gently leading him to her left side. Then looking up to the craft, she simply said, "We're ready."

Watching open-mouthed from the bedroom window, Phillip saw the huge craft descending towards his family. Frantically racing down the stairs and out the front door, he found himself frozen in his tracks by a beam of light coming from the ship, leaving him to helplessly watch his wife and sons float upwards and through an opening in the front of the craft.

Once inside the ship, the boys were taken to one room, Alice to another. JD and Bobby looked around the stark room. Brightly lit, it held only a bed-like platform that extended from one wall opposite the door. What looked like cabinets lined the remaining two walls, although neither boy saw handles or hinges. JD and Bobby were placed on the platform in turn and a number of devices were passed over their bodies. Neither of them experienced any pain, even when the small tracking devices were implanted in their scalps. Alice's examination took less time than the boys' as they were new to the study.

Ten minutes later, Phillip's prayers were answered as Alice and the boys were deposited back in the yard. Finally, able move, he watched the craft rise until it was but a fading star that finally disappeared. Gathering Alice and the boys into his arms, he made sure they were unharmed, then peppered them with questions, most of which they were unable to answer, for the next hour. He was very disappointed to learn he didn't possess the abilities needed to participate in the visitors' study. Alice explained it was something passed through her family somehow. According to the visitors, all communication is pure thought, but most people have to process the thought into language to be understood. Somehow, members of Alice's family, and others around the world, had the ability to communicate with the visitors by thought alone.

By breakfast, Phillip and the boys had regained their composure enough to not tip Margaret off to the visit. The boys were instructed not to speak to anyone about the encounter. As the day went on, Phillip's excitement over the visit gave way to his concerns for the situation in San Francisco.

The family's routine returned to normal over the next several days. JD resumed school and Alice and Phillip slowly learned the extent of the tragedy in San Francisco. They heard that several of their friends had been injured by falling debris in their homes, but none of them seriously. Two of the businesses Phillip had interest in were destroyed, others damaged, and many employees had been killed. Phillip wanted desperately to travel north to try to help, but Alice wouldn't hear of it. The risk was too great and the news still reported of fires burning out of control. There would be time later to travel to San Francisco, she said, when it was safe. He reluctantly agreed. Another minor earthquake a few days later, yet another aftershock from the main quake, gave Alice's objection even more weight. It also worsened the cracks in the stucco on the buildings, giving Phillip and Jorge more work to do.

Two months later, Phillip finally made the trip north. The Southern Pacific had repaired track as far as San Mateo, where he located a business associate and borrowed a horse to ride into San Francisco. The devastation was nearly beyond his comprehension. He found himself lost several times, unable to find landmarks that were no longer there and streets blocked with rubble. Entire families still wandered the streets seeking food, shelter, and hope. They paid little mind to Phillip as he rode by.

He finally succeeded in finding friends whose homes had not been severely damaged and were allowed to stay while repairs began. From them he learned of others who were staying out of town and got their contact information before he headed home. It struck him how quickly he had become dependent on the telephone for communication now that the area was without service.

He was also struck to learn the true nature of some of the people he had befriended over the years and whom he thought he knew well. One partner went on for an hour talking about how he had broken a bone in one finger and how inconveniencing it was, then complaining how he was having difficulty replacing ten dead employees. Another openly wept for a broken chandelier. When he asked the man about his employees, Phillip was sickened by the response of, "Who cares?" The partnership was dissolved on the spot and Phillip returned home.

Back in Glendale, he was able to contact most of his associates at their temporary offices and homes. He was thankful that most of these people had shown more empathy towards employees injured or killed in the quake due to their own serious losses. Insurance would likely leave their losses at a minimum, but resuming normal business would take years. Fortunately, Phillip was also an owner or partner in several construction companies in the area that would be very busy for a long time, and he used this advantage to move as many employees as possible from his other businesses to the construction firms to provide them with a job.

PART TWO

Growing Pains

Fourteen

May 20, 1915
Glendale, California

Alice walked out of the barn and into the afternoon sunshine. A Steller's jay jabbered at her from one of the oak trees along the driveway. It had been an easy spring for her with only four two-year-olds to start training and two three-year-olds to finish. They had purchased three new young mares in the spring of 1911 in order to retire three older mares who had failed to conceive the previous two years. Over the summer nine of their twelve mares aborted their foals and one died, leaving only two live foals born in 1912. The new mares were sold immediately, suspected of having brought a disease onto the farm, but the foal crop in 1913 was a disappointing four head. Phillip was embarrassed to have purchased the mares from a stranger without consulting Alice, but she held no blame for her husband. The pedigrees of the mares were exactly what they had been looking for and Alice was as enthusiastic over their arrival as Phillip was. Fortunately, the foal crop of 1914 returned to normal and three new mares with foals at side were purchased. There were now twelve yearlings that JD and Bobby could begin halter breaking, and in the pasture were twelve new foals with their mothers.

Phillip had used the extra time away from the horses to consolidate some of his business interests, selling out of some enterprises while buying out partners in others. He and Alice were astounded when a certified letter arrived in April from none other than Oscar Templeton informing them that Hanna Nelson had died and, with no children of her own, willed the ranch and all her assets to Alice. While Alice had written to Hanna regularly, she hadn't received a reply in several weeks but knew Mrs. Nelson was in ill health, as reported by the nurse Alice had hired to care for her. She had no idea, however, that she was the beneficiary of the estate. Will, Peggy, and Matt were immediately notified and at Phillip's suggestion, the partnership was reorganized and incorporated as Three S Land and Cattle, Inc.

Matt, thinking he wanted something different than ranching before college, had taken the bulk of his share of the partnership in cash to finish his studies. He made an about-face after his third year in Albuquerque, however, and moved to Fort Collins, Colorado, where he graduated with degrees in animal husbandry and veterinary medicine from Colorado Agricultural College in 1910. Setting up practice in Las Vegas, he still assisted at the ranch and when the Nelson Ranch came under family ownership he moved to Sunnyside, now officially merged into Fort Sumner, and bought back in as an active member of the corporation. He divided his time between operating the ranch and practicing, running up and down the roads in his Ford Model T.

Phillip also had purchased a new car, a Cadillac, in 1914, and took to driving everywhere he could make an excuse to go to, including giving the boys rides to and from school every day. He had taught JD how to drive and sometimes allowed him to drive home from school, to the envy of his classmates.

Now a senior in high school, JD was as tall as Phillip,

but was the ruddy-faced image of his father Delbert. Blessed with a sharp intellect and his mother's natural balance and agility, he was an excellent student and athlete. He and Bobby spent six weeks every summer in New Mexico, working for their uncles. They had become horsemen of considerable skill and when at home were glued to the back of a horse. As much as he loved the ranch and horses, though, JD loved the sea and was captivated by the thought of serving in the United States Navy. His grades and extracurricular leadership were impressive enough to encourage him to apply to the United States Naval Academy. Phillip had become acquainted with Congressman Charles Randall, as he had been with Randall's predecessors. Although not politically active, Phillip's money made him attractive to politicians as a potential donor. After talking with JD, Phillip and the Principal of JD's school sought and received the Congressman's recommendation for JD to the Academy. A discrete but generous contribution from Phillip to the congressman's reelection campaign for 1916 followed.

As she made her way back to the house, Alice heard the familiar honking of the Cadillac's horn as it turned up the driveway. Phillip was driving and JD was standing in the front passenger seat, shouting to her and wildly waving something in his hand.

"I'm in! I'm in!" JD kept yelling as Phillip slid to a stop. Vaulting from the seat, JD swept his mother into a hug, lifting her off the ground. "I'm in! I made it!"

Phillip and Bobby got out of the car, both beaming.

"James Delbert, settle down!" Alice was taken aback by JD's exuberance. "You're in what?"

"Sorry, Momma," JD said as he stepped back. He handed the letter he'd been holding to Alice. She looked at the envelope as she collected herself. The return address read, "Capt. W. Fullam, Supt. United States Naval Academy, Annapolis, Maryland."

Eyes widening, Alice quickly removed and skimmed the letter, over Captain Fullam's signature, welcoming JD to the Class of 1919. As the realization sank in, she began to tremble, then shrieked, "You're in! You're in!" and wrapped JD in her own bear hug.

Phillip and Bobby howled with laughter. Drawn by the commotion, the entire staff had come to the house and, learning the news, all joined in the celebration.

The letter ordered JD to report for registration and orientation at the academy on August 1st. Over dinner, the family decided to accompany JD to Annapolis and spend some time touring the area. Alice's grandfather had fought for the Union Army and she wanted to see some of the Civil War battlegrounds, as did Phillip. They also wanted to go to Washington and New York. It would be their first trip east of the Mississippi and they began planning immediately.

JD graduated from Glendale Union High School as valedictorian in June and immediately departed for New Mexico with Bobby for one final, abbreviated summer with his beloved uncles, aunt, and cousins Sylvia and Frances. The extended Stevens family was thrilled to learn of JD's appointment to Annapolis. Matt feigned disgust, however, when he heard the news.

"What's wrong, Uncle Matt?" JD asked, truly concerned, "I'm sorry if I disappointed you somehow."

"Well, what would you expect?" Matt grumbled, trying to maintain the charade. "Now I have to find another good roper to help at branding time." He scowled at JD for a moment before playfully pulling the boy into a headlock. Matt's powerful build had increased as he matured, and as a veterinarian his strength was considerable. Where JD had inherited his father's lanky build, Bobby was a slightly smaller version of Matt. Nobody could escape the grasp of Matt and Bobby if they caught them. JD howled in mock pain and laughter.

The summer flew by for the boys. The year before, Will had introduced Bobby to shooting, as he had JD when he was fourteen. Bobby became completely fascinated with firearms. He learned not only how to shoot, but the characteristics of every rifle, handgun, and shotgun Will and Matt owned. He studied how the different calibers and bullet weights behaved at different ranges and in different conditions. His favorite was Matt's Winchester .30-40 lever action Krag rifle. The week before he left, Bobby dropped a pronghorn with a single round from the rifle in a crosswind. Matt stepped off the shot at two hundred seventy-five yards. Asked how he managed to drop something as small as the antelope from such a distance, Bobby tried to explain, but couldn't. He simply had a knack for knowing the behavior of a projectile.

On July fourteenth, JD and Bobby boarded the train in Fort Sumner and thanks to a newly constructed rail line headed for Albuquerque, where they met Phillip and Alice for the trip east. Their trip was very comfortable in the Pullman car Phillip had booked, despite the rising humidity as they travelled further east, and they arrived in Washington, D.C. five days after leaving Albuquerque. Three days were spent touring the capital, then on to Manassas and Gettysburg, and finally looping south to Baltimore before ending their trip in Annapolis, arriving on the thirty-first.

They attended a welcome reception for families at the Naval Academy, then said good-bye to JD. He seemed completely calm and confident in his new independence, and Phillip beamed with quiet pride. Alice and Bobby, however, couldn't contain their emotions as well as Phillip. Weeping with pride and sadness, they held JD for a very long time. Finally, JD had to gently pull himself away from them.

"Easy, you two," he said, "I'm going to school, not the gallows. I'll be home at Christmas."

Alice calmed down but still worried about JD. Despite Phillip's stating that the war in Europe would not involve the United States, she knew he had moved funds into companies like Remington and Winchester, along with steel, aircraft, lumber, and textile companies. She also knew from JD that the navy had commissioned two new battleships and was building four more. Both her husband and the Navy thought war was a definite possibility, in her opinion.

From Annapolis, they traveled to New York. While accustomed to the business district of Los Angeles, they were struck by the sheer density and volume of activity in New York. It reminded Bobby of an ant colony, thousands of people swarming to and fro, all accomplishing some form of work. The height of the buildings was also a surprise. Their rooms at the Biltmore were on the sixteenth floor, with more floors above them. Phillip quipped that it was easy to build that high when you didn't have to worry about earthquakes, not knowing that the occasional temblor did affect the area. The Call Building in San Francisco was the tallest building on the west coast at fifteen stories. Los Angeles forbade buildings higher than one hundred fifty feet high, not for fear of earthquake, but for appearances.

For three days the family walked for miles through Manhattan, enjoying the different cultures of neighborhoods, and sampling the dizzying variety of foods. Their final stop was Philadelphia, touring Independence Hall and other landmarks of the founding of the nation. At one point they found themselves on the banks of the Delaware River looking across at the shipyard in Camden, New Jersey and the Navy's new battleship, USS *Oklahoma,* now nearly complete. Alice shuddered.

The return to California was altered to allow a stopover in Fort Sumner. Alice had not been back to New Mexico since Matt had moved to the Nelson Ranch. Matt was anxious to show her the improvements he had made, including building a new main residence, but guarded his enthusiasm as he was unsure if she wanted to return. He tentatively mentioned the new house before heading home the first night they were together and received no reply. When he returned the next day, Alice surprised him and asked when they could go to what she now referred to as "the west place".

"Why, we can go anytime you please Alice," Matt said, "It only takes a little more than an hour to get there by car."

"Could you take us now?" Alice asked.

"Absolutely. I'll have to clean out the back seat a little, but we can go as soon as I do."

Alice and Phillip waited patiently in the house while Bobby helped his uncle unload the "two boxes" of equipment, along with a half-bushel basket of instruments and bottles of medicine, from the back seat of the Model T touring car into the barn. Bobby offered to stay behind to save Matt some work but Matt insisted he come. He had a surprise for Bobby, he said. Soon Phillip and Alice came out of the house and, after a little more ribbing of Matt, piled into the Model T and headed west. The roads had been improved dramatically with the influx of automobiles in the area and true to Matt's word, the car turned into the ranch seventy-five minutes after they left. Where the original ranch house once stood was a large two–story frame house with a wide veranda completely encircling the building.

"Oh, my!" Alice exclaimed when they stopped at the front door, "what on Earth do you need a house this size for?"

"To be honest," Matt answered with a smile, "I built it in the hope that I could talk Will and Peggy into moving and I would stay at the home place. But I hope in time I can fill it up." Just then the door to the house opened and a woman in her late twenties stepped out.

"Can't you give a girl a chance to clean up a little for company?" she scolded Matt with a smile.

"Oh, honey, you're so pretty you don't need to do anything," Matt said as he jumped out of the car to kiss her cheek. "Phil, Alice, I'd like to introduce you to my wife Ellen."

Alice froze in her tracks, looking back and forth at Matt, Bobby, and Phillip in delighted, open-mouthed confusion. She finally found her voice.

"Matthew, you are a rascal of the first order. Just when were you planning on telling your sister you had gotten married?" and then, to Bobby, "And just what made you think you could keep a secret like this from your own mother?" She gave Bobby a playful cuff to the shoulder.

"I wanted to pay you back a little for not telling me that you and Phil got engaged," Matt laughed mischievously. "Actually, it was a bit of a fluke. Ellen was my secretary and bookkeeper in Las Vegas and when I decided to move down here, we suddenly realized that we didn't know what to do without each other. So, we had the Methodist minister in Las Vegas perform the ceremony and here we are."

Phillip and Alice walked to the veranda and after properly hugging Ellen and welcoming her into the family, toured the house, as well as the improved barns and corrals. It was a very different place from the one Alice had left fifteen years before. She still had many memories, but they were softer now, without grief. As they started back towards the house, Alice asked to be excused from the group. They all knew where she needed to go.

The simple gravestones for both James Nelson and Delbert Roberts had been replaced with larger, polished granite stones, personally selected by JD and paid for by Matt and Will. Hanna Nelson was buried next to her husband and their monument memorialized them both. Delbert's monument bore the epitaph, "Husband and Father." The cottonwood trees still shaded the grass and the breeze seemed to blow back sounds of laughter from two teenagers growing up faster than they should have, of squealing broncs and bawling calves and work that Alice thought would surely kill her. She remembered all that and more, and considered where she now found herself in life. She stared at the stone a long time with a wistful smile before she whispered, "Good-bye, dear," and walked back to the house.

When she entered the front door, she found Bobby beaming, proudly holding Matt's .30-40. This was the surprise Matt wanted Bobby to come for. The rifle was now his. Alice thanked Matt for his generosity. She had heard the story of the shot on the pronghorn several times from both of her boys, and was proud of every useful skill they mastered. They visited through lunch, and then Matt further surprised them by driving the Model T into a large shed he used for a garage and returned driving a brand new Chevrolet Series H out of the building.

"You *are* full of surprises today, Doc," Phillip crowed. He was completely thrilled with all the happy news of the day. The Stevens and Jenkins families rode back to Will and Peggy's in comfort and style. There was a full house for dinner that evening with the entire family, save for JD, present. A toast to his success concluded the meal. With more rooms available at Matt's house, and the surprise for Alice sprung, The Jenkins family returned with Matt and Ellen for the night. Two days later they returned to California.

Fifteen

April 7, 1917
Glendale, California

The *Times* arrived at the farm by mail the day after it was printed. Both Phillip and Alice had read that President Wilson asked Congress to declare war on Germany due to its total war campaign against American shipping and the shocking discovery of the German plot to support a Mexican invasion of the United States. They knew the Senate had already passed the resolution and now the paper reported that it had also passed the House. America was at war.

Neither Phillip nor Alice knew what effect the official declaration of war would have on JD. They hoped the war would be over by graduation in 1919, but later would learn that JD and his classmates would graduate early, in 1918, to fill the need for officers in the expansion of American forces in the war. The news of the deadly German submarine activity in the Atlantic made Alice very aware of the risks her son would face. JD didn't help with his enthusiasm over America's entry into the war and his champing at the bit to get into the fight. Even Bobby was starting to talk about being in the military.

JD was not always focused on his studies, however. The Naval Academy always included social functions to round out the lives of the midshipmen, from ice cream socials to dances, inviting young ladies from the best families of Maryland, Virginia, and southern Pennsylvania. It was at one of these dances in 1916 that JD was introduced to Jeanne Sommerville.

Jeanne, a city girl from Baltimore, was the grand-daughter of a retired army colonel who, as a young Lieutenant, once served at Fort Sumner. The coincidence wasn't lost on JD, who became infatuated with the beautiful young socialite. He played his one card master-fully and over the next year won her heart, thanks, in part to Jeanne's memories of her grandfather's stories of the cavalry in the wild west. She was fascinated by JD's stories of horses and horsemanship, never revealing to JD that she was an accomplished equestrian herself, trained first by her grandfather, then by expert instructors.

She eventually let JD know of her ability with horses and invited him to her home for a ride one weekend. JD cemented himself in her heart when he fell off his mount his first time on an English saddle. Conceding superior horsemanship to Jeanne, he also confessed his love. The courtship was brief, but the two knew they were meant for each other. Jeanne accepted JD's marriage proposal in early 1917, and the couple were married January 4, 1918. The entire Jenkins and Stevens family traveled to Baltimore for the ceremony at the Old Otterbein Methodist Church.

JD graduated in June the following year and, after two weeks of crash-course anti-submarine sea training, was assigned to the destroyer USS *Tucker,* operating out of Brest, France in July. A few weeks later, on August 8th, the destroyer was credited with sinking a German submarine. JD was exhilarated by the action and his confidence and ease at leading his men was noted by his superiors. His enthusiasm did nothing to stop his mother's worrying, though. She knew the German Navy cared little about her son's enthusiasm. She prayed for the end of the war and her worry. *Maybe someday*, she thought.

Sixteen

September 13, 1918
Glendale, California

"I got a curious call today from a man who claims he wants to buy all the yearlings," Phillip said at dinner.

"Really?" Alice asked. It was rare for them to hear from people interested in untrained horses, much less twelve of them. People were very happy to buy three-year-olds from them and pay a premium for a nearly finished and gentle young horse. "I don't really fancy the idea. If it's someone who doesn't know what they're doing it could certainly harm our reputation should they not like what they get."

"I agree. And reputation aside, this group is pretty special. If they come back in the spring like I think they will, we could name our price when they're three. I've talked with our Arizona and New Mexico customers, as well as the locals and they're all very happy. Everyone wants to buy more. This fellow said he'd like to make a name for himself as a trainer and wants good, solid stock to start with."

"It sounds to me like he wants to get his hands on some good, halter broke yearlings and sell them fast," Bobby snorted, "just take advantage of our good breeding and then he gets the credit for it. If he wants to be a trainer he should take in outside horses and send them back to their owners.

That's how you get a good reputation."

At nearly seventeen, Bobby had become an integral part of the management of the horses. Over the summer he had stayed at home to work with the yearlings, halter breaking them and breaking them to lead, as well as working with the three-year-olds, most of which had been picked up and sent to their new owners. He had learned much from his parents and uncles and was becoming an accomplished trainer in his own right. Now that school was back in session, he still worked every weekend with the horses.

"I agree with Bobby," Alice said, "This thing just doesn't add up. Did this fellow give you a name?"

"I wrote it down in the office but I can't be positive now. I think it was Schmidt . . . yes. Yes, it was. Walter Schmidt."

Alice stopped chewing and brought her napkin to her mouth, as if she were about to get sick. Her face was as pale as death.

"What's wrong, Momma?" Bobby asked as he left his chair, thinking she was choking.

"It can't be," she whispered. "It simply cannot be."

"What is it, dear?" Phillip rounded the table and knelt at Alice's side, with Bobby hovering over her.

"Oliver Sinclair," was all she could say.

Bobby looked at his father, baffled by her reply. It took Phillip a moment to recall the story Alice had told him, but it finally clicked. He gently took her hand and kissed it. "It can't be him, Alice. What are the chances?"

"But what if it is?" she snapped at Phillip.

"Well, if it was, he had no idea who he was talking to," Phillip assured her.

"You're probably right. I'm sorry. It couldn't be him."

Bobby interjected, "I'm sorry if I'm rude, but who the

heck are you talking about?"

Alice had regained her composure. "Bobby, a man named Oliver Sinclair killed JD's father. He used the alias Walter Schmidt when he stole the cattle Delbert was taking to market with Mr. Nelson. He was never caught."

Bobby was quiet for a moment. "I'm really sorry, Momma. I didn't know that part of the story. But Dad's right. There's just no way this could be the same man."

"You didn't know his name because I didn't think it was important, son. And both of you are quite right. There's bound to be more than one Walter Schmidt out in this world. But that being said, Phillip, I'm dead set against selling those yearlings. To anyone."

"Agreed," Phillip nodded and returned to his chair at the table. "I told him the chances of him getting them weren't good, but that I'd discuss the matter with you two before I gave him my final answer. He's supposed to call me back tomorrow morning. When I say we're not interested in selling, the matter will be closed."

"Well, I had an unsettling thing occur today as well," Alice said as they resumed their meal. "I was riding the hillside near the artesian well and I happened upon a set of tracks that have to be from a cougar."

"That's not good at all," Phillip said.

There had been a good population of mule deer in the hills around Los Angeles, but with the continued growth of the city the deer had become less common. They still were seen in the hills adjacent to the farm, however, and on occasion a few were even spotted in the horse pastures. The summer had been drier than usual and Phillip and Alice had noticed the deer more frequently. It made sense that a predator would follow its prey. The problem with a cougar was it would have no problem taking down a foal instead of a deer if it chose to.

"Sounds like I'm going cat hunting tomorrow," Bobby said.

"Just be careful," Phillip reminded him, "Which horse will you take?"

"Old Reliable," Bobby replied. Alice smiled, thankful once again that she didn't let Phillip sell Diablo. Now twenty years old, the former menace was the steadiest and most trusted horse on the farm and despite his advancing age, was still capable of doing almost anything. Bobby had even shot coyotes from the horse's back at a full gallop. He also made for good advertisement when prospective buyers came to look at three-year-olds.

"Don't let him get hurt," Alice said with a twinkle in her eye.

"And thank you, dear mother, for your concern for *my* safety," Bobby laughed. "Don't worry. We'll be fine."

Bobby caught Diablo in the pasture as soon as it was light the next morning and brought him to the barn to saddle. He slipped the .30-40 into a saddle scabbard and rode off to the hills behind the farm. He quickly found the tracks his mother had discovered leading from the artesian well downhill towards the farm. Bobby decided to back-track and find out where the cougar might have come from. Seeing the tracks from the back of Diablo became increasingly difficult as the scrub became thicker on the hillside, and at several points Bobby had to dismount to follow them. The trail took him along the first ridge of hills behind the farm and he was almost two miles from home when he topped the ridge.

As he paused at the top of the ridge, a glint of light on the next ridge to the north caught his eye. Pulling a set of binoculars from his saddle bag, he glassed the ridge until he spotted a buckskin horse, barely visible as it blended into the brush on the hillside, with a man, also looking through binoculars, standing next to the horse. The man wore the khaki uniform of a California Game Warden. Bobby remained sky-lined at the top of the hill and the warden spotted him quickly. Waving to each other, the warden mounted his horse and began coming Bobby's way. Bobby started Diablo down the hill and the two met in the draw between them. Bobby noticed the man had a rifle in his scabbard and a revolver on his belt.

The Game Warden introduced himself then asked Bobby what he was doing armed. Bobby explained the discovery of the cougar tracks and how he had backtracked them to where the two had spotted each other. The man confirmed he was looking for the cat as well, as it had killed a calf and several dogs north of Glendale a few days before. Two other Wardens with hounds were working their way towards them from the southeast, he said, and a fourth Warden was on the next ridge over. The Warden politely but firmly told Bobby he needed to head back to the farm for the day, but he would drop by the house and give the family a report when they had finished their hunt. Wanting to stay but knowing better than to argue, Bobby wished the man good luck and headed back for home.

As he came down off the top of the ridge, Bobby took a long and gently sloping route down the south facing slope. He promised he would go home but didn't specify his route to the Game Warden. He did, however, want the hill between him and any bullets fired on the other side. And he still hoped he might catch sight of the cougar himself. Thirty minutes later, he heard several rifle shots in quick succession, followed by one final pistol shot. It was clear that the cougar had been found and killed. Thankful that the threat to the horses was gone but still wishing he could have had a shot at the cat, Bobby turned Diablo to a more direct route home.

The hill above the farm offered a beautiful view of the pastures and trees on the farm as well as a view of the valley leading into Glendale. Bobby noticed an odd looking truck travelling down the road that ran by the farm. It appeared to be the size of a Mack freight truck but had wooden side boards on the back. He took out the binoculars again and confirmed that this was exactly what the vehicle was. He was even more surprised to see it slowing down as it approached the driveway. He spurred Diablo to a trot as they angled more steeply down the hill towards the farm.

The previous night's conversation about Walter Schmidt had Bobby on high alert as he approached the back gate to the pasture. Stripping his tack and leaving it in the tall grass, he took the .30-40 from the scabbard, levered a round into the chamber, and carefully released the hammer. He removed his spurs, then led Diablo through the gate, keeping a single rein around the horse's neck. Using the horse as cover, he angled across the pasture to the rear of the barn.

The truck had stopped in the center of the driveway near the barn. Bobby looked between the barn and carriage house and saw an "ON" brand painted on the door of the truck, but it meant nothing to him. He couldn't see any people because of the truck, but heard his father's voice and another unfamiliar male voice. While he couldn't make out the words, the strain in his father's voice was unmistakable, as was the menace in the other man's voice. Bobby quickly ran around the back side the carriage house and the cottage his mother once occupied and, peeking around a corner, was shocked at what he saw.

Phillip stood in the yard to Bobby's left about seventy-five feet from the cottage. Just to the right, and twenty feet closer, a man stood with his back to Bobby. His left arm was wrapped tightly around Alice's waist and his right hand held a revolver that he would wave as he ranted and then point at her temple.

"Get that ramp and them sideboards down, you two," the man screamed at Jorge and Emilio, "and get them horses loaded!"

"Please, Mr. Sinclair, calm down," Phillip pleaded, "I've already told you to take the best horses on the place. Even the stallion if you want him. Just put the gun down and we'll talk."

"There ain't nothin' to talk about, mister. I just need to decide if your wife gets to live after those horses get loaded. I should've killed you eighteen years ago," he growled at Alice, "but now I think it might be better just to kill another husband for you. How does that sound, Alice?" He broke out in a hoarse, evil laugh and fired a shot into the ground near Phillip's feet.

"Nobody has to die," Phillip cried, "just take the horses and let us be. Let her go and we'll get the horses and you can be on your way. I swear you can just leave." He tried very hard not to turn his eyes toward Bobby at the corner of the cottage.

"Oh, you're wrong there, mister. Somebody's gonna die here. I just can't decide if it'll be both of you or just one. Maybe all four of you!" The demented cackle began again as he pointed the revolver at Jorge and Emilio.

His mouth dry as dust, Bobby had seen and heard enough. He pulled the hammer back on the rifle, picked up a small rock and silently stepped to his left. He tossed the rock high into the air, then quickly shouldered his rifle. The rock landed behind Alice and the man and ten feet to their right. Reflexively, the man turned his head towards the sound, unconsciously pointing the revolver in the same direction to ward off any threat.

The two hundred twenty-grain bullet struck Oliver

Sinclair above his right ear and exited just behind his left eye in a mist of blood and fragmented bone. His hat prevented most of the gore from hitting Alice as his body crumpled to the ground, dead before he fell. Alice stood frozen in shock and fear, finally turning to see her son lower the rifle as Phillip ran to her side. She collapsed into his arms as he pulled her away from Sinclair and sat on the ground, holding him close. Bobby laid the rifle on the ground and ran to his parents, sobbing in fear and relief. The three sat and held each other, not noticing Jorge, Carmen, Emilio, Dorothy and Theresa coming to their aid, forming a protective circle around the family.

After a long while, Phillip helped Alice back to her feet. She was still in a state of shock, but had regained enough of her faculties to walk back to the body lying in the gravel, where a large pool of blood had spread out from the head. Sinclair's remaining right eye stared back at her. She stared at the shattered head in silence, then spat in the lifeless eye and walked into the house.

Margaret was the first to speak. "I called the sheriff. They're on the way," she said quietly.

"Don't move anything. Everyone, get inside," Philip said quietly to the staff as he and Bobby followed Alice to the house.

Phillip walked down the hallway to his office. As he passed the downstairs bathroom door, he heard Alice retching inside. He made sure Bobby was not in a similar state. The boy was shaken, but in control of himself as he sat in the front room. Alice emerged from the bathroom a few minutes later, still quite pale but coherent. Phillip guided her to the front room to await the sheriff.

Two deputies arrived quickly and after hearing Phillip's initial report, came inside and called the department headquarters in Los Angeles, requesting a detective, coroner, and additional deputies. Hearing a vehicle approaching, one deputy walked back outside, his hand on his revolver. To his surprise a Fish and Game Commission car was coming down the driveway. Stopping the car at the house, the deputy was told by the Game Warden that he promised a report on the cougar to the Jenkins family and wanted them to know the animal had been shot. The deputy thanked him and sent him on his way, not divulging the reason for his presence nor allowing him to drive further onto the property. He relayed the news of the cougar and Phillip and Bobby nodded numbly.

It took another half hour for the detective and two deputies to arrive from downtown. After walking the area with the responding deputy, he sent his subordinates to take statements from the staff while he interviewed the family individually, starting with Phillip, in his office. With the door closed, Phillip relayed how he had been contacted by a man named Walter Schmidt regarding the purchase of the yearlings. Schmidt said he was going to call back but instead showed up in his truck unannounced to negotiate a price. Phillip told him that the horses were not for sale. The news angered Schmidt, who then began haranguing Phillip to sell him the remaining three-year-olds, only to learn that they were all spoken for. Alice had been working a colt in the arena behind the barn when she saw the truck come down the driveway, and tied up the colt to investigate. She realized who the man was after it was too late to get to the house unseen, and also missed seeing Bobby sneaking in from the pasture.

Sinclair didn't recognize Alice at first but ordered her over to Phillip and became increasingly belligerent. Alice finally had had enough and asked if he planned on killing them like he did Delbert and James Nelson. It was at this point that he recognized Alice and pulled her away, producing the gun from inside his coat. He demanded Phillip get the remaining three-year-olds he had and ordered Jorge and Emilio to set up the loading ramps attached to the sides of the truck. As Jorge and Emilio set to work, Phillip continued to try to calm Sinclair to no avail, assuring him he would bring the best horses he had if Sinclair would release Alice. Sinclair was shot moments later.

The questioning paused after the detective took Phillip's statement with the arrival of the coroner and the removal of Sinclair's body. He then took Alice's statement, collecting the background information regarding the murder of Delbert and James Nelson. She had some difficulty getting the detective to understand how county lines in New Mexico had changed since 1900, and which county sheriff to notify regarding the still-open murder case there. The detective finally took Bobby's statement. To the absolute shock of Phillip and Alice, Bobby emerged from Phillip's office in handcuffs, under arrest for second-degree murder.

Two deputies escorted Bobby to one of the cars as the detective and the remaining deputy restrained his hysterical parents. Only after the car had left did the detective explain that by law, he had to detain Bobby until a judge could hold a preliminary hearing in Los Angeles, probably on Monday. The news did nothing to soothe Phillip and Alice, however. The moment the detective was out the door Phillip was on the phone to his attorney's home to find the best criminal defense lawyer in Los Angeles. J. H. McNally was mentioned immediately by Philip's real estate attorney, James Norville, who volunteered to call on Phillip's behalf. Half an hour later, the telephone rang. Phillip sprang to answer it. It was J. H. McNally.

"Mr. Jenkins, I understand you've had quite the

ordeal."

"To say the least, Mr. McNally. Thank you so much for calling on the weekend."

"Well, in light of the circumstances, I think we should move quickly. Mr. Jenkins, I doubt that you remember, but we met briefly a few years back at the hospital benefit."

"Of course, I do. Thank you for your recall."

"It was your charming wife that made me remember. Please extend her my sympathy. Now, tell me what happened today."

Over the next several minutes Phillip relayed the events leading up to the shooting of Oliver Sinclair, leaving out no detail, starting with the Nelson Ranch eighteen years before.

"Do you have any reason to believe that he knew he was coming to Alice's home?" McNally asked.

"No, I don't," Phillip answered. "The look on his face when he finally recognized Alice was absolute shock, followed by fear, then hatred. I've never seen anyone act like that before. I think he's just been making a living taking advantage of people through intimidation and fraud and today, when he saw Alice, he panicked. My question is, why on Earth did they arrest my son for protecting his mother?"

"Unfortunately, it is procedure, and prescribed by law. He did admit to killing the man. But to hold a boy in jail over the weekend is intolerable. I'll petition one of the criminal court judges for an arraignment today. The problem may be posting bail. Forgive me if I pry, but do you have some cash on hand?"

"I have around three thousand in the safe. Would that be enough?"

"I'll make sure it is. In fact, I think bail may not be set since your son is a minor, but you'd better bring the cash just in case. I'll call you back as soon as I know something. In the meantime, and I know this will be difficult, but I want you and Mrs. Jenkins to clean up and dress for court. I'll want you there to vouch for Robert."

"We'll be ready for your call, sir. Thank you again."

The simple act of washing up did much to pull Phillip and Alice back to a semblance of normality. Margaret made a bite of food and that helped as well. At 4:30 p.m. the phone rang again. It was Mr. McNally advising them that Bobby would be arraigned at 6:00 at the Los Angeles County Courthouse. He was currently being held by himself in Glendale, which was a minor relief to Phillip and Alice. They couldn't bear the thought of their boy in a holding cell with grown men in the downtown jail. Not wanting to be a minute late, they immediately set off for Los Angeles.

The courthouse doors were locked when Phillip and Alice arrived, but they were early and waited in the circle drive at the front of the ornate building. At 5:45 p.m., another Cadillac pulled in behind them and a distinguished, silver-haired gentleman stepped out and strode to them with the quiet confidence men of influence and ability acquire over a career. The face was immediately familiar to both Phillip and Alice as Mr. McNally. He removed his hat and bowed slightly as Alice extended her hand and her thanks for his trouble on a Saturday. He dismissed the inconvenience, assuring her it was something somewhat common for him.

A few minutes later a deputy inside the building opened the door and led the trio to a courtroom on the second floor. They found Bobby handcuffed and sitting on a bench next to the deputy who had removed him from the house earlier in the day. McNally informed the deputy he needed to speak to his client in private and was led to a small room across the hall. The deputy removed the handcuffs and stood guard outside the room. Once inside, McNally asked the Jenkins to sit down. He was suddenly all business.

"Robert, Phillip, Alice, I'll be honest with you. Today will be a piece of cake. The prosecutor will be whoever the District Attorney can find to come in. The judge is a practical man that I've argued cases before in the past. However, in light of your confession, this matter will proceed and if the right prosecutor gets hold of this, we could have a fight on our hands. But, today, I want you all to be totally cooperative, meek and mild and let me get Robert out of jail. Agreed?"

"Agreed," all three responded.

McNally spent the next several minutes having Bobby recount his interrogation at the Glendale Sheriff's office. He was thankful the boy had said nothing more than what he told the detective prior to his arrest and that the deputies had not forced the issue with any rough handling to obtain any more information. Soon the Clerk of the Court informed them that the judge had arrived, and led them to a courtroom, the deputy following the family.

McNally was right. The prosecutor for the county was a young lawyer named Reeves who had only a preliminary report from the Sheriff's detective that he received in his office at 5:30. Judge Grant Jacobson mounted the steps to his bench in a hurry. He was irritated at having his Saturday interrupted. The clerk read the docket number introducing the matter of the People of the State of California versus Robert Phillip Jenkins on the single charge of murder in the second degree.

"Master Jenkins, how to you plead?" Jacobson demanded.

"Not guilty Your Honor," McNally replied. "In fact, I

move for dismissal of the charge as my client acted in the defense of himself and others."

"Your Honor, the defendant is accused of ambushing a man and shooting him from behind while his father watched," Reeves countered. "The State requests the defendant be remanded without bail."

"Your Honor, my client is a sixteen-year-old boy and was defending his family from an armed assailant," McNally parried. "The facts will show that my client had no choice but to act as he did. His family is of impeccable character and very well known in the community."

"Which I'm sure you will argue at trial, Mr. McNally. Mr. Reeves?" Jacobson looked at the young lawyer, who was still furiously reading the sheriff's report.

"Your Honor, the defendant presents a flight risk. His parents have the means to easily move him out of the jurisdiction."

"Oh, please," McNally scoffed, "Your Honor, my client is no more a flight risk than I am, and to place him in the general population of the county jail is tantamount to condemning him to assault, or worse. He will appear for trial. I request that the defendant be released to the custody of his parents."

"Your status as a flight risk is not germane to the debate, sir. Mr. Reeves?" Jacobson was getting tired of this.

"At the very least your honor, the State requests that bail be set at . . . five hundred dollars."

"Mr. Reeves, are you familiar with the Jenkins family name?"

"No, your honor."

"I didn't think so," Jacobson grumbled as he looked at the docket calendar. "The defendant is released to the custody of his parents. Jury selection is scheduled for Thursday, October third, with trial to begin October seventh." The gavel slammed before Reeves could draw a breath.

When they arrived back at the farm, Alice, Phillip and Bobby were relieved to see Sinclair's truck had been removed, according to Jorge, by the Sheriff's Department. Emilio had found Bobby's tack and spurs and had put them away as well. Phillip made sure Alice and Bobby were settled before he quietly walked to his office and shut the door. He called the Western Union office in Los Angeles, asking how he could send a transatlantic telegram to JD.

It was almost a week before JD learned of the incident, when the *Tucker* docked in Brest and the telegram was delivered. He worried terribly for Bobby, but couldn't deny his vindictive pleasure in learning that his own father's murderer had fallen to his brother's rifle.

Seventeen

October 1, 1918
Glendale, California

"Alice, it's Mr. McNally," Phillip called to the front room where Alice was reading. As she entered his office, Phillip asked if she knew where Bobby was. Alice replied that he was riding after returning from school. Phillip uncovered the mouthpiece on the telephone and held the earpiece so that he and Alice could both hear. "Alice is here. Go ahead."

"I just got off the telephone with the judge in Robert's case," McNally explained, "He wants to meet with us and the district attorney at 9:00 a.m. tomorrow. It appears that influenza cases in the city are increasing at an alarming rate, and he's not confident we will be able to impanel a jury that will remain intact for the entire trial. He said the mayor may declare an emergency before the week's end which may postpone everything for an indefinite period of time. He'd like to try the case tomorrow."

"Just what does that mean?" Alice asked.

"Well, he has all the reports from the sheriff and the coroner. He also has reports from the authorities in New Mexico that confirm Sinclair was the prime suspect in the seven cattle-theft murders, including Delbert's, which should help. However, if I were a prosecutor, I would try to use that to show you wanted revenge and took it, using your minor son to do the dirty work. We also have your employees' statements regarding how Sinclair seemed to be unhinged, but Judge Jacobson may discount them. All my background investigations into Sinclair show him to be violent and unstable, and I have several sworn statements to that effect from people I planned on calling as witnesses. We just have to see what the judge wants to do."

"What do we need to do?" Phillip asked.

"Just show up and be prepared for a long day. And bring Jorge and Emilio with you as eyewitnesses," the attorney said, "I don't know if they will testify, but I want them there if needed. This is uncharted water for all of us."

The next morning, Judge Grant Jacobson met with McNally and District Attorney Thomas L. Woodbine in his chambers. Outside chambers, Los Angeles County Sheriff John Kline, the detective in charge of the case, and the Jenkins family waited in separate rooms across the hall. They then moved to a courtroom where the judge announced he would try the case immediately. Through the remainder of the morning the judge heard opening arguments and testimony. The prosecution's case essentially consisted of testimony from the detective, who conceded on cross-examination that he had no evidence of a revenge motive in the shooting, based on sworn statements he obtained from officials in New Mexico, as well as employees and friends of the Jenkins family. Woodbine then called Bobby to the stand to confirm his confession to the shooting, and again attempted to prove premeditation in Bobby's actions. McNally had several objections to the questioning sustained and invoked Bobby's Fifth Amendment rights, blunting Woodbine's examination. McNally's cross-examination further deflated Woodbine's strategy.

Before his opening statement, McNally again asked for a dismissal of charges, but was again denied. Phillip and

Alice testified in Bobby's defense. Woodbine spent a great deal of time in his cross-examination of Alice trying again to establish a revenge motive. It proved to be a mistake, as on redirect McNally again referred to the sworn statements of the staff given to the sheriff's deputies and by the authorities in New Mexico—all over the prosecution's objections—noting the absence of any mentions of revenge by Alice. He then offered to call Jorge and Emilio, but the judge ruled that their sworn statements were sufficient.

At two o'clock, Judge Jacobson called a recess until the next morning to allow him time to review the written statements, with closing arguments to be presented at nine the next morning. McNally discussed the morning's session with his clients over lunch. He had tried to get the charges dismissed in chambers, but Woodbine was adamant that the case merited a charge of second-degree murder, as defined by law. He then tried to persuade the judge to at least attempt a jury trial, which he was positive he could win, but Jacobson refused, probably due to pressure from powers above, to prevent the county from being blamed for furthering the spread of influenza.

At nine o'clock the next morning, Judge Jacobson called the trial back in session. Only the Jenkins family, counsel, two bailiffs and the recorder were in the court room. McNally and Woodbine presented their closing arguments very briefly, compared to what either would have done with a jury and more time to prepare. Judge Jacobson shocked everyone when he stated he would render his verdict immediately. He began by thanking them all for coming on short notice. He reiterated his grave concerns for holding a jury trial in the face of what appeared to be a highly infectious and potentially very deadly influenza outbreak. Although he felt that this case did merit a jury trial, he was confident that it would end in

mistrial for lack of jurors or worse, resulting in post-
ponement past what he considered constitutional, not to
mention the risk of infecting all parties involved. He
complimented Misters McNally and Woodbine for their
flexibility and brevity in arguments and examinations.
Finally, he asked Bobby to rise for the verdict.

"Robert Phillip Jenkins," he began, his voice grave, "I
have no doubt you did what you thought you had to do to
protect your mother from what appeared to be a life-
threatening situation. I wish time and circumstances had
allowed for Mr. Sinclair to have been arrested and
extradited to New Mexico to stand trial for murder.
However, I'm convinced by the evidence presented that,
had you waited for the authorities to arrive, your mother
and perhaps others would now be dead.

"I believe that your family took no sorrow in Mr.
Sinclair's death, but likewise I see no evidence of premeditation in this act. Indeed, the evidence shows that you
were not even on the property when Mr. Sinclair appeared
at your home unannounced and uninvited, using an alias,
and apparently unaware of whom he was dealing with
when he arrived. Your knowledge that 'Walter Schmidt'
might be Oliver Sinclair and the fact that Sinclair was a
suspected killer, gave you pause to be cautious in how you
approached him. That, in my mind, is far different from
premeditation.

"I also have to be mindful of the fact that this act was
committed by a minor, so I am loath to consider a charge of
murder. Still, a life has been taken and therefore, Robert
Phillip Jenkins, I find you guilty of manslaughter. During
the recess yesterday, I learned that there is no room for you
at any of the state's juvenile institutions to serve a sentence
of any length. Therefore, I give you the choice of serving
five years in the general population of a state penitentiary

or eight years of service in the armed forces of the United States. After successful completion of one half of this sentence with good behavior, I will consider suspension of the remainder of the sentence and the sealing of your record. I expect your answer within one week."

Woodbine objected, "Your Honor, this sentence is lenient in the extreme. We have testimony proving that the defendant deliberately put himself in a position to ambush the victim prior to killing him. That hardly fits the definition of manslaughter."

"Overruled, Mr. Woodbine. You're free to file an appeal. Of course, the press might wonder why you would want to lock up a boy from a good family for most of his life for saving his mother from certain death at the hands of a murderous cattle rustler."

"Oh, I can assure you sir, the press *will* be fascinated with that story," McNally interjected, looking Woodbine dead in the eye. It was a promise, not a threat. He had friends at the *Times,* and it was an election year for Woodbine.

"If you'd like, your honor, I'll give you my answer now," Bobby said in a trembling voice. "I'll join the Navy."

"Are you sure about that, son?" Jacobson asked quietly.

Bobby looked at his parents and attorney. Despite the tears in his parents' eyes, all three nodded their approval. "Yes sir. I'm sure."

"Your Honor, I would request a continuance in sentencing until Robert reaches the age of seventeen on the second of November, so he can enlist legally." McNally was going to buy as much time as he could.

"Granted. I will expect to have documentation of Robert's enlistment by close of business on Friday the fifteenth. We are adjourned."

As they descended the courthouse steps, the Jenkins family held each other, trying to come to grips with their new reality. McNally tried to show the silver lining to the cloud.

"You know, Phillip, four years is not all that long. Robert can learn many valuable lessons in the service that will serve him well. And then all this can be put behind you."

"Maybe someday," Phillip said bitterly, "maybe."

Eighteen

November 12, 1918
Glendale, California

News of the armistice reached the Jenkins family with great relief. JD sent a telegram to Jeanne reporting that he would remain on the *Tucker* until December, then return to the United States.

When he and his destroyer squadron returned to the United States, he was promoted to Lieutenant, Junior Grade and transferred to USS *Utah.* Assigned to the Engineering Department, he began learning the complexities of maintaining the electrical systems and propulsion of the battleship. It was back to France again for JD as *Utah* was assigned to an escort fleet for President Wilson aboard the liner SS *George Washington* for the peace conference at Versailles.

A new problem was arising with Bobby, however. With the end of hostilities, it was unclear what the Navy would do with so many new recruits coming out of basic training. Between delays in recruit classes graduating due to the influenza pandemic and now the end of the war, there was a real concern that Bobby might actually have to go to prison. Over the following week, Phillip made a dozen phone calls to J. H. McNally, and a dozen more to influential friends, to make sure Bobby stayed in the Navy. JD even entered the fray for his brother, asking colleagues from the academy whose fathers were senior officers to help where they could. As a result, Apprentice Seaman Robert Phillip Jenkins graduated basic training and was assigned to the armored cruiser USS *Pueblo* on December fifteenth. He had already earned two ribbons: the Navy Distinguished Marksman and the Navy Distinguished Pistol Shot badges.

During his tour aboard *Pueblo,* he was promoted to Seaman First Class in the Gunnery Department, serving as a loader on one of the six-inch guns. He worked very hard on the ship, doing whatever menial work he was ordered to do. The fear of making a mistake and landing in prison made him a model seaman. It also made him an easy target for bullying from other sailors.

When *Pueblo* docked in Philadelphia in August of 1919, she was placed in reduced commission status. Bobby remained in Philadelphia through October for *Pueblo*'s "mothballing" process, then received additional training in gunnery and ordnance. He was thrilled to learn he would be transferred to the Navy's newest battleship, USS *Idaho,* after his training ended. It also meant he would be transferred to the Pacific Fleet from the Atlantic, putting him closer to home. In mid-November, he received thirty days leave before reporting to duty aboard *Idaho* in California.

JD remained aboard *Utah* through 1919. He and Jeanne welcomed their first child, a daughter named Katherine, on November eighteenth. JD was in Europe when the baby arrived, but Phillip and Alice traveled east, arriving on November tenth, and stayed through December to help Jeanne. Uncle Bobby spent Thanksgiving with the family prior to reporting for duty on *Idaho* in December.

Nineteen

22 March, 1920
Long Beach, California

"I can't get over how sea water beats up a ship," Bob said to nobody in particular.

He and a detail of seamen were scraping and wire-brushing peeling paint from the exposed barbette, the huge pedestal that supported fourteen-inch gun turret number two, on USS *Idaho*. Maintaining the ship at sea and in port was dull compared to training exercises and tours at sea, but was always the most important job. As part of the gun crew for turret two, Bob felt personal responsibility for its care and upkeep. Now a Gunners Mate Third Class, he found that the rank carried only the responsibility of blame if men under his command screwed up, but rarely praise if they did well. He tried to lead by example, but often found his size and strength carried more weight with some of the men in the form of a slap to the back of a swabbie's head.

This day, his detail was well-behaved and actually productive. He had just stepped back to inspect the prep job prior to opening paint cans when a familiar voice spoke from behind him.

"How is your work progressing, men?" the voice asked.

Bob turned to see JD smiling at him. Maintaining his military bearing, Bob snapped to attention and ordered his detail to do likewise.

"Very well, sir," Bob replied with a wink under his salute, "I believe we're ready to start painting."

"You certainly appear to be. Well done."

"Is there a problem, *sir*?" A Chief Gunners Mate approached JD and Bob. JD had to stop himself from laughing at the man. He looked to be well over fifty years old, overweight and poorly shaven. The stump of a cigar was clamped between his teeth. He approached from Bob's rear, giving Bob time to mouth, "Asshole," to JD.

"No problem at all, Chief. Just getting to know the men. I'm Lieutenant Roberts. I just arrived on board and wanted to get acquainted with the gunnery divisions. And you are . . . ?"

"*Chief* Gunners Mate Alfred Polanski, sir."

"And I take it, *Chief* Polanski, that standing at attention before an officer is optional on this vessel?"

"No sir," Polanski sighed as he attempted to draw in his gut to a semblance of attention.

"And is smoking permitted by a crew member while at attention on this vessel?"

"It ain't lit, *sir*."

JD plucked the cigar from Polanski's mouth, walked to the rail, and tossed it overboard. "If I'm out of line, *Chief*, please feel free to report me to your superior officer. I work on the assumption that assignment to the newest and best ship in the fleet is an honor, and requires exemplary behavior by all hands. Now I can see that you've been in the Navy a *long* time, but that is no excuse for looking and acting like a slob. And since we are both in Gunnery, we'll have to learn to make nice with each other. And the way to make nice with me is to go by the book. Understood?"

"*Yes sir,*" Polanski hissed.

Bob and his paint detail were still at attention, but were

struggling to maintain their composure. It was obvious a few lips were being bitten to hold off laughter. JD stared at the Chief for a full minute without speaking, a bemused smile on his lips. Polanski finally couldn't take any more.

"Anything else, *sir?*"

"Carry on," JD smiled and walked away. He was thankful that the Gunnery Officer had given him the lowdown on Polanski twenty minutes before, as well as suggesting JD rattle the man's cage as the new junior officer in the fold. The Chief was a veteran of the Spanish-American war and the recipient of the Navy Cross. He was once a top-notch sailor and, had he maintained any ambition, he could have been a Warrant Officer, but he became complacent after making Chief Gunners Mate. It was hoped he would retire after the war, but now it was obvious he would have to be forced out when his current enlistment ended in August. There just wasn't room for him in the post-war Navy and he knew it. He contented himself to bide his time doing the bare minimum required. He was ignored by the other Chiefs and stayed just inside the lines of insubordination with the officers. Bob stayed on his good side, the fear of violating the terms of his sentence still steering his course. Plus, the Chief had been in the Navy longer than Bob had been alive. There had to be *something* he could learn from the man.

The incident began what JD and Bob later jokingly referred to as the "Battle of the *Idaho.*" JD made it very clear to the other junior gunnery officers that while much could be learned from an experienced Chief, Polanski didn't fit the bill and they were in no way to be intimidated by the man. The Gunnery Officer approved of this new leader among his Ensigns and Junior Grade Lieutenants and over the next seven months Polanski was actually whipped into shape to a degree.

He snapped on his last mission, however, and spent his final days in the Navy sitting in *Idaho's* brig for spitting on an Ensign. The Captain took pity on him and did not recommend a court-martial, allowing him to keep his pension with an honorable discharge.

It was also on this deployment that a problem was noted with the accuracy of the ship's fourteen-inch, Mark Four guns. It seemed that at maximum range, the projectile placement became erratic. The problem was also noted on the other *New Mexico*–class ships, as well as the brand-new *Tennessee* on her shakedown cruises. Several theories were put forward for the problem. Bob noted that the shells behaved like a bullet fired from a rifle with a worn out receiver, remembering an old .22 rifle that he literally wore out shooting. The more rounds he shot, the closer to his target he needed to be to remain accurate. Replacing the .22's receiver solved much of the problem. He brought the idea up to his lieutenant, who sent it up the chain to the Gunnery Officer. At one point, the crew loaded a projectile and sent the skinniest sailor aboard down the barrel with a headlamp and crowbar. The sailor was actually able to wiggle the sixteen-hundred-pound projectile with the crowbar. This "play" inside the chamber would cause the projectile to begin to wobble in the air, and the farther it flew, the more erratic it would become. It took several modifications and twenty years before all the Mark Eleven gun's problems were solved.

Although JD and Bob were both in the Gunnery Department, they seldom crossed paths. JD was assigned to FC Division, which dealt with fire control. Despite the name, Fire Control did not involve hoses and flames. On warships, Fire Control involved the men who operated the range finders and optical directors that aimed and fired the ship's guns. Bob was in Second Division, the men who operated and maintained the number two fourteen-inch turret. They still met on occasion while at sea. JD developed a habit of walking the deck for exercise whenever he could. He would stop and visit with many of the enlisted men, but always with Bob. Some of the men who constantly pushed Bob around noticed him talking to the new Lieutenant more than the others, resulting in even more harassment. The brothers only talked when they absolutely had to after this new pattern of abuse began. If a conversation was necessary, one would tip back his cap as a signal to the other and then a discreet conversation was had later.

Twenty

December 15, 1920
Glendale, CA

JD and Bob were lucky enough to have both been granted thirty days leave over the holidays. Jeanne had packed up Katie and their things and moved west from Philadelphia when JD was transferred, and was adapting to the vagabond life of a Navy wife. Phillip and Alice invited her to stay with them temporarily and they found they enjoyed each other so much Alice asked her to stay. Katie was the apple of Alice's eye, and at only forty she made for a very active grandmother. She quickly became more of a big sister to Jeanne than a mother-in-law.

The day after JD and Bob arrived home, the family set off for New Mexico to celebrate Christmas with Will and Matt and their families, and to meet the newest addition to the family, Matt and Ellen's son Richard. While Matt had hoped to fill his new house with children, he and Ellen had been heartbroken by two miscarriages. Richard was born a month early but survived. Ellen experienced complications from the delivery and she was strongly cautioned against attempting to have another baby, dashing hopes for a larger family.

The Jenkins returned to California on January sixth. On the night of the eleventh, Alice and her boys were uneasy, each experiencing the telltale little headache. They stayed up after everyone else had gone to bed, knowing they were going to have company soon. Just after midnight, they heard their names being called in their minds and walked out into the front yard. Soon the craft was hovering just above the orange trees and the three were lifted into the bay of the craft for their examinations. Phillip stood at the bedroom window as he always did when the visitors came, watching again as his family was levitated through the open door of the craft like it was something everyone did on occasion.

A few minutes later they were back in the house and everyone went to bed. While Jeanne knew about these visits, she hadn't worked up enough nerve to actually watch when JD was taken aboard the craft, and quietly hoped Katie had not received the genes required for the visitors' study.

Bob and JD returned to *Idaho* on January fourteenth and served together on the ship through 1922, when JD was transferred to USS *Pennsylvania*. Bob remained on *Idaho* another year, then was transferred to the new light cruiser USS *Omaha*, where he was introduced to the new six-inch, fifty-three-caliber turret guns. Both brothers continued to advance in their training, but in the post-war Navy, promotions were slow in coming, generally dependent on the retirement of more senior officers and enlisted men.

After four years with good conduct, Bob surprised the family by announcing his plan to re-enlist. His fascination with gunnery made him want to stay until he had learned all he could. Judge Jacobson vacated Bob's manslaughter conviction and sealed the record.

Bob also had another, less noble reason for re-enlisting. He had a few scores he wanted to settle. The removal of the sword of his conviction above his head allowed him to find some of his old tormentors when on liberty and soon any bullying was put to a sudden and violent end. After putting his oppressors in their place, he never looked for trouble, but his size made him a popular target for drunken sailors who thought they could always lick the biggest man around. Prohibition kept the drunks somewhat in check in America, but trouble always seemed to find Bob when on liberty outside the country. His problem was that, if attacked, he rarely stopped before his opponent required medical attention, and he didn't cool off when the Shore Patrol tried to stop the melee, resulting in some stays in the brig. Even so, he loved his job on the big guns and seriously considered making the Navy his career.

Twenty-One

August 17, 1923
Glendale, California

"You must be joking," Phillip said, his features reflected his incredulity and his grip on the telephone was tight. "What on Earth possessed you to do such a thing?" Four hours earlier, Phillip had been elated by a telephone call from JD announcing the birth of a baby boy named Phillip to honor his grandfather. Now he sat in disbelief at the news from his younger son.

"Dad, I'm nearly twenty-two years old now. I think I can make up my mind about whether or not I want to get married. You never said a word to JD when he got married and he was just twenty," Bob countered.

"But we have no idea who this girl is, son! We don't know who her parents are, or what kind of person she is, or . . ."

"She's *my* kind, Dad. Nancy doesn't care about status or money, or who she's supposed to impress. She cares about making me happy and enjoying our time together. And her father works for you."

"Really?" Phillip was taken aback, "Who is her father?"

"Jack Stuart. He works for Bayside Construction Company in San Francisco."

Phillip paused before he spoke, trying to place the

name. "Well, yes, son. I believe a Jack Stuart does work for Bayside. He's a bricklayer if I recall."

"So, a bricklayer's daughter isn't good enough for me, in your eyes?"

"I'm not saying that, Bob, I'm saying that your different upbringings make you very different people."

"I can't agree, Dad, I'm a whole lot more saddle tramp than businessman, with all due respect to you and Momma. I just get along with simple people better than with rich people, that's all."

"Does she know that you get sucked up into a spaceship every now and then?"

"Yeah, that," Bob said after a long pause, "I guess we'll cross that bridge when we come to it. They were here the other day. I should have some time to let her know before they come back."

"Bob, do you ever plan any further ahead than the next two minutes?" Phillip's exasperation was quickly turning to anger.

"Dad, if I wasted as much time mulling over all the 'what ifs' in life as you do, you'd be dead. You know that, right?"

Phillip paused. His son was right, and it infuriated him. "Do you love her son? Would you walk away from everybody to stay with her?"

"Please don't ask me to do that, Dad, because I would."

"Then you have my blessing, Bob. Because that's exactly what I told my father when I married this cowgirl from New Mexico. I wish you'd spent more time to get to know her, but what's done is done. You two be sure to come by next time you have leave, alright?"

"Maybe someday. We'll need to save a little before we take any trips. Thanks, Dad. I was hoping you'd understand."

"Well, don't expect your mother to be all daisies and angel farts about this. I'll remind her of how she and I got our start, but you know she would have wanted to be there when you got married."

"It was at City Hall. She would have had a fit."

"Maybe. Just expect a butt chewing next time you see her."

"Aye, aye. Take care, Dad."

Phillip sighed as he hung up the phone and turned his office chair to the window. His emotions had been on a rollercoaster ride over the last twelve hours, starting at 3:00 a.m. with Alice being visited again by the spaceship and taken aboard for yet another examination. He had been awake since then.

He watched Alice working a three-year-old in the arena for a long time, thinking of Bob's surprise marriage and remembering how his father reacted when he announced his engagement to "the rustic widow Roberts and her whelp," as his father phrased it. His father asked him if he would walk away from everything for her, just as he had asked Bob, and his answer had been the same. ". . . *forsaking all others* . . . ," the wedding vow said, he recalled. It took several years for his parents to fully accept Alice and JD, but he certainly had no regrets after nearly twenty-three years. He hoped Bob wouldn't either.

Twenty-Two

February 25, 1929
Glendale, California

"Phillip, are you angry with me?" Alice asked during breakfast.

"Not particularly. Should I be?" Phillip smiled as he finished his coffee.

"Don't be a smarty pants with me, sir. You haven't spoken ten words since lunch yesterday. Something is bothering you. You haven't been this quiet in years."

"Sorry, I just have a lot of things on my mind and don't quite know how to talk about them."

"How about one at a time?"

"Alright, you asked for it. Bob called me day before yesterday. He said Nancy wants a divorce."

Alice sighed, half with frustration, half with relief. "So she finally accepted the fact that he's a career Navy man and we don't subsidize our sons if they don't work in a family business?"

"In a nutshell, yes. I don't quite understand it, either. Bob makes decent money as a Petty Officer First Class. He gives her every red cent, they live on base, and everything is cheaper at the Naval Exchange. It won't be long before he makes Chief Gunners Mate if he keeps his nose clean. She should be relatively comfortable."

"But she knows his father is a millionaire and his

brother is a Lieutenant Commander and *everybody* makes more money than Bobby does. He's the only one that doesn't seem to be bothered by his income."

"Well, according to Bob, she's met somebody who makes 'real' money and she and Allison have moved out. She's claiming adultery with the judge. The old 'Girl in every port' story."

"But that could mean a court-martial! So, what's Bob going to do?"

"From what I gather, Nancy will drop the claim of adultery if she gets a check every month for Allison. Poor thing. Only four and having to go through this. I thought we could have a trust set up so Nancy can't get to it, and allow Allie a monthly stipend until she's eighteen. We both know Nancy is going to spend every penny Bob sends if we don't limit it somehow. I'm hoping you'll agree to us adding a little just to spite Nancy."

"Phillip, you are a sly devil. That is a wonderful idea. And we need to specify that, as trustees, we know Allie's address at all times."

"You're not so dumb yourself, Miss Alice. You know, we ought to do something similar for Little Phil and Katie as well. Not that I fear trouble between JD and Jeanne, but to be fair."

"Agreed. Now, what else is bothering you?"

"I've got a bad feeling about business. I was at a board of directors meeting at the bank yesterday and they were all quite happy about the volume of business loans that are out. I got to digging through the details and there are a lot of businesses out there that are over-leveraged to a dangerous degree. They're fine now, and will be in five years, but if a few key debtors fail in between, there's going to be a lot of trouble. That's the situation nationwide, too, from what I read. And I don't like what's going on in Europe one bit.

Germany is not going to be able to keep paying war reparations at the current pace, and if that banking system begins to fail, it could topple everything."

"What do you think we should do?"

"You may think I'm crazy, but I think we should literally put as much cash in our hands as we can safely keep. I think we could see a banking collapse and depression worse than 1896. And if we do have a banking collapse, we obviously don't want cash in the banks. Same thing with stocks. I don't think we should have any stocks other than the absolute cream of the crop, and many, many fewer shares than we hold now."

"Do you think we need to sell any businesses? What about real estate?"

"A few of the businesses should go. And as to the real estate, we'll probably lose some tenants in the commercial properties and have to wait that out. The oil revenues should remain somewhat stable, and if consumption falls, the companies themselves will survive. And even if the worst happens, we still own the land. Real estate will always come back, especially the properties we hold. The only real estate I would really consider selling is this place."

"You can't be serious!" Alice was sincerely shocked, "Why would you want to sell this beautiful place? Phillip, I love this farm and you do, too!"

"I do love it, dear, but the reality is, Los Angeles continues to grow north and Glendale east, and sooner or later we'll be forced to sell it rather than naming our price. You've seen farms sell out and others forced out for development just as I have. This place isn't immune. I seem to be the only person worried about things, so I think we could sell now and walk away with enough money to buy or build another place better than this almost anywhere."

"Where would you want to go after here, then?"

"Would you consider going back to New Mexico?"

"I think I'd rather go there than anywhere. We're starting to get a little too old to be riding colts all day long. I think we could easily sell green-broke two-year-olds there to the ranchers and just keep the best one or two to finish as threes."

"I'll give Will a call and see if he knows of any places for sale. I want to talk to him and Matt both about their investments as well."

In late March, Phillip and Alice traveled to New Mexico and purchased twelve hundred acres southeast of Fort Sumner, drilled two irrigation wells and one domestic well, and began construction on a house and barn facilities similar to the one in Glendale, but this new house would also have a basement with a built-in vault. He paid the contractor handsomely and promised a bonus if construction was completed by the end of August. He also hired a farmer and planted three hundred acres to alfalfa and irrigated grass for hay, leaving the rest in native pasture.

Over the next few months, he discretely sold almost all of his stocks for good profits and, using his coming relocation as an excuse, closed all but one bank account in Los Angeles, keeping it open with a minimal balance for any necessary expenses. He left his attorney in charge of managing the real estate holdings in California, and left his managers and partners in charge of the remaining businesses he owned or shared, having sold several. The funds generated from these sales and liquidations were wire transferred to the bank in Fort Sumner, where Jacob Gray, now the president of the bank, deposited them either into an account for Three S Land and Cattle, Inc., or into Phillip and Alice's personal account, as ownership dictated.

The farm was sold to Ben Silverman, another real estate developer that Phillip had known for years. Scoffing at Phillip's concern over the economic future, Silverman paid Phillip and Alice their asking price with no hesitation, planning on developing an upscale neighborhood from the pastures and tree groves and living in the main residence himself. Phillip and Alice gave every member of the staff five thousand dollars as a good-bye gift. Only Emilio stayed as an employee; everyone else moved on or retired. The horses were shipped to the new farm on August twenty-fifth. Despite looking forward to his retirement at age seventy, Jorge sobbed as the trucks headed down the driveway for town. Alice held her friend a long time before they were able to say good-bye.

On August 27th, Phillip and Alice watched the moving van pull away with the belongings they decided to take with them and headed for the train in Glendale. Emilio drove them and was reduced to tears when Phillip handed him the keys and title to the Cadillac.

They arrived in Fort Sumner on the first of September and were greeted by the entire family at the station, then drove to the new farm with Phillip leading the way in the new Cadillac he had ordered, which Matt had driven home from Albuquerque. At dinner, he received some good-natured ribbing from his brothers-in-law regarding their conversion of so many assets to cash, as the stock market had reached a new high for the year.

Phillip drew less good-natured treatment from Jacob Gray when he, Will, and Matt quietly withdrew more than four million dollars in cash from the bank over the course of the next six weeks. A few days later, they all sighed in relief at Phillip's foresight as the stock market plummeted. When the bank later experienced a run from panicked depositors, the family stepped in. Quietly loaning five hundred thousand dollars to keep the bank solvent, they saved Jacob Gray and perhaps Fort Sumner.

Phillip surprised everyone again when he began reinvesting in the stock market in 1932. Convinced things couldn't get any worse, he invested nearly one million dollars in companies like 3M, DuPont, Babcock and Wilcox, Electric Boat, and Owens-Illinois Glass. Many of the shares were purchased at one tenth to one third of the value Phillip had sold them for just three years before.

Alice noticed again how Phillip's instincts were leading him to invest in companies with national defense connections. Phillip had been watching European politics very closely, and was wary of the increasing power of Adolf Hitler in Germany and his buddy-buddy attitude towards the Italian fascist Mussolini. He also knew from conversations with JD that Britain and France were politically exhausted from the Great War and would not be likely to violently oppose the two radicals. Japan's invasion of Manchuria the previous year also made Phillip think national defense business would pick up sooner or later.

While Phillip had saved the family from financial ruin, even he couldn't get the family through the Depression completely unscathed. The drought that ravaged the western United States had no respect for planning and intelligence, and by 1932 both ranches were empty of cattle. On their thirty-second wedding anniversary, Alice and Phillip tearfully loaded the last of their mares and weanlings onto a rail car to be taken to their temporary home with oil industry friends near Houston, Texas. Christmas for the family was one of mixed emotions: gratitude for having the reserves to survive, but uncertainty for when they would able to do what they loved again.

They spent the spring of 1933 investing in every soil and range conservation improvement they could, and what little rain that came kept the grass alive and held the soil to some degree. Even so, the winds came, bringing dust from Texas and Colorado, leaving drifts across roads and filtering into homes as a haze that crept into nooks and crannies and lungs. Will seemed to cough continually despite all the treatments the doctors prescribed.

They kept their ranch employees through it all, paying them from their cash reserves and dividends from Phillip's timely reinvestments. They worked hard to save the land, and by April of 1936, the drought had eased enough to allow them to bring cattle back and start again. Will's manager and hired man handled eighty cows on the home ranch and Matt's son Richard, now sixteen, began helping their manager with the cow herd on the old Nelson Ranch, making sure what few cattle they had didn't overgraze the pastures. It seemed he was constantly moving the little herd of sixty cows over land that used to allow four hundred to graze. With no horses to feed, alfalfa and grass hay from Phillip and Alice helped supplement the cattle through the winter.

"Do you think we'll ever get back to where we were, Dad?" Richard asked one day as he and Matt yet again moved cattle to a new pasture.

"I don't know, son. Maybe someday," the dejected veterinarian said.

Twenty-Three

May 20, 1936
Fort Sumner, New Mexico

Bob was thankful to be home for a while. After his first two enlistments, he had struggled in the Navy. Promotions had been hard to come by and his temper had not helped him. Fights and demotions just seemed to happen every couple of years. He thought his marriage to Nancy would provide stability, but she had quickly became disenchanted with the life of a Navy wife. Bob had been able to keep his encounters with "the Visitors" from Nancy by sneaking away when he sensed their presence, but this only led to her suspecting him of being unfaithful. Their divorce was inevitable. He had begun drinking too much after his transfer to the Asiatic Fleet and the repeal of prohibition.

In November of 1933, he found himself in the brig of the heavy cruiser USS *Augusta* for sixty days, demoted to Gunners Mate Third Class from First Class, and docked four months' pay thanks to yet another fight—this time while on duty. He was told by his commanding officer that while he should be court-martialed, he would be spared the inevitable conviction and dishonorable discharge not so much for his sake, but for the sake of his half-brother and the embarrassment it would cause JD. Plus, he was too good a gunner to just throw away. Bob was surprised to know that his CO, as well as a handful of other officers, were aware of his and JD's relationship, and his loyalty to JD motivated him to try harder. He also never failed to provide for Allison. He used every penny he had saved to continue payments into her trust fund, plus having to borrow money from JD.

Bob had been granted thirty days' leave and found himself at the old Nelson Ranch with Matt, Ellen and Richard. He needed a sympathetic ear, but couldn't bring himself to look for one with his parents. One day during his visit, feeling especially sorry for himself, he tagged along with Matt, making a single veterinary call, then working on a windmill that had been damaged in a recent wind storm. He spent a good portion of the time lamenting his current state and struggling with whether he should stay in the Navy or return home to work on the ranches with the family when his current enlistment was up.

Matt had patiently listened to Bob all day but had finally heard enough. He had just finished repairing the gearbox and brake at the top of the windmill. After returning to the ground, he walked over to Bob, handing him the wrench he carried. Bob reached for the wrench and Matt took advantage of the distraction to deliver a haymaker right hand to his nephew's jaw. Knowing Bob's temper, he kicked the wrench away before Bob could pick it up and then pulled him to his feet, holding him like a vice by the collar. Their noses almost touched and Matt squeezed Bob's neck hard, allowing him to just remain conscious.

"Now you listen to me, Bobby," Matt spoke quietly and evenly. Even though dazed, Bob knew that this meant his uncle was absolutely enraged. "I have had a bellyful of listening to a grown man whine like a little kid. You've been in the Navy for almost eighteen years and you're still acting like you're seventeen. You haven't learned a damned thing about how to act like a man or to take responsibility for your own dumb actions and that is going to stop, because if you think for one minute you can leave the Navy and come here to work for us and act like you have been, you're nuts. I wouldn't hire you right now to feed the chickens, much less give you any responsibility. Hell, you were better help when you were fifteen than you are now. Dick's twice the hand you are and half your age. You're drunk half the time and the other half you can't decide what to do. Well, I'll tell you one thing—you're not about to come here and even think you can act like that.

"Now, you're still part of this family, and you've had your ups and downs, but so have all the rest of us. Do you see a thousand mother cows? Do you see any green grass? Your folks have two mares now. Two! How can you contribute anything to this family if you leave the Navy? There isn't anything here for you to do. All that will happen is you'll get bored and start drinking, and you'll end up like your grandfather or worse. And I just won't allow that. Now you just proved to me that you have enough self-control to not get in a fight every time somebody throws a punch. You need to start right here, right now, and walk away from the man you're turning into and turn back into the man I know you are. You're going to act like you did when you were afraid of going to prison, because if you don't change and if you leave the Navy now, you by God *will* end up in prison! Do you understand me?"

"You're right, Uncle Matt. You're damn sure right." Bob's initial anger had subsided, replaced with shame. Tears ran from his eyes as he looked into the weathered, worried eyes of his favorite uncle. He felt the grip on his shirt release as Matt shoved him back.

"You bet your ass I'm right. Now let's get these tools picked up and go get some supper."

They retrieved the tools and put them back in the toolbox Matt welded to the bed of the Model A pickup he used to drive around the ranch. They were silent for a long while before Matt started to chuckle.

"What's so funny?" Bob asked.

"I was just thanking my lucky stars that I hit you like I did. That windmill would have been an unglamorous place to die if I had missed," Matt smiled as he looked at Bob.

"I was thinking it was an unglamorous place to die when I was lying there in the dirt," Bob laughed.

"When we get to the house, remember that I dropped a wrench from the platform on the windmill and it hit you on the jaw. Right?"

"Right. Does it look like it's starting to feel?" Bob asked, gingerly feeling the swelling that was already noticeable.

"Oh, yeah," Matt replied.

Bobby was surprised that the older man still had that kind of strength. Secretly, Matt was, too.

At the end of his leave, Bob returned and devoted the next two years to restoring his reputation as a model sailor. The Depression gave him pause to be thankful he was still employed. Many men sought to get into the service now, and Bob realized there was real competition to keep his job. In 1937, he was transferred to a destroyer, USS *Chew,* where he served under JD in his older brother's second command. He was promoted to Gunners Mate Second Class and re-enlisted in 1938. JD promoted him back to Gunners Mate First Class later that year before being transferred himself and promoted to Commander.

As older World War One veterans began to retire, advancement in rank became a little easier and Bob heaved a sigh of relief when, in February of 1940, he was finally promoted to Chief Gunners Mate and transferred to USS

Tennessee. Battleship assignments were always considered something of an honor in the Navy, and Bob was thankful to be back on one after fifteen years. With war raging in Europe and Japan's aggressions in China and Southeast Asia, it looked like American involvement in the war was inevitable, and Bob wanted to be on a capital ship when it came.

He had taken only two liberty calls since 1938, both times while in Bremerton, Washington to spend the weekend with JD and his family, who had moved to Seattle. He had tried to visit his daughter when he was in San Francisco, but was refused by Nancy, who had married a police lieutenant. Bob didn't push the issue for obvious reasons. He still wrote to Allison regularly, but had little confidence she was given any of the letters by her mother. He still deposited the bulk of each paycheck into her trust fund. He lived either on board ship or in base housing, and allowed himself two beers each pay day at the CPO club wherever he was stationed, if he was ashore. He spent one week of those two years on leave in New Mexico visiting his parents. He still couldn't face his uncles.

Twenty-Four

17 April, 1940
USS *Tennessee*

The memory was so powerful JD nearly laughed out loud. He walked aft on the forecastle of the battleship towards turret two, where a detail of sailors was scraping and wire brushing the barbette in preparation for repainting. Their Chief Petty Officer was supervising them and another detail on turret one. The Chief had his back turned to JD as he spoke to the young sailors.

"How is your work progressing, men?" JD asked.

"Pretty good, sir," a Gunner's Mate, Third Class replied, standing at attention and saluting the unfamiliar face. The rest of the detail stopped and came to attention as well. One of them stole a glance to the side as he saw the Chief approach as JD returned their salutes and ordered them at ease.

"Just about ready to start painting, I see . . . ."

"Is there a problem, *sir*?" the Chief asked JD, trying his best to mimic Chief Polanski from *Idaho*.

JD just couldn't keep from breaking up. "Damn, Jenkins, how did you remember that?"

Bob remained at attention, holding his salute above his smile. "Some things are hard to forget, sir. Forgive me for not having a cigar to properly welcome you aboard." Then he silently mouthed, "Happy birthday."

JD regained his composure and returned the salute. "The cigar won't be necessary, Chief. Good to see you again."

"Likewise, sir. Am I correct in assuming you're the new Executive Officer?"

"That's correct."

"Then welcome aboard the best ship in the fleet, Commander Roberts."

"Thank you. It's also good to be able to call you Chief. Lessons learned?"

"In spades, sir. You won't have any trouble from me. I graduated from all that on the *Chew*."

"That's good to know, Jenkins. Well, I'd best be about my rounds. Carry on."

"What 'lessons' was the Commander talkin' about, Chief?" a seaman asked when JD was out of earshot.

Bob didn't seem to notice as he watched his brother walk away. He remembered again how JD and Matt had gotten him to turn his life around.

"Chief, you okay? What lessons were you talking about?" the seaman repeated, bringing Bob back to turret two and his paint detail.

"None of your damned business is what," Bob growled. "Now get back to work."

Twenty-Five

15 June, 1941
Maili, Oahu

JD and Bob had enjoyed a rare weekend pass together. Borrowing a car from a fellow officer, JD met Bob and the two struck out to have some fun. Avoiding the places frequented by the military, where an officer might be recognized fraternizing with an enlisted man, they explored the places where the locals ate, drank, and relaxed. They were happy to have each other's company to soften spending Father's Day away from home again. They were making their way back to base, driving along the western shore of Oahu, when the car sputtered to a stop.

"Damn it, JD, did you run us out of gas?" Bob sighed.

"No," JD sighed as well as he looked to the west. "Bearing two-seven-zero."

The craft was approaching them from the west, only a few yards off the surface of the ocean. It stopped in front of the car as the door in the nose of the craft began to open. JD and Bob obediently stepped out of the car and were soon floating toward the open door. Their examinations took longer than usual and were more invasive. JD asked the commander of the craft about it.

"*We have attempted to contact your children for further study, but are unable to communicate with them,*" the commander replied. "*We needed genetic material from the two of you to further define what gives you the ability to communicate with us, and why your children cannot."*

Bob became concerned immediately. "So, have you taken our kids onto your ship to compare our genes?"

"We have obtained samples from them, yes. But because they are not fully a part of our study this is all that is required for now. Be assured they have no memory of their contact with us."

"Well, I can't stop you, but you need to know I don't like what you did."

"I do regret that, Robert, but they will not be contacted for the remainder of this study."

Back on the ground, the brothers watched as the craft moved out over the Pacific, then darted up into the late afternoon sky. The car started immediately for JD, and the two drove on towards Pearl Harbor. JD finally spoke as they turned east towards the base.

"Well, at least the kids don't have to worry about getting picked up all the time."

"I'm not so sure, brother. The captain only said they wouldn't be contacted for the remainder of their study. He didn't say what would happen if there's another study later."

THE FOLLOWING Thursday, Bob had just finished his watch and stretched out on his bunk to relax before chow when *Tennessee's* general announcement system, or 1MC, barked, "Chief Jenkins report to the XO's office." Wondering what JD had on his mind, he immediately headed aft to the Executive Officer's office on the starboard side of the ship.

"Chief Jenkins reporting, sir," the Desk Yeoman said to JD.

"Send him in," JD replied. The door opened and Bob stepped through.

"Chief Jenkins reporting as ordered, sir."

"Close the door, Chief," JD ordered.

"Aye, aye, sir," Bob replied as he closed the door. "What's up, JD?" he asked once the formality was removed.

"Three things," JD smiled, "first of all, how are you feeling?" After their examinations on Sunday, Bob had complained of dizziness for two days after they returned to the ship.

"Fine now," Bob replied. "The Doc blamed it on me staying onboard ship too much and the car ride messed up my inner ear, so he gave me some pills for sea sickness. Shows what he knows."

"Good. The other two things I wanted you to know firsthand. One, your nephew has been accepted to the Academy. I just received Jeanne's letter with the official notification."

"Hot damn! I didn't have any doubt, but it's still good to know officially. I'll send him my best, but it's sure going to be tough calling both of you 'sir'. What's number two?"

"I'm being transferred for further training at the Naval War College. I'll be leaving in seventy-two hours to report on two July."

"Well, that's great, too. It means you'll most likely get promoted to Captain and get a command when you finish. But I do hate to see you go. You've made a big difference on this ship, I can tell you that."

"Thanks, Bobby. I really like it here and I'm really going to miss it. Captain Reordan has taught me a lot. You've really made a comeback and I want you to know I'm very proud of you. So are Momma and Dad. Uncle Matt, too."

"I couldn't have done it without Matt kicking my butt, and you getting me back to first class like you did. I owe you a lot, JD, more than you'll ever know, and more than I can ever repay."

"Just keep out of trouble and you'll repay me."

"Done."

"Well, I may not get to say good-bye later so that's why I called you in. I'll tell Little Phil you send your congratulations. I'm sure I'll see him before your letter gets to him."

"Thanks. Hug Jeanne and Katie for me, too."

"Will do."

"I'll see you around, big brother," Bob said as he rounded the desk to hug JD, "have a safe trip stateside."

"Stay safe, Bobby," JD said as they embraced. Bob stepped back, and after taking a second to compose himself, left the office. He wandered topside, and stood looking out at the few ships in the harbor. Only Battleship Division Two and its escort ships remained in port. The rest of the battleships and aircraft carriers were on training maneuvers between Pearl and Midway, along with most of the cruisers and destroyers. *Tennessee* was moored along the eastern side of Ford Island on "Battleship Row." Her sister ship, USS *California,* was moored ahead and USS *Oklahoma* astern. The trade wind blew a gentle north breeze as the sun began to drop on the western horizon. Tonight, he'd get off a letter to his parents and nephew, along with one to Allison, still hoping she might get one. *Maybe someday*, he said to himself as he headed back in for chow.

PART THREE

Surprises

Twenty-Six

6 December, 1941
Pearl Harbor Naval Base

The harbor was crowded. Ninety-six warships were at anchor, including eight of the Pacific Fleet's nine battleships, all moored along the east side of Ford Island with the exception of USS *Pennsylvania*, which was sitting in dry dock. *California, Oklahoma, Maryland, West Virginia, Tennessee, Arizona,* and *Nevada* made "Battleship Row" an impressive sight as thousands of sailors headed into Honolulu on weekend passes.

Bob had liberty as well but, as usual, preferred to stay close to *Tennessee*. Honolulu offered nothing but trouble as far as he was concerned. Hotel Street, with its bars and brothels, just sounded like a one-way ticket to the brig. He spent that Saturday double-checking the ammunition handling room of turret one in preparation for Monday's inspection. Later, he and another Chief took a launch to the CPO club for dinner, where they each enjoyed one beer. They cheered on *Tennessee*'s band as it advanced in the Battle of the Bands competition at Bloch Arena, had some ice cream, and were back aboard ship and in their racks by 2300.

He was up at 0530 as usual on Sunday the seventh and wrote letters to JD and his parents, praising the band's performance the night before, then cleaned up and went to breakfast at 0700. He took his time eating, visiting with the other Chiefs as they came and went, seeing how the other divisions were doing in preparation for the inspection. His crew in the handling room for turret one had finished their work on Saturday morning, prior to taking liberty call. Since he had no duty assignment, he decided to go topside for some fresh air and sunshine.

The band was assembling on the quarterdeck for morning colors when Bob heard the sounds of aircraft engines screaming as they pulled out of a dive to the south, over Ford Island, followed by muffled explosions. Trotting forward along the starboard rail, he could see smoke rising from the area of the seaplane hangars as a second round of screaming engines drew his attention to the sky above. A single-engine aircraft with fixed landing gear pulled out of its dive and banked to the west over the ship. Red circles on the bottom of the wings were easily visible in the morning sun.

"Holy God," Bob said aloud as he sprinted through the knee-knocker door in the forward superstructure. He collided with a lieutenant, nearly knocking him down.

"Damn, Chief, where's the fire?" the lieutenant asked good-naturedly.

"Out there!" Bob yelled, "Ford Island is under attack! Japanese planes! Look!"

"Sound General Quarters!" the lieutenant yelled after one glance at the sky. Someone on the bridge had already noticed, as the general alarm sounded immediately and the 1MC ordered general quarters, air defense. Throughout the ship, men left their bunks and breakfasts, donning what clothes were handy, and began moving to their battle stations. Bob hustled down to the handling room of turret one and his station. He arrived to hear the phone ringing. Answering it, he was ordered by Lieutenant Commander

John Adams, the Gunnery Officer and, for the moment, Commanding Officer of the ship, not to load the main batteries and stand by. It made sense. The only things the big guns could fire on were the *Oklahoma* and *Maryland* ahead, *West Virginia* to port, *Arizona* and *Vestal* astern and Ford Island to starboard. He relayed the order to the turret captain and the Ensign who was senior officer aboard for Bob's division.

A few minutes later, a lieutenant from Seventh Division ordered Bob to go above and check on the status of the machine gun platform. Crew members, including Chiefs, were in short supply with many men still on liberty in Honolulu, and every man would have to do double and maybe triple duty. A muffled explosion above him vibrated through the ship, making Bob wish someone else had been ordered above. At one point, he was shoved out of the way by a Seaman Second Class with a pair of three-inch anti-aircraft shells balanced on each shoulder, charging up the ladder to his gun. Bob assumed something was wrong with the ammunition hoist. The sailor had already run up two decks from the magazine and had two more to go to reach his station, but carried the one hundred-plus pounds of ordnance like it was weightless.

Bob continued up, coming out on the fifty-caliber machine gun platform above the signal bridge. He found the cause of the explosion: horizontal bombers were flying over the rows of battleships. A bomb appeared to have struck the center gun on turret two and fragmented when it detonated, disabling the gun as well as damaging shielding and killing the sailor manning one of the machine guns. Another lay wounded nearby. A stretcher detail appeared and carried the wounded sailor below. Unknown to Bob, the same bomb fragments had mortally wounded Captain Mervyn Bennion, skipper of the *West Virginia*.

"Damn. He was a good guy," the sailor said, looking at the body.

Bob turned to see the seaman who had knocked him aside carrying the three-inch shells standing beside him. The two had bumped heads before. He was a good kid, the son of an oil rig roughneck from Wyoming, but was headstrong and kind of liked to fight. Bob saw a lot of his younger self in the kid.

"What the hell are you doing here?" Bob yelled. "Get back to your station!"

"I'm the only man *at* my station, Chief!" the sailor said. Bob knew he was a trainer on one of the three-inch anti-aircraft guns. "I just came up here to see if I could help," the kid said, his lip quivering in fear and anger.

"Go back to your station, Roy. Hunker down and wait for the rest of your crew. If nobody shows up, assist another three-inch crew. *Stay calm!*"

They started moving down and aft when an explosion and shock wave from astern struck them like a hammer. They looked up to see *Arizona*'s bow rise thirty feet out of the water as a fireball raged forward over *Tennessee*'s quarterdeck, showering the ship with burning debris. As Bob continued down from the signal bridge, he watched as *Oklahoma* rolled over into the mud of the harbor. *West Virginia* appeared to be next. Her masts leaned precariously over the water, her fires out of control. He returned to the relative safety of his station, where the Ensign asked why he had returned.

"Because there ain't any machine gunners alive to command, sir," he said.

A few minutes later a call came from Damage Control for help manning hoses on the main deck and second deck aft. The heat from the inferno on *Arizona* had spon-taneously ignited fires in wardroom country, where the officers' staterooms were located, and on the quarterdeck. Bob was sent aft to assist. He remained on second deck, where at least he had cover from the strafing fighters above.

Below, three of the powder magazines were ordered flooded because of the intense heat to prevent an explosion akin to that on *Arizona*. At one point, he felt a bump and then a gentle movement to starboard, followed by another bump. Later he discovered that it had been due to *West Virginia*. Thanks to rapid counter-flooding, her crew had righted her and she rolled back to starboard, gently pushing *Tennessee* against the large concrete mooring quays as she sank.

The entire attack lasted just a little more than two hours but Bob felt like it should be dark when it was over. The fires had been controlled and now the firemen played their hoses out onto the water, pushing the burning oil from *Arizona* away from the stern. Unable to move, but with a full head of steam, *Tennessee* made turns for six knots, the screw current assisting in keeping the flames away. Bob came out on the forecastle later in the day and looked at the devastation that yesterday was the United States Pacific Fleet. He remembered how he had seen *Oklahoma* in Philadelphia years before, brand new and awesomely powerful. Now she sat on the bottom of the harbor, her hull turned to the sky with shipyard crews frantically trying to cut through her bottom to rescue the men trapped inside.

The fires were out, for the most part, on *West Virginia,* but *Arizona* still burned astern. More than eleven-hundred men had died in the explosion and fire. *Tennessee* had lost only four men with two missing and twenty-two injured, despite taking two bomb hits. It occurred to Bob that the smoke rising from the fires had obscured his ship and *Maryland* from the bombers of a second wave of attackers.

They couldn't bomb what they couldn't see.

The rest of the day was spent anxiously watching the skies and keeping the ship as battle ready as possible. Scuttlebutt of another attack coming, an invasion of the island of Oahu underway, and other fantastic stories passed through the ship, with nobody having any idea of the facts. At 1800 another fire broke out in the aircraft crane room that took over an hour to extinguish, then at around 2100 Bob heard the anti-aircraft guns firing again. Later he learned the gunners had been firing at American planes from USS *Enterprise* attempting to land at Ford Island.

Bob and *Tennessee* were stuck in place by the wrecks surrounding them. *Maryland* was towed away from *Oklahoma* on the ninth. Finally, on the sixteenth, demolition crews blew away enough concrete from the mooring quays to allow *Tennessee* to be towed free from *West Virginia* and around *Oklahoma* to the navy yard. The heat from the fires had warped plating and loosened rivets, all of which had to be repaired before the ship could sail to Puget Sound for further repairs.

Twenty-Seven

January 6, 1942
Fort Sumner, New Mexico

"Thank God," Phillip said as he placed Bob's letter on the table. The letter written on the morning of December seventh never got mailed, but Bob did send a very brief letter home on the eighth letting everyone know he was alive and unharmed. It was all the Navy censors allowed. Phillip and Alice didn't know that Bob had beaten the letter back to the mainland and was in Bremerton, Washington, working to get *Tennessee* back in fighting shape. All they knew with any certainty was that the fleet had been attacked with one battleship and one destroyer sunk and other ships damaged. They also knew that after declaring war on Japan, Germany had declared war on the United States. JD was unable to divulge any more official news for security reasons when they called him, except to thank them for letting him know about Bob.

EIGHTEEN HUNDRED miles away in Newport, Rhode Island at the Naval War College, JD still had not heard from Bob, but did know *Tennessee* was relatively undamaged. He assumed that if Bob had been injured or killed in the number one handling room, the ship would have suffered severe damage or been sunk, so he assumed his brother was safe. The news from his parents was welcomed and helped blunt the frustration he felt when he saw his next assignment.

"*Wyoming*? I get stuck with *Wyoming*?" he ranted to his roommate, Lieutenant Commander Ed Hathaway. The two were nearing the end of a two-month course in intelligence gathering and interpretation. JD had completed a four-month course in command tactics prior to that, and with the outbreak of war was ready to leave the classroom and return to the wardroom. USS *Wyoming*, once a battleship, had been reconfigured to provide training for new sailors on anti-aircraft guns. JD had been promoted to Captain and given command of this ship.

"Well, look at it like a father," Hathaway's rich baritone voice always added weight to his words, "why would you let your son drive the Cadillac first if you have a jalopy to start him in? Learn to drive an old battleship then the new one will be easy. You're going to get a battle command, JD, I know it. But you're also going to be one of the youngest Captains out there. You're only forty-four, for Pete's sake. We currently have a surplus of skippers with no ships to sail. We have six battleships to fix, three of which have to be refloated, plus three cruisers. They're still getting the bugs out of the *North Carolina*-class battleships and the next class doesn't even have a ship commissioned, not to mention a whole slew of cruisers under construction. Be patient. It's going to take time to gear this machine up."

"Thanks, Ed. You always have a way of putting things in perspective. Where are they sending you?"

"Back to Washington, for the time being," he sighed, "They'll probably put me to bird-dogging a suspected Nazi spy that's actually some poor schmuck who's having an affair again." At five-feet-seven with a receding hairline, Hathaway could certainly blend into a crowd.

NEAR THE opposite coast, Bob took advantage of the Sunday evening off to take a walk. He actually used his weekend pass to leave the main gate of Puget Sound Naval Yard and walk the streets of Bremerton. He wasn't looking for entertainment, which was good since entertainment was hard to come by in the blacked-out city. He simply wanted to clear his mind.

He found a little park where he sat on a bench for the better part of two hours looking up at the stars, wondering where this new war would take him. A meteor streaked across the sky and made him think of the visitors. They hadn't come around for a year, giving Bob hope that they were finished with their study.

He wondered how much of the old crew would remain, including himself, when *Tennessee* was repaired and underway to defeat the Japanese. His current enlistment ended in November, but he also knew he was in for the duration. He hoped he could someday be back in New Mexico on a horse before he ran out of room on his sleeve for hash marks. Or simply ran out of time and luck.

"Maybe someday," he said to the stars.

Twenty-Eight

July 22, 1943
Fort Sumner, New Mexico

"Hello?" Alice said into the receiver as she tucked it under her chin. She was putting milk and a rare find of fresh vegetables in the refrigerator and didn't want to stop. They had started to get warm on the drive back from town and she wanted to keep them as fresh as possible. Her victory garden was not yet quite ready to yield much.

Now sixty-three, she still rode on occasion and even would rope a few calves at branding time just to show she still could, but her training days had passed. She was happy with tending her garden, remembering all the lessons Carmen and Margaret had taught her so many years ago. She also helped Phillip manage the family assets as well as supervising Frank, the trainer they had hired for the horses.

"Is this Alice Jenkins, Robert Jenkins' mother?" a quiet female voice asked.

"Yes, that's correct. To whom am I speaking?" Alice asked, and to herself, *"Please, God, let him be alright."* There was a gut-wrenching pause before the caller replied. Alice closed the refrigerator door and sat at the table, bracing for bad news.

"My name is Allison Grady," the voice replied, "I'm ... I think you're my grandmother."

Alice was dumbfounded for a moment by the relief that

no harm had come to Bob, coupled with the surprise of the caller's identity. She fought for the right words.

"I think you may be right," Alice finally said. "What's your mother's name, dear?"

"Nancy."

"And what's your address?"

"Three seventeen Fifteenth Avenue, San Francisco. Why are you asking me these questions?"

"I'm sorry, Allison. I don't mean to be rude. I just wanted to be sure it's you. I'm very happy you found us! Happy belated birthday. Did you receive our cards in the mail?"

"Oh . . . thanks for remembering. I haven't seen a card, though."

"Well, you know how the mail is with the war. You'll get them in due time, I'm sure, the same as every year."

"What do you mean, 'every year'? I've never seen any cards from you or my father or anything my whole life. That's why I'm calling, actually. I got a certified letter from some lawyer in Albuquerque about a trust fund that I'm supposed to have. My mom says it's all fake, but my Dad said he checked it out and it's real."

"That's correct, Allison. When your parents divorced, your mother demanded that you receive a monthly payment to assist her with expenses. The trust was established to provide those funds. Your grandfather and I managed the trust's investments and added some money as well, but almost every dollar your father has made the past fourteen years has gone into that fund. And now that you're eighteen it's yours to use as you see fit. Your two cousins had similar funds set up for them, also."

"But there's over *fifty thousand dollars* in it! Dad says there has to be a catch, and he's a police officer."

"I know he is, dear. And there's no catch, but it will

take a long time to explain. Could I call you right back so your folks don't have to pay the long-distance charges?"

"I suppose," Allison sounded a little suspicious, but said, "Butterfield six, four-four-two-seven."

"I'll call you right back," Alice said.

She did so immediately, and then spent the next hour visiting with her granddaughter. According to Allison, she grew up being told Bob was nothing more than an abusive drunk that abandoned her and her mother with little more than the clothes on their backs. After answering very delicately put questions from Alice, however, she started to see a pattern of deception from her mother that had carried on to the present. As childhood memories came into focus, she began to recall how she knew who her stepfather was before her mother divorced Bob, and even had fuzzy memories of her father, all of them pleasant. Nancy always got the mail and always sorted it for her new husband into bills and correspondence. She was sure to have seen the many letters Bob, Phillip, and Alice had sent over the years, all of which she must have destroyed, except for the checks from the trust.

Allison said she looked through the mail once in early 1942 and found a letter addressed to her from Bob. She wrote back, saying she wasn't sure she was his daughter, but wished him good luck. She never saw another letter. As the conversation continued, Allison became increasingly distraught with her mother.

"Mrs. Jenkins, I just don't know what to do," Allison said, near tears, "this is so hard to believe! My Mom and Dad have always taken such good care of me and my brother and sister, I can't believe what you're telling me is true."

"I know it's hard, Allison. And don't think harshly of your mother. I'm sure she did what she did to protect you.

Your father went through some tough times during those years, and your mother did what she thought was right at the time. And your stepfather adopted you and loves you as his own. I just want you to know you have another family that cares about you and would love to meet you, if that's what you want. If you don't, we'll understand. In any event, the trust fund is now yours. Your grandfather and I just wanted to make sure you could go to college and have a good start in life. Now that you're an adult, you're free to do as you choose."

"Thank you, Mrs. Jenkins. This is very generous of you. I would think you'd be bitter about all this. Obviously, my mother still is."

"I have to admit I was for a while, but that was many years ago. I do wish she had let you hear from us, though."

"Me too." Allison paused. "Mrs. Jenkins, could I call you from time to time? It's going to take me a while to sort all this out and I hope you'll be willing to answer any questions I may have. I'm sure Mom won't give me an honest answer, and it's obvious my Dad doesn't know the whole story, either."

"Of course, you can dear, and call collect. That way the call won't show on your phone bill, which I'm sure your mother will start watching like a hawk."

Over the next two months, Alice received four more calls from Allison. Her mother had attempted to take control of the trust fund almost immediately, and Alice and Phillip enlisted an old attorney friend in San Francisco to represent Allison's interests. Nancy and her husband, Neil, realized quickly that they were outgunned in the legal department and relented. The dust-up greatly strained Allison's relationship with her mother and stepfather, but she kept the peace by paying her way through school. She had started college at the university in Berkeley and began writing Alice frequently, along with the occasional telephone call. She still was unsure about contacting Bob, though. With him in harm's way, Allison was afraid to make an emotional investment only to have it ruined at the hands of the Japanese. "Maybe someday," she would say to Alice, with whom a solid bond was building. She now trusted Alice and Phillip, whose advice had never been wrong and whose affection always seemed genuine.

Through their letters, Allison was introduced to the extended Jenkins and Stevens family, and became fascinated with the ranch lifestyle which was so different from her urban upbringing. She had a small album of photographs that Alice had sent of all the family members, including a photo of Bob in his dress blues with an American flag in the background. Bob didn't like having his picture taken but was proud to send two prints to Alice when he was promoted to Chief Gunners Mate. The dark uniform highlighted the five hash marks on his sleeve, marking his twenty years of service. Allison looked at that picture more often now as news of the vicious fighting in the Pacific let her know what danger this man and so many others were facing on her behalf. She even clipped a stock photograph of USS *Tennessee* published in the *San Francisco Chronicle* and taped it to her vanity mirror.

Twenty-Nine

21 June, 1944
Puget Sound Naval Shipyard

Bob stood staring in wonderment at the huge building. It was more than a thousand feet long, over three hundred feet wide and the top of its rounded roof towered at least one-hundred fifty feet above him. Two huge motorized sliding doors, each easily one hundred feet tall and at least that wide, dominated the center of the structure. A single, standard steel door was at the corner of the building. The entire structure was painted battleship gray with mottled gray-green patches to resemble trees, and was far enough away from the other moorings in the navy yard to be surprisingly well camouflaged against the backdrop of buildings, especially on overcast days like this one. It was camouflaged so well, in fact, that Bob suddenly realized that he had never really noticed the building before.

Why did those idiot Marine sentries give his driver directions to this monstrous airship hangar when he clearly stated he was ordered to report to Dry Dock C-2? He looked from the building to the young Seaman First Class behind the wheel of the jeep, who simply shrugged and raised his hands.

"Don't ask me, Chief," he said, "I just got here yesterday myself. I barely know I'm in Washington. This is where the jarheads said to take you. You heard them same as me."

"Alright. Alright. I'm going in to find out where I *really* need to go," Bob growled. "You sit your butt right there until I get back."

"Aye, aye, Chief," the sailor replied as he fished a pack of cigarettes from his shirt pocket.

"Typical BUPERS nonsense," Bob groused as he approached the single steel door on the front of the building. BUPERS, the Navy's acronym for the Bureau of Personnel, was a very busy agency at the time. As a result, details sometimes were lacking in orders for the individual serviceman, regardless of rank or seniority. He still had no idea why he had been transferred so abruptly, having just been transferred to USS *Maryland* in December.

He grabbed the handle on the door and nearly fell when the door failed to yield, his hand jerking out of the handle and throwing him off balance. "God almighty!" he roared as he began pounding on the door, "open this damn door right now before I find a grenade and blow it in!"

The door flung open and struck with such force that Bob was knocked backwards, tripping and landing hard on his backside. The old, fighting version of Bob made him spring to his feet, ready to deliver swift justice to the fool who just signed his own death warrant. He paused, though, when he found himself staring at the barrel of a .45 caliber pistol leveled at his chest. The broad "SP" armband of the Shore Patrol covered the sailor's rank insignia. The man holding the gun was every bit as brawny as Bob, but clearly also twenty years his junior.

"Sorry, Chief," the SP drawled in a voice straight from the heart of Dixie, "but this is a secure area. I need to see your authorization to enter."

"Now you listen to me, General Beauregard," Bob growled as he brushed off his dress khakis, "I was sent here by two numbskull Marines who think this is a dry dock. I have orders to report to Dry Dock C-2 tout suite. Now you lower that weapon and tell me how I get to my duty station before I stick it where the sun don't shine."

The SP considered Bob for a moment then lowered the .45. "Wait here, Chief," he said as he unlocked the door and went back inside. A moment later he reappeared. The .45 was still in his hand and he was accompanied by a slightly built Lieutenant Junior Grade who appeared, if possible, younger than the SP. The j.g. looked confused and more than a little exasperated by the interruption. Bob noticed he also had a .45 on his belt. Behind him were two more SP's with M-1 rifles.

"What seems to be the problem, Hadley?" the lieutenant asked, looking Bob square in the eye.

"The Chief claims he was sent here by the gate sentries, sir," SP Hadley replied, his drawl far over-extending the time required to speak, in Bob's opinion.

"Yes sir," Bob chimed in. Then, realizing his gaff, snapped to attention and saluted. He had grown weary over the years of having to salute these snot-nosed kids, but he still believed in the strict discipline of "the book" and lived by it, never wanting to turn into a Chief like old Polanski on *Idaho*. He waited until the Lieutenant returned the salute before speaking again.

"Begging your pardon, sir, I was ordered to report to Dry Dock C-2 the minute I arrived. The sentries sent me here and I'm not familiar with this part of the yard. I thought I'd ask for directions since I was already here."

"Chief Gunners Mate Jenkins?" the lieutenant asked, one eyebrow raised quizzically.

"Yes, sir." Bob was taken aback by the kid knowing his name.

"Your orders didn't mention reporting to base HQ to

receive security clearance?"

"No, sir. The orders are in the jeep. I'll get them if you'd like to read them for yourself, sir."

"That won't be necessary, Chief. You didn't get where you are by not following orders exactly as given. But we do need to get you credentialed. Come with me." Without waiting for a reply, the lieutenant headed for the jeep at a brisk walk.

"Aye, aye, sir," Bob chirped as he fell in behind the j.g.

The driver nearly fell out of the jeep attempting to come to attention. The j.g. snapped a return salute, then sharply ordered the driver to take them to the sentry post. Bob barely had time to crawl into the back seat before the jeep wheeled back to the guard post and screeched to a stop. The j.g. was out of the jeep and beat the Marine sentry to the door, storming in and slamming the door behind him. A muffled, but obvious butt chewing of the Marines ensued.

A few minutes later, the j.g. shot out of the guard post. Slamming himself into the seat of the jeep, he barked, "Get us to HQ. Now!"

"Aye, aye sir," the driver shot back as he dropped the clutch. "Begging the Lieutenant's pardon, sir, but could you direct me to the HQ? I'm kind of new here myself."

There was an ominous pause. "Mary mother of God," the j.g. sighed. "Doesn't anybody do anything to orient anybody here anymore?" The driver cringed, waiting for a similar fate as the poor Marine at the sentry post, but the j.g. had spent his wrath. Instead, he laughed. "Okay, okay. Let's get you two lost lambs to the barn."

The driver sighed in relief as the j.g. calmly guided the sailor through the busy base traffic. After a few turns, the jeep pulled into a small parking lot alongside the headquarters building. Bob credited the young officer for his self-control.

"Chief, grab your orders and come with me," Wilson ordered. The two entered the building and marched down a corridor to a staircase, then up to the second floor and further down the corridor to a door guarded by another Marine, a sergeant, at a desk. As the pair approached, the Marine rose to attention and recognized the j.g. by name.

"Lieutenant Wilson. What can I do for you, sir?"

"This is an unusual situation, Sims. I need to see Commander Hathaway immediately. It's urgent."

"One moment, sir," Sims said as he picked up the telephone on the desk. "Lieutenant Wilson would like to see Commander Hathaway. He says it's urgent." There was a pause of several seconds before Sims looked up at Lieutenant Wilson. "Commander Hathaway will see you now, sir." Sims unlocked the door and opened it, stepping aside to allow Wilson and Bob to enter.

"Thank you, Sims," Wilson said as he passed.

"Of course, sir," Sims replied as he closed the door and returned to his desk. Bob's opinion of the j.g. continued to improve. They entered an office with at least a dozen enlisted men working at desks. "As you were," Wilson said before most of the men could even get out of their chairs, and continued to a door in the rear of the office. A Chief Yeoman stood as they approached and knocked on a heavy wood door with a frosted glass window stenciled, "CDR E. Hathaway."

"Come," commanded the rich baritone on the other side of the glass. The Yeoman leaned through the door.

"Lieutenant j.g. Wilson to see you, sir."

"Send him in," the baritone replied.

Wilson and Bob entered a small but immaculate office. The dark maple desk was in stark contrast to the steel desks in the outer office and the room smelled of very good pipe tobacco. Behind the desk was a small, slightly pudgy man with a receding hairline and a pencil thin moustache. The silver oak leaf cluster on his collar identified him as a Commander in the U.S. Navy. Bob wondered how anyone that short could be a commissioned officer. He wanted to look around the office for the man with the baritone voice, but stood at rigid attention. Amazingly, the voice came out of the man behind the desk.

"Wilson, what's all this about—and who is this man?"

Bob just couldn't reconcile the body and the voice.

"Sir, this is Chief Gunners Mate Robert Jenkins. He stated he was ordered to Dry Dock C-2 but was not instructed to obtain credentials prior to entering a restricted area. The Marine sentries allowed him and his driver to pass, and now here we are." Wilson looked at Bob, who passed his orders packet to Commander Hathaway. Hathaway opened it and scanned the paperwork. It occurred again to Bob how odd it was that Wilson knew his name. After a moment Commander Hathaway looked up from the orders, a smirk on his face.

"I see Lieutenant Commander Davis wrote this transfer order in Hawaii. Do you know him, Chief Jenkins?"

"Only by name, sir. I've mostly been at sea. I'm not all that familiar with HQ staff at Pearl," he lied. He knew Davis was an officer in the Naval Reserve and a Class-A screwup, as well as the nephew of a member of the House Naval Affairs Committee. As a Lieutenant, he was briefly given command of a destroyer escort that he beached on a jetty trying to leave Mare Island on his first deployment, tearing a hole in the hull. The Navy decided the safest place to put him seemed to be in Personnel. He couldn't sink anything there, at least.

"Well, let's just say his attention to detail is a bit lacking. Anyway, no harm done. We'll get your clearance chop-chop and get you to your duty station," he smiled as he picked up the phone. "Jackson, bring me Chief Jenkins' security packet."

Not twenty seconds passed before there was a knock at the door and the Chief Yeoman placed an oversized manila envelope on the Commander's desk. As he turned to leave, Wilson murmured something to the Yeoman, who then nodded and left.

Hathaway opened the envelope and removed a file marked "Top Secret: Eyes Only." He took his time looking through the stack of documents, making sure that everything required was in the packet. Clipped to the file was a new Navy ID card with Bob's name, rank, and serial number, along with a red stamp reading "C-2 S-1." Hathaway removed the card and handed it to Bob. "Give me your current ID card, Chief. It will be destroyed." Bob complied as Hathaway continued, "Starting tonight, you commit everything in that folder to memory, and you better be a quick learner because you're putting to sea in the next few days. You will be working in a restricted area performing duties classified as top secret. You will correspond with no one except through official channels. So far as the world and most of the Navy knows, you're still on the *Maryland*. Understood?"

"Yes, sir," Bob replied. He didn't understand much of anything at the moment, but hoped he would in time.

"Very well, then. Lieutenant Wilson will accompany you to Dry Dock C-2 now. Dismiss."

"Yes, sir," the two replied and simultaneously turned to leave. Bob opened the door for Wilson and followed him back through the building the way they came.

Commander Hathaway picked up his phone and ordered a secure line. He dialed a number and when the operator answered, he requested to be connected to the operator's commanding officer.

"He's on his way. No, it was another Davis snafu at Pearl. He's just fine . . . No, he's not in dutch with me or anyone else that I know of . . . Alright . . . Your welcome, friend. Anytime."

Bob and Lieutenant (j.g.) Wilson exited the building to find a different jeep waiting for them, and now a Marine was driving. Bob hoped the poor kid who drove him through the sentry post would get off easy. He also noticed his luggage was missing.

"Your gear is already in your quarters," Wilson explained when he saw Bob looking in the back seat, "and that sailor is headed to an orientation. He's not in trouble. But just so you know, those sentries really should have shot, or at the very least arrested, both of you. I'm glad for all of us they didn't." Bob was beginning to kind of like this kid.

The Marine dropped the jeep into gear and started back the exact way they had come. At the sentry post, two different Marines stopped the jeep and this time one demanded to see both Wilson's and Bob's ID while the other held his M-1 rifle at the ready. Satisfied, they saluted the young officer through. Bob was thoroughly confused when the jeep stopped back in front of the massive hangar building. He guessed Wilson was just returning to his post and that the driver would take him on, but Wilson hopped out of the jeep then looked back at Bob, slightly irritated at him.

"Well, are you getting out or not?" Wilson asked at length.

"Yes sir. Sorry sir. I thought you were being dropped off at this hangar and the driver would take me to Dry Dock C-2."

"Hangar?" Wilson chuckled as he headed for the steel

door. "Wow. They really didn't tell you squat, did they Chief?"

"I guess not, sir," Bob admitted as he followed.

Wilson took a key from his pocket and unlocked the steel door. They entered a small cell-like room with concrete walls and ceiling. A heavy, solid steel door like one would find in a prison was at the other end. Next to it, a telephone with no dial hung on the wall. Wilson picked up the receiver. "Mayflower 4739. Two to enter." As he hung up, a slot opened in the door and Wilson showed his ID. The sound of several heavy bolts being retracted could be heard and the door swung open. On the other side was yet another, but larger, concrete-walled room and in it stood the burly southern Shore Patrolman and his two colleagues that Bob had seen earlier, along with two desks and several chairs. Bob signed a check-in form stating his reason for entry as one of the SP's bolted the door behind him.

What the hell kind of an airship needs security like this? Bob asked himself as the next door swung open and they entered the huge expanse of the building. It took a moment for his eyes to adjust to the dimmer light provided by skylights, punctuated by bright electric work lights, but when he realized what he was looking at Bob stopped in his tracks. What he saw was no airship—and the building was no hangar.

"What the hell?" Bob breathed. He realized he was indeed looking at a dry dock. An indoor, covered dry dock. To further his disbelief, the dry dock held a battleship, or a ship the size of a battleship at any rate. He could only clearly see the vessel from the bow to the forward turret along the port side. The rest of his view was obstructed by cranes, trucks, work shacks, cables and generators. Work-men swarmed the ship like ants. Among them, Bob could see both officers and enlisted men. The dry dock had obviously been drained, as the foredeck of the ship was level with the dock. The three sixteen-inch guns of the forward turret loomed over the foredeck.

Lieutenant (j.g.) Wilson looked at Bob, smiling to see the door beating Chief nonplussed. "Welcome aboard, Chief. Some blimp, huh?"

"What? Oh. Yes, sir. It's . . . well it's quite a surprise," Bob stammered as he continued to stare at the ship.

"Come with me," Wilson ordered, still smiling, "I'll escort you aboard. They don't take well to strangers in this building."

Bob fell in behind the officer and headed for the ship. *This kid's alright*, he mused as he walked. Wilson wasn't kidding about suspicion of strangers, either. Every nearby head turned to look at the pair as they passed. Bob noticed that every officer had a .45 holster and in strategic areas, and tucked away in the shadows stood sailors with M-1's.

Weaving through the tangle of cables and air hoses, they reached and crossed the brow. Both men stopped before crossing onto the deck, saluted the ensign, and then saluted the Officer of the Deck, a lieutenant.

"I request permission to come aboard, sir. Lieutenant j.g. Wilson escorting Chief Gunner's Mate Jenkins," Wilson said as he showed the OOD his ID card.

"Very well," the lieutenant replied.

Bob then observed the custom. "Permission to come aboard, sir. Chief Gunners Mate Robert Jenkins reporting for duty."

"Very well and welcome aboard," the OOD responded as he returned Bob's ID. "I've been ordered to instruct you to report to Commander Olson on the bridge."

"Aye, aye, sir." Bob turned to Wilson. "I thank you for your courtesy, sir. I probably should be in the brig."

"Or the morgue," Wilson said with a twinkle in his eye. "I'm glad Commodore Roberts gave us a heads-up about you. Carry on." He grinned again before requesting permission to leave from the OOD, who was stifling a grin himself.

Bob was again dumbfounded at the mention of Commodore Roberts. It was now his turn to grin to himself. *Commodore Roberts? That slick little devil*, he thought as he shook his head.

The OOD brought him back to the moment. "Anything else, Chief?"

"One thing if I may, sir. Do you reach the bridge on this ship like on a *North Carolina*–class?"

"More like a *Colorado*," the lieutenant replied, "or so I'm told."

"Thank you, sir."

"Carry on."

Bob turned and headed across the teak deck for a door situated at the base of the superstructure. He couldn't help noticing that the second turret held triple twelve-inch guns rather than the expected sixteen-inchers. *I hope that danged JD can explain some of this,* he thought as he headed up the series of ladders leading to the conning station platform. As he entered, a Chief Boatswains Mate noticed him and stepped in front of him, blocking his way.

"Can I help you, Chief?" he asked. The words were an offer but the tone was a challenge. They said, *"And just what are you doing on my bridge?"* Bob didn't take the bait.

"I was ordered by the OOD to report to Commander Olson. I was told he was on the bridge." Bob's words were noncommittal, as was his tone. The Chief Bos'n seemed disappointed that the challenge was not accepted. They stared at each other for a long second before the Bos'n turned and walked forward.

"Commander, someone to see you, sir."

The Commander looked up from what appeared to be an electrical schematic he was examining with two junior officers.

"Thank you, Chief," he replied, "Carry on." He left the others and walked toward Bob. His bearing commanded instant respect. He was a good six feet two and although he appeared to be pushing fifty, the muscular build was obvious even in his khakis. That build, coupled with a rock-hard jaw and steel-blue eyes that seemed capable of penetrating armor plate, left no doubt he was not a man to trifle with. Bob knew this Commander Olson had to be the Executive Officer for the ship. He stood at ramrod attention and looked the officer directly in the eye.

"Chief Gunners Mate Jenkins reporting for duty, sir. I was ordered by the OOD to report to you."

"You're late." Olson's tone was similar to the Chief Bos'n. He didn't seem interested in an explanation. "Come with me. The Commodore has been waiting." He immediately walked past Bob to the ladder and headed down.

"Yes, sir." Bob immediately fell in behind the XO. Nine ladders down and several hundred feet aft, they arrived outside the Captain's cabin. Olson's knock was answered by JD's voice.

"Come," the voice boomed.

The two entered the portion of the cabin that served as the personal office of the ship's commanding officer. His state room was aft of the office, through a door behind the large oak desk which was bolted to the deck. JD looked older than the last time they had met, Bob noticed. Gray hair had begun creeping up his temples and his face was more lined. The collar tabs of his khaki shirt bore the single star of a Commodore. Olson and Bob stopped behind the two chairs that faced the desk. Olson spoke first.

"Chief Gunners Mate Jenkins reporting for duty, sir." Bob remained silent.

"Welcome aboard, Chief." JD didn't seem perturbed at being made to wait. "What kept you?"

"I'm afraid my orders weren't complete, sir," Bob replied. "I was not informed of the need for security clearance. I'm sorry to say I made Lieutenant Wilson's day a little difficult. He was most helpful, by the way." *Can't hurt to let the Old Man know,* he thought.

"Sounds like Dumbass Davis did it again," JD chuckled. Olson gave his CO a look. It was not proper to disparage a fellow officer in the presence of an enlisted man. JD noticed. "Don't get your shorts in a bunch, Mr. Olson. The Chief and I have served together before. I doubt he'll fire off a letter to Lieutenant Commander Davis. That will be all, thank you."

"Yes sir. Chief, come with me and we'll get your orders processed—"

"That won't be necessary, Mr. Olson. I'll have someone get the Chief squared away later. Carry on."

Olson stood for a moment, trying to digest his dismissal while leaving an enlisted man with the CO. A tense second passed before Olson spoke. "As you wish, sir." He closed the door a little too hard as he left.

Bob chuckled. "Looks like I'm just pissing *everybody* off today."

JD rose from his chair and walked around the desk. "Why should today be different from any other with you? Good to see you, Bobby." He extended his hand.

"Good to see you, too, JD," Bob replied, clasping his CO's hand before pulling him into an embrace. How are Jeanne and the kids?"

"They're doing well. They think I'm commanding a

cruiser division, which worries Jeanne to death. Momma too, I suppose. It's the one part of this assignment that hurts. Your family has to worry about nothing. Katie got engaged to Bill in April, and of course you know Little Phil graduated day before yesterday. They're sending him to sub school so we all get to *really* worry about him soon. Still no word from Allie?"

"Just that one letter two years ago. I wrote back but never heard anything else. Momma said she calls her from time to time and writes, though. Last time they talked, Allie said she would like to meet. Maybe someday."

"I sure hope so. She was such a sweet little girl."

"By the way, just what the heck did you get me into? What is this tub?"

"Sit down and I'll give you the short story," JD said, gesturing to one of the chairs facing his desk. He walked behind it to a cabinet set in the bulkhead and produced a bottle of scotch and two glasses. "Care for a snort?"

"Something tells me I will before you shut up."

"I really have missed that mouth of yours," JD chuckled. "You did keep things interesting on *Tennessee*."

"Then you had to go off and get smarter just when the fun started."

"But it got me a fourth stripe. How were the Aleutians?"

"Cold. But it made for good gunnery practice. God knows we needed it. They turned almost the entire crew over during repairs. There were maybe two hundred of us left with all those green kids."

"Did you ever make nice with that one kid? You were both so much alike I knew you'd never be able to get along."

"What the heck was his name? Newsom? Newlin? We made peace. He was one of the few that stayed, so I was kind of happy to have him. He got transferred to the Atlantic, though. He's on a jeep carrier chasing U-boats now."

"He has a kid brother in the Navy, too. Nice kid from what I hear."

"God help us all!" Bob took a sip of scotch, then leaned forward and put his glass on the desk. "Now will you please tell me what this ship is?"

"This, little brother, is a ship that doesn't exist. She was supposed to be USS *South Dakota* back in 1920 when they started construction, but she was officially scrapped thanks to the Washington Naval Treaty. And I guess in a way she was. She sure wasn't finished out the way she was drawn up. The Navy decided they would finish the ship out as a lightly armored vessel to be used as a testing platform for all the new improvements designed for all the refits on current and future battleships and cruisers. If you have a high enough security clearance like you now have, you know she is officially BX-1. Battleship, Experimental, Number One. Every man aboard has received security clearance and has a cover story involving another duty station. Hell, even the tug crews that take us out and bring us in are sworn to secrecy.

"Everything on the ship is the most advanced version available, from gunnery to baking ovens. The aerial search radar is the only exception. We've had to take out the most recent SK-2 version to reinstall the SK units currently on the carriers and battleships. Our sea commanders keep reporting anomalies showing up on their displays."

"Anomalies?" Bob interrupted, a sly smile coming over his face. "Do you think maybe our boys might be tracking something like . . . oh, I don't know . . . a spaceship?"

JD's smile matched Bob's. "All of this is in the packet you got when you checked in at HQ. You need to get up to speed on all gunnery and fire control centers as soon as you can. You'll be the Gunnery Officer's senior Chief. It won't hurt to be good buddies with the Chief Radarman, too. You're also senior enlisted man aboard."

"So that's why that Chief Bos'n on the bridge was so charming."

"Carlisle? Yeah. He didn't take that well and he's Olson's puppy. He could be a problem if you let him. But you'll get used to each other. And he's in Navigation. You'll rarely cross paths except at meals, and the weekly Chiefs meeting. I want all my Chiefs to formally meet once a week with any issues with the crew or ship. You'll now run that meeting."

"And Olson?"

"So far as I can figure, his biggest problem is that he graduated the Academy two years ahead of me and is still a Commander. He's an incredible electrical engineer, though. After the academy, he got a master's from MIT before he began active duty. He really deserves to be promoted and be teaching at Annapolis, but he wants to command a warship, and I just can't bring myself to recommend him for a command. He was instrumental in developing the radars we're using now. I've let him basically run the ship while I tended to the evaluations of the new gear."

"So, speaking of promotions, how did you manage that pretty little star?"

"The Navy kind of painted itself into a corner, to be honest. *Soda*—we call the ship *Soda* for South Dakota because she was never christened—she was run by a four-striper, with the escort ships commanded by another Captain. With the rapid growth of the Navy, a lot of senior Captains were promoted to Rear Admiral, including Bill Spencer, who was the skipper before me. The Navy decided to unify command of this little task force under a single officer. Then they suddenly noticed that they didn't have any other Captains that knew all the things that I know in terms of gunnery and electronics with the security clearance necessary for this command except me, so they made me a Commodore. It doesn't ruffle any feathers among the two stars and the more senior Captains kept their combat commands. Plus, the rank allows command of a task force of this size."

"Okay, so now for the big question. Why am I so damned indispensable to this ship?"

"Two reasons, actually. One, you're the best gunner in the Navy. If there's a bug in a system you can find it and fix it. Two, you're no spring chicken. This war has a way to go. The Navy won't make you retire until it's over, you won't retire unless the Navy makes you, and I don't want you to die. So here you are." JD finished his drink. "Well, I'd better get you to the Admin. Officer and get you processed. Your gear is in your quarters. You have a stateroom as Senior Enlisted Aboard. The bad news is we live on the ship for security reasons." He picked up the phone and ordered a Yeoman to help Bob get squared away. "And as always, outside this door I'm just the Old Man and you're just Chief Jenkins."

"Aye, aye, Cap'n," Bob smirked before his face became serious again. "Thanks, JD. I'm getting too old to get shot at anymore, but I don't know what to do outside the Navy."

"Don't give me that. The ranch is in your blood."

The knock at the cabin door interrupted. "Come," JD ordered. A Yeoman Third Class entered. "Take Chief Jenkins to the Captain's Office to process his orders and show him to his quarters."

"Aye, aye, sir," the sailor replied.

"Dismiss."

The sailor led Bob through the passages to the Captain's Office to process his orders, then the pay office, and finally forward to the Chief Petty Officers' quarters, keeping up a nonstop chatter as they went. They entered the CPO quarters and the sailor pointed to a small stateroom on the starboard side of the berthing area reserved for the Chiefs.

"Here ya go, Chief." the Bronx accent was so heavy it almost seemed contrived. "Commanduh Dougherty said he'll show youz around aftuh suppuh. Youz seen the Chief's Mess?"

Bob rolled his eyes. "Yes, I *saw* it. Chow at 1730?"

"You gottit, Chief. My name's Russo. If youz need anything, look me up."

"Thanks Russo." Bob closed the door and looked around. This was different than other battleships he had served on. All the others had a common berthing area for the Chief Petty Officers. His empty sea bag and suitcase were on the bunk. A quick inspection of the closet locker found his belongings neatly stowed. He wasn't very keen on someone else handling his skivvies until he realized that his belongings had not only been stowed, they had probably also been closely inspected by someone from Naval Intelligence. *Oh well*, he thought. He had nothing to hide in his gear and at least that chore was finished. He looked at his watch: 1430. It seemed later.

He sat at the desk and removed the stack of documents from the packet Commander Hathaway had given him at headquarters. Many of the documents were classified top secret. *Might as well get started*, he sighed. He really wanted to catch forty winks before he ate, but orders were orders.

The first document was the history of BX-1, elaborating on the thumbnail sketch of the ship given to him by JD. Most of the armor belt was removed and most of the secondary armaments and anti-aircraft batteries never installed. The crew was reduced by almost seven hundred, mostly through the reduction of gunnery divisions. Instead of the usual sixty-plus chief petty officers on a battleship, *Soda* had only forty-five. *And now I know why I have a stateroom,* Bob smiled.

The second item was a thick operational manual for BX-1, including line drawings for the entire ship. Bob was happy to see that the basic design of the ship was very similar to that of the *Tennessee-* and *Colorado*-class battleships, and his tours on *Tennessee* and *Maryland* gave him a solid knowledge of the ship very quickly. The rest of the documents in the envelope were technical manuals for the ship's armament and fire control systems, including the sea and air radars currently being updated. He was just beginning to review the operational manual when mess call piped over the 1MC. He secured the documents in a lock box mounted to the bulkhead before leaving. As he stepped out of his stateroom, he met several Chiefs coming out of the forward berthing compartment.

Introductions and handshakes followed as the men made their way up to the Chiefs' mess. With the smaller group of men present, conversation at dinner was easier and less hurried, and as men came in after cleaning up from working below decks or on the dock, more introductions followed. Bob was pleased to see some familiar faces. He noticed that the conversation quieted down when Chief Carlisle entered the room. He was mildly surprised when Carlisle got his chow and sat down in an empty chair across from him.

"I need to tell you something," Carlisle said after taking a few bites, "it's kind of bothered me to step down for you. But, from what some of these men tell me, you're a good egg and you know your stuff. I have to make up my own mind."

"I respect that," Bob replied after a moment. "The guys that said I'm a good egg tell you I can be a real jerk sometimes?"

Carlisle chuckled. "Well, yeah, actually."

"Good!" Now it was Bob's turn to laugh. "I'd hate to think somebody I'd served with was a liar. Listen, I've got a lot to learn on this tub. I didn't volunteer for this job and I don't plan on pissing anybody off. I've been in your spot myself. I'll give you and everybody else their due."

"Well, they tell me nobody knows more about gunnery than you. I hear you can drop a sixteen-inch round down the stack of a tin can making thirty knots at thirty thousand yards." He extended his hand, "Fred Carlisle."

Bob set down his fork and wiped his hand before extending it. "Bob Jenkins."

"Where you from, Jenkins?" Carlisle asked as coffee was refilled.

"California, with a big dose of New Mexico. You?"

"Montana by way of South Dakota."

"Sounds kind of ranchy."

"Worse. Wheat farmers."

"So now I know why you joined the Navy."

"Pretty much, yeah. Why did you join up?"

"That's a long story. Straight out of a Tom Mix movie."

The conversation was interrupted by the squawk of the 1MC, announcing throughout the ship that Chief Jenkins was ordered to report to Main Battery Plot.

"Duty calls," Carlisle smirked.

"Guess the Gunnery Officer is finished eating. What's the skinny on him?" Bob asked as he stood.

"Good man. Cruisers and battleships his whole career.

Real math whiz."

"Well, I better get my butt in gear. Good to meet all of you."

"Welcome aboard."

As Bob began heading down the ladders three decks to meet the Gunnery Officer, he couldn't quite put a finger on what Carlisle's angle was in light of what JD had told him earlier. Cordial distrust seemed to be the best tack to take with him for now, he decided. As he descended below the water line, the little twinge of claustrophobia hit him as it always did. Memories of the men trapped on *Oklahoma* at Pearl were never too far away. His mind was back to business by the time he entered Main Battery Plot, however. A tall, lanky, balding Commander looked up from across the plotting table. Bob closed the door and faced his new boss at attention.

"Chief Gunners Mate Jenkins reporting as ordered, sir."

"Welcome aboard, Jenkins. I'm Commander Dougherty. I'm your new boss." His voice was impassive, but his face had a slight smile. "I've heard a good deal about you. You were the man who figured out the problems with the Mark Four guns, right?"

"Well, sir, I don't know about that. I'd have to credit Captain Hussey on *Idaho* with most of the improvements," Bob replied.

"You're too modest, Chief. Anyway, have you had a chance to look over any of the technical manuals yet?"

"Just scratched the surface, sir. I ran into some trouble getting aboard. I'm afraid it put me off schedule."

"I heard. Do you always make this much trouble?"

"My apologies, sir. I guess I was a little edgy after bouncing around in that plane on the flight here. My B.S. tolerance wasn't very high today."

"Guess I can't blame you. Well, let's get you up to speed with the physical ship."

Dougherty spent the next three hours walking Bob through every inch of the ship, concentrating on the differences between BX-1 and other battleships. They started in the Main Battery Plotting room, then worked their way systematically through all the ship's gunnery components, finally finding themselves high above the deck at the surface radar antennas. As they made their way back down to the superstructure, Dougherty became more conversational, but still all business regarding the ship.

"Our sole purpose is to install every new piece of equipment perfectly, then do everything we can to find every flaw under any condition so that the flaw can be corrected. If a new gadget gets put on a warship, it's with our guarantee that it will work. Your experience is going to prove very valuable. I want you to feel completely free to speak your mind about any concern you have for anything to do with the guns and fire control on this ship, including how we conduct our trials and drills. We have some really good men on this ship, but sometimes it's not easy to get them to push the equipment the way they would if someone was shooting back at them. I'll need you to help keep them sharp."

"I understand, sir." Jenkins was impressed with Dougherty. "I can see how that can happen. I'll do my best."

"Well, you've had a long day, Chief. Turn in and get some sleep. There's a meeting scheduled for 0800 with all CPO's to get to meet you and get an update on how the radar installations are going. Any questions?"

"Too many for the hour, sir, but none pressing. I'd imagine most of them will get answered soon."

"If not, pipe up. Carry on."

"Yes, sir. Thank you."

Bob was appreciative of the walk-around, but was thankful it was over. He was worn out from the day. He only wanted a final cup of coffee before he turned in. The Chiefs' mess didn't disappoint him. He even treated himself to some pie that had been left out before he headed back to his state room. He switched on the light and looked at the lock box. *Not tonight*, he thought as he set his alarm clock for 0500. He could study before turn-to in the morning. For the first time in the past few months, he was going to sleep with no risk of having his ship blown out from under him. He was asleep in a few minutes.

Thirty

"I don't want to take a great deal of time this morning, but I do want to formally introduce you to Chief Jenkins."

Commander Olson seemed less than enthusiastic that he had to present Bob to the other Chief Petty Officers. Instead of a more formal setting, he had ordered the Chiefs to assemble in the crew's messing area after breakfast. The tables had been secured to the overhead and Olson chose to lean against the counter of the ship's soda fountain, or gee-dunk as the crew called it.

"Chief Jenkins comes to us from the *Maryland*, where he was also Chief Gunner. His skills are considerable and I expect him to put our gunners through their paces. He is also Senior Enlisted Aboard so besides reporting to Commander Dougherty he will also be providing the Commodore and me with updates on crew performance, just as Chief Carlisle did. Your weekly meetings will continue to update Chief Jenkins. I'm sure you'll all find time to get to know him better soon.

"To update you on the installation of the SK radar units, the installation is complete and testing and inspection will commence today. We hope to be able to put to sea in less than seventy-two hours. Dismiss." Olson turned on his heel and was the first man out of the area, nearly running down the starboard ladder to the second deck and wardroom country.

"Wow. Who pissed in his cereal?"

Bob turned to see Carlisle standing next to him.

"I thought it was just me," Bob replied.

"I think he's pissed that after finally beating me down, he has to start all over with a new guy."

"What the hell are you sayin', Carlisle?"

Carlisle looked over Bob's shoulder at a small group of Chiefs that had stayed to visit. "Men, can we have this area?"

"You bet, Fred. We'll catch up later, Bob," one of them replied.

"Thanks. Carry on," Bob said.

As the other men left, Carlisle returned his attention to Bob and said, "The first thing you need to know is that Olson is a Class A, two-faced, self-serving ass. He would shoot his own mother to get a command, and his own kids to get a promotion to Captain. He makes sure to tell the department officers one thing, then the junior officers something else. He keeps his thumb on every CPO and junior officer on this ship, one or two at a time, until they're half nuts. Chain of command doesn't mean much to him. If he doesn't like how you do things, Dougherty will be the last one to know. He'll just chew you out, tell you how he wants something done, and then wait for Dougherty to see you doing things different so Dougherty chews you out again. Oh, and by the way, he's a damn liar. I tried to work this out through channels when I started, but he is so smooth at what he does the other senior officers didn't believe me."

"Did you ever mention this to the skipper? What about those meetings he talked about?"

"The skipper doesn't make many meetings. Olson sees

to it. He usually invents a problem with a junior officer to distract him. And when the old man does come, Olson makes sure to take up all the time running off at the mouth. After so long, I just gave up and became Olson's yes man. I'm actually glad you showed up, Jenkins. I didn't realize how much I was starting to hate my job."

"Well, the Old Man and I go back a way. This is the fourth time I've served under him. Maybe I can do something," Bob ruminated aloud, and to himself thought, *Oh, Mr. Olson, you are so screwed.*

"I hope so. Every petty officer on this ship came here because he was considered a hot shot by his superiors and now, they all just go through the motions. If they really perform well it's either out of spite for Olson or devotion to duty."

"So, when do the Chiefs all meet?"

"Usually on Thursdays after breakfast, at 0800. We would have had one today, but Olson cancelled it. And you meet with Olson and the skipper Thursday afternoons at around 1500. Also cancelled today."

"Huh. Convenient. I really appreciate you letting me know all this, Carlisle."

"Fred. All the chiefs are on a first name basis when we're together. We started it to kind of help morale. You know, the 'us versus them' thing."

"Fair enough, Fred. Just don't be offended if I slip up and forget that until I get used to you men. As few of us as there are, I kind of like it. And call me Bob. The only person that ever calls me Robert is my momma, and only then when she's pissed."

"Good enough Bob," Carlisle chuckled, "See you around."

"See ya. Thanks again."

Bob headed to the port side ladder to report to

Dougherty in Main Battery Plot. Dougherty wasn't present but his junior officer, Lieutenant Commander Dwight Williams, was. He was sitting at a desk against the aft bulkhead and turned to look at Bob.

"Chief Jenkins reporting, sir," Bob said at attention.

Williams seemed a bit confused. "Reporting for what, Chief?" he asked.

"Duty, sir," it was now Bob's turn to be confused, "I assumed all hands would report to their duty station for daily orders."

Williams glanced at the clock on the bulkhead and smiled. "At ease. You're kind of early, Chief. We generally don't turn-to until 0830."

"My apologies for interrupting, sir. I should have known that, considering I should still be at the CPO meeting."

"No problem, Chief. Welcome aboard. I'm Lieutenant Commander Williams."

"Pleased to meet you, sir."

"Commander Dougherty should be here soon. He and the junior officers go over daily orders before the men arrive. Have a seat. I need to finish this report."

"Thank you, sir," Bob replied and found a chair near the plotting table.

Williams returned to his work at the desk. He had just slipped his report into a manila envelope and was turning to speak to Bob when the door opened and Dougherty entered, followed by several junior officers and two warrant officers. Bob hopped to attention.

"As you were, Chief," Dougherty smiled at Bob. "No Chiefs' meeting this morning?"

"No sir, just a quick meet and greet."

"I got so busy with my tour last night I forgot to fill you in on the schedule. When in port, I generally meet with my junior officers daily at 0815, and the crew reports by divisions at 0830 in their duty areas. We meet back again at 1700 for report and orders. As Chief Gunner you are welcome at these meetings and you may spend your watch with any division you choose after that, provided I have no specific job for you that day. And as Senior Enlisted Aboard, I understand the Captain or XO may require you elsewhere. During exercises involving other departments you go where you see a need, but I want you here for all main and secondary battery exercises, and, God forbid, if we ever have to go to battle stations."

"Understood, sir."

Dougherty introduced Bob to the gunnery division officers and warrant officers, then quickly gave the orders for the day. In anticipation of the completion of the radar inspections, the gunnery divisions would be cleaning and inspecting all gunnery stations, then stand by pending the final inspections of the radar installations. The ship would begin taking on fuel and stores during the radar inspections and ordnance taken on after radar inspection had been completed. With the dismissal of the junior officers, Bob requested permission to remain in plot to get to know the men he would be working closest with.

At 0830, Dougherty gave his daily orders to the men of the main and secondary battery plots after introducing Bob. Organizing and cleaning the station and plot rooms took little time as they were both spotless to begin with. The men then moved on to the main battery magazines and handling rooms to assist the respective crews for each turret. Bob was pleased to see how meticulous the cleaning had been. He could still remember working for days on end in the magazines on *Tennessee* after the attack on Pearl Harbor, cleaning the magazines that had been intentionally flooded during the attack. Bob thought he would never see those compartments clean again, or get the smell of powder soaked in oily water out of his nose. He could never inspect a magazine without that memory.

The gunnery divisions broke for lunch at different times between 1145 and 1215. Bob ate with the Chief of the secondary plot room and the secondary battery Chiefs. He was just exiting the Chiefs' mess when he spotted a familiar figure coming down the port side ladder.

"Hey, Morris," he called, "you actually work hard enough to deserve to eat?"

A harried-looking Chief glanced at Bob before rolling his eyes back in his head and giving Bob the bird as he disappeared into the mess. Bob made sure the man could hear him howling with laughter.

"Friend of yours?" the plot Chief asked Bob.

"From way back," Bob replied, still chuckling.

The afternoon consisted of cleaning and inspection of the main and secondary battery guns and turrets. Bob learned that because of *Soda's* limited scope in testing weapons, the crew reduction resulted in only enough crewmen to man two of the four main batteries at any given time. A similar situation existed with the secondary and anti-aircraft crews, a fact that caused him more than a little concern should the ship be threatened.

Several times he saw Chief Morris scrambling up and down ladders. It seemed that every time he saw Morris heading up, Olson's voice would blare over the 1MC ordering him below, and vice versa. Olson was being a real prick, Bob thought. Finally, the two passed close enough to share a smile.

"Can we talk at supper?" Bob asked as they passed.

"Sorry, old man, not tonight. No time for chow. Breakfast?"

"Deal," Bob replied as Morris started up a ladder to the

forward 40-millimeter anti-aircraft director. As he disappeared up the ladder, Olson's voice barked over the 1MC ordering Chief Morris to the aft radar control room. Bob had heard enough. *Might as well stir the pot early,* he thought. He glanced at his watch: 1450. He headed for the bridge, hoping JD would be there. Stepping out and feigning a look at the 5-inch anti-aircraft director beneath the conning platform, he heard JD's voice from above, answering his prayer to be noticed.

"Things looking up to standards, Chief?" JD called down.

"Very satisfactory, sir," Bob called back, "Forgive me for running late for the meeting today. I'll be right up." Bob tipped his cap back on his head, the old signal he and JD developed on *Idaho* that said, "We need to talk."

"The meeting was cancelled, but come up to the conn."

"Aye, aye, sir." Bob hustled up the ladder to the conning platform. As he rounded the ladder running up to the conning platform he paused, allowing a Lieutenant and Ensign to pass as they came down the ladder. Word might get to Olson quickly, so Bob wasted no time in climbing to the conning platform. The Commodore was alone.

"What's up, Bobby?"

"Too much to tell you here. Nothing operational. We're fine gunnery-wise. But have you been listening to the 1MC today?"

"Only with half an ear, I admit. Why?"

"Olson is running the Chief Radarman to death. He sends him up then down then forward then aft. You know how you told me to get to know the Chief Radarman? No need. I've known Carl Morris for years and he knows his stuff. Olson's just jerking his chain today and the man has real work to do. I don't know what he thinks he's doing but it ain't right. One thing's for sure. We need to have this weekly meeting with you, me, and Olson *every* week, and I need some way to meet with you in private."

"I'll take care of that. You still walk laps when at sea?"

"Every day. How about you?"

"I'll start again."

"Thanks. I'd better get below and check in with Dougherty," Bob said as he headed for the ladder. His head was level with the deck when the 1MC once again summoned Chief Morris. He stopped and turned to his brother with a look that said, "See what I mean?" JD nodded.

Bob took his time working down the ten decks to Main Battery Plot, stopping in several different areas of the ship to meet with his subordinate chiefs and be introduced to some of the junior officers. The young Ensigns and Lieutenants junior grade were always of interest to Bob, although sometimes a bother. He always liked the ones that listened to and watched how their Chiefs went about their leadership roles. They were the ones the older Chiefs called "son" when out of other peoples' earshot. They were also the ones that usually wound up with promotions first, it seemed.

He checked the progress of fueling operations and checked the boiler rooms and machinery rooms before finally reporting to Main Battery Plot at 1655. Dougherty was already present, as was Lieutenant Commander Williams. The plot room personnel reported in a few minutes, and after a brief report specific to plot they were dismissed. The remaining gunnery officers gave their report as well and Dougherty dismissed all hands. While in port, no night watch was set. Bob retired to his stateroom and studied manuals until chow time. He stayed in the Chiefs' mess until every man had eaten, visiting with every Chief. He never saw Carl Morris, whose name he heard twice over the 1MC while he ate. Stifled curses hissed from several men after the second summons.

Bob lingered over one final cup of coffee, visiting with the mess stewards as they cleaned up. Carl Morris never came in for chow. Bob finally headed for his stateroom to study and turn in. He woke at 2330 and had to go to the head. Quietly entering the berthing area from his stateroom, he saw Carl Morris getting ready for bed.

"Did you ever get to eat?" Bob whispered so as not to disturb the other men.

"I grabbed a sandwich," Morris replied.

"You alright?"

"Yeah. See you at breakfast."

Thirty-One

23 June, 1944

Bob was awake at 0530, the same as always. He turned off the alarm on his clock before it went off, then grabbed his Dopp kit and headed up to the Chiefs' head. Washed and shaved, he was in the Chief's mess at 0615, where he waited for Carl Morris. Morris came in a few minutes later, apparently none the worse for his short night. Bob got in line with Morris and the two took seats together. After a few minutes of brief reunion chat catching up with family news, Bob got straight to the point.

"So, I have to ask. Did you need to be in ten places at once yesterday, or was Olson jerking you around as bad as I think he was?"

"You still get the pulse of a ship as fast as ever, huh?" Morris replied with a wry smile.

"One of my many talents. Now answer the question."

"One of my boys screwed up wiring a junction box and the Lieutenant threw him and me to Olson. It was a ten-minute fix but Olson made us pay in spades. The poor Lieutenant had to recite the temporary wiring schematic for the radar reinstall from memory and every time he screwed up, I had to run and verify that he was wrong. The damned schematics were right in front of us but Olson wouldn't back off, even when the Lieutenant Commander tried to step in. But we were able to test almost everything else around the nonsense. We should be able to fire everything up and test all continuity this morning and then make ready to get under way."

"Well, at least your other men could keep inspection going. Your legs stiff?"

"Like a couple of boards. I woke up twice with cramps."

"So, let me get this straight. We're retrofitting the radar to try to see why our ships are picking up targets that ain't there? Why don't they just install the SK-2 equipment we're currently using on lead carriers and battleships?" Bob was commonly frustrated by decisions made by the Navy, and this was no exception.

"Simple. Until we give the okay to the equipment we're removing, they can't put it into production. We haven't done that yet. So there simply aren't enough of these new SK-2 units to do any good." Morris was patient with his superior. They had served together for the first time on *Pueblo*, long before radar was developed. A master electrician, as well as curious and ambitious, Morris quickly moved to embrace the new technology of radar, and his skills grew with each advance. "So, we have to debug what we originally said was good to use. It's pretty embarrassing, to be honest. The brass ain't happy, and I'm taking this kind of personally. So is Olson. He helped develop it. We tested this equipment against every kind of plane we have. I can't for the life of me figure what the problem is. So, we're going to reinstall the same units that the fleet has and put them through the wringer."

"Well, I know one thing for sure. If you can't figure it out, ain't nobody goin' to." Bob's frustration was replaced by sympathy and concern for his old friend. Carl had a lot riding on this, both professionally and personally. "What kind of anomalies are they reporting?"

"Weird stuff. Targets at fifty, sixty thousand feet. Targets the size of an entire squadron that don't move, or move at speeds that are impossible. Targets that look like they're crashing into the ocean. It has to be an electrical problem somewhere that causes the display to be messed up."

"That seems logical," Bob lied, knowing full well what the anomalies had to be. "Did you do a complete rewire of all the trunks between the antennas and screens?"

"Yup. The reinstall of the older units was easy, but the new wiring has been a royal pain. Nobody wanted to remove the wiring we have because it's working on the new radars. So we're running temporary wiring trunks alongside the existing lines. It's taken twice as long as it was supposed to. Olson's been riding me like a mule. Yesterday was just one of many like that. But we're finished. Once we perform the full start-up we can go to sea. By the way, you *have* heard how we leave port, right?"

"I'm not looking forward to that. I've never heard of a ship this size entering or leaving port at night."

"Oh, it gets better. We're completely blacked out. Even the tugs. Nobody ever gets to see us come or go."

"Lovely."

"It really isn't as bad as it sounds. The channel is shut down. It is every night. And the tug skippers are wizards. And remember, this is a lot nimbler a vessel than a normal battleship. The lower displacement and the more powerful turbines give us a lot of maneuverability. We ride pretty high in the water until we get out in the sound and take on ballast. Until then we can pretty well stop on a dime. It's quite a show."

"Glad I'll be below decks."

"Like hell. I bet the skipper sticks you on the bow with the First Lieutenant to watch the angle of the bow and signal when we're clear of the dock."

"Well, at least I can't screw that up too bad," Bob chuckled as he wiped his plate with a piece of biscuit. "Thanks for meeting me, Carl. I know you have a ton to do but it's good to work with you again."

"Same here, Bob. You're going to be kind of busy yourself today, huh?"

"Maybe. It depends on how you boys get along. If you're happy with the electronics, I have to take on ordnance. I don't know if Dougherty wants to work through the night or stop and finish in the morning."

"Probably stop and start again in the morning, provided you start today at all. We pretty much operate on banker's hours. The crew just isn't big enough to go all night and I bet you won't take on anywhere near a full load of ordnance. You won't even have much anti-aircraft ammo. We never load to combat capacity except for individual weapons when we test gunnery upgrades."

"Huh. Good to know. So, what happens if we actually run into trouble?"

"Expend all available rounds and run like hell. This tub can really move when she has to. We can out run everything the Japanese have on the surface that's bigger than a destroyer, and we never get far enough from home to worry about carrier aircraft."

"Yeah. I keep forgetting the lack of armor and surplus of turbine. What about torpedo defense?"

"We always have a screen of six destroyers, all loaded for bear, and they have all the newest and best toys, too. It would take a really good sub captain to get a shot off at us, but if we take a hit, we are well and truly screwed. Well, I got'ta get my happy little butt to work. See you around."

"See you later."

The two men separated as they left the Chiefs' mess,

Morris up to the radar antennas and Bob down to the Gunnery Office. Morning orders were to assist dry dock crew in clearing decks and taking on stores. Ordnance would not be brought to the dry dock until the other supplies had come aboard and the final radar inspection complete. Bob pitched in, supervising his men under the direction of the supply officer. The process was completed by 1230. The gunnery crews were then dismissed for lunch and then to ship liberty, with orders to stand by.

With nothing left to do until the electronic tests were completed, Bob went below. Even though Dougherty had completed his inspection, Bob triple checked every main battery magazine and handling room. Skipping lunch, he inspected the five-inch turrets and each anti-aircraft station. It didn't take as long as it would have on a normal battleship with the greatly reduced number of batteries. *Soda* was never intended to go very far from home, so defensive weaponry was limited to just enough to adequately test the equipment. It still bothered him that even with these limited armaments he couldn't test them all at once on multiple targets.

Finally, at 1600, the 1MC barked, "All gunnery Division Commanders and Chief Petty Officers assemble on the fantail." Bob chuckled at his good fortune; he was just getting out of the barber's chair. He exited straight from the barber shop to the quarterdeck and, after walking around the aft turrets, was on the fantail. As opposed to all the commissioned battleships, *Soda* had no aircraft or catapult mounted on the fantail, for reasons unknown to everyone except Admiral Cochrane at the Bureau of Ships. As a result of this mystery, the area provided a roomy assembly point. Soon all the gunnery leadership was present and accounted for. Commander Dougherty stood before the men.

"I have been informed that the final radar test and inspection has been completed. I've met with the Captain and XO and we agree that attempting to take on our ordnance at this hour and being able to depart on the tide tonight would force us to take unnecessary risks in the interest of speed. So, consider this your morning orders meeting for tomorrow. Mr. Williams . . ."

Lieutenant Commander Williams stepped forward as Dougherty continued. "You will assemble by division in the magazines and on the starboard rail at 0800 and prepare to take on ordnance, commencing with turrets one and two and progressing aft for all main batteries, then five-inch ordnance, then anti-aircraft ammunition. We will be loading the standard defensive minimum as this deployment will not involve gunnery testing. Available Engineering and Navigation personnel will assist as usual. The Chief Master at Arms and Marine detail will be responsible for machine gun and small arms ammunition. As always, all safety protocols will be followed to the letter. Enlisted personnel are ordered to report any concern immediately, repeat, immediately to the nearest officer or Chief Petty Officer. If all goes as planned, we will finish up around 1700 and we can plan on getting underway around 2400 hours.

"Dry dock Security Condition One will be in place as usual tomorrow. All officers and Chiefs will report to the Chief Master at Arms office at 0730 to receive their sidearms. Questions?" None were raised. "Dismiss."

The assembly broke up and headed for their respective messes. Bob was thankful to have finished the ship's operational manual the night before. He knew it took over twenty-four hours for a full crew to load the arsenal that a ship like this could carry. The "standard defensive minimum" was a term unique to *Soda* as far as Bob knew, and consisted of only twelve rounds of armor-piercing shells for each main battery, with three water-dye rounds for turret one plus three star-shells for turret four, along with the minimum number of powder charges. The five-inch guns and anti-aircraft batteries also had a bare minimum of ammunition. He assumed that with only twelve fifty caliber machine guns and thirty Marines on board, they would have an easy day as well. Carl Morris was right. They had just enough ordnance to shoot as they ran away. He hoped the escort ships were better armed like Morris had said.

At dinner, Bob was joined by Carl Morris, Fred Carlisle, and Chief Quartermaster Bill Zimmerman. After congratulating Morris for his good work and not being in the brig for killing Olson, the topic turned to departure the next night. Bob had plenty of questions, despite his reading. Carlisle was happy to oblige.

"The XO always directs the tugs. Olson stands on turret three. The senior Chief or Chief Quartermaster stands with Olson and relays commands for rudder adjustments to the helm and course adjustments to the tug by walkie-talkie. First Lieutenant Sharpe sets up a transom on the bow and relays the angle of the bow to the helm as well. There's a black line painted up the wall in front of the bow that lines up with the center of the dry dock. I don't know if you've noticed that yet, Bob."

"Actually, I have, I just had no idea what it was for until now," Bob replied.

"Well, when we pull out, there is one light on in the whole building and it's on that black line. Sharpe sets the transom directly amidships ahead of turret one and lines up the jack staff with the transom, then figures the angle of the bow against the jack staff and the line on the wall. One of us will be on the radio transmitting those readings. Up to now, Bill has been on the bow."

"Sounds like we need to get some guidance from Mr. Olson."

"Orders and assignments for getting underway are posted at 1700 the evening we get underway, but I suggest you be ready to double check fast just in case Olson tries to get cute."

"No kidding," Zimmerman interjected, "He would love to pull a trifecta and bust all three of us at once."

Carl Morris suddenly laughed. He had been quiet through the entire meal, mostly from exhaustion. "Well, if he follows form for the last two days, he'll have you three running relays from stem to stern!"

The others chuckled their agreement, and then headed down to turn in.

Thirty-Two

24 June, 1944

Bob awoke at 0300, surprised he had slept for three hours at a stretch. He always had trouble sleeping before departing on a mission, but this night seemed worse for some reason. After staring at the overhead for ten minutes, he dressed and took a walk, coming out on the starboard forecastle deck near turret two. On the dry dock, trucks were beginning to unload ordnance, guarded by Lieutenant (j.g.) Wilson's shore patrolmen. At one point, Wilson looked up to see Bob leaning against the rail chains. Bob straightened and saluted the young officer, eliciting a smile as he returned Bob's salute.

"He's a good kid, huh?"

Bob jumped, then he realized his brother had snuck up on him yet again.

"Damn you, JD, you're goin' to be the death of me yet," he laughed softly.

"Yeah, well, I had a good teacher on how to be sneaky."

"Can't sleep either?"

"Not well, anyway. This ship has never given me worries like some have. Can't figure out why I'm wound up tonight."

"I can. I think we're goin' to have company on this mission."

JD glared at Bob in the gloom and sighed as he turned his attention back to the work on the dockside. "I really wish you hadn't said that."

"Because you know it, too."

"Yup."

Somehow, since their first encounter with the alien beings, they believed they had a sixth sense about knowing when they would have another encounter, just as their mother did: a slight headache that wouldn't go away and a dull, hollow uneasiness that settled in their gut. Had they known about the tracking devices implanted in their scalps, they would have known it was the activation of the devices that caused their physical response. The two stood silent for several minutes, watching the workmen unloading the last of the twelve-inch projectiles, before Bob finally spoke again.

"You got Carlisle all wrong."

"How so?"

"Olson plays the senior officers against the junior officers and Chiefs. From what I hear, almost constantly. Carlisle wasn't his puppy. Carlisle gave up trying to fight Olson and just went along. From what he and the other Chiefs tell me, I'm next. I noticed one of the Warrants kept an eye on me all day. I think I shook him before we talked, but he picked me up not long after I left the bridge."

"I noticed how he was running Morris after you mentioned it. That went on all day?"

"Until 2330 by the clock. I kid you not."

"I got stupid after I got this command, then. I've been so busy with the administration end of things, I quit being a skipper somewhere along the way. I'm really glad you're here. You get me back on the straight and narrow."

"Anything you need."

"We'll start tomorrow. You'll see how sneaky I can be

when I really try. And just so you know, you'll be on the bridge when we put to sea. I don't need a dog and pony show from Olson while leaving dry dock."

"Thanks. I'll see how many times I spot you."

"I have a feeling it might be tough. Something tells me you might get the run-around like Morris did."

"I don't know if I have the legs for that," Bob chuckled.

"Well, you dang sure won't if you don't get some sleep. Turn in, Chief. That's an order."

"Aye, aye, Skipper. See you later."

The two men returned to their respective quarters. Both were able to doze until 0530, then both were up and about their business. Bob ate quickly and was soon walking the starboard rail, visualizing the process of lifting the huge projectiles, the sixteen-inch shells weighing over a ton, onto the deck, then gently lowering them through hatches down into the handling rooms where they would be strapped to the bulkheads. They were followed by the powder charges, bags filled with gunpowder, the largest weighing over one hundred pounds each. He always did this, trying to spot problems before they happened. At 0715, he looked up to see Olson striding toward him. *Oh goody*, he thought, *here we go*. He turned to Olson and saluted. Olson ignored him until the last moment, returning the salute with his first salvo of the day.

"Were you exempted from morning orders, Chief?"

"Begging your pardon, sir, but Commander Dougherty gave orders yesterday afternoon."

"Morning orders were scheduled for 0700, Chief. I was just there."

"My apologies, sir. I wasn't aware of the change."

"The orders were posted on the Gunnery Office door at 2000 last night. You don't check that daily?"

"I was never informed of that, sir." The heat was beginning to creep up Bob's collar. "I regret I didn't ask Commander Dougherty of such practices. If you'll excuse me, sir, I'll get down for the last of the meeting."

"Don't worry about it now, they're nearly finished," Olson's volume was beginning to rise.

"Well, then, I'll find Commander Dougherty after I collect my sidearm."

"Why on Earth do you think you need a sidearm? What the hell are you playing at, Jenkins?"

"Lieutenant Commander Williams ordered all Chief Petty Officers and officers to have a sidearm today, sir." Above him, he saw a familiar silhouette peeking over a twenty-millimeter gun tub. Time to play the fish a little, Bob thought. "If you'll excuse me, sir, I'm supposed to get my sidearm at 0730."

"You're not going anywhere, mister, until you explain to me why you are so ignorant of onboard procedures, as well as telling me how you think that the number one handling room is clean," Olson's volume was steadily rising. Early-arriving crewmen were beginning to take notice.

"Beg pardon sir?"

"The questions are simple, Jenkins! Why don't you know shipboard procedure, and why is the handling room dirty?"

"Sir, to answer your questions in order, there is no mention of posting of orders at any other times than 0800 and 1700 hours, per the standing orders for this ship as noted in the operational manual. As to the condition of the number one handling room, Commander Dougherty inspected all handling rooms personally yesterday with Lieutenant Commander Williams and found them satisfactory. I also inspected them after that. I will report your dissatisfaction to them immediately."

"You'll do nothing of the sort. You will personally supervise the cleanup with the handling room crew immediately. That's an order."

"Aye, aye, sir." Bob noticed the silhouette had left the gun tub. "Right away, sir."

"Dismiss."

Bob raced down the ladders to the number one handling room. On the way down, he had to cool off and think about Olson's tactics for the day. The crew was already there, preparing to receive the sixteen-inch shells from above. They looked surprised to see Bob, and perhaps a little fearful. A glance around the area showed Olson had lied.

"Ready to start your day, men?" Bob asked

A Gunners Mate Second Class spoke up, "Ready and willing, Chief."

"Outstanding. You men didn't encounter anything amiss or dirty when you arrived, did you?"

"You mean this?" The second class reached into his dungarees pocket and incredulously held out a chewing gum wrapper. "I picked this up off the deck when I got here."

Bob looked at the wrapper and snorted. "Lord. Carry on." Bob left without further comment. Racing up three ladders in the hope of still getting his sidearm, he arrived at the Chief Master at Arms's office to find it locked. He looked at his watch: 0758. He was going to be late for assembly topside now, too. As he turned, he bumped into JD, smiling and holding a gun belt with a .45.

"There wasn't a change in orders. Dougherty knows. Get topside. Keep your cool."

Bob had just exited the starboard hatch on the fore-castle when morning colors stopped him at precisely 0800.

He found Dougherty immediately after and reported. He started to speak when Dougherty held up his hand.

"I know. Keep your mouth shut. I want to watch this. I'm going to babble at you and you stand at attention listening and don't move a muscle. Act like you're really getting read the riot act," the Gunnery Officer said, looking to his left without turning his head.

"Yes, sir," Bob replied, wishing he could look as well. Over the next thirty seconds, Dougherty quietly talked about the muzzle velocities of the guns and the superiority of the fifty caliber guns over the forty-five calibers, and how the newer forty-millimeter directors were so much faster at locking onto the target. As he spoke, he jerked his head in serious inflection, even pointing a finger at Bob's chest at one point. Finally, he looked at Bob again. "You don't look like you've been chewed out, Chief. You should."

"With all due respect, sir, I better not. The men on the ship that know me know I have a great poker face when I get bawled out. I'm honestly looking exactly like I would if this had been real."

"Good to know. Carry on," and then, bellowing over Bob's shoulder, "Mr. Williams!"

Bob began to head for the handling crane. He watched Lieutenant Commander Williams walking towards his boss. Williams, unlike Bob, didn't have a poker face for a butt chewing, and he had just received one from Olson. This is what Dougherty had been watching while using Bob as his decoy. As Williams approached Dougherty, Bob watched Olson's back storming aft towards the superstructure, casting sideways glances at Dougherty and Williams. It was obvious to Bob that Dougherty was giving the same sham to Williams he had received. Olson suddenly stopped in his tracks, as if he'd had an epiphany, and turned to stare at the gun belt Bob was wearing. Out of the corner of his eye, Bob watched Olson mutter something to himself before heading below. As soon as Olson disappeared through the knee-knocker door, Dougherty finished his talk with Williams and with a sly smile walked away. He glanced up at the bridge, then clapped his hands and good-naturedly shouted, "All right men, let's get a move on!" Sixteen-inch shells began moving up and over the rail, then down to their racks.

Bob almost laughed twenty minutes later when he heard Olson's voice crackle over the 1MC, "Chief Jenkins report to number four Turret Captain's booth." He headed aft to turret four, then through hatch to the booth located in the overhang of the turret. He found Olson in the Turret Captain's booth, looking at a photo of Betty Grable taped to the aft bulkhead. Dougherty had personally assured Bob that Betty was there with his permission and had been there for months. This couldn't be about the photo.

"Chief Jenkins reporting, sir," Bob obediently reported.

"Chief," Olson said with little interest, looking at the most famous legs in America, "do you know if Commander Dougherty is aware of this?"

"He was day before yesterday at 1045 when he inspected this booth, sir." *You jerk*, Bob thought.

"I see. Do you know who the Turret Captain for the aft batteries is, Chief?"

"Yes sir. Chief Warrant Officer Lopez." *Ass*.

"And the gunnery officer aft is Lieutenant Adams, correct?"

"That is correct, sir." *Pompous Ass*.

"Do you happen to know his whereabouts at the moment?"

"He was five feet away from me when you paged me, sir. I would assume he's still on the fo'c'sle." *Oh, you miserable son of a . . . .*

"Inform Lieutenant Adams and Chief Warrant Lopez that this is not acceptable on a naval vessel and it needs to be removed immediately."

"Yes sir."

"That will be all, Chief."

"Yes sir."

Back through the ship Bob went. Per regulations, he immediately reported to Lieutenant Adams, who was supervising the lowering of the projectiles down to the handling room, and relayed the order to remove the photograph of Betty Grable immediately, and informed the lieutenant he needed to relay the order to Chief Warrant Officer Lopez as well. Adams sighed and told Bob to let one of Lopez's men handle the order. Bob complied. A seaman was dispatched aft to remove the offending photo—and save it to put back up later. A few minutes passed before the 1MC came to life and squawked, "Chief Jenkins report to the Butcher Shop."

"The old dull knife ploy. He hasn't pulled that one in a while," Lopez said, and couldn't help but laugh.

The trip across the ship to the butcher shop didn't take Bob two minutes. Olson was waiting.

"Chief, who is responsible for the sharpening and care of these knives?" the XO asked, absently touching the blade of a butcher's knife he had removed from a block.

"I would imagine that would be Chief Commissary Steward Olivetti, sir," Bob replied with honey-sweet patience.

"Inform Chief Steward Olivetti that these knives require sharpening."

"Yes sir."

"Carry on." Olson touched the doorknob when the 1MC blared, "XO to steering gear room." It was the Engineering Officer's voice.

Bob smiled as Olson disappeared from view on his way to the steering gear room in the stern, four decks down. "And so, it begins. JD, you *are* sneaky," he whispered.

He found Chief Steward Olivetti and relayed the order to sharpen knives and returned to the forecastle and his regular duties. Dougherty winked at him when he returned. Ten minutes later, the XO was ordered to the conning station, twelve decks above and five hundred feet forward of the steering gear room. Slightly winded, he entered the conn, where JD was waiting for him.

"Everything alright in steering?" JD asked as he looked over a set of weather charts.

"Yes, sir. For some reason Stapleton wanted me to inspect a repair on a housing. I have no idea why he thought I needed to see that."

"Well, I'm sure he appreciated your input."

"I suppose so, sir." Olson waited a good thirty seconds for JD to explain why he ordered him to the conn, but his CO seemed lost in the weather forecasts. Finally, he asked, "Beg pardon, sir, but what did you need me for?"

"Hmm? Oh. Yes, sorry. I need you to go to HQ and get the intelligence brief from Commander Hathaway. See if Lieutenant Wilson can arrange a driver for you."

"Excuse me, sir?" Olson was incredulous. "Doesn't Hathaway bring the report over himself on days when we leave port?"

"Yes, normally. However, he called me a few minutes ago and apparently his gout has flared up. He regrets he is barely able to move around HQ, much less navigate the ladders on a ship. He asked if I could pick up the packet but I'm waiting on a call from Admiral Fletcher, so you'll have to pick it up."

"Very well, sir." Olson could smell the rat. He just had

no idea how big it was going to be.

"Good man. I should still be up here when you get back. Meet me here when you return. Carry on." JD had already returned to his weather charts. He waited until he saw Olson on the starboard forecastle, calling to Wilson to get him a driver, before he picked up the telephone and ordered a connection to the base Intelligence Office and Commander Hathaway.

"Ed? JD. He's trying to find a ride now. Make damn sure he's there for at least an hour after he arrives."

"You are a vindictive bugger, you know that?" Hathaway's voice was full of conspiratorial mirth.

"If I were vindictive, I'd have you investigate him for no reason. This is just a little comeuppance."

"The ass has it coming. I promise I'll frustrate him to the point of murder or tears, whichever comes first."

"Thanks. And don't forget—you're crippled!"

"Oh, I'm dyin'! I'm dyin'!" Hathaway laughed.

"Thanks again, Ed." JD hung up, smiling.

It took Lieutenant Wilson several minutes to decide which of his SP's was least critical to relieve from security duty and drive Olson to headquarters. He also advised Olson that it was raining outside and the Commander may want to consider a raincoat, even though the jeep would be covered. Olson dashed down to his cabin for his rain jacket before he crossed the brow. It took even longer to stow the SP's rifle and get the jeep started. The Marine guards at the check point were chatty as well, until Olson barked that he needed to be on his way.

Arriving at headquarters, there were no parking spaces, and the SP wasted more time looking for one before Olson jumped out at a stop sign and marched through the drizzle into the building. The sentry at the Intelligence Office announced Commander Olson for Commander Hathaway, but Hathaway couldn't seem to be found. Olson was finally granted admittance and escorted to Hathaway's clerk, who invited Olson to have a seat. Commander Hathaway would be back any minute, the Chief Yeoman explained.

Fifteen minutes later, Hathaway entered the office, moving slowly and leaning heavily on a cane. He stopped at several desks on the way to Olson, asking questions of every man he passed. Finally reaching Olson, he stopped and extended his hand. Olson shook hands briefly, already short on patience.

"Harold, I'm so sorry I made you wait," Hathaway gushed in apology, "I know you must have a million things on your plate, and I just made everything that much worse. Come on in." He gestured to his office door. The Yeoman opened the door for Olson and Hathaway followed, grunting in apparent pain with every step. "I haven't had a flare-up like this in years. Guess it's fish for dinner for a while."

He finally was able to plop down in his chair. There was a stack of thick envelopes on his desk. He began rummaging through them, looking for the report for BX-1, but it was nowhere to be found. Perplexed, Hathaway called the Yeoman into the office, asking for the intelligence briefing for Commander Olson's ship. For the next twenty-five minutes Hathaway prattled on about base gossip and baseball, much to the detriment of Olson's blood pressure.

The Yeoman appeared again with the report, which Hathaway opened and reviewed with Olson, almost word for word, while adding extraneous tidbits regarding the Yankees and Cubs along the way. After taking nearly forty minutes to report that no enemy activity had been reported in *Soda*'s operational area, and no hard evidence of enemy activity in the Northern Pacific Theater in the past week,

Hathaway meticulously replaced all the report documents in the envelope, took out a locking attaché case, placed the envelope in the case and locked it. Handing it to a fuming Olson, Hathaway asked if he had any questions.

"Keys?" Olson asked through clenched teeth.

"Oh Lord, yes! Of course! They're right here . . . somewhere . . . ." Hathaway's voice trailed off as he rummaged through his desk drawer, "They were right here!" After going through the drawer twice, Hathaway slowly limped to a file cabinet across the room, where another five minutes were spent looking for the keys. He closed the drawer and turned to Olson with a concerned look on his face. After what seemed to Olson to be a week, Hathaway asked, "You don't think the Navy will actually put Ted Williams in combat, do you?"

"Ed, I need those keys and I need to return to my ship and I don't give a damn if Ted Williams winds up shining Hirohito's shoes right now." Olson's voice was controlled but his face was beet red.

"The keys. Right." Again, Hathaway struggled back to his desk. Opening the same drawer he had already gone through twice, he chuckled, "Well I'll be damned. Right in front of my nose. If they had been a snake, they would have bitten me." He produced a ring with two keys on it and held it out to Olson, who nearly took a finger with him as he snatched the ring from Hathaway's hand.

"I'll have the driver return the case," he growled as he stood.

"No need for that. Just drop it off when you get back from your mission. I'll still be here." Hathaway was speaking to Olson's back as he left the office. A few minutes later, Olson was back, seething.

"Get me . . . a . . . damned . . . jeep!"

Twenty minutes later—and nearly two hours after

leaving—Commander Olson returned to Dry Dock C-2. He made a beeline for Lieutenant Wilson and his SPs.

"Lieutenant!" Olson bellowed as he approached, "just what were you thinking when you recalled my driver? You have put me seriously behind schedule and you are on report!"

"With all due respect, sir," Wilson replied, "You do not have the authority to put me on report. You are free to contact my commanding officer, but I remind you, sir, that we were at Security Condition One when you ordered that driver. Under Security Condition One, I am authorized to deny any person leave of, or access to, this facility and detain or arrest anyone who attempts to violate that authority. I authorized your departure and the dismissal of one of my sentries as a courtesy to you as the Executive Officer of the ship I am charged with protecting. My orders to my sentry were to take you to HQ and return as quickly as possible so as to ensure the compliance with the Security Condition set by the Commanding Officer, North Pacific Area, for the taking on of ordnance by this vessel."

"Well, we'll just see about that," Olson fumed as he turned to go around the bow to come aboard. As he crossed the brow, he never slowed for the OOD, never saluted, and never requested permission to come aboard. The OOD, a young Lieutenant from Supply, called to him to stop. Olson turned, pointed a finger at the OOD, and simply replied, "Don't," before continuing on.

As he entered the superstructure, Olson began asking for the Commodore's whereabouts, hoping JD had come down from the heights of the conning platform. The best responses he could get were, "Sorry, can't tell you," or "Up in conn, last I knew." He finally arrived on the conning platform, out of breath, to find two Ensigns and a Quartermaster first class testing the helm in the conning tower.

"Any of you know where the Commodore is?" Olson demanded.

"Oh, yes sir. He's in CIC." The young Ensign was very happy to be of assistance. "He ordered me to tell you he's waiting for you there."

The CIC, or Combat Information Center, was situated just forward of the ammunition handling room for the number one turret, eleven decks below. Olson sighed and began the trek back down through the ship. As preparations to get under way continued, the entire crew was busy doing something and was on the move. More than once a sailor shot down a ladder as Olson roared, "Make a hole!"

He finally entered the CIC, where JD was waiting, sipping a cup of coffee with Jesse Sharpe, the Damage Control Officer and First Lieutenant of the ship. First Lieutenant in the Navy is a title, not a rank. On a battleship or aircraft carrier, the position was usually held by an officer of equal rank, but lower seniority, to the Executive Officer. Jesse Sharpe held the rank of Commander.

"I thought maybe you and Hathaway slipped off for a round of golf," JD quipped.

"Hardly, sir. That arrogant little ass Wilson made my driver leave me at HQ to come back here and then had the nerve to lecture *me* about security in front of his men, telling me he had control over who comes and goes out of here."

"I hate to tell you, Hal, but the kid's right. You know full well his group runs the show once you cross the brow," Sharpe reminded Olson. Of any man on the ship, Sharpe was the closest thing to a friend Olson had. He was a class behind Olson at the academy, and looked up to Olson. He saw him as an under-appreciated genius, only learning later how hated Olson was among the midshipmen. He had come aboard *Soda* at Olson's high recommendation, but his loyalty was weakening after seeing Olson in action.

"And I also hate to tell you," JD added, "I was asked by Admiral Fletcher an hour ago for an opinion on security and gave Wilson a glowing review." There was a tense silence for a moment. JD could tell Olson wanted to pop off, but knew better. He finally asked Olson for the security briefing.

Still chafing, Olson unlocked the attaché case and brought out the security briefing from Naval Intelligence. "In a nutshell, we have an all clear for our operational area," he reported. "No reports of any enemy activity in the theater."

"I have a problem with this," Sharpe said, staring at the report as if there was something in it that only he could see.

"How so?" JD asked. He knew Sharpe had a memory like a steel trap and could recall details from months ago that at first seemed insignificant, but when added with other insignificant details over time became a major concern.

"Three weeks ago, there was a report of radio traffic near the Kuriles involving what ONI thought could be a Japanese battleship and its escorts. The code name they were using for the battleship was for the *Mutsu*, which we had considered sunk. Then two weeks ago, one of our subs thought they saw a battleship and two destroyers come out of a fog bank then go right back in. They were six hundred miles east of the Kuriles, and the skipper was convinced enough of what he saw that he dove fast. Then a patrol plane out of Adak reported a possible ship sighting southeast of the Aleutians a few days later, but couldn't confirm due to low cloud cover and fog. Maybe I'm just paranoid, but if—and I mean *if*—all these things are real, and if—and I mean *if*—they are related, there may be a Japanese battleship sneaking around out there and it may—

and I do mean *may*—be headed our way."

"Those are an awful lot of ifs, Jesse," JD said with a cautious grin.

"I know sir. But you know me. Always remembering too many extraneous facts. I think there are way too many unconfirmed things in this to string together a threat."

"Which is why it's not in this brief," Olson stated with a note of finality.

"I tend to agree," JD said. Olson was beginning to push back from the table before JD could continue. "But let's go over this once just to be sure." Olson sighed and scooted his chair back to the table.

JD took a chart of the northern Pacific from a rack and spread it out over the table. He had Sharpe show what he recalled to be the positions mentioned in the previous security briefs and plotted them on the map. They described a rough course toward the western coast of North America. "One thing we know, they don't fear sneaking across the northern Pacific to hit a target," JD said, remembering Admiral Nagumo's northern route to attack Pearl Harbor. "The question is, why would they do this at this junction of the war?"

"Suicide attack on the west coast?" Sharpe speculated. "Hoping to draw forces away from other areas for coastal defense? Have a string of subs attack the ships we recall?"

"Even if this is the case," Olson added, "what good would we be in stopping even a small task force?"

"Report location, fight a harrying retreat while help comes by air and sea," JD replied. "Look, I don't think this is anything real, but just in case, I want our lookouts both on this ship and the escorts to be sharp. If this hypothetical threat is a battleship our surface radars will have him before he even knows we're around, unless he's launching air reconnaissance and gets lucky. However, if there is a carrier involved in this hypothetical, I'm not thrilled to have questionable air search radar and no protection from an aerial attack."

"With respect, sir, I think we're thinking at the extreme of 'what if'," Olson said.

"Agreed," Sharpe added.

"Very well, then," JD knew they had covered the topic sufficiently, "let's get some lunch."

Olson was securing the attaché case in a lock box mounted on the bulkhead as he spoke.

"If you'll excuse me, sir, I really should check on the ordnance loading."

"They're ahead of schedule. Mr. Sharpe and I checked not long before you got back. Mr. Dougherty is rotating his men through lunch and they should have the main magazines secured by 1300. He'll take his extra help to start taking on five-inch ordnance when turret three is finished. The Marines are finished with the machine gun and small arms ammunition already."

"I'm happy to hear that, sir," Olson replied, "but if I may, I'd like to check once again for my own peace of mind."

"Suit yourself. But I want the two of you in my office at 1400 to draw up orders and stations for tonight."

"*You'll* be setting orders and stations, sir?" Olson's ego was reeling. The skipper hadn't done work like this for over a year. Orders for getting underway were always Olson's job, occasionally assisted by Sharpe. Their last three missions, it had been his sole responsibility.

"Sorry. Fletcher was kind of grumpy with me this morning. Apparently, he has received information from an officer on this ship that I appear to be disengaged from onboard operations. I've always thought commanding officers shouldn't second guess their men, but someone thinks

I've swung too far. So, on this mission, I'll be inserting myself more frequently."

"I see," Olson replied. He seemed thoroughly deflated. "Nonetheless, if you would humor me to go topside . . . ."

"Just be on time," JD warned.

"Thank you, sir. I'll be at your office at 1400."

"Very well."

The three officers left the CIC and headed up. As they walked around the barbette of turret one heading for the ladder, JD couldn't resist. Stopping the procession, he turned to Olson.

"Mr. Olson, I heard there was some sort of problem in the Number One handling room this morning. I trust it was corrected quickly." His tone was neutral, but his look said he knew every bit of what had happened.

"Frankly, sir, I haven't had an opportunity to follow up. I trust Chief Jenkins handled it as he was ordered to." His arrogance had not completely gone yet. There was contempt in the reply.

JD turned and the procession continued to the next deck up, where Sharpe split off to head to the wardroom. Olson went up one more deck before going aft to turret four, and JD retired to his cabin to eat alone. He was behind his desk in the Captain's Office at 1345. Sharpe arrived a few minutes later. Olson arrived at the stroke of the hour, liberally chastising an Ensign all the way to the office door.

JD was direct with his two senior officers. "Gentlemen, I don't want to beat around the bush. The two of you, and Mr. Olson in particular, are still responsible for drawing up orders and stations for the operation of this ship. However, to satisfy Admiral Fletcher, I may interject here and there where I think I can help. As far as our getting underway, I have only one order. I want Chief Jenkins in the Conn so he can get the overall picture of the process of leaving dry dock. Chief Zimmerman will still be on the bow, and Chief Carlisle will be with you, Mr. Olson, same as we have done. On future deployments, I'll have Chief Jenkins alternate with the two of you so that we have him, and you, comfortable with him in all positions. Other than that, set your orders as you normally do. Questions?"

"None, sir," Sharpe answered.

"Just a few logistical details, sir," Olson answered. Turning to Sharpe, he said, "Jesse, could you meet me in my office in about five minutes to finish this?"

"I'll be there," Sharpe replied.

"Very well. Carry on Mr. Sharpe," JD said in dismissal.

As the door closed, Olson began, "High tide tonight is predicted at 0020. The dock is currently flooded and flow into the dock is even with the tide. I would recommend all six boilers lit by 1800, and General Quarters for departure at 2330."

"Very well. That will give the men a chance for a cat nap if they want one. Anything else?" JD wanted to give Olson a chance to comment about his day.

"No sir," Olson replied after a pause.

"One last thing," JD leaned into Olson's face as he spoke with a controlled anger, "don't you ever, *ever* come aboard a ship I command without permission again. I don't care how mad, drunk, hurt, late or happy you are, you observe the custom and respect the ensign and the ship. Am I clear, mister?"

Olson thanked his lucky stars he hadn't popped off. "Yes sir."

"And unlike Lieutenant Wilson, you *are* on report. Carry on."

The last of the ordnance had come aboard and Dougherty dismissed his men until 1700 for reports and orders. Bob and Lieutenant Commander Williams made one last whirlwind trip through the ship, inspecting every magazine. They returned to Main Battery Plot just before 1700 and found the rest of the officers already there. Dougherty wasted no time getting the meeting started.

"Reports?" he asked. The junior officers quickly relayed the success of the day's activities and status of their divisions.

"Very good. Orders for getting underway have been issued and are standard for our divisions," he said as he passed out copies of the orders. "General Quarters at 2330. Chief Jenkins, I see you will be on the bridge tonight."

"Yes sir," Bob acknowledged.

Commander Stapleton ordered the remaining four boilers lit at 1800 to complement the two boilers already supplying power to the ship and had full steam at 2130. At 2330, JD summoned the crew to general quarters for departure. Each side of the dry dock had been lined with bumpers by the shipyard crew assigned to Dry Dock C-2 during the day. The mooring lines were cast off and the massive lock door slowly opened at midnight. A *Sotoyomo*-class fleet tug eased back to *Soda's* stern. Lines were secured and at 0025, JD ordered the center pair of *Soda's* four screws idle astern. The slack slowly pulled out of the lines as the tug eased ahead under Olson's direction.

Lieutenant Commander Garrison, the Navigation Officer, had the helm with JD standing next to him. He only had to correct the rudder once when the angle on the bow reached two degrees port and the dock was cleared at 0039. Bob stood silently in the conn, listening to and watching the slow-motion, thirty-thousand-ton ballet playing out over the radios between JD, Olson, and Zimmerman. He was amazed at how smoothly the process went.

Thirty-Three

After the fleet tug cast off lines, two smaller type-V tugs gently turned the battleship and eased her through the channel around Point Glover. Once in Puget Sound proper, JD ordered to make turns for fifteen knots and the ship moved through the empty waterway to the Pacific, guided only by shadowy landmarks and Lieutenant Commander Garrison's abilities with a chart, compass and stopwatch.

At 0200, JD secured the ship from general quarters and retired, handing the conn to Garrison. JD again took the conn with the change of the watch at 0800, and *Soda* rendezvoused with Captain H.E. Geiring's Destroyer Squadron Forty-nine just outside Puget Sound. Once assembled, the small task force set course for its designated operational area 100 miles southwest.

JD slowed BX-1 to eighteen knots to conserve fuel in the destroyers. After reaching their operational area, the ships would slow and zigzag in a large circle until the next morning, when the Navy and Army would conduct a series of flyovers by various aircraft in different formations. The timing and types of planes were known only by JD, his department commanders, and Captain Geiring. Only the radiomen, JD, and the Officer of the Watch knew when the planes were approaching. JD planned to have his anti-aircraft batteries drill on these flyovers as well to make sure the anti-aircraft fire control systems were still working properly.

Late that afternoon, the ships were scheduled to rendezvous with the submarine USS *Roughy*. The sub would recharge her batteries on the surface, protected by the ships, and the destroyers would conduct sonar drills the next day as they worked their way back towards the coast. The SK radar seemed to be functioning properly, with no anomalies noted as *Soda* and her escorts steamed to their designated operational area.

Thirty-Four

26 June, 1944

JD relieved Lieutenant Commander Garrison of the conn at 0800 as the watch changed. One of Garrison's junior officers arrived as the watch commander. At 0820, the shipboard telephone rang in the conning station. JD leaned over and picked up the receiver. "Conn," he said.

"Conn, Radio. Coyote One reports inbound, bearing zero-six-eight relative, altitude one-six thousand, speed one-eight-zero, estimated range one-nine-zero miles," the Communications Officer reported.

"Radio, Conn. Roger. Advise escort commander of drill commencing," JD replied as he scribbled the information on the incoming planes. This flight was a group of eight Douglas SBD Dauntless dive bombers that would conduct a mock bombing run. The escort ships would have received the radio message as well, but safety required confirmation from the group commander and acknowledgement from Captain Geiring.

Upon receipt of the message, the destroyers picked up speed and maneuvered out and away from the battleship to their normal defensive positions several hundred yards further away. Eighteen minutes later, the phone rang again. JD smiled as he answered this time. It was radar.

"Conn, Radar," Carl Morris got the honor of reporting, "Aerial contact. Bearing zero-five-eight degrees relative, zero-seven-zero degrees magnetic, course two-seven-zero, range one-five-zero miles, altitude one-six thousand, speed one-eight-zero knots."

"Radar, Conn. Commence tracking and report."

"Conn, Radar. Aye."

JD turned to the watch commander, "Sound General Quarters," then, to the helmsman, "Steady as she goes." As the General Alarm sounded, JD keyed the 1MC, "This is the Captain speaking. This is a drill. General Quarters, General Quarters, aerial contact. All hands man your battle stations. Do not load ordnance. This is a drill. I repeat, General Quarters, aerial contact. Do not load ordnance. This is a drill. Set Defensive Condition Zed throughout the ship. Flow of personnel is up and forward starboard, down and aft port. This is the Captain. This is a drill."

The ship sprang to life, men rushing to their battle stations while donning helmets and life jackets as they readied for the mock attack. Soon all department commanders reported to JD their ready status. Olson reported the Central Station was at ready status and CIC was operational.

Bob entered the Main Battery Plot just behind Dougherty. "Chief," Dougherty said, "Feel free to go topside if you'd care to. I'd like your evaluation of the anti-aircraft crews."

"Aye, aye sir. I'd like to observe them myself." Bob was back out the door and sprinting to get topside before the massive "Zed" doors, watertight doors made of sixteen-inch armor designed to seal the interior of the ship, were closed. He just made it to the foredeck before the Zed doors were secured. From there he took a more leisurely pace to the superstructure deck where the forty-millimeter and twenty-millimeter guns were manned.

"Conn, Radar," Morris called.

"Conn," JD replied. He was happy with the speed of his crew. All stations were manned and ready.

"Conn, target now bearing zero-five-seven degrees relative, zero-eight-three degrees magnetic. Course three-five-six. Range one-zero-zero miles. Altitude one-zero-thousand feet. Speed one-eight-zero knots."

"Very well." JD assumed that the dive bombers would most likely execute a turn, then peel off and dive towards the bow of the ship, so that their "bombs" would release in line with the ship's course. When their dives commenced, JD would put his ship into a series of turns to avoid the mock attack. He planned on using this tactic to make sure his anti-aircraft directors functioned properly as well. He called the radio room to verify Coyote One's position for safety's sake. Coyote One confirmed and, as JD predicted, advised they would approach the ship bow-on. The minutes seemed to pass slowly for JD. It wasn't all that exciting when he knew where and how his "enemy" was going to attack, and even more so when he knew they were unarmed. Morris reported the planes turning to a southerly course towards the ships, and then half an hour later called in with a hint of excitement on his voice.

"Conn, Radar. Target range now two-zero miles, bearing zero-zero-zero relative, zero-two-zero degrees magnetic. Altitude ten-zero-thousand. Speed one-eight-zero. I think he's ready to dive, sir."

"Radar, Conn. Advise when dive commences." He ordered the helm to increase speed to twenty-five knots. Seconds later, the Mark 28 radars picked up the planes and the anti-aircraft gun controls activated. The five-inch guns shot up towards the sky and the forty-millimeter guns spun forward and up. Lookouts strained through their binoculars for a glint of sunlight off metal, hoping to be the first to sight the target.

"Conn, Radar. Target on rapid descent through eight thousand. Here they come, sir," Morris reported, happy for some action.

"Radar, Conn. Roger. Five degrees right rudder, bearing zero-five-zero."

"Five degrees right rudder, zero-five-zero, aye," the helmsman answered.

Soda heeled to port as the turn progressed. The radar-guided five-inch gun directors adjusted the port side turrets to swing with the turn and keep the guns trained on the target. The port side forty-millimeter gun swung as well as the dive bombers continued on their runs. Bob noticed his gun crews were enjoying the ride, looking up and trying to find the planes, but not with their gun sights.

"What the hell do you numbnuts think you're watching? A football game?" Bob roared at the gunners. "Get your butts in those seats and your eyes on those sights! The damned director isn't God! Be ready to adjust your fire, trainers! Loaders, act like you actually have to feed shells! Someday you may be on a carrier with a Japanese dive bomber coming at you—and you'll just be standing there with your finger up your nose! NOW MOVE!" Looking at the twenty-millimeter crews, he saw similar lack of activity and pounced on them like a cougar on a lamb. Above them, they heard the scream of the first SBD's engine as it pulled out of its dive.

"Six degrees left rudder, bearing three-five-five," JD calmly ordered. He was looking down at the anti-aircraft platform, working very hard not to laugh at the sight of Bob pacing up and down the line of twenty-millimeter guns in a full rant.

"Six degrees left rudder. Three-five-five. Aye." The big ship now heeled hard to starboard. As she came out of the turn, he ordered speed reduced to fifteen knots. The radio room reported Coyote One had completed their run and were returning to base. JD ordered the crew to stand at ease at battle stations.

The drill continued through the day. The watch changed at 1200 to allow the most men practice at testing of the radars, especially the junior officers, and allow those on lookout a rest. The destroyers continued their underwater surveillance, as well as testing their own radars and fire control systems. Bob was happy to see one coordinated "attack" by eight TBF Avengers on a torpedo run with two B-26 bombers on a horizontal bombing run. At one point, he thought JD was about to roll *Soda* over in a high-speed turn, but she somehow stayed upright through the exercise.

The final exercise of the day was tracking four B-29 bombers, all at different altitudes and speeds. The planes were out of gunnery range, and Bob let his gunners finally relax. He had grilled every gun crew between "attacks" on the capabilities of their weapons: range, rate of fire, ballistics, care and maintenance, and anything else he could think of. He found his men were knowledgeable, but just a little lazy.

The crew was ordered to secure from general quarters at 1400. All officers were to prepare preliminary reports for the Captain by 1700. JD recalled his destroyers back to a more compact formation and set course for their rendezvous point with USS *Roughy* for anti-submarine training the next day. JD transferred the conn to the watch commander and headed down for his office at 1430. As he walked through the main deck, he caught Bob's eye, and tipped his cap back. Bob nodded slightly.

JD received his department heads' preliminary action reports by 1700, and was pleased with what he saw, except for Dougherty's report on the anti-aircraft batteries. He wasn't worried. Bob would have them at combat readiness before their next gunnery drills. The SK radar appeared to work perfectly. However, at 1240 both radar and radio reported a brief but high-powered burst of static, for which no explanation beyond "atmospherics" could be offered, that appeared to have come from the southwest. JD ate his dinner quickly, then headed to the quarterdeck for a walk. He saw Bob already walking the rail. Bob waited for his brother, letting him take the lead and walking the required one stride behind. "Looked like you had to kick some tail today," the skipper commented casually.

"A little," Bob replied, "Just enough to get their attention. It's tough to stay motivated when you're not scared to death. You haven't lost your touch at hot-rodding a ship, though."

"That wasn't my doing. The kid on the helm turned too far too fast. He made a hell of a recovery, though."

"That he did. So, what's up?"

"They're out there somewhere, Bobby. They're close. Radar and radio reported a 'burst of static' at 1240. They can't explain it. I think I can."

"Yeah? What do you think? Did Radar report any anomalies?"

"No anomalies reported, but I believe our 'friends' caused that burst of static. I'm not sure why, but I think I'm sleeping in my uniform tonight."

"Good idea. When do we meet up with the sub?"

"Any time now. In fact, I'd better go in and see about that."

"Holler if you need anything."

JD left Bob and headed down to the radio room. As he passed through the second deck, he heard Olson paged to the same location. Technically, Olson would be the first officer to receive an urgent message, not the Captain. *This isn't good,* JD thought as he headed down the ladder. He met Olson in the passage leading to the aft radio room. Seeing Olson's quizzical look, he explained.

"No offense, Mr. Olson, I was stretching my legs and decided to come check on the status of our rendezvous with the sub when you were summoned."

"No offense taken, sir," Olson replied as they reached the radio room door, "after you."

JD led the way into the room, Olson on his heels. The lieutenant in charge of the watch in radio looked up in surprise to see both the XO and the Old Man enter. Olson took the lead.

"What's going on, Wallace?" Olson asked.

"Sirs, I wanted to report that we have been transmitting to *Roughy* for the past half hour and have received no response," the lieutenant explained.

"Are you sure we are on course and on time?"

"Yes sir. Navigation confirmed that before I called for you."

"And the destroyers report no sonar contacts?"

"No sir. I also asked them to verify our radio transmissions, which they confirmed."

"Is it possible we are transmitting using the wrong code?"

"I guess anything is possible, but I triple checked our orders for the code and I'm using the right one."

"What do you think, Captain?" Olson looked at JD, who considered the options for a moment before speaking.

"A half an hour isn't all that late, but it is concerning. Order the destroyers into a spread pattern and commence active sonar search. Continue to hail *Roughy* using the same code. If we don't get a response or sonar contact in another half hour, notify me and Mr. Olson."

"Yes sir," the lieutenant replied.

The senior officers left the radio room and headed up

to the wardroom.

"What do you suggest we do if we don't hear from the sub?" JD asked Olson over coffee.

Olson thought for a moment. "I would suggest we notify Fleet of the overdue ship and request permission to hail *Roughy* in plain English, then continue the search and request further assistance."

"I concur. You have the watch at midnight, right?"

"That's correct, sir."

"So, Sharpe has Central Station for General Quarters."

"Also correct, sir."

"This makes me a little more concerned about that half-baked idea Sharpe had about those possible enemy ship sightings."

"I still think that theory is far-fetched, but I don't fault you for your concern."

"Well, you had better try to catch forty winks before your watch—"

JD was interrupted by the 1MC.

"CO and XO to radio."

"Maybe we found our sub," Olson smiled.

The two picked up their coffee cups and headed back down. There was no smile on the lieutenant's face as they entered. He held a typed sheet of paper out to JD and Olson as he spoke.

"We just decoded this message from Fleet. It has been confirmed. I thought you should see it immediately sirs." JD took the sheet of paper and read it, then passed it to Olson without comment. Olson looked at JD when he finished. Neither spoke for a moment, then JD walked to the microphone for the 1MC.

"Now hear this. Now hear this. This is the Captain. All Department Commanders assemble in the wardroom immediately." He then looked at the radio officer, "Confirm receipt of this message and advise Fleet that *Roughy* is overdue with no contact. Confirm that Captain Geiring has received this message along with my orders to cease active sonar and resume a defensive formation."

JD and Olson retraced their steps to the wardroom, where several junior officers were wolfing down the last of their dinners and clearing the room for what was obviously something important. Soon all the senior officers aboard were present. JD stood before his men, the message in his hand.

"Gentlemen," he began, lifting the message, "We have received a message from Fleet. It appears that the B-29's that flew over us today were on a training run that took them further west before they returned to base. They reported sighting several ships some two hundred eighty miles west-southwest of our position. They circled back to confirm this sighting from low altitude and reported what appeared to be five Japanese warships. They also reported that the ships appeared to be adrift, as they saw no wakes and they were not in a normal formation. This appears to be a force consisting of three destroyers, one heavy cruiser, and one battleship. We have been ordered to plot an intercept course and engage this force when contacted. Two heavy cruisers have sortied from Mare Island and will be here in thirty hours. *Massachusetts* is preparing to sortie from Puget Sound with a destroyer squadron escort, and should arrive shortly before that. But for the time being we will be alone.

"Search aircraft will be over the area of the last reported contact at dawn. We will have tactical command of the operation as I am senior officer afloat. I'm hoping that we have time to rendezvous and coordinate with the other ships and land-based bombers when we attack. I have no idea how battle-ready *Massachusetts* will be. She was in port to have her main battery guns re-lined.

"Most significant to us at the moment is we don't know for sure if these ships are, or are not, adrift, and we do not have any course upon which to act to intercept, other than the last coordinates the B-29's reported. My plan is to close on this location tonight and hope, if we make contact, that our radar will let us monitor the enemy from beyond their horizon. Mr. Garrison, our intelligence says these ships are adrift. As best you can, use currents and winds to give me a best guess course."

"Yes sir," Garrison nodded.

"Mr. Dougherty, if we must engage alone, I'm going to go for the battleship first and have our destroyers attack the cruiser with torpedoes, then deal with their destroyers on the fly. You will fire your sixteen-inch and fourteen-inch rounds on the battleship, then concentrate on the cruiser with the remaining main batteries. Load turrets two and three now. We won't have time to move your crews *and* load if we have to attack."

"Yes sir," Dougherty replied.

"One last thing. As you all know we were to rendezvous with USS *Roughy* for training tomorrow. We are at that rendezvous point and have received no word from her. Before we received these new orders, I had ordered a surface and sonar search for her. I have broken off sonar search. We will continue surface search through the night. I am hopeful that she may have encountered this enemy force and is waiting to engage it as well, but I have no reason to believe this. Questions?" None were raised. "Dismiss. Mr. Garrison, I'll be in the Conn when you get that course."

"Very well, sir," Garrison said, and was on his way to the chart room.

After the officers were gone, JD turned to Olson. "I

think rather than Conn you should be in CIC for your watch tonight. It'll keep you close to Central Station if something happens."

"That makes sense to me sir. Do you have a preference on my replacement?"

"Van Buskirk. Garrison won't like losing his number two, but he's very capable."

"Good man. I'll let him know," Olson said.

"I can do it. I'll stop by the chart room on my way to Conn. I'll bet a hundred Garrison will have him in there. Try to get some sleep."

"Yes sir," Olson said, and headed aft to his stateroom.

JD folded the orders into his shirt pocket and headed up to the chart room. He was going to have a lengthy log entry for the day and hoped he could get some of the work done before he took the conn. As he entered the chart room, he found Garrison and Van Buskirk busy with their calipers and slide rules.

"How are you getting along, Mr. Garrison?" he asked.

"Well, considering this is just a guess, I know I can't be wrong," Garrison replied with a wry smile. "The current can be pretty strong in this part of the ocean and winds are probably around eight to ten knots, so a large ship could be drifting as fast as three to six knots. I'm going to guess five on a rough course of zero-two-five. If the time of the sighting is right, the current location of the enemy ships should be here," he said as he pointed to an X drawn on the chart. "If we close at twenty knots, we should intercept that course in about twelve hours."

"Very well. I'll call you when I reach the Conn. Mr. Van Buskirk, I want you as Officer of the Watch at midnight. Mr. Olson will have the watch in CIC."

"Yes sir," Van Buskirk replied.

JD arrived in the conning station and immediately

called Garrison. Writing down the new course and speed, he verified with Garrison, then contacted radio giving the course change orders to be relayed to the destroyers. When the acknowledgement came back from Captain Geiring, JD ordered *Soda* to her new course, two-five-five, at a speed of twenty knots.

The ships turned to the still light western horizon. He called the radar room and made sure the SL surface radar was working properly, giving strict orders to report any contact to him in the conn immediately. He returned the conn to the Officer of the Watch and retired to his sea cabin. On all battleships, the captain, besides his large cabin and stateroom below decks, had a small stateroom, usually adjacent to the conning platform, for his use while at sea. He was only steps away if needed. He worked on his log until 2100, and then stretched out on his bed. He awoke at midnight for the changing of the watch, and returned to bed. He was awakened by a knock on the door at 0240.

PART FOUR

Revelation

Thirty-Five

27 June, 1944

"Sir, radar reports an aerial contact," Van Buskirk said.

JD was on the horn to radar immediately. A nighttime radar contact this far from land in this part of the ocean was odd, to say the least.

"Radar," Lieutenant Commander Williams answered, picking up almost immediately.

"Williams, this is the Captain. Report."

"Sir, I have a possible contact, bearing zero-zero-zero relative, two-five-five magnetic, range one-four-zero miles, altitude four-two-thousand feet."

"Radar, repeat altitude. Did you say four-two-thousand?"

"That is affirmative, sir. Four-two-thousand."

"Very well. What's the course and speed?"

"Course and speed indicate stationary target, sir. I believe this is an anomaly with the SK, sir. It's just like what our commanders in the fleet have been reporting. And it's huge. It would have to be a tight formation of aircraft, but that makes no sense, either."

"You may well be right, Mr. Williams. Start a plot and report any change to me immediately. Contact Radio and relay your findings to Fleet with our position and target position."

"Yes sir," Williams replied as he hung up.

JD called the CIC. Olson answered. "What do you make of this radar contact, Mr. Olson?" JD asked.

"I believe that this is probably an anomaly, sir" Olson confirmed, "there's just no known aircraft that can behave like this."

"Agreed. We'll see what happens."

Fifteen minutes later, Williams reported that the contact was gone, but appeared to shoot straight up at an apparent speed of 1600 knots before it was lost to the range of the SK radar.

I wonder what they're up to? JD thought. He had no doubt as to what the target was, but didn't tip his hand to the crew. JD reasoned that it was far better they think of the target as an anomaly than a craft not of this world. He returned to his sea cabin, where he dozed fitfully until 0440, when he thought he heard is name. He woke just before the knock on his door.

"Sir, Radar has another aerial contact," Van Buskirk reported.

JD again picked up the receiver connecting him to Lieutenant Commander Williams. The new target was closer, only fifty miles away, but off the port bow thirty degrees. It was again at forty-two thousand feet altitude, and still stationary, apparently having dropped from extremely high altitude to its current position in a matter of seconds. Radio reported that Captain Geiring reported the same contact.

Suddenly, Williams' steady monotone voice rose almost an octave. "Sir, target is moving rapidly up and down! It's oscillating between three-seven-thousand and four-two-thousand every five seconds!" The officer of the Watch reported lookouts had visually confirmed the possible target as well: what looked like a bright star was dancing up and down in the sky.

"Signal Captain Geiring, radio silence. Come to port, new course two-two-five, maintain twenty knots. Sound General Quarters," JD ordered quickly. Then, into the 1MC, "General Quarters, General Quarters, aerial contact. This is not a drill. Repeat, this is *no* drill. All hands man your battle stations. Set Defensive Condition Zed through-out the ship. Flow of personnel is up and forward starboard, down and aft port. This is the Captain. This is not a drill." He repeated the announcement and waited for his departments to report status. For the second time since leaving port, the interior of the ship was sealed behind the massive, watertight Zed doors, designed to keep the ship afloat in the worst conditions. JD could see the flashing of an Aldis lamp from Captain Geiring's destroyer acknowledging his orders. The signal bridge confirmed this. All battle stations were manned in a few minutes. CIC and Central Station were operational.

JD picked up the telephone receiver and asked for Main Battery Plot.

"Main Battery Plot," Dougherty answered.

"Mr. Dougherty, do you have turret one loaded yet?"

"Number One gun is loaded, number two loading now, sir."

"Order a water dye round loaded in your number three gun. I have a hunch."

"Yes sir."

Grabbing a pair of binoculars, JD stepped out onto the exposed conning platform deck for a clear view of the target. It did look like a bright star, oscillating up and down in the predawn sky. As the ships completed their turn, the target was now dead ahead. As soon as the bearing to target reached zero-zero-zero, it shot straight up, radar reported, again at 1600 knots. It disappeared from sight in a few seconds, and from radar in less than a minute.

So that's what you were doing, JD thought, *Thank you, Captain.* It was clear now to JD that the enemy ships were now dead ahead, and that the visitors knew where he was. He had ordered the ship to battle stations for that reason, not the aerial target. Walking inside the conn, he ordered the crew to maintain general quarters, speed and course. He ordered the galleys to have donuts and coffee distributed.

Thirty minutes later, the ship received a message from a PBY, one of the Navy's "flying boats," out of Naval Air Station, Sand Point. He reported he would be over the area where the enemy ships had been sighted in thirty minutes. Behind him was a group of four B-17 bombers that would circle fifty miles south of the last reported enemy position. *Soda* responded with one long dash, hoping the PBY would read between the lines. The PBY pilot acknowledged radio silence from the ship. Radar picked up the PBY and began tracking it as it zigzagged towards them. By 0530, the sun was rising and JD ordered speed reduced to ten knots. At 0720, Radar called. JD picked up the receiver.

"Conn, Radar. Surface contact. Bearing three-five-two relative. Range four-zero-thousand yards. Course zero-two-two, speed four knots. The signature is consistent with a large ship."

"Very well. Advise when we reach range three-five-thousand yards."

"Aye, sir."

"Helm, come to port, bearing two-four-three. Signal the destroyers. Maintain ten knots."

The phone rang again, this time from CIC. It was Olson.

"Sir, I need to verify with you that you plan to shadow this target until our other ships arrive."

"That is still the plan, Mr. Olson, if time and circumstances allow, but we won't have help for several more hours. If the Japanese ships move against us, I plan to try to decoy them towards *Massachusetts* and coordinate an attack with them."

"Very well, sir. I would advise against engaging the enemy alone."

"Point taken, Mr. Olson, But I don't like the way this PBY is behaving. If he does something stupid, we may have our hand forced."

"Then I would advise we disengage if that happens, sir."

"And lose tactical advantage? I don't think so, Mr. Olson, but let's not get ahead of ourselves."

A few minutes later, Dougherty notified JD that he had a firing solution for both turrets, and that the number three sixteen-inch gun was loaded with a yellow dye shell. Fifteen minutes after that, radar reported the range to target was thirty-five-thousand yards. JD turned *Soda* to a new course in parallel with the target and reduced speed to four knots. The main battery directors turned the massive turrets to port, the barrels rising. JD ordered Captain Geiring's destroyers to take up a position ten miles ahead of the target and ready torpedoes. He then called Main Battery Plot.

"Main Battery Plot," Dougherty answered.

"Mr. Dougherty, plot a solution for your number three gun in turret one to place the water dye round two thousand yards astern of the target. If they execute a bombing run on their own, I want those B-17's to know they have the right ships. You will fire the dye round on my command and then redirect to the target solution."

"Aye, aye, sir."

Dougherty made the adjustment for the dye round and relayed the adjustment to Fire Control when Bob spoke up from the other side of the plotting table.

"Sir, if I may, I would suggest we aim one-half degree ahead of the solution on turret four."

"And why would you say that, Chief?" Dougherty wasn't really in the mood for a debate.

"At this range, the spin of the projectile will cause a drift away from the direction of the spin, sir. With minimal forward momentum provided by the ship, they'll drift further astern than the sixteens."

Dougherty stared at Bob a long time. "You're sure?"

"I'll put my next month's pay on it, sir."

"You better be right, Chief," Dougherty sighed. He ordered the new solution into the fire control analog computer and the rear turret adjusted accordingly.

A few minutes later, the PBY radioed visual contact of a single destroyer thirty-two miles away trailing no wake, then reported what appeared to be the cruiser and the battleship adrift and in contact with each other abeam as if they had collided or were somehow locked together. The plane made a wide circle around, and reported sighting *Soda* and her destroyers. Again, *Soda* replied with one long dash. The PBY dropped altitude and made another pass on the Japanese ships at ten thousand feet, then again at five thousand feet. No activity was seen on the enemy ships; no anti-aircraft fire was noted. The pilot reported he was calling in the four B-17's to bomb the enemy ships.

Infuriated by the continued open-air radio traffic generated by the PBY pilot, not to mention apparently taking command of the attack coordination, JD broke radio silence and advised he was firing one yellow dye round two thousand yards astern of the enemy battleship. He didn't want the B-17 pilots to make a mistake, even though they would be almost twenty miles away.

The number three sixteen-inch gun sent a billowing cloud of fire and smoke off the port side and forty seconds later a geyser of canary yellow water erupted a little more than one mile behind the Japanese battleship. The PBY circled at ten thousand feet and saw no response from the ships. The pilot reported the successful round placement to JD and the bomber pilots, who began their run. The SK radar picked up the bombers and reported that they were on course to intercept the enemy ships, much to JD's relief. Twenty minutes later the bombers dropped their loads of ten five-hundred-pound bombs each. The PBY reported multiple hits on both the battleship and cruiser. No fire was returned by either ship or the destroyer that the PBY had located, and none of the ships changed course or speed. Both the battleship and cruiser were reported on fire.

JD acknowledged the PBY's report and asked if the pilot had enough fuel to continue searching for the other Japanese destroyers. He was informed the plane had forty-five minutes worth of fuel left and would resume his search. The B-17's turned and made a low-level pass to assess bomb damage and reported both the cruiser and battleship ablaze, with the cruiser settling by the stern. Soon the smoke plume was visible to JD.

The PBY made one last report before heading for home. It was a surprising one: the plane had searched ahead of the battleship and found nothing, then backtracked to the first destroyer he sighted. Six miles further southwest, he sighted what appeared to be a submarine on the surface, some forty miles astern of the battleship and cruiser. Making one final pass, they saw men on the conning tower waving an American flag. The deck of the sub was barely level above the water and the sub appeared to be in distress. The pilot gave *Soda* the sub's coordinates and headed home.

JD glanced at his watch: 1030. *Massachusetts* and the cruisers were still over an hour and a half away. The sub had to be the *Roughy* and if she was in trouble, she needed help immediately. She obviously had no radio. JD sent a brief report of the engagement to Fleet, reporting the sighting of the submarine, and informing Fleet they were setting course for the crippled sub and would examine and fire upon the enemy ships as they passed. He then ordered Captain Geiring to make a torpedo attack on the cruiser and battleship. As the destroyers turned, he ordered one salvo fired from turret one and turret four. Radar recorded two hits from each turret. In Main Battery Plot, Dougherty looked at Bob incredulously, then smiled and shook his head.

"I guess what they say about you really is true, Chief. How do you do it?"

"I wish I could explain it, sir, but I just kind of know," Bob replied. "Plus I've fired a lot of fourteen-inch rounds in practice, and a few for real in the Aleutians."

JD ordered *Soda* turned and closed on the enemy ships at twenty-four knots to cover the destroyers. He was informed that turrets one and four guns were reloaded, but he ordered Fire Control to fire only on his order. He didn't want to be surprised by another large ship and have empty pockets, especially with no resistance being offered by the ships within range.

Captain Geiring divided his destroyers in two groups and attacked. Four of the tin cans fired two torpedoes each at the battleship's starboard side. The other two destroyers trailed by ten minutes and attacked the cruiser on her port side. The two ships did indeed appear to have collided then drifted together. No return fire or any other signs of life were seen, only fires raging. Two of the main batteries of the battleship had been destroyed and the bridge tower was so badly damaged that the class of the battleship could not be determined. The first flight of destroyers scored six hits, ripping the starboard side of the battleship open and setting off a large explosion. She rolled over and sank before *Soda* was out of sight. All four torpedoes fired at the cruiser found their target amidships, blowing the ship in two. The bow and stern bobbed like buoys for ten minutes before disappearing into the deep, leaving only a burning slick of fuel oil.

As they steamed on, JD contacted *Massachusetts* and the cruisers from Mare Island and gave them orders to commence a search for the second and third destroyers, assuming they were leading the formation when disabled. Captain Warwick of the *Massachusetts* reported his sixteen-inch guns were all relined and operational and he was itching for a chance to test them. JD also reported the sinking of the battleship and cruiser, and that he was underway to assist the disabled *Roughy.*

The course JD set to reach the submarine would take them within range of the one known Japanese destroyer. Radar reported contact and reported her to be seemingly adrift, making only four knots. JD ordered two of Captain Geiring's destroyers to make a pass and report any activity on the enemy ship, attacking it if challenged. She was confirmed to be an *Akizuki*-class, definitely adrift, with no signs of life on deck. JD ordered the destroyers back into formation, and ordered all ships to secure from general quarters They could deal with the destroyer later. Right now, there were American lives at risk.

A surfaced submarine offered a very poor visual profile. The main deck was only twelve feet above waterline when running on the surface. It had an even smaller radar signature. The PBY pilot said the sub he sighted had her deck awash, so the only thing visible would be the conning tower and gun decks, a speck of gray steel barely ten feet out of the water and thirty feet long. Luckily the seas were calm, with only a gentle three-foot swell to obstruct visibility. JD doubled the lookouts and the seven ships under his command spread out abreast as they approached the location given by the PBY at twenty knots. There was still a lot of daylight, but they had a lot of ocean to search.

JD once again cursed the fact that *Soda* had no aircraft. He was mulling over how to execute an orderly turn for his formation of ships when a lookout on the SG antenna mount, some one hundred and thirty feet above the water, spotted the sub. Two destroyers maneuvered alongside while the remaining four peeled off into a defensive pattern. JD ordered *Soda's* motor whale boats into the water to bring the sub's crew aboard and soon seventy men and four junior officers were safely brought aboard. The sub's captain, XO and engineering officer remained aboard until the last man was accounted for, then finally stepped into the whale boat.

JD made sure the skies and sea were clear, and then ordered Olson and Chiefs Jenkins and Carlisle to meet him at the starboard accommodation ladder to welcome the sub's officers and crew aboard. JD noted that although they were exhausted, the submariners were giving *Soda* an incredulous once-over as the whale boats cruised down her starboard side and as they assembled on the quarterdeck.

As the sub's skipper mounted the last step, he smartly saluted the ensign and JD.

"Request permission to come aboard, sir. Lieutenant Commander Kelly Bennett, Commanding Officer, USS *Roughy.*"

JD wanted to simply shake the skipper's hand, but the lesson to Olson was too valuable to pass up. Olson felt a twinge of guilt as he and JD returned Bennett's salute.

"Permission granted and welcome aboard," JD replied.

"Commodore JD Roberts, Commanding Officer, BX-1. My XO, Commander Olson." Only after saluting did JD extend his hand.

"Permission to come aboard, sir. Lieutenant Gerald Kreiger, Executive Officer, USS *Roughy.*" The young XO looked like something the cat dragged in, his uniform stained top to bottom with hydraulic fluid. JD's thoughts immediately went to his son. Little Phil who would soon be out there somewhere.

"Welcome aboard, lieutenant," JD snapped a salute and extended his hand.

"Permission to come aboard, sir. Lieutenant Wallace Pierpoint, Engineering Officer, USS Roughy." Pierpoint was also soaked in hydraulic fluid.

JD returned his salute and shook his hand as well. "You three look like you've had one hell of a fight keeping your sub afloat."

"That we have had, sir," Bennett replied, "I need to fill you in on our last twenty-four hours as soon as possible."

"Can it wait for you to get a wash and change of clothes?" JD asked with only half a smile.

"I think you and I should speak now, sir. But it might be better for all of us if Mr. Kreiger and Mr. Pierpoint got cleaned up. I'm afraid they may spontaneously combust in their current condition."

"I think you may be right," JD chuckled, "Chief Jenkins, show Mr. Kreiger and Mr. Pierpoint to the officers' showers and arrange for a change of clothes."

"My pleasure, Captain," Bob said. "Sirs, if you'll come with me, please . . . ."

"Thanks, Chief. And thank you, sir," Kreiger said as they headed in.

"Chief Carlisle, assist the *Roughy*'s junior officers and arrange berthing for the crew. Let Chief Olivetti know we have company and plan his meals accordingly."

"Aye, aye, Captain," Carlisle said as he set off to the quarterdeck.

"Now," JD said, "what is the condition of your boat?"

"I fear she's doomed, sir," Bennett said with sad resignation, "we've been manually pumping for twenty hours. All electronics on board failed at once yesterday. Everything. We barely blew enough ballast to surface—and we've had a slow leak for weeks that needs dry dock work, but it wasn't a problem the pumps couldn't handle. The only way to tow her would be to leave a skeleton crew aboard to continue pumping, and my men have had it. We were preparing to take to the rafts and scuttle her when that PBY showed up. I figured you were close, but with those Japanese ships we had no idea what to expect in terms of rescue."

"Well, you know your boat better than I," JD replied, "and we still have a potential threat in those destroyers. If you don't think she can be saved, we'll let her go."

"I really don't think she'll make it home, sir. I don't want to give up, but I know it's the smart thing to do. My officers will confirm that."

"If you say she's doomed, she's doomed."

"Oh. And I doubt you'll have any trouble with the Japanese ships."

"Well, the cruiser and the battleship are on the bottom. Our only concerns are with the destroyers. But what do you mean?"

"When we were damaged yesterday, I was observing the trailing destroyer and the cruiser through my periscope. We couldn't rendezvous with you on time because we had to dive and hide when we spotted these ships. How the destroyers missed us is beyond me." Bennett paused. "Forgive me, Commodore, but could I get some water?"

"Dear God, yes! I apologize, of course you can. Let's get you to the wardroom."

Seated in the wardroom with a pitcher of water, a pot of coffee, and a plate of sandwiches, JD and Olson ate with Lt. Commander Bennett. Lieutenants Kaiser and Pierpoint, freshly washed and sporting clean khakis, joined them. *Roughy's* other junior officers were already eating at another table in the wardroom. JD and Olson waited patiently while the submariners ate their first meal in over twenty-four hours. The water pitcher was refilled before they slowed down enough to talk more. Washing down the last of his sandwich with a fourth glass of water, and after thanking JD and Olson, Bennett picked up his story.

"So, as I said, I was tracking the cruiser, working a firing solution when she and the battleship suddenly picked up speed and turned hard to starboard. They brought their guns to bear port and then this . . . this *thing* just drops out of the sky abeam of the battleship. I lowered the scope and ordered an emergency dive. We were down about thirty feet when we lost power. How my men stopped the dive I'm still not sure, but we were able to stabilize the boat and blow enough ballast to surface the tower and ten feet of freeboard. The electricians were able to get the lights on long enough to man the pumps, but the batteries completely died shortly after that. We didn't even have flashlights that worked."

"So, what was this 'thing' you saw?" Olson asked.

"Commander, you're going to call me crazy, but with God as my witness it was an airborne craft, triangular in shape, and at least three hundred feet long on two sides and a hundred fifty feet wide at the tail. Maybe eighty feet thick. It just frigging dropped out of the sky and hovered about two hundred feet off the surface. While the scope was coming down, my sound man reported what he thought to be the sounds of big guns firing, then a blast of static and everything shorted out." Bennett paused when he noticed JD's and Olson's eyes lock at the mention of the static. "What?" he asked.

"Our radio and radar both recorded a large static burst yesterday," JD explained.

"Around 1230?" Kreiger asked, hoping for some confirmation of the insanity he survived.

"1240, if I recall," Olson confirmed.

"I'll be damned," Bennett responded. "Well, after we got the boat stable, I figured we were dead meat and would be sunk or captured, but nothing happened. The enemy ships slowed, like they lost their steam. No smoke, no fires. They just slowed down and started drifting, as did we. A flight of B-29's came over a few hours later, then made a second pass. We drifted and pumped and watched the wind take the other ships away and we trailed. Then today we were sighted by the PBY and saw the smoke column and hoped you had found the enemy. And now here we are. Of course, we'll prepare formal reports, but that's the short version."

JD and Olson sat silently for a moment. JD finally broke the silence.

"Well, Skipper, you've had one hell of an ordeal. Do you think your boat will stay afloat long enough for a quick inspection by our two Engineering Officers?"

"If we hurry, yes. I'd like to literally shed some light on this. All we've had for light has been Zippo lighters."

"Very well. Mr. Olson, get some lanterns and order the whale boat back in the water. Have Mr. Stapleton report to the accommodation ladder. I'll catch up with you when you return, but in the meantime, I'd better get this task force organized."

"Yes sir," Olson hopped to his feet. "Gentlemen, if

you'll follow me . . . ." He and the *Roughy's* officers head-ed back topside. Stapleton joined them and they set off for the sub, which had already settled another foot.

JD headed for the CIC, where he could check the status of the other ships now under his command. The cruisers had met up with *Massachusetts* and were searching for the Japanese destroyers and any other contacts fifty miles to the northeast, assisted by another PBY, and would continue through the night.

Half an hour later, the detail from the submarine returned. JD met the men as they came back aboard. He was surprised the see the sub's gun decks were awash and she was settling quickly. Lt. Commander Bennett and his officers watched in silence as *Roughy*'s conning tower slipped beneath the surface.

"She was a good boat," Bennett said, his voice quaver-ing.

"And you saved your entire crew to man another," JD replied. "That doesn't happen to many submarine crews. You all are to be commended."

"Thank you, sir."

"Were you able to determine anything?"

"Every circuit we could examine looked as if it had taken a massive surge of current. Insulation melted, every circuit breaker and fuse blown, you name it."

An idea was forming in JD's head. "I wonder if the same thing happened to the Japanese ships," he mused.

"Only one way to find out," Commander Stapleton said, "board that Japanese tin can and have a look."

"What about her crew?" Olson didn't sound fond of the idea from his tone.

"Well, we've seen no signs of life on any enemy ship encountered so far," JD countered.

"Something tells me whatever it was that disabled

these ships also killed the crews, sir," Bennett said, "and I think the thirty feet of water between us and that craft gave us enough . . . I don't know . . . insulation, I guess, to survive whatever happened. We had battery power for just enough time to save the boat. I don't think the surface ships were that lucky."

"I tend to agree with you, Mr. Bennett," JD said, looking at the sun, now beginning to dip towards the horizon, "but I don't think we'll have time to find out today. If we patrol tonight looking for the other destroyers, we could come back in the morning and have a look-see. Depending on what Fleet says, of course. I'll send a briefing to Admiral Fletcher and see what he says."

"I hope he doesn't say I'm nuts," Bennett worried.

"I'm just going to say you reported an unknown aircraft, Mr. Bennett, and leave the details for your report. We can discuss that more after you get some rest. But," JD paused, a smile creeping across his face, "if we can show some proof of what you said, it may make you saner. In fact, if we find what we think we may find on that destroyer, we'll just tow her back and show the admiral what happened!"

"Sir, you can't be serious," Olson said, getting more nervous by the minute. "What if the Japanese have other ships looking for this group?"

"Your concern is duly noted, Mr. Olson, but I would bet that right now the news of our engagement with these enemy ships is being broadcast across America. I'm pretty sure the Japanese know their ships are lost. This is too important an opportunity for us not to pursue—for a variety of reasons. We can study their sonars, their depth charges, their tactical orders. That ship is a little treasure chest. Not to mention the propaganda jackpot she'll provide. I assure you, I will relay your concerns to Fleet in my message."

JD hoped Olson would see his last comment as the veiled threat it was, telling Admiral Fletcher he thought his XO was a coward. He was wrong in assuming the engagement would become news, however. Due to *Soda's* involvement, as well as how close the enemy ships had gotten to the American coast, Naval Intelligence quashed all reports to the public.

JD contacted Fleet with his report on the rescue of Roughy's crew, and requested permission to board the Japanese destroyer in the morning after hunting the remaining destroyers during the night. He also requested to be relieved of command of the task force so as to minimize exposure of *Soda* to the other ships. Two hours later, he received a reply from Admiral Fletcher himself ordering the boarding, seizure, and towing of the Japanese destroyer, and relieving him of command of the task force, transferring command to Captain Warwick on *Massachusetts*.

JD dispatched Captain Geiring with five destroyers to try to locate the remaining Japanese ships. *Soda* kept an eye on the destroyer they had located from a range of five miles, with one destroyer circling on submarine patrol. He secured the crew from general quarters, with the exception of Main Battery Plot and turrets one and four, who kept their guns trained on the destroyer with strict orders to blow her out of the water if she moved one foot under her own power.

Thirty-Six

28 June, 1944

At 0600, JD maneuvered *Soda* to a point two hundred yards from, and parallel to, the Japanese destroyer. He ordered the motor whale boats into the water once again. One boat held twenty sailors headed by Bob Jenkins. The second boat carried twenty men of the ship's Marine detachment. The boarding party was under the command of Lieutenant Richard Barnes, USMC. All were heavily armed.

Prior to the boats getting underway, JD ordered the destroyer strafed stem to stern by the twenty millimeter and machine gun batteries. There was no response from the enemy ship. Barnes and his men shoved off and approached the destroyer. The machine gunners kept their thumbs on the triggers of their weapons.

The boarding parties made it onto the fantail of the destroyer, then split up, each team working forward on each side. Bob quietly approached the hatch of the aft turret, housing two one-hundred-millimeter guns. Two riflemen held their muzzles just clear of the hatch and Bob swung it wide. They found the crew dead at their stations, both guns loaded. As they worked their way forward, the grim reality became obvious. Every man on deck was dead at his battle station. The pace of their search picked up as they checked every compartment on the ship. Every man aboard, from captain to cook, died at his station. There was not a drop of blood anywhere. Lieutenant Barnes notified JD that the ship was secured, and JD came aboard himself to inspect it accompanied by Commander Stapleton.

The electronic components of the ship were ruined. Generator coils and rotors had melted and the shafts fused. Most of the insulation on the wiring had melted off. Radios and sonars were scorched. It appeared the boilers simply went out when the fuel oil pumps died. There was no hope of making anything electrical function. Stapleton noted that the damage was far worse than what he saw on *Roughy*. He also noticed, as did several others, that the entire ship seemed to be magnetized. The crew working below decks found this curiosity very handy as they could easily position metal flashlights and lanterns on pipes and bulkheads to assist with their work. JD wondered if the same thing happened to the battleship and cruiser, causing them to be somehow magnetically connected after colliding.

Within an hour, there were a hundred men on the destroyer recovering bodies, wrapping them in their bedding and whatever else could be found, weighting them with everything from shells to chains and slipping them over the side. More men continued to ferry across and by 1400 all the bodies had been removed with the exception of two, the captain and an enlisted man. JD ordered those bodies to be saved for autopsy, and the crew began readying the ship to be towed.

While machinist mates worked by lantern light to manually lock the rudder amidships, others rigged bilge pumps to diesel-powered generators and boatswain's mates rigged the tow lines from the bow of the destroyer to the stern of the battleship. Rations and water were ferried over for the skeleton crew that would man the destroyer for the trip to Bremerton. The crew began to ferry back to *Soda* and at 1800 she eased forward. The lines drew tight, and the two ships crept forward. JD slowly increased speed to six knots. With calm seas they would reach the coast in sixty to sixty-five hours. He was thankful he had two hours of daylight to get any bugs out of the tow. If something was going to go wrong it would most likely happen in the first few hours.

Everything was in good shape and the sun set on the task force as it steamed northeast. Admiral Fletcher was informed that they were underway, and he acknowledged. Just before he turned in, JD learned that Captain Warwick reported the other two Japanese destroyers had been sunk and his ships were returning to port, as continued intensive aerial searches had reported no other enemy ship sightings. JD stretched out in his sea cabin and was asleep in minutes.

Thirty-Seven

29 June, 1944

The sharp knock at his cabin door jolted JD awake. "Captain, aerial contact!" It was Olson. JD jumped into his uniform trousers and shoes and crossed the few feet from his sea cabin to the conning platform, buttoning and tucking in his shirt as he came. He glanced at the clock: 0412.

"What is it, Mr. Olson?" he asked.

"That!" Olson said, pointing out the windscreen. "It just dropped out of the sky! Radar says range is thirty miles, altitude one-zero-thousand, course zero, speed zero."

JD leveled his binoculars at a bright light dead ahead, hovering in the night sky. "*Hello, James,*" he heard in his mind. He held the binoculars steady so as not to tip off Olson. "*Hello, Captain,*" he silently replied, then said aloud and calmly, "Mr. Olson, call Lieutenant Commander Bennett and Chief Jenkins up here. I have the conn."

"CO has the conn, aye," the Helmsman acknowledged.

"I'll sound General Quarters," Olson said, reaching for the general alarm.

"No," JD replied patiently as he contacted the radar room. "Page Mr. Bennett and Chief Jenkins, Mr. Olson. Now." Then, lifting the handset to his ear, "Radar, Conn. Can you estimate the size of the aerial target?"

"My best guess is a hundred feet wide, sir, but it's too

far away to really tell. If it were moving, I would call it three aircraft in tight, triangular formation," said Lieutenant Commander Williams, who had been pulled from his bed as well. "The destroyers have it also. Same range and altitude."

"Very well, advise any change in aspect." JD replaced the receiver and picked up the 1MC microphone, looking at Olson as he did. "Now hear this. Now hear this. Lieutenant Commander Bennett, Chief Gunners Mate Jenkins, report to the conning station immediately. Chief of the Watch, escort Mr. Bennett. That is all."

"Sir, I would *strongly* advise putting the ship on alert."

Olson's voice was difficult to read, JD thought, a mixture of frustration and perhaps fear.

"Not yet," JD replied calmly. "I think this is the same craft that basically led us to the enemy battleship and cruiser. I also believe it's the craft that disabled six warships, and from all appearances killed over three thousand men. I really don't think I want to provoke it. Signal the destroyers not to go to General Quarters."

"Sir, that is insane! You're putting this ship and her crew in jeopardy. We need to be able to defend ourselves."

"Mr. Olson, you have been given a direct order. You've already ignored one. Signal the destroyers."

Olson stood motionless, his face white. JD's face flushed red as he picked up the receiver and contacted Radio, ordering that the destroyers be told in plain English not to go to general quarters. They acknowledged, also in plain language. A few minutes later, Bob appeared, bounding up the ladder.

"Chief Jenkins reporting as ordered, sir," Bob said as he stepped onto the deck. JD handed him binoculars. Bob stared at the light in silence. "*Hello, Robert,*" he heard. "*Hello Captain,*" he replied as he lowered the binoculars.

A few minutes later, Lieutenant Commander Bennett arrived. After looking at the light, he turned to JD.

"Is that the 'thing'?" he asked JD.

"I was hoping you could tell us," JD answered.

"Too far away to say for sure, sir. Sorry."

Radar came back on the phone. "Sir, target is moving. Course one-eight-zero relative, two-zero-five magnetic, speed one-five-zero knots. Altitude three hundred. It's coming straight at us, sir."

"Very well." JD hung up the receiver, saying, "Steady as she goes."

"Steady as she goes, aye," Helm replied.

Olson reached across JD's face and sounded the general alarm. JD grabbed his arm just as the alarm sounded. He switched it off and yanked Olson's arm away from him.

"Chief of the Watch!" he barked. The Chief had waited below at the foot of the ladder. Now he charged up. JD was still outwardly calm, but his voice had gravel in it. "Mr. Olson, you are relieved. Chief, escort Commander Olson to his office and post a guard."

"Aye, aye, sir," the Chief said grimly.

"You *cannot* be serious," Olson hissed, "you are going to get us all killed."

"Take Mr. Olson below, Chief. By force if necessary."

"I'm going," Olson said, shoving past Bennett and Bob.

JD thought for a moment before taking the 1MC. "Now hear this. Now hear this. This is the Captain. Set defensive condition Zed throughout the ship. Central Station, CIC, firemen and damage control parties, man your battle stations. All other personnel retire behind Zed doors. Repeat, set defensive condition Zed throughout the ship. Central Station, CIC, firemen and damage control parties, man your battle stations. All other personnel retire behind Zed doors. Do not man guns. Repeat, do not man guns. Commander Sharpe, report to Central Station. Commander Sharpe is acting XO. This is the Captain. That is all." JD replaced the microphone on its hanger. "Mr. Bennett, you'd better get below."

"All due respect, sir, I'd like to stay," although the sub commander really wasn't asking. "I want to lay eyes on this thing, even if it's the last thing I see."

"Very well, but just don't be surprised by anything you may see or hear." JD ordered the helmsman to the armored conning tower and the other sailors below decks.

The light steadily grew larger as it approached the ship. As it got closer, its shape became easier to discern: the familiar, narrow triangle, just as Bennett reported seeing, almost as long as the destroyers. It slowed, then stopped and began reversing, matching the ship's speed of six knots. The craft had no external lights, but emitted a glow from what appeared to be a bank of windows that ran the length of the craft on each side. At the front of the craft, silhouettes, human-like in shape but smaller, could be seen through the window. A low frequency humming sound reverberated softly through the steel of the bridge structure.

"That's what I saw through my periscope," Bennett whispered.

"*Do you command this ship, James?*" the voice asked.

"I do," JD answered silently as he stepped through the door to the outside platform. "It's been a long time since we've spoken."

Bennett looked at JD, then Bob, "What's he doing?" referring to JD.

"Danged if I know, sir," Bob replied, knowing Bennett couldn't "hear" the telepathic conversation.

"*We returned home for a while,*" the voice replied.

"This war on your planet has become quite serious. Many of our contacts cannot be found. I assume this war has been a deadly one."

"It has been, sadly. Many, many people have died."

"Sad, indeed. Your enemy appears to be very determined. We were attacked ourselves, as you might have guessed."

"I assumed so. What happened?" JD remained on the platform.

Bob and Bennett moved closer to the windscreen as Bennett watched, spellbound.

"We attempted to communicate with a study participant on one of the ships. He had changed since our last visit. He referred to us as his enemy, and before we could visit the large ship fired her weapons. Our shields are not as strong as those of our war ships. We sustained damage and were forced to defend ourselves."

"I'm sorry you were attacked. I'm also thankful you didn't attack my country's ships."

"We are strictly forbidden from interfering in the affairs of your nations. Our mission is still purely scientific. But we had no choice in this instance but to defend ourselves."

"Why have you returned?"

"This will be our last mission. We will monitor our participants for four more of your years, then return home. Another ship will then continue our studies of your planet."

"Do we need to come aboard your ship again?" Bob thought.

"No, Robert, we have newer devices that allow us to examine you from a greater distance now. In fact, the examinations on both of you have already been performed during our visit."

"Have you examined our mother?"

"We examined your mother in her sleep recently. We don't need to contact her directly any more. She is quite healthy for her age."

"We're grateful to know that," Bob replied silently.

"Before you go, I must ask," JD thought, "what sort of weapon did you use against the Japanese ships? This man with us had a submarine underwater when you fired your weapon. He and his men lived, but his ship was severely damaged."

"I'm not permitted to say, James, but I regret his ship was damaged. Please let him know I'm thankful that he and his crew survived. Good-bye, James."

"Good-bye, Captain."

The craft slowly backed away and gained altitude until it was about one thousand feet above the water. The entire craft then began to glow brightly and shot straight up into the air, disappearing from sight. JD came back inside the conning station as Bennett took a handkerchief from a pocket and wiped his face.

"What the hell did I just see, Commodore?"

"We'll discuss it in my cabin. Dismiss, Chief," JD said.

"Aye, aye, Captain," Bob said as he exited.

JD reached for the 1MC and quickly ordered *Soda* to resume normal watch activity, and ordered Lieutenant Commander Garrison to take the conn in Olson's absence. Before they left the conning platform, Radio notified JD that Captain Geiring requested to speak with him. They patched the radio to the handset.

"JD, what the hell was that thing?" Captain Geiring asked in a voice JD almost didn't recognize.

"I'm not sure, Hank," JD lied to his old Academy roommate, "I'm just happy we didn't try to shoot at it. My submarine skipper thinks that was the thing that killed the Japanese ships."

"What do we do if it comes back?" Geiring was rattled.

"Calm down, Hank. Keep a grip on yourself. We're still alive and in one piece. If that thing wanted us dead, we would be. If it comes back, we make nice and hope. It's all we can do."

"You *are* going to put this in your report, right?"

"Absolutely. As will you—exactly as you saw it. We have to."

"Our careers are over, you know."

"Maybe, but we have to do this. Plus, I'm towing our evidence."

"That you are. I'll make my report."

"Don't worry, Hank. It'll work out."

"I hope so, JD. I hope so."

On the way to his stateroom, JD stopped by the XO's office and ordered Olson taken to his stateroom, where he was to remain under guard. He also stopped in the wardroom and got a pot of coffee to take with them.

Over the next hour, JD explained the purpose and function of *Soda*. No mention was made of his and his family's previous experiences with the alien craft. JD was careful to explain how Bennett and his men would certainly be sworn to secrecy about BX-1, and most likely how all of them were going to be thoroughly grilled by Hathaway's men about the craft they had seen. As to his ordering Bob to the bridge, JD explained that he wanted extra beef available if Olson required forcible removal, as well as to have someone to escort Bennett back to his quarters if necessary. He confessed that Bob was his half-brother and wanted an ally handy as a witness, but asked Bennett to keep that to himself.

"Sir, you saved my life and the lives of my crew. You allowed me to witness the most fantastic thing I'll ever see before heaven. I owe you much more than this confidence.

I'll never speak of it."

"I thank you for that, Mr. Bennett. You and your men make yourselves at home on the way back," JD said.

"Thank you, sir. Once they've rested up, I'm sure they'll appreciate the elbow room. Are we free to move about topside? I'd like to assemble them and inform them of our circumstances."

"Feel free, but remember the quarterdeck is restricted for safety reasons. Just ask anyone to hail them on the 1MC when you're ready. Now, let's get some breakfast. We have a long day of paperwork ahead of us." At JD's invitation, Bennett ate with him in his cabin.

The wardroom was eerily quiet as the officers ate. As the department commanders arrived, JD made a brief appearance to remind them of his need of their after-action reports. No one asked about Olson, although everyone wanted to. The tension was eased by conversations with the submarine officers.

The Chiefs' mess was far less subdued. Bob fended off questions from every angle regarding Olson. Finally, he'd had enough.

"Listen, men. What happened with Mr. Olson was serious. Damn serious. You don't need to be running your mouths about it. And no matter what you think of the man, Mr. Olson is an officer in this man's Navy. I expect every enlisted man on this ship to treat Commander Olson with the respect his rank entitles. You start having a damned party over this and the men will pick up on it. Keep yourselves and your men on a tight leash about this and I'm not kidding. Got it?" The silence in the room let him know they did. Later, Bob let Carlisle and Morris in on some of what had happened.

JD returned to his sea cabin and remained there through the morning. He first prepared an interim report for

Admiral Fletcher regarding the incident with the alien craft, as well as his relieving Olson for insubordination. There would be an inquiry, no doubt. He didn't necessarily want to see a court-martial for Olson, but he did want him off his ship. As to the encounter with the alien craft, he had no clue what would happen. Normally, his reports were typed by an Ensign in Communications. JD typed this report himself, and hand delivered it to his Communications Officer, Lieutenant Commander Charles Haney, to personally encode. He was sure this incident was going to go all the way to Chief of Naval Operations, Admiral Ernest J. King. Probably even the White House.

As his department commanders brought their reports, JD began putting his final report together. Shortly after lunch, Haney knocked on JD's door. He had his formal report from Communications, as well as a reply from Admiral Fletcher. BX-1 would transfer towing of the destroyer to a fleet tug off Cape Flattery and hold off the coast until 1900, then come into port under cover of darkness as usual. JD was to report to Fletcher's office at 1000 the morning after their arrival in Bremerton to present his final report. Olson was ordered to remain confined to quarters and prepare his own report, to be presented to the admiral at 1100, at which time he would be quartered on base. Bennett and Chief Jenkins were to report to the admiral at 1300.

Thirty-Eight

At 0530, still ten miles from the mouth of Puget Sound, BX-1 contacted the Harbor Master, Puget Sound Navy Yard, requesting a tug for the captured Japanese destroyer. The Harbor Master reported the tug was holding station off Cape Flattery.

The two ships rendezvoused at 0700. The men on the destroyer cast off lines from *Soda* and secured lines from the tug, then boarded the motor whale boats to return to their ship. *Soda* and her destroyers cruised twenty miles off the coast until 1900, when *Soda* left her escorts and headed into Puget Sound. The tugs gently nudged the big ship into Dry Dock C-2 at 0420, and by the time the sun came up the building was secure and looking like an abandoned airship hangar.

JD didn't bother with trying to sleep after *Soda* was secured in dry dock. He knew he'd feel even worse waking from a sound sleep after only a couple of hours. Instead, he pored over his final report, going over every detail of the events that prompted him to relieve Olson. He even went over Olson's last performance reviews, in which JD characterized his XO as a capable officer but never recommended him for promotion or command. He was thankful for his reserve in those evaluations. He was vaguely aware of Olson's behavior with his subordinates, but it took Bob's frankness to let him actually see the character flaws in the man.

An ambulance arrived outside the building shortly after 0600 and JD supervised the transfer of the bodies of the Japanese crewmen to the SP's, who rolled them away on gurneys. After breakfast he watched his tired crew as they offloaded ordnance, ordering Commander Dougherty to take his time and to not clean guns or perform any other maintenance until his men had a decent night's rest.

At 0930, he crossed the brow, where Lieutenant Wilson waited to personally drive him to the headquarters of the Commander, North Pacific Area. Wilson had a little worry over his orders to personally drive Commodore Roberts and Commander Olson at different times to the same place. Something was up, and he hoped his dust-up with Olson didn't fit into the equation anywhere. He drove in silence, letting JD off at the front of the building. JD thanked Wilson and headed inside, but not before pausing to watch as USS *West Virginia,* finally overhauled and rebuilt after being sunk at Pearl Harbor, left her dry dock in preparation to rejoin the fleet.

Admiral Fletcher's clerk looked up and rose to greet JD as he entered at the stroke of 1000. "Good morning, sir. I'll let the admiral know you're here."

He crossed the few feet between his desk and the door and knocked. He announced Commodore Roberts had arrived and Fletcher ordered JD in. JD entered and stood at attention before Fletcher's desk.

"Sit down, Commodore," Fletcher said as he watched *West Virginia* through the window. It wasn't an invitation.

JD laid his report on Fletcher's desk and sat, but didn't relax. Fletcher finally turned from the window and sat at his desk. None of his normally affable demeanor was evident. He picked up JD's final report, sighed and looked across the desk.

"JD, what the hell is all this?"

Vice Admiral Frank Jack Fletcher received his commission as an Ensign in 1908 and in 1912 was awarded the Medal of Honor, along with his commanding officer and uncle, Frank Friday Fletcher, for their actions during the invasion of Vera Cruz. Trained as a cruiser and battleship commander, Fletcher found himself suddenly commanding aircraft carriers in the early stages of the war, leading the U.S. forces in the battles of the Coral Sea and Midway, although he was not an aviator. His actions in these engagements drew a fair amount of animosity and criticism from the naval aviation fraternity, all the way to Admiral King. The fact that his commands had sunk six Japanese carriers was apparently, in their eyes, insignificant. His one ally, it appeared, was Chester Nimitz. Thanks to Nimitz, Fletcher still had what was considered a combat command, albeit a backwater compared to others.

"Just what it says, I'm afraid, sir," JD replied, "I have very little in the way of explanation or analysis. The enemy ships we encountered showed no resistance or attempted to evade us. Based on what I saw on the destroyer, these ships were all completely disabled through their electrical systems, and every man aboard died at his station. I'm hopeful the autopsies on the two bodies we kept will shed some light on what happened. Lieutenant Commander Bennett may be able to provide more detail in his report, but from what he told me he's as baffled as anyone."

"I'm curious as to why you took on the cruiser and battleship alone, instead of waiting for the rest of the task force."

"I had several reasons for that, sir. First, our air support forced my hand. I assumed the task force would assemble and then I would call for air support, when in fact the opposite happened. The actions of the PBY and the B-17s seemed coordinated, but not by us. I assumed their orders came from your desk and didn't question it. After the bombing of the two ships, all aircraft reported the ships to be adrift. They reported no anti-aircraft fire, no changes in course or speed, none of the enemy ships were trailing a wake, and that they had sustained significant bomb damage. I concluded the risk to my ships was minimal and ordered them in to finish off the battleship and cruiser.

"My second reason was to be prepared to assemble the task force and move to any new sighting quickly. Additionally, we had the report of an American sub in distress and my ships were closest. I had to recall my destroyers to respond to *Roughy,* and since they were ahead of the Japanese ships, it made sense to execute the battle plan while they were returning. That way we could dispatch the enemy and proceed to assist *Roughy* in one turn. Finally, by executing the battle plan as we did, it minimized exposure of BX-1 to unauthorized eyes."

"Alright, now what about this 'aircraft' you encountered? You believe it was what caused the radar anomalies reported earlier?"

"I do, sir. The SK radar worked perfectly during testing. It picked up and accurately tracked every target as soon as it was in range."

"So, you're convinced the radar is not defective?"

"Based on this test, absolutely."

"Could this craft you saw be what's showing up on other ships' radars?"

"Possibly. I don't think it's a problem with the radar. The first two unexplained targets we picked up directed us right to the Japanese battleship and cruiser. And the craft we encountered was absolutely real. I can't explain how it operated, but it obviously operated under intelligent control. I anticipate Captain Geiring's report to support that, as well Lieutenant Commander Bennett's." JD didn't lie. He had no idea how the craft worked.

"You know ONI will be all over you, right? This thing isn't going away."

"I'm sure. I assume Hathaway and his men will be busy with us for some time."

"Hathaway has been relieved. He never put together that there might be enemy activity approaching the coast. The top brass isn't happy that I didn't, either."

"My First Lieutenant thought he saw some clues, but Olson and I dismissed it as well, sir. It was pretty thin evidence at the time the intelligence was collected."

"I agree, but you know the Navy. Hindsight always proves you needed greater foresight. Just ask Admiral Kimmel. The Navy was sure he should have known Pearl Harbor was going to be attacked—without ever naming Hawaii as a potential target in their intelligence briefs. Now, explain what happened with your Executive Officer."

JD took a long breath before he began. This was going to be tricky. "Well sir, it came to my attention just before we put to sea that Mr. Olson had begun a pattern of behavior that had started undermining both the chain of command and morale. It appears that he had been managing some of the junior officers and Chief Petty Officers in ways that were sometimes contradictory to the orders of their Division Commanders or Department Heads and then, quite frankly, lying to the superior officers about this. This behavior bordered on abuse at times. During the forty-eight hours preceding our departure, I was made aware of him running my Chief Radarman nearly to the point of exhaustion chasing red herrings during the radar inspection. I personally witnessed him lying to Chief Gunners Mate Jenkins regarding orders prior to taking on ordnance. Then he attempted to pull the red herring trick with Chief Jenkins by sending him on frivolous chores while ordnance was being taken on."

"Define frivolous," Fletcher said.

"Specifically, he was ordered to personally inspect and clean turret one handling room over a gum wrapper found on the deck, then to turret four to see an unauthorized photo taped to the bulkhead, then relay to the division officer Mr. Olson's order to have the photo removed. Olson then summoned the Chief to the butcher shop and ordered him to relay orders to the Chief Commissary Steward to sharpen knives. At this point, I ordered Mr. Olson to pick up the intelligence brief from Commander Hathaway and did so with the sole purpose of keeping him from being a distraction during our preparations to get underway. I believe I mentioned this to you in our telephone conversation on the twenty-fourth. I should add that when he returned to the ship, he did not observe the custom and boarded without permission from the OOD. This incident was reported to me by the OOD, and Mr. Olson was verbally reprimanded, placed on report, and the incident was noted in the log."

"Alright. Continue."

"During our mission, Mr. Olson expressed caution regarding our engagement of the enemy ships when our orders were received, and recommended withdrawal from the area should we be forced to engage the enemy prior to the arrival of *Massachusetts* and the cruisers. He also objected when I considered towing the captured enemy destroyer back to port, fearing that other enemy ships could be in the area searching for the task force. You'll recall I mentioned this when requesting permission to take the destroyer under tow. On the night we encountered the unknown craft, he disobeyed a direct order to summon Mr.

Bennett and Chief Jenkins to the bridge, then disobeyed another direct order by sounding the general alarm after being ordered specifically not to."

"And you didn't sound General Quarters because you were convinced this craft was the one that killed the Japanese crews?"

"Yes sir. Lieutenant Commander Bennett said his Sonarman reported the sound of large guns being fired just before he lost power. I wanted Bennett to see this craft and confirm it was what he saw through his periscope before I took any action that could jeopardize my ships and men. Mr. Bennett confirmed that this was the craft he had observed, and I surmised that any outward offensive action on my part could result in a similar response from the craft that the Japanese suffered. As it turned out, the craft just seemed to observe us for a few minutes then left. I'm now convinced that if I had acted otherwise, I and every man under my command would be dead and you would be finding our ships adrift in the Pacific."

"What would you recommend for Olson?"

"It's my opinion that he is unfit to command a warship, sir. By the letter of the book, he should be tried for disobeying orders, but I don't know if he deserves that in light of these extraordinary circumstances. I believe he could be of great service teaching, or in design and development of radar and other electrical systems. That opinion is in my final report, as well."

"Well, just so you know, I have no idea where this incident is going from here. Obviously, I have to forward the report of your attack on the Japanese forces, as well as the encounter with the unknown aircraft, to CINCPAC. I'll include Captain Geiring's report, Lieutenant Commander Bennett's report, and Chief Jenkins' oral report as well. My opinion of your performance on this operation is commendable in terms of your aggressive action against an enemy force and your swift rescue of the submarine crew. As to Mr. Olson, I'll hear him out and refer it to the Judge Advocate to see if charges should be filed.

"Off the record, I want you to know that in my opinion you were either incredibly tolerant of Commander Olson or woefully ignorant of what was going on. Either way, I'm not particularly pleased with your performance as a commanding officer in the way you managed your XO. You will report back to your ship and await further orders. You will not converse with Commander Olson, Lieutenant Commander Bennett, or Chief Jenkins before I finish with them today. Dismiss."

"Yes sir."

JD stood and walked out of the admiral's office without further comment. As he left the building, Olson was getting out of the jeep driven by Lieutenant Wilson. The two men locked eyes until they passed. Neither spoke.

Arriving back at the dry dock, JD did a walk-around of the ship, checking the status of each department, and finally met with Commander Sharpe in his office. He informed Sharpe that until further notice he would continue as Executive Officer. They drew up orders and stations for the night together. Lieutenant Wilson arrived after returning Bennett and Bob to the ship with orders to pick up Olson's belongings and take them to his new quarters ashore.

Later that afternoon, buses arrived to transport the crew of *Roughy* to temporary housing, where they would await debriefing by ONI. JD stood at the brow to send them off. Bennett smartly saluted as he prepared to leave.

"On behalf of my officers and crew, I want to thank you again for all you've done, Commodore," he said.

"On behalf of my officers and crew, it was our pleasure." JD smiled as they shook hands, adding, "Good luck to you, sir."

"And to you, sir. Just so you know, I told the admiral that I believed you were completely justified in relieving Commander Olson."

"Thank you, Mr. Bennett. I appreciate that, especially coming from another skipper."

"Well, the truth is the truth. Take care."

"You, too."

THE WARDROOM was crowded for dinner that night, with only a minimal number of the officers and crew on watch. As the Executive Officer commands the wardroom, and as the Captain customarily eats alone, Commander Sharpe invited JD for dinner and to address the officers. As dessert was finished up, JD stood and tapped his glass with a spoon. The room settled quickly.

"Gentlemen, I feel it is important to inform you of the events regarding Commander Olson. In the early hours of 29 June, BX-1 encountered an aircraft of unknown type and origin. During the course of this encounter, Mr. Olson refused to obey two direct orders from me. He was relieved for this reason. On orders from Admiral Fletcher, he has been temporarily detained on base pending an investigation of the incident. That is all I care to say on the matter for the moment and would appreciate your using this information judiciously with your men. I don't want any scuttlebutt to get legs. Until further notice, Commander Sharpe will remain as Executive Officer and First Lieutenant. I expect your full assistance to him in performing this double duty. Carry on." JD retired to his stateroom.

Thirty-Nine

JD and Bob walked along the dry dock at a brisk pace. The work area was free of equipment and activity, partly due to the holiday, and partly because *Soda* simply didn't require any maintenance except for cleaning the guns on turrets one and four and the magazines.

The ship and crew seemed oddly imprisoned. JD had requested grills, hot dogs, ice cream and beer brought to Dry Dock C-2. Later that day, the crew would be treated to a subdued Independence Day celebration, ending with a movie. Just before 1100 that morning, JD welcomed Commander Lawrence Gilstrap aboard as Damage Control Officer and First Lieutenant. Commander Sharpe, with Admiral Fletcher's approval, would remain as Executive Officer. JD spent the afternoon introducing Gilstrap to the ship and crew, and then met with Sharpe in his office to set orders and stations for the night watches. Sharpe had just been dismissed when the telephone rang.

"Admiral Fletcher for you, sir," the switchboard operator said.

"Very well, put him through," JD replied. He heard the line click open. "Hello, Admiral."

"Happy Independence Day, Commodore," Fletcher sounded more like his good-natured self.

"And to you, sir. What can I do for you?"

"Pack a bag for three days. Tomorrow morning you'll be picked up at 0630 and taken to Ault Field then flown to Pearl Harbor. Nimitz's orders. You can imagine why, I guess."

"Yes sir. I'll be ready."

"They'll have someone waiting at Hickam to take you to your quarters. You meet with Nimitz at 0800 on the sixth. Wear dress khaki. Oh, and bring your brother."

"Beg pardon, sir?"

"Don't worry, JD. I've known for quite a while."

"Yes sir. We'll be there."

"Carry on." The line went dead.

JD sat, holding the receiver for a full minute, contemplating the call. Finally, he hung up and walked to the XO's office and informed Sharpe that he would be in charge of the ship for the next couple of days, and ordered Bob removed from duty that night as Chief of the Watch so he could pack and get some sleep. A few minutes later Bob reported to the Captain's office where JD relayed Fletcher's orders. At 1800, JD announced to the wardroom that he had been ordered to Pearl Harbor for three days and introduced Commander Gilstrap to the officers he hadn't yet met, encouraging their assistance to him and Mr. Sharpe in conducting the activities of the ship. Bob informed Carlisle that he would be Senior Enlisted Aboard again for a few days. Both men packed and went to bed before the movie was over topside. Neither man slept well.

Forty

5 July, 1944

Showered, shaved and fed, JD and Bob crossed the brow at 0615 and passed through the security room at Dry Dock C-2. Lieutenant (j.g.) Wilson was waiting outside in the jeep. JD laughed as he and Bob got in.

"Lieutenant, just when do you sleep?"

"I don't work very hard, sir. Don't need much sleep," Wilson smiled.

He drove them through the sentry post to the motor launch dock. A covered launch flying a Commodore's flag was waiting. The launch took them across Puget Sound to a small craft dock used by the Navy in the port of Seattle, where a staff car drove them to Ault Field. A Douglas R5D transport plane waited on the tarmac, where an Aviation Boatswain's mate took their bags and stowed them on the plane, as JD and Bob were introduced to the flight crew. An awkward silence ensued for a few minutes before JD finally asked the pilot what the holdup was.

"Well, sir," the pilot replied, "we *do* have to wait on the admiral, right?"

"Of course," JD said with a wry smile, "the admiral. Yes."

Bob turned away to hide his smile. A few minutes later another staff car flying three stars arrived. The boatswain's mate opened the rear door and saluted as Admiral Fletcher and a Lieutenant, introduced as his secretary, stepped out. The other men snapped to attention and saluted as Fletcher approached. Returning their salutes, he smiled at JD and Bob.

"You didn't think I was going to get out of this mess, did you?"

"You play your cards pretty close, sir," JD smiled.

"Well, we have ten hours to talk," Fletcher said. He looked at the pilot. "Ready to go, Commander?"

"Yes sir," the pilot replied.

"Then let's get going."

The crew bounded up the stairs to their positions on the plane, followed by Fletcher and the other men. As they strapped in, the Pratt and Whitney engines on the starboard side sputtered, then roared to life. The boatswain's mate secured the cabin door as the port side engines were started, then the plane taxied and started down the runway, gently rising into the air above Puget Sound and turning to the southwest and Hawaii.

Fletcher and JD exchanged some small talk but JD remained reserved. He had been to Fletcher's office a few times and had never seen this Lieutenant before. He assumed him to be from Naval Intelligence. The conversation lapsed into silence for several hours until the bos'n brought sandwiches and coffee for lunch. As they ate, Fletcher rekindled the conversation.

"I suppose you're wondering how I know about your family connection. Apparently, some officers were aware of your relationship going back to your Academy days, JD, but nobody took much notice until the Chief's little dust-up on the *Augusta*. Because of the nature of service on BX-1, you get heavily vetted by Naval Intelligence before you are assigned to the ship and receive your security clearance. It didn't take Sherlock Holmes to notice each of you had a mother with the same name who lived at the same address. From there, they found your adoption records, JD. Now, as you know, since the start of the war there's been an unwritten rule barring brothers from serving on the same ship, but I approved Chief Jenkins coming aboard based on his ability and—in one notable case—the recommendations from a former commanding officer, as well as your own opinion. It's my opinion that having the two of you on BX-1 posed little risk to either of you, and was a benefit to the ship and the Navy."

"I appreciate your candor, Admiral," JD replied, "my primary motivation for requesting Chief Jenkins on board was based on his exemplary skills as a gunnery expert and leader of men. As you probably know, we have served together several times before—by chance I might add—and while he can be a royal pain in the ass, he does get the job done."

"Thank you, brother, I think," Bob smirked at JD. "If I may, Admiral, I'd like to add that the Commodore has always insisted that he and I maintain the strictest military bearing with respect to each other while on duty."

"A fact your former superiors have confirmed, Chief. But for the record, the two of you were not stationed together on the *Chew* by chance. Someone recommended that then-Lieutenant Commander Roberts might be able to get you back in line."

"Thank you, admiral," JD said. "Now I have a question for you, if I may. Other than the obvious, why exactly does Admiral Nimitz want to see us?"

Fletcher eyed JD evenly for a moment before he replied, "JD, you're one of the most intelligent and capable officers I've ever met. The way you adjusted your plans and managed your forces in dealing with those Japanese ships when air support arrived early—and succeeded in sinking them on the fly to rescue the *Roughy*—was brilliant seamanship. But this unknown aircraft story is something that is nearly unbelievable. Nimitz wants to hear the story from both of you, unfiltered, just like it happened."

"Well, that he'll get," JD promised.

The men all took advantage of the long flight to catch forty winks after lunch. Toward the end of the flight Fletcher again asked JD and Bob random questions regarding the encounter with the alien craft. His "secretary" tried to appear to be doing paperwork, but both JD and Bob noticed he only wrote while they were responding to Fletcher's questions.

The RD5 landed at Hickam Field adjacent to Pearl Harbor at 1620 local time. As they came down the stairs, a staff sergeant saluted them and led them to two staff cars that whisked them off to Pearl Harbor. Admiral Fletcher, his secretary and JD were driven to their quarters, and Bob to a separate building for noncommissioned officers.

Forty-One

Two staff cars pulled up in front of CINCPAC headquarters just before 0800. JD, Admiral Fletcher and his secretary exited one car, and Bob from the other. They all came to attention for morning colors and, after the ceremony, entered the concrete building. A few minutes later they were escorted into a conference room.

At one end of the table sat Admiral Chester Nimitz, Commander in Chief of the Pacific Fleet, flanked by Brigadier Gen. J.J. Twitty of the Royal Army, Assistant Chief of Staff for Intelligence, and Captain Edwin T. Layton, Combat Intelligence Officer. Nimitz rose and walked towards the men as they came in. He extended his hand to Fletcher.

"Frank, how are you doing?"

"Very well sir. Thank you for asking. And you?"

"Sometimes I feel like a one-armed paper hanger, but I'm doing well. Commodore, it's been a long time. Good to see you again."

"Thank you, sir. It's always a pleasure," JD replied.

"And Chief, we're both a long way from the *Augusta,* aren't we?" Nimitz smiled.

"That we are, Admiral. I'm surprised you remembered." Bob answered.

"You're a little hard to forget, Chief," Nimitz said with

a sardonic smile. It was then-Captain Nimitz who had demoted Bob and thrown him in the brig for his fight with a Chief Gunners Mate while skipper of the cruiser USS *Augusta* in 1933. The Chief was beaten so badly that he and the Executive Officer wanted Bob court-martialed for assault. Nimitz, perhaps remembering his own court-martial as an Ensign, stood firm with his ruling at the Captain's Mast, stating that the Chief "needed to learn how to retreat in the face of superior firepower."

Nimitz then introduced JD and Bob to General Twitty and Captain Layton. Layton had become a bit of a legend for believing, then proving, that the Japanese were going to attack Midway when the top brass and others in Washington insisted the attack would be elsewhere. Nimitz's faith in Layton and his crew was steadfast. Motioning to the table, the admiral invited the men to have a seat.

"Well, now that the pleasantries are over, let's get down to the bare bones of why we're here," Nimitz said, never changing his even tone. "Commodore, this is quite a tale you told," he said as he held a copy of JD's final action report. "First, my congratulations on your actions against the enemy ships. The capture of that destroyer was a brilliant idea. Not only for intelligence purposes, but it may wind up saving your hide."

"Saving my hide was not my reason for bringing her in, sir," JD replied, "I brought her in for the intelligence we could gather from her. My only selfish reason was the hope that the intelligence we gathered might save my son's hide someday. I'm also hoping to figure out what killed her and her crew."

"That's right, your son *is* in sub training. Well, the people going through the tin can are completely at a loss as to what could cause that kind of damage, I can tell you that.

And the autopsies of the two men you brought back initially show they may have been electrocuted somehow, which is logical in light of the damage reported. Lieutenant Commander Bennett stated his sub suffered similar damage, correct?"

"Yes sir. That's what he reported, and what my Engineering Officer saw as well."

Captain Layton cleared his throat and asked, "Commodore Roberts, Lieutenant Commander Bennett reported this event occurred at about 1740 Zulu, is that right?"

"That's correct," JD confirmed.

"And you noted a large static burst both on radio and radar at that time as well?"

"That is also correct."

"Admiral, our radio surveillance recorded a static burst emanating from the northeast at the same time that day also. Whatever killed those ships had to be electromagnetic in nature."

Nimitz digested the information for a moment. "Well, we'll wait and see how that pans out. Now for the elephant in the room. Off the record, what is your opinion of the unknown aircraft you saw?"

JD took a deep breath. He was going to have to choose his words carefully. And he knew he was on the record regardless. "Admiral, this craft was of a design and performed in such a way that I can't believe it was built by man. I don't see how a human body could take the acceleration I saw when the craft took off. And it had to be intelligently controlled. General, if it is man-made, you would know better than I."

"I can say that I have no knowledge of any British or American craft of this nature, and it would be contrary to reason to think it was German, considering it attacked

Japanese ships," Twitty said. "As for our Soviet friends, I can't say, but what you described seeing in terms of its little 'yo-yo' trick and hovering at forty-two thousand feet, plus a vertical climb at sixteen-hundred knots, implies a technology that's simply unknown at the moment."

"So, are you two implying this thing is extra-terrestrial?" Nimitz asked.

"I think it's the only conclusion we can draw, sir," JD said.

"And you concur, based on your observation of this craft, Chief?"

"I would, sir. I'm no engineer, but this thing was as long as a destroyer and climbed like a scalded angel. I've never seen anything man-made like it," Bob replied.

Nimitz sighed. "Well, this is why this discussion is off the record for now. If this was just some officer reporting a possible radar anomaly and a distant visual sighting, I would discount it. But when the commander of the most secret vessel in the Navy says he saw something like this up close, I have to believe him. And I have to tell Admiral King that I believe him. JD, my intelligence people will need to go over this with you and Chief Jenkins again today. I want you two to be as patient as you can be because they're going to ask you the same questions twenty different ways. But I want Admiral King convinced that this thing is real, understood?"

"Understood," both men said.

"Very well. Ed, will you escort these men to your torture chamber?"

"Yes sir," Layton chuckled. "Commodore, Chief, if you'll come with me, please?"

General Twitty accompanied the three men as they left the room. Nimitz waited until the door was closed before he looked at Fletcher.

"Well, what do you think, Frank?" he asked

"Chet, Commodore Roberts has not given a single word of inconsistency in this matter. I think he's completely convinced he saw what he said he saw. And Chief Jenkins is the exact same in terms of detail down to the letter."

"You don't think Jenkins is just sticking up for his half-brother, then?"

"I don't. Plus, we have Bennett's report, both from his sub and from BX-1, along with Geiring's report from his destroyers. It's all consistent."

"I still wouldn't believe any of this if it weren't for one thing."

"What's that?"

"Ray Spruance described the exact same craft to me two months ago."

"Spruance said what?" Admiral Fletcher asked incredulously. "He actually saw that thing?"

"Apparently," Nimitz replied, "or, God forbid, another one just like it. He said he was returning from the Caroline Islands when he saw it from his aircraft. He swore the flight crew to secrecy, but then made the connection between the 'thing' and the anomalous radar signatures his ships were picking up. He stewed on it and finally told me just before he headed back out to relieve Halsey."

"And Halsey hasn't reported seeing it?"

"You know Bill," Nimitz smiled, "he's convinced that the anomalies are strictly a radar malfunction. He wouldn't say he saw anything like this if it flew him back here and set him down on Ford Island. But, with his habit of shooting first and asking questions later, I'm inclined to think he really hasn't seen it simply because he's alive and the fleet is intact."

"So how are you going to play this?"

"Well, there's no getting around the fact that I have to report this to King. He'll surely move it up to Secretary Forrestal. Maybe even the President. They'll set official policy. But I'm issuing a general order today to all commanding officers to consider these anomalies as real and that any craft associated with these anomalies encountered are to be treated in a non-hostile manner."

"What about MacArthur?"

"I think I'd better send the General a personal message regarding this one. He and I are supposed to meet with the President here in three weeks. By then we'll know a lot more about that captured destroyer and the stories from all the men who saw this thing. If the President knows about all this and wants to, we can discuss it, but in the meantime, MacArthur needs to know my position on the matter. I bet King will tell Marshall as well, and Marshall will notify MacArthur, too. Now, how are you going to handle this incident with JD's Executive Officer?"

"There is no doubt he refused to obey two direct orders. All present on the bridge agree on that point. Even Olson. The question is whether he was justified given the circumstances. Roberts doesn't think charges are warranted. He just wants him off the ship. Olson legitimately wants Roberts court-martialed for dereliction of duty, and from what I hear his lawyer wants to follow through with it. I was hoping the JAG would think Olson was nuts, but now they know this story, too."

"Well personally, I don't see ONI allowing this kind of information brought out. There's no way you can prosecute this case without the details of the incident being presented at a general court-martial."

"Chet, what I'd really like to do, in all honesty, is give Olson a swift kick in the pants and a non-combat position for the rest of war in return for a nondisclosure agreement and dropping the counter-charge against Roberts. He's a first-rate fink and he could turn a tricky situation into an absolute fiasco."

"I agree. I'll discuss this with Twitty and have him contact the Judge Advocate in Bremerton. He also has Admiral Schuirmann's ear. If the ONI Director likes the idea, I'll bet that will be exactly what happens."

"Thanks, Chet. This thing could get some really long legs really fast."

"Well, this incident is going to put a lot of people in uncomfortable positions. I'm glad I don't have the final say, I can tell you that."

"How long do you think Twitty is going to keep my two men?"

"If their story is as solid as you say, all morning. If Twitty thinks they're lying, then all day and well into the night. He's a nice guy, but a brutal interrogator if he suspects you're holding out on him. I wouldn't plan on leaving for home today. Consider yourself at liberty, or free to use my staff if you have things that need done. And feel free to join me for dinner tonight. If Twitty cuts those two loose early, I'll tell them to be here at 0700 for your flight home."

"Very well, then. I have a couple of things I need to do before I head back to my quarters, but I'll take you up on your dinner invitation. Where and when do you want to meet?"

"Meet me out front at 1800. I'll buy you a steak at the Royal Hawaiian."

"That sounds great. Thanks Chet."

General Twitty released JD and Bob at 1500 to their liberty. They both returned to their quarters, neither one in the mood to go into Honolulu and unable to fraternize with each other while on base. JD had dinner and drinks at the

Pearl Harbor Officers Club. Bob ate a hamburger with French fries, washed down with a cold beer, at the NCO Club, while the admirals dined in Waikiki. Neither saw a familiar face. Prior to the war, the Navy was small enough for career men to know a large number of people, but it had quadrupled in size. With the bulk of the fleet in forward areas, most of JD's and Bob's friends were either in harm's way, wounded, or dead.

Forty-Two

Bob and JD entered the headquarters building just before 0700 the next morning. Admiral Fletcher was coming down the hallway from Nimitz's office. His secretary was nowhere to be seen, confirming JD's suspicion that he was with ONI.

The staff car took them back to Hickam Field, where another RD5 waited to fly them back to the mainland. They boarded quickly and were airborne by 0740. Banking over Diamond Head, the plane pointed northeast and settled in for the ten-hour flight.

After the bosn's mate had served coffee, Fletcher took a manila envelope from his brief case and handed it to JD. "This was waiting for me when I got to HQ this morning. It's from Bureau of Ships. You might as well see it now."

"Thank you, sir," JD said as he opened the envelope. A single typed sheet of paper was inside, orders from Vice Admiral Cochrane, Chief of Bureau of Ships to Commanding Officer, BX-1, with copies sent to Commander, North Pacific Area, and Commander in Chief, Pacific Fleet. BX-1 was ordered to reinstall SK2 search radars and put to sea as soon as possible for testing of the radar. Upon completion of testing and evaluation of the radar, BX-1 was to return to port for immediate deactivation. JD handed the orders to Bob as he looked at Fletcher.

"Any idea why we're getting fired, sir?" JD asked.

"Two official reasons, JD. First, the days of the battleship as the Navy's frontline weapon are over. You know that as well as anyone. The cancellation of the *Montana* class made that opinion obvious. So, there's no need for a testing platform like a battleship. All other improvements can be tested on cruisers. I seriously doubt that the *Alaska*-class cruisers will be continued past two or three ships, so even the twelve-inch gun is obsolete. Second, keeping a crew together with the necessary security clearances just for testing new equipment is simply an expensive pain in the tail."

"So, my crew will be . . . ?"

"Transferred to where they are most needed. I imagine you two will be put on another battleship. You may even get a divisional command, Commodore. My recommendation is that you get either a battleship or a cruiser division. And I expect your recommendations for your officers as well."

"Thank you, sir." JD fell silent for the remainder of the trip. Bob never spoke except to thank the bosn's mate for his lunch. He had, in two short weeks, become very comfortable with being out of harm's way. Even the engagement with the Japanese ships was more gunnery practice than combat. He didn't relish the prospect of returning to the fight and he struggled with the thought of having turned soft or worse, afraid. He decided he wasn't a coward; he was just tired of war. He wanted to sit a horse again, to be with his family, to try to somehow be a father to Allie. He was tired of saying, "Maybe someday."

The sun was setting when the plane touched the runway at Ault Field and it was nearly 2300 when they arrived at Dry Dock C-2. Before they split up for their quarters, JD stopped and looked at his brother.

"You alright, Bob?"

"Yeah. I will be. I'll talk to you later. G'night JD."

"Good night, Bobby."

Forty-Three

10 July, 1944
Puget Sound Naval Shipyard

"Chief Jenkins, report to the Captain's Office," the 1MC barked. *Damn it, JD, how do you know?* Bob said to himself. He grumbled under his breath as he hastily finished the job at hand, then hustled off, much to the amusement of everyone in the Chiefs' head at the time.

"How do you always manage to page me when I'm on the crapper?" Bob asked as soon as the Captain's door was closed and he was alone with JD.

"Sorry Bobby. It's just a talent, I guess," JD chuckled.

"So, what's so important?"

"I just got an intelligence memo. You and I need to coordinate letters home so our cover stories jibe. *Maryland* docked in Pearl today with torpedo damage sustained in an aerial attack off Saipan. You need to get a letter off to Dad and Momma, dated today, letting them know the ship was damaged but you're not hurt. I have to send one dated a week before saying that I heard you're safe. Apparently, there's a picture of *Maryland* that leaked to the press and they want anyone on *Soda* with a *Maryland* cover story to be aware." JD slid a photograph stamped 'Top Secret' across the desk to Bob showing a large hole in *Maryland's* starboard side, forward of turret one, just below the Chief Petty Officers berthing. Bob let out a low whistle.

"I hope to God she was at General Quarters when that happened."

"She was. Casualties were surprisingly low and minor."

"Good thing. If a sub had snuck in and done that, the Navy would need a whole lot of new Chief Petty Officers. Damn, JD, that could've been me in that compartment. You saved my butt again—and didn't even know it." Bob was a little shaky when he slid the photo back across the desk.

"Don't think about it that way, Bob. It's not healthy."

"I wonder if I should write Allie," Bob said absently.

"The memo's orders are specific. Don't. Momma will get word to Allie if she thinks it best."

"Orders are orders," Bob said, pulling himself together, "I'll have my letter ready by morning."

"Thanks, Bob. Remember to date it today or yesterday. By the way, you still haven't told me why you were so quiet when we came back from Pearl. What's up?"

"I'm tired, JD. I'm tired of the Navy and I'm damn sure tired of the war. I don't much like the idea of having to go back to it. Seeing things like that don't help, either," he said as he pointed at the photo. "It's going to take a lot more blood to win this war, and I don't want any of it to be mine. I'm not afraid, I just don't want the stress anymore."

"I know what you mean, Bobby. But on the bright side, we're almost sure to be behind some heavy armor. I just can't see us on anything besides a battleship or a heavy cruiser."

"Amen to that. But, like I said, orders are orders. We go where they say, but I sure hope to wind up working for Oldendorf or Lee. They know battleships and how to keep them in one piece."

"Amen to that. Well, we better get back to work."

"Aye, aye Cap'n."

Forty-Four

26 July, 1944

Soda cleared Dry Dock C-2 at 2210 and began her final mission. Under orders from Fletcher, only JD and Bob knew the fate of the ship. They both suspected that part of the mission was to see if the SK-2 radar would detect the visitors more quickly should they happen by. They would drill through a number of mock attacks as they had done previously, testing the SK-2 thoroughly. JD was to make a general announcement to the crew regarding the fate of the ship only after returning to port.

Earlier that afternoon, the heavy cruiser USS *Baltimore* entered Pearl Harbor carrying President Roosevelt. In meetings on the twenty-seventh through the twenty-ninth, Nimitz and MacArthur presented two strategies for the next phase of the war. MacArthur argued for the liberation of the Philippines and Nimitz for the liberation of Taiwan. No written records of the meetings were kept.

At one point on the 28th, the President ordered all aides out of the room for twenty minutes. During those twenty minutes the President, MacArthur, Nimitz and Admiral William Leahy, President Roosevelt's top military advisor, discussed the unknown aircraft report of BX-1. Nimitz and MacArthur were informed that similar sightings had been reported in the Atlantic and European theaters, and that the policy of the United States was to be one of strict neutrality in encounters with such craft. All such encounters were to be classified as top secret and any violation of this policy would be dealt with immediately and severely. This policy had also been adopted by Great Britain, France, Canada, and Australia. The Soviet Union, predictably, had scoffed at the suggestion that such craft existed, which most experts interpreted as an admission to their knowledge of the craft and that no policy statement would be forthcoming. The President departed Pearl Harbor aboard *Baltimore* for the Aleutians the evening of the twenty-ninth.

Forty-Five

6 August, 1944
100 miles off the Oregon Coast

After a full week of rigorous testing of the SK-2 radar, JD was informed that it had performed perfectly in every respect with no anomalies noted. He sent a preliminary report to Admiral Fletcher and Admiral Cochrane and notified them that *Soda* was returning to port. At 0430 on the morning of the seventh, the ship was secured in Dry Dock C-2. Breakfast was served as usual, and JD ordered all hands to ship liberty until 1200.

At 1330, JD keyed the 1MC, "Now here this. Now hear this. This is the Captain. I have been ordered by the Chief, Bureau of Ships, the Commander in Chief, Pacific Fleet, and the Commander, North Pacific Area, to inform you that as of 2400 hours on 21 August, 1944, BX-1 will be deactivated. Transfer orders for all crew members will be issued beginning 10 August at 0800, with dismissal and security debriefing commencing twenty-four hours after orders are received. All hands will report by division daily at 0800 for morning colors and receipt of orders. Department Heads will meet in the Captain's Office today at 1900.

"I personally wish to commend each and every man aboard for your dedication and discipline in the performance of your duties. The nature of this ship and her mission have placed hardships upon you and demanded sacrifices from you above and beyond the call of duty. I want to personally thank each of you for that sacrifice and dedication. At my request, the Bureau of Personnel has granted sixty days leave for each member of the crew prior to your next assignment, and special commendations for dedicated service at your cover-story stations will be placed in your service records. Well done, *Soda*. That is all."

At 1900, the Department Heads and Commander Sharpe met with JD. He once again thanked them for their service and let them know he had recommended all of them for promotion, except for Commander Gilstrap, who had just received a promotion from Lieutenant Commander three weeks before. They were then informed of what JD knew regarding how the crew would be relieved. Gunnery and Navigation divisions would depart first, followed by Hull, Communications, Medical, Engineering and Supply. JD, Commander Sharpe, and Chief Jenkins would be the last three to leave the ship, turning her over to the Superintendent of the Yard. There would be no decommissioning ceremony, as was typical for other warships, because BX-1 was never commissioned. He also ordered all department heads to provide him with their recommendations for promotion of junior officers, warrant officers, and petty officers.

The crew had *Soda* secured from sea ready status in two days. The first gunnery division left the ship on the eleventh as scheduled. Over the next ten days, one or two divisions left the ship daily.

On the morning of 21 August, breakfast in the form of corn flakes and coffee was served and the galleys secured before the Supply Division departed and Engineering extinguished the last operating boiler. JD then turned the ship over to Rear Admiral C. S. Gillette, Yard Manager.

Commander Jesse Sharpe was given his orders and JD and Bob saluted him farewell. As they crossed the brow, Bob looked at JD with a crooked smile.

"So, what's the deal? We get taken out back and shot?" Bob asked.

"I have been ordered to instruct you to accompany me to Admiral Fletcher's office," JD replied. "Our gear will follow us, I'm told. You *are* packed, right?"

"Holy crap. That ain't good."

"My thoughts exactly. Let's get going."

They walked through the nearly deserted building to the security office. The ever-present Lieutenant (j.g.) Wilson waited for them to drive them to headquarters. JD couldn't stay glum for long. Hopping in the jeep, he turned to Wilson.

"One more time to headquarters, Rochester," he said in his best Jack Benny.

"Yes sir, Mr. Benny," Wilson replied, doing his best to sound like Eddie Anderson.

They drove in silence to the headquarters building. As JD and Bob got out of the jeep, JD looked at the young officer and extended his hand. "Mr. Wilson, I want to thank you for your excellent work during my command. I hope you have a long and successful career."

"Thank you very much sir. It was my privilege. I wish you and Chief Jenkins all the best, as well," Wilson said.

"Good luck to you, sir," JD said as he saluted Wilson. Wilson smiled and winked as he returned Bob's salute.

Fletcher was waiting for them when they arrived at his office and welcomed them in personally. Coffee service was sitting on a table near the admiral's desk. After their cups were filled, Fletcher sat at the table with JD and Bob. Two manila envelopes lay on the table in front of him. After taking a sip from his cup, he looked at the two.

"I want you to know that you two have caused a fair amount of discussion the last month. I have it on good authority that your unknown aircraft was reported to the President, and as you know he has issued a policy for our military response should this thing show up again. The problem now is, Naval Intelligence has somehow come to the conclusion that you two were, for lack of a better term, 'targeted' by this thing. It is the opinion of Admiral King that this could make you both security risks to the Navy. Admiral Nimitz and I agree that if you are indeed somehow targeted by this craft, and if you were to have another encounter with this craft, another officer with less restraint than you and Captain Geiring, JD, could jeopardize an entire task force or land installation, despite the standing order. Commander Olson's actions on BX-1 have bolstered that opinion.

"It is therefore the opinion of the Navy Department that it is in the best interests of the United States for the two of you to be honorably discharged. Since you each have over twenty-five years of service, you will receive a full pension for the rank held on the date of your discharge. Admiral Nimitz has recommended and the President has approved your immediate promotion to Rear Admiral, JD. Chief, on my authority you are to be immediately promoted to Chief Warrant Officer," Fletcher said as he slid the envelopes across the table.

"Your promotion and discharge papers are in these envelopes along with letters of commendation from me, Admiral Nimitz, and Admiral King. You will both be in the Reserve until further notice. I've arranged for base housing if needed while you make travel plans. Your commission and enlistment end 31 August, and you're at liberty until then."

"I suppose there is no appeal of this decision," JD said

in the hope of staying in the Navy. He still desperately wanted a command and wanted to serve through the end of the war. Bob was silent, but was privately celebrating. He was finished with the Navy and wanted nothing more than to go home.

"I'm sorry, JD, but not at this time. I know you would like and deserve another command. However, your reserve status still keeps that door open."

"Well for me, sir, I would like to get to Fort Sumner, New Mexico as quickly as possible." Bob surprised himself a little with his blunt response.

"As you know, my wife is in Seattle, sir. I just need a cab," JD said, cheering at the thought.

"You won't need a cab, Admiral," Fletcher chuckled. You're free to use a staff car. If I were you, I'd wear out my flag just driving around. You are completely free to utilize my staff if you have any administrative needs. Before you leave today, I do need to have both of you go through a short debriefing with ONI, but it's basically you signing a nondisclosure agreement regarding your time of service on BX-1, and receiving the official cover story and service record for the duty stations you were supposed to be at during your tour on BX-1. And when I mean nondisclosure, I mean about *everything* that *ever* happened aboard that ship. Questions?"

"Just one, if I may sir," JD asked, "what became of Commander Olson?"

"*Lieutenant* Commander Olson, thanks to his over-bearing attitude during the investigation, is now on the staff of Captain Gingrich in the Joint Purchasing Board in Auckland." Fletcher's face was impassive.

"That really is a shame. He's such a brilliant engineer. I hope he's learned something that will help him when the war's over."

"We can hope. Now I want you two to head for the Intel Office for your debriefing and then to the Supply Office to collect your personal items. Supply will set you up with uniforms for your new ranks. You're welcome to head to home or housing after that."

"I would guess we'll both be at my house until Bob gets his travel orders, sir. Right Bob?"

"If that's an invitation, you bet," Bob replied happily.

"Then it's settled," Fletcher said, rising, "your staff car is outside, and I have your home phone number, JD, so I'll let you know when Chief Warrant Jenkins' travel orders are ready. Personally, I want to thank both of you for your service, and sacrifice, on behalf of the Navy and country. Your talents will be greatly missed and you should both stand very proud of your service."

"Thank you, sir," they replied in unison as they rose to attention prior to dismissal.

"One last thing," Fletcher said as he walked to his desk. He picked up a medal and walked to JD. "Rear Admiral James Delbert Roberts, for your distinguished service in command and defense of Battleship, Experimental, Number One against enemy forces, and in directing the successful rescue of the crew of USS *Roughy,* and upon the recommendation of the Commander in Chief, Pacific Fleet, I award you the Navy Cross with my thanks and congratulations."

JD stood at ramrod attention as the medal was pinned to his jacket. Being indoors, he was unsure if he should salute or not, but answered with, "My privilege, sir."

Fletcher then returned to his desk. Apparently, the salute wasn't necessary. He picked up another medal and turned to Bob.

"Chief Warrant Officer Robert Phillip Jenkins, for your courage in combat aboard Battleship, Experimental,

Number One against enemy forces, and your exemplary skills in directing fire to quickly destroy said enemy force, and upon the recommendation of the Commander in Chief, Pacific Fleet, I award you the Bronze Star with V attachment, with my thanks and congratulations."

"My privilege, sir," Bob replied.

"Admiral, Chief Warrant, you are dismissed."

Leaving Fletcher's office, JD stopped at the desk of one of the aides. He requested that a message be sent to his son, Phil, who was still attending submarine training in New London, Connecticut, informing him of his father's and uncle's retirement. The officer assured him the message would be sent to Ensign Roberts immediately. JD wrote out the message and handed it off.

The debriefing with Commander Hathaway's replacement took less than an hour. The Supply Office staff acted like JD and Bob were visiting royalty, making sure they had enough of each uniform. JD mischievously called Jeanne to let her know she had "company coming" in the form of Bob, but didn't mention he would be there as well. They left the building and found the car, with a two-star flag on the fender, waiting for them. The car slowed down just enough for the main gate sentry to see the flag and wave them through, and after the drive around Puget Sound, they were in front of an attractive home in suburban Seattle. Since he was expected, Bob got out the car first. Jeanne was waiting on the porch and met Bob on the sidewalk. He wrapped her in a big hug, turning her away from the staff car. JD then snuck out to tap Jeanne on the shoulder.

"Got one of those for me?" he smiled, then nearly toppled over as Jeanne jumped into his arms.

After hearing that both brothers were being discharged, Jeanne wept for ten minutes in relief and joy. JD's driver discretely moved luggage from the trunk of the staff car to the porch during the reunion. Not knowing quite what to do with him, JD asked the driver how he should contact him if he needed a ride, and was told to just call the motor pool at Bremerton and give them a pick up time. JD thanked the driver and dismissed him.

Going inside the house, Bob called Alice and Phillip to let them know he would be home within a few days. Alice was so overcome with joy her crying made Phillip take the phone from her, fearing the worst for one or both of his sons. He was barely able to contain himself when he learned the news. Next came a call to Katie, who appeared at the door within the hour to greet her father and uncle.

Forty-Six

22 August, 1944

"Bobby, what are you doing in uniform?" JD asked as he walked into the kitchen. They were both up at 5:30, despite being on liberty, out of sheer habit. Bob had already made coffee. JD still wore his bathrobe.

"Sorry, Admiral, but it's either uniform or just skivvies."

"Do you mean to tell me you have no civilian clothes?"

"I have one old Hawaiian shirt, but it has blood stains on it that won't come out. I figured Jeanne didn't need to hear the story behind it."

"Is it the one you were wearing the night after your divorce became final? I can't believe you kept that thing."

"Uh-huh. I'd still like another crack at that SP without his billy club."

"As I recall, I had to tell you about it the next day before I took you back to your ship."

"Yeah, yeah. Remind me again how you kept saving my butt."

"Well, we better get you some clothes today, then."

"I don't know if Seattle even has a western wear store."

"Something tells me a department store will have something close. You may have to wait on a good pair of boots, though."

"What are you two heathens doing up at this hour?" Jeanne grumbled as she made her way to the coffee pot.

"Sorry dear," JD said, "You just don't jump back into civilian life."

"Well, start walking towards it, at least," she smiled as she sat at the table. "What big plans have you been hatching this morning?"

"Believe it or not, shopping," JD replied, "Chief Warrant Jenkins isn't going to be Chief Warrant Jenkins that much longer and *Mister* Jenkins doesn't have any civvies to change into."

"Why, oh why, am I not surprised? Bob, what on Earth did you do for fun?"

"Mostly just sailor fun Jeanne," Bob replied, "I didn't even change into civvies when I went to the ranch. I didn't have much time to work when I visited, so a work uniform was enough."

"Well, Momma Alice is going to be so excited to have you back, you could show up in a hula skirt and she wouldn't notice."

"Speaking of Momma," JD said to Jeanne, "what would be the chances for us to head down to the ranch while I still have some clout?"

"I really don't think you have that kind of clout, Admiral. I was talking to Mrs. Fletcher the other day and she said wives can't travel on the military's dime except for emergencies. And a commercial flight out of here is out of the question. Plus, Katie and I need to start wedding planning. But I don't have a problem with you going if you'd like, though."

"Are you sure?"

"I've made do without you full time for nearly twenty-six years. What are a few more days?" Jeanne laughed. "Besides, I'll have you all to myself after that."

"Thanks, hon. I'll make the call before we go shopping."

"And I'm sorry but there's not much in the way of breakfast fixings. I'll have to use some ration cards before we can have bacon or eggs. I think I still have some oats and corn flakes somewhere in the cupboard."

"Don't worry about it, Jeanne. We'll eat in town," JD said. He'd forgotten that the burden of war wasn't just borne by the armed services.

"And we'll raid the Naval Exchange before we come home," Bob added. JD gave his brother a curious look.

Jeanne took her coffee back to bed and the brothers talked through the early morning as they read the paper. JD was getting antsy to get going by 7:00 and got dressed, returning to Bob in the kitchen. In deference to his brother's wardrobe plight, plus having to go back to the base NEX, JD also wore his khakis. He did enjoy pinning the two stars onto his collar tabs, though.

"Well, I'd better get us a ride and see about that plane." Lifting the receiver off the wall phone in the kitchen, JD called the motor pool for a car to pick him up at 0900. He then called Admiral Fletcher's office and added himself to Bob's trip to New Mexico, along with his return. He was surprised to learn that, since he was now accompanying Bob, he could pick his dates and they would fly directly to Fort Sumner Army Airfield. He had no idea that the Army had taken over the old abandoned airport northeast of town. Covering the mouthpiece, JD asked Bob when he wanted to leave. Bob replied that now was fine, but the day after tomorrow would be alright, too. JD ordered the plane to depart at 0800 on the twenty-fourth, returning on the twenty-ninth. He hung up the phone with a slight look of amazement on his face.

"If I had known about stuff like this, I would have

worked harder," he laughed.

Bob simply smiled and shook his head. A few minutes later, Alice and Phillip were informed that Bob would be home on the twenty-fourth. Bob "forgot" to mention that JD would be tagging along.

The driver pulled up in front of the house at nine o'clock precisely and JD and Bob got in. Thanks to the Yellow Pages, they actually located a western wear store and went there first. Both JD and Bob were brought back to the real war on the home front when they saw the pitifully small collection of work jeans and shirts. There was a good collection of gaudy "dude" clothes, as they referred to the fancy shirts with bright colors, bib yokes and tassels. A dogged search turned up one pair of denim jeans that were too long for Bob but would fit his waist after a wash or two, and two chambray shirts. There were no work style cowboy boots that fit, and only one felt hat in Bob's size: a huge thing like the ones popularized by Tom Mix and Hopalong Cassidy in the movies.

Bob paid for the jeans and shirts and they left for the department store. There, they found one pair of dungarees and a plaid cotton work shirt, along with a wider brimmed fedora that Bob said could be reshaped into something resembling a cowboy's work hat. They found a pair of boots designed for loggers with a narrower toe and higher heel than a regular work boot. Both brothers thought the heel might hold a set of spurs, although neither liked the idea of a lace-up boot that wouldn't pull off if trapped in a stirrup. Bob decided against them and hoped the store in Fort Sumner would have something when he got home. He had a pair of work boots in his gear that would work for the time being.

Shopping finished, they realized they hadn't eaten yet. Crossing the street to a café, they were greeted with a large sign reading, "NO NAVY, NO MARINES." Obviously, the place had seen one fight too many. They finally found a lunch counter in one of the stores and ate. The blue-plate special consisting of one pork chop, a spoonful of mashed potatoes with gravy, and some sliced carrots with no dessert, humbled both men. Compared to this, they had been eating very well. They returned to the car, where the driver had finished his sack lunch provided by the motor pool. JD ordered the driver to Bremerton and the NEX.

The sentries saw the two-star flag and saluted the car onto base after a cursory glance at the driver's ID. The NEX wasn't big at Bremerton, and neither JD nor Bob had ever been there. Their hopes weren't high as they looked at the building.

"Jeanne has a little freezer besides the one in the refrigerator, right?" Bob asked.

"Yes," JD said, a little confused, "why do you ask?"

"Just follow my lead. She's scrimped too long, plus she has to feed you when you get back and she won't have more ration stamps till next month. Just act important and aloof."

Bob got out of the car and waited while the driver let JD out, then opened the door to the NEX for JD, who paused and looked around as Bob approached the Commissary Steward First Class behind the counter.

"Admiral Roberts here is planning a little get-together for some fellow officers and was wondering if he could pick up a few items," Bob said with all the authority his new rank allowed.

"Yes sir," the First Class said at rigid attention. He didn't look like he'd seen many admirals.

"Good," Bob smiled. He figured he might as well play a strong hand since he had it. "The Admiral would like eight pounds of rib steak, four pounds of bacon, six pounds of ground beef, two pounds of cheddar cheese, ten pounds of potatoes, two dozen eggs and three pounds of coffee. Also, two cases of beer, six bottles of merlot, and two quarts of scotch."

JD struggled not to look shocked at the audacity of the request his brother had just made.

"Did you say bacon and eggs, Chief Warrant?" the Commissary Steward asked incredulously as he looked up from his list.

"Bacon to wrap the steaks and eggs for deviled eggs. Do you have a problem with the Admiral's menu choices?"

"No sir, not at all, sir. I'll have to check the freezer though, sir. I'm not sure we have that much rib steak," the First Class said as he looked up from his list.

"Just do your best, son," JD said. He had decided on the kindly uncle approach to counter Bob's demanding approach. A few minutes later two seamen appeared from the rear with two large boxes.

"I'm sorry sir, but I didn't have enough rib steaks. I had the butcher cut ten pounds of fresh top sirloins for the same price, if that's alright. Also, I only have three pounds of bacon and the only whisky I have is bourbon."

"That's fine, son. We can make do with that," JD smiled.

He and Bob then worked through the rows of canned goods until a third, smaller box had been filled. JD complimented the sailors on their efforts as he signed for the groceries, the cost to be deducted from his final paycheck. The two seamen took the boxes out to the car, stowing them safely in the trunk. Bob hovered over them like an avenging angel, threatening hellfire if an egg got broken, and death if a bottle of bourbon or wine broke. Back on the way to the main gate, JD stared at Bob, a sardonic smile on his face.

"You, sir, are a damned pirate, you know that? Where did you learn to pull that kind of crap?"

"I made some friends in Supply along the way," Bob replied. "They always have good stuff like this stashed in the back for the brass. In fact, I bet they had enough rib steaks and scotch, but held out in case Fletcher wanted them. It was too bad you were stuck onboard ship so much. You missed out on a lot."

Back home, Jeanne looked at the treasure trove of food open-mouthed. "When should I expect the FBI to show up?" she asked.

"No crime was committed, I swear," Bob smiled as he put the eggs in the refrigerator, "I just had to show your hubby how to pull a little rank."

"Too bad he won't be able to pull it longer," she said.

"On the contrary, Jeannie girl. Rear Admirals tend to get shot up following the orders of full Admirals. Be thankful."

Forty-Seven

24 August, 1944
Ault Field, Washington

JD and Bob rolled onto the tarmac to find the R4D waiting for them. The flight crew greeted the Admiral, informing him they had been cleared to fly directly to Fort Sumner, arriving around 1800 local time. The thirteen-hundred mile trip was safely in the range of the aircraft. JD thanked the pilot, a Lieutenant Commander, and at 0810 the plane was airborne, angling around Mount Rainier and bearing south-southeast.

The flight allowed the two brothers time to talk, reminiscing about their careers and plans for the future. JD confessed his frustration over the situation. He truly wanted another command, so much so that he would have gladly taken a demotion to Captain for another ship. Bob was sympathetic, but knew the dangers of fighting the Japanese were only going to increase as the allied forces clawed closer to the home islands, despite the fact that the Imperial Japanese Navy was severely weakened. He was far happier JD would soon be a civilian, and feared for his nephew. He never could fathom the thought of being crammed into a sub. Watching the *Roughy* sink before his eyes confirmed that submarine service just was no place for him, and he prayed that every Japanese destroyer be sunk before Little Phil's sub was.

JD was unsure what he wanted to do. There surely would be demand for a mechanical engineer with his level of leadership experience, but the ranch was hard to get out of his mind. He and Jeanne would have to discuss it seriously when he returned home. Plus, he needed to see if he—and Bob for that matter—could actually be of use to the ranches. While his parents and uncles were getting along in age, he knew his cousin Richard, now twenty-four, had received an agriculture exemption from the draft and was doing a fair amount of the work, plus each place had at least one other employee. And while cousins Frances and Sylvia and their families were not directly involved in the ranch operations, JD certainly didn't want either Bob or him to become a fifth wheel or cause any reduction in the corporate income for the rest of the family.

The R4D touched down in Fort Sumner at 1828. Bob and JD were surprised to see several B-17s and B-24s lined up along the taxiway. The abandoned municipal airport had been rebuilt as a training facility and had just begun training bomber crews. They were even more surprised to be greeted by the base commander when they taxied to a stop near the headquarters building. It appeared that a plane crashed on the home ranch the year before, and Will and Peggy helped the crew members out of the wreckage and provided first aid until medics arrived. The family had befriended most of the officers and enlisted men permanently assigned to the little base, even hosting barbecues for the men.

The Lieutenant Colonel led them towards the former airport terminal, now the headquarters building. As they approached the entrance, the door flew open and Alice raced to her sons, unable to wait for them another second and overcome with the surprise of seeing JD. Phillip walked behind her at a brisk pace. The four embraced and held each other for a long time, Phillip and Alice alternately crying and laughing.

Finally, Bob raised his head. Standing a few feet outside the door was a girl who looked to be around nineteen years of age, clutching a small purse and smiling self-consciously. Bob had held his tears in check to this point, but they began to flow freely as he gently released himself from his mother and walked to the girl.

"Allie . . . Allie . . . ," he repeated softly as he took his daughter gently into his arms. He buried his face in her hair, his body bouncing with sobs of joy.

Allison had not completely prepared herself for this type of reception, but finally accepted everything Alice had been telling her for the past year. She wrapped her arms around Bob's broad frame, gently patting his back.

"It's me, Daddy. It's me," was all she could manage for the moment.

"I'm so, so sorry I had to leave you, baby. I'll never leave you again," Bob said when he was finally able to speak.

"It's alright, Daddy. We're both home now."

"Then welcome home, Miss Grady."

"Miss Jenkins, if you please." Allison smiled, then again wrapped her arms around her father. It was her turn to sob now.

JD watched, his arms draped over his parents' shoulders, beaming as he watched the reunion. *It's finally someday,* he thought.

Forty-Eight

July 16, 1945
Fort Sumner, New Mexico

JD hadn't slept well. A line of thunderstorms passed through during the night and the thunder had kept him awake. Still, the moisture was appreciated for the grass. He finally gave up trying to get back to sleep and went into the kitchen to make coffee at 5:00. He went out on the front porch, drinking his coffee and smelling the wet ground. His schedule today now included checking water gaps, the fences built across washes to make sure they had held through the runoff in the night.

At about 5:30, he thought he saw a distant lightning flash to the southwest, but he could only see what appeared to be a small thunderhead in that part of the horizon. He didn't know the flash was from the detonation of an atomic bomb over one hundred miles away. He went inside to fix breakfast before Jeanne got up.

It hadn't taken long for JD and Jeanne to decide to move to New Mexico. After his discharge, JD had attempted to stay close to the war effort, taking a job with Boeing as an engineering supervisor. The job was interesting and paid well, but only served to remind JD that he wasn't commanding a ship. He became withdrawn and quick-tempered, to the point that Jeanne finally sat him down to hash things out. JD finally admitted that he could only be happy in the Navy or on the ranch, but didn't think Jeanne would want to move. Much to his surprise, she confessed that she was ready to get away from the war and the city. They had moved shortly after Katie's wedding in February.

The ranches had finally recovered from the trials of the Depression, but the work had taken its toll. Matt, the youngest of the Stevens siblings, was now nearly sixty-three, and both he and Alice at sixty-five were becoming arthritic from their years in the saddle. Will, at sixty-nine, had developed chronic lung problems stemming from dust pneumonia contracted in the wind storms of the Dust Bowl days. Phillip, now seventy-one, only rode while moving cattle and other easier jobs, preferring to use a pickup whenever possible, and had even delegated some of the investment management of the family's assets to a brokerage firm in Albuquerque.

Bob had begun training horses for Alice and Phillip within days of his arrival the previous August, and everyone was grateful to have him back working the ranch with them. Once JD and Jeanne got settled from their move, Matt's son Richard, especially, welcomed JD's experience and knowledge managing the cattle and the remaining two cowboys.

Will and Peggy's manager, a twenty-three-year-old bachelor, had been drafted into the Army not long before JD and Jeanne moved back, so they happily took up residence in the manager's house at the home ranch. Neither JD nor Bob took any salary from the ranches and were surprised to learn that their cousins, like them, were not stockholders in the corporation. Richard was well paid as a rightful employee and cousins Sylvia and Frances were happily disengaged from the business end of the ranches, although they and their families visited often. JD and Bob did well, living off their pensions and dividends from the stock portfolios Phillip had set up for them during the recovery from the Depression.

Allison had transferred to the University of New Mexico to complete her education and was spending her first full summer vacation with her new family. She and Bob spent hours on end together with the horses, where they found she had inherited her grandmother's instinctive abilities with a horse, and they rode for miles daily. He taught her the different species of plants and animals in the area as well as horsemanship and cattle sense, along with the philosophy and values of "the cowboy way." She still maintained cordial ties with her adoptive siblings, but had parted ways with her mother and stepfather completely, having fallen completely in love with her newfound family and rural lifestyle. She was studying Elementary Education and could think of no better career than teaching in a small-town school, hopefully nearby.

JD grudgingly conceded his brother was right about their leaving the Navy at the right time. News of the kamikaze attacks on American ships struck home when the brothers learned of hits to *Tennessee, New York, California, Nevada, Mississippi, New Mexico, Maryland,* and *Colorado,* not to mention the aircraft carriers and dozens of destroyers and cruisers. JD admitted that command of a battleship in these last campaigns wouldn't be his cup of tea, although both brothers wished they could have been present at the battle of Surigao Straight, where American battleships and cruisers destroyed a Japanese task force with minimal losses.

Each naval victory made the family breathe a little easier, knowing that Little Phil was still aboard his submarine, and therefore still in harm's way. While the exact number wasn't disclosed, JD knew the Navy had lost at least thirty subs by the time he and Bob had left the service, a fact he kept to himself. He took comfort knowing the Japanese Navy was nearly nonexistent and that most of the American submarines were working hard just to find targets worthy of a torpedo.

Three weeks after the night of the thunderstorms and the "flash of lightning" JD thought he saw the morning after, President Truman announced that a new weapon of massive destructive power, the atomic bomb, had been used against Japan and eight days later Japan surrendered. Celebrations erupted across America. The celebration at the ranches was muted. Nobody was going to get too excited until Little Phil contacted them to say he was safe in port.

On August nineteenth, their wait was rewarded when a letter arrived from Pearl Harbor dated August tenth. Little Phil was safe and had been since the ninth when his sub docked for repairs and maintenance.

Christmas of 1945 saw a full family reunion. Every member of the extended Stevens-Jenkins family was gathered together for the first time in twenty years at the insistence of Alice. Even Little Phil had obtained leave, having been promoted to Lieutenant Commander and assigned to the office of the Commander of Submarines, Pacific.

Along with the celebration, a very cordial but very serious meeting of the family was held to discuss the future of Three S Land and Cattle Corporation. Alice, Will, and Matt agreed to identical estate plans that would secure a fair transfer of ownership of the corporation, while fairly providing salaries for JD, Bob, and Richard as the operational managers of the ranches upon the passing of the three family shareholders and their spouses. Both JD and Bob again refused salaries from the corporation while Alice and Phillip were alive.

Forty-Nine

July 7, 1947
Fort Sumner, New Mexico

JD closed the wire gate that separated the Stevens Ranch from their neighbor to the north, who just happened to be his Aunt Peggy's cousin, Everett Osterhaus. He and Everett's hired man had just finished cutting one of Everett's bulls out of a group of Stevens Ranch cows and trailed him back to where he belonged. JD volunteered to repair the gap in the barbed wire fence that was created when the bull decided to pay his uninvited visit, so the hired man could keep the bull moving on towards home. He removed his hat, wiped his forehead with his shirt sleeve, and looked at his watch. It was only nine o'clock, but already getting hot.

He rode the quarter mile back to the damaged portion of the fence where he had parked the pickup and trailer. He took the canvas water bag from the shade under the pickup and took a long drink, washing down two aspirin tablets for the all-too-familiar headache that announced an impending "visit."

He heaved a sigh and got his tools out to fix the fence. Thirty minutes later it was repaired. He was just about to take another drink when the familiar triangle began descending. JD was surprised to see it in broad daylight like this. The visitors had almost always come at night before this.

"Good morning, Captain," JD said aloud, "what brings you here in the middle of the day?"

"*Hello James,*" the voice replied in his mind, "*I'm sad to say I'm here to ask for your help.*"

"My help? What can *I* do to help you?"

"*I dispatched a small scout craft last night to obtain soil samples. We've been studying the radiation spread by your atomic bomb, as you call it. While my crew was obtaining these samples, I took this ship to rendezvous with a supply vessel outside your atmosphere. While I was away, my scout craft suffered a malfunction and crashed nearby. Two of my crew on the craft were killed.*"

"I'm truly sorry to hear that. But what does that have to do with me?"

"*It appears your military took the bodies of my crew before we returned. I was hoping you might assist me in getting them back so I can return them to their families.*"

"As you can see, I'm not in the military full time now, Captain, but I'll try." JD sympathized with the loss of crewmen and a commander's desire to bring them home. "Where was the crash?"

"*About eighty of your miles from here. If you'd like I could show you. It will only take a few minutes.*"

"I think that would help, yes."

The door on the craft began to open and JD felt the familiar sensation of weightlessness as he rose to the door. Crewmen escorted him to a room with a large, flat screen on the wall. A moment later, JD could see an aerial view of jeeps and trucks in a pasture strewn with debris, obviously the crash site. The view zoomed out, showing a town, then zoomed out again, showing the location of the town, the crash site, and the exact location of JD's pickup.

"*Do you know the town we're showing you, James?*"

"I do, Captain—and I'm fairly sure where your crewmen would have been taken. But it may take some time for me to find out for sure. I know you can find me easily, but it might not be safe for you to follow me until I know more. I'll keep my brother informed of developments and if you will contact him, he can tell you when it's safe to come to wherever I wind up. Does that make sense?"

"*It does make sense. One of the flaws in our capabilities is that our tracking devices stop working upon the death of any individual that has them. My crew and I have them as well as you and your brother, and all our test participants. But with my scout craft crew dead, I have no way to locate them.*"

"You have always been honest with me and my family, Captain. I'll do my best to help you, I promise."

"*Thank you, James.*"

He was escorted back to the door of the craft and gently deposited next to his pickup. The craft was gone in seconds.

JD quickly tossed the rest of his tools in the pickup, then walked several hundred yards to his horse which had spooked and run off from the ship. Riding back to the trailer, he loaded the gelding and started back to the ranch headquarters. His mind worked through how he could penetrate the bureaucracy of the military quickly enough to do any good. By the time he had bumped along the pasture road back to headquarters, he had a plan. He quickly unloaded and unsaddled his horse and after putting him in his pen, jogged to the house.

"Well, you finished that job quickly," Jeanne said cheerfully as JD came through the door.

"Sorry dear, but I don't have time to chat," JD said as he headed straight for the phone in his office.

"What's wrong, JD? Is somebody hurt?" Jeanne had

learned a great deal about ranching, and knew anything could happen when a bull was involved.

"No, nothing like that. I'll explain in a minute," he replied as he dialed the operator. "Hello, operator, I don't know the number, but I need to place a call to the Navy Department in Washington, D.C. immediately. It's a matter of national security. This is Rear Admiral James D. Roberts." JD prayed silently for some form of success. Finally, a receptionist at the Navy Department answered. JD explained who he was and that he needed to speak to the Chief of Naval Operations immediately. The civilian receptionist seemed almost amused, but humored him and transferred JD to another office, where a Lieutenant Jameson answered. JD used his security clearance this time to try to impress the urgency of the matter, but the Lieutenant just acted confused and placed him on hold. After a wait of several minutes, JD heaved a sigh of relief when a new voice answered.

"CNO's Office, Captain Dougherty," a calm voice answered. JD wanted to cry out in relief at his good fortune.

"Thomas Dougherty? From Minneapolis?"

"Yes, who is this?"

"Thom! This is JD Roberts. Thank God it's you. Listen, I don't mean to be rude but I need to speak with the Old Man and I mean immediately. This is absolutely a matter of national security."

"Wow, Skipper, it's good to hear from you. What's going on?"

"I used my Reserve rank to get through. I'm a Rear Admiral in the Reserve now. But I need to talk to the CNO immediately. It relates back to the incident you had on *Nevada* in late June of '44." JD was thankful he instantly remembered Dougherty's cover story for his assignment on BX-1, just in case ONI was listening. He added, "Is this a secure line?"

"No, but I'll put you through to the CNO on one right now. Call me back sometime and we'll catch up."

"Thanks, Thom. I will." *Maybe someday,* JD thought as he heard a series of clicks as he was transferred. Finally, the phone was answered again.

"JD, I assume this isn't a social call," the Chief of Naval Operations answered, sounding somewhat perturbed.

"I'm afraid not, sir. Admiral Nimitz, I was contacted an hour ago by the same alien craft that contacted BX-1. Believe it or not, the commander of the craft told me they launched a small scout craft that crashed here in New Mexico. Two crewmen, if you want to call them that, were killed, and their bodies were taken by our military. The commander would like the bodies back to take home."

"Are you serious?" Nimitz asked after an incredulous pause.

"Absolutely, sir. If I'm lying, I know the consequences. I'm telling you this as honestly as I did three years ago at Pearl, sir. I had no idea what else to do but start at the top and hope."

"JD, your luck with timing baffles me. I just got off the phone with Eisenhower, who just got off the phone with General Spaatz at the Army Air Force. I've just learned about this crash myself. Nobody knows about it yet except them and General Ramey, who's in charge of the Eighth Air Force and Roswell Army Air Base—so once again, I have to believe another crazy story from you."

"Do you know if General Ramey would have the bodies?"

"I really don't know much of anything, JD. I just know an unknown gizmo of some sort crashed in New Mexico," Nimitz paused for a moment, "and you know, JD, I think I should know more than that. Ike said even he didn't have all the details yet, either, but he has a more direct link. How fast can you shine up your stars and get to Roswell?"

"Two hours, maybe less."

"Well, as of right now you're back on active duty. Ramey is a brigadier, and he isn't in Roswell. Eighth Force HQ is in Fort Worth, so don't be afraid to pull rank as my liaison. The base commander is a colonel named Blanchard, I believe. I'll tell Ike you're going there and why, and ask him to order Ramey to cooperate."

"Am I free to demand the bodies?"

"Do you think it's really necessary, JD?"

"They asked me nicely, sir. The last time someone told them no, they fried three thousand Japanese sailors."

"You do have a way of turning a phrase, Admiral. I'll remind Ike of that little fact as well. By the way, just what do you plan to do with the bodies once you have them?"

"I have a feeling they'll find me, sir. And when they do, I'll return the bodies."

"Then get going. Report directly to me as you learn more."

"Yes, sir." JD hung up the phone to see Jeanne looking at him from the doorway, a gentle smile on her face.

"Want some sandwiches for the road?" was all she asked.

"You, my dear, are the most unflappable person I have ever known," JD smiled.

"Get in the shower. I'll pack a bag. Three days?"

"I guess. Who knows?"

JD emerged from the bathroom a few minutes later to find his dress khaki uniform laid out and a small, packed suitcase next to it, left open for his Dopp kit. He dropped it in and closed the case then put on his uniform. Grabbing the suitcase, he walked into his office, where he stopped to call Bob. Once aware of the situation, Bob agreed to keep the visitors apprised and would make sure Alice was made aware in advance. Jeanne met him at the front door with a sack of sandwiches and two thermos bottles, one with ice water, one with coffee.

"Be careful, JD," she said as she kissed him.

"I will be. Let Uncle Will know I got the bull put back and the fence fixed. I'll be back as soon as possible," he said. The two walked out together to the new Ford sedan JD had purchased just the month before. JD tossed his bag in the trunk and Jeanne set the food and thermos bottles in the passenger seat.

"Sorry for the short notice," he apologized as he hugged Jeanne.

"Such is the life of an interplanetary ambassador," she quipped. "Call me tonight when you can."

"Soon as I'm able," he promised.

The eighty-plus-mile drive to Roswell across the short-grass prairie was easy but hot. JD went through the water quickly, and stopped at a gas station on Highway 285 to refill his thermos, topping off his gas tank as an excuse for getting more water. He stopped again in downtown Roswell to get directions to Roswell Army Air Field located on the southern outskirts of town.

At the main gate, he took a deep breath, hoping word had gotten to the sentries. He showed his Navy ID card to the staff sergeant at the main gate, who looked at his clipboard and then saluted JD through, giving him directions to the headquarters building. Driving through the base, JD could see the sun glinting off the aluminum fuselages of the B-29's lining the taxiways. The 509th Bombardment Wing, part of the Eighth Air Force, was stationed here and trained pilots to drop atomic bombs. The thought chilled JD.

A Major was waiting outside the headquarters building

and escorted JD directly to Colonel William Blanchard's office. The Colonel had the no-nonsense look of an officer who ran a very tight ship, in JD's initial opinion. He also looked like he had already had a harrying day, and was now resigned to the rest of it going straight down the tube. Blanchard greeted JD with respect and a pitcher of iced tea, both of which JD was grateful for. Once behind closed doors and seated across from Blanchard at his desk, JD got straight to the point.

"Colonel Blanchard, I am aware that there was an incident up near Corona early this morning. I know that this incident involved the crash of a craft of unknown origin and type, and that the bodies of two nonhuman occupants in that craft were recovered along with the wreckage. As Admiral Nimitz's representative, I'm here to recover those bodies."

"You don't mince words, sir," Blanchard replied, his hard-featured face neutral. JD was glad they weren't playing poker.

"Unfortunately, I don't have the time for small talk. I'm hoping that General Ramey has briefed you based on information he should have received from General Eisenhower regarding my mission. If we had time to get to know each other, you'd find me a really nice fellow, but my mission is urgent."

"Admiral, I have received orders from General Ramey to inform you that this matter will be handled through his office in Fort Worth. That is the extent of my ability to comment on the matter, sir."

"I understand," JD replied evenly, as he mulled over his options. "Pass me your telephone, Colonel, and connect me to your base operator."

Blanchard dialed a number, turned the phone to face JD, and then reached for the pitcher on the end of his desk.

"More tea, sir?"

"Yes, thank you," then, to the operator, "this is Rear Admiral James Roberts. Get me the office of the Chief of Naval Operations in Washington and contact me in Colonel Blanchard's office when you're connected to Captain Dougherty. Tell him I need to speak with Admiral Nimitz immediately." He took a long drink of tea after he hung up, then looked across the desk at Blanchard.

"Don't take offense at what I'm going to say, Colonel. I know you're under orders. I ran a top-secret operation during the war myself and if I was General Ramey, I would order my subordinate to stonewall if some jerk from another branch showed up in my shop, too."

"You have a unique way of courteously insulting someone, sir."

"I really intend no insult, Colonel. It's the way things are done and we both know it. The simple truth is, I have information I can't share with anyone below General Ramey and was sincerely hoping General Eisenhower had communicated this to him before I got here. I just don't think General Ramey got the full picture and thus neither did you." The buzz of the phone interrupted JD, who gestured to Blanchard that it was his phone to answer or not.

"Yes?" Blanchard handed the phone to JD, saying, "Captain Dougherty." His poker face stayed impassive, but the color had retreated a little.

"Thom?" JD asked.

"I've got the Old Man on the line, sir," Dougherty replied, "I'm connecting you now." JD heard a click in the line, then Admiral Nimitz's voice.

"What do you have for me, Admiral Roberts?" he asked, his even tone sounding forced.

"Sir, I'm in the office of the Commanding Officer here

in Roswell, and he has been ordered to inform me that General Ramey's office in Fort Worth is running the show with regard to my mission," JD said.

"Nothing else?" Nimitz asked after a pause. JD made sure to keep the receiver away from his ear so that Blanchard could hear.

"Anything else?" JD asked Blanchard.

Blanchard's face had gone from pale to red. He simply stared at JD.

"Colonel Blanchard has nothing else to tell me, sir," JD added.

"Wait there, Admiral. Tell the colonel to wait, too."

The line went dead. JD hung up the phone and looked at Blanchard.

"So where are you from, Colonel?" JD asked nonchalantly.

Blanchard remained silent. For the next hour the two sat in silence. Blanchard began to show signs of stress, fidgeting in his chair, then pacing the floor. He wasn't sure who he should be mad at: this Rear Admiral with ties to the Pentagon, or General Ramey for squeezing him into this crack between the two most powerful officers in the United States.

JD was a little surprised at the lack of patience in an old bomber pilot after many long missions. He sat placidly, relying on the patience gained sitting in the Captain's chair at sea, knowing that even at ten knots you can eventually sail around the world. The phone buzzed again and Blanchard pounced on it.

"Yes? Very well, put him through." Blanchard looked at JD. There was a hint of a smug smile on his face, the first emotion he had shown. "Hello, General . . . Yes sir . . . Yes sir . . . Yes sir." The smile had faded. His face again began to flush. "But they're . . . Yes sir, but . . . And he . . . I see.

Yes sir." He hung up and looked at JD. After a long pause, he spoke.

"That was General Ramey. I apparently owe you a debt of gratitude, sir."

"How's that, Colonel?" JD was taken aback by the change in Blanchard's demeanor.

"In 1944, my bomber group began operations out of India. Every now and then we'd see this thing flying above us, sometimes as high as fifty thousand feet, and it would just zip right past us like we were standing still. Then in August, we were ordered to treat any unknown aircraft as a neutral. One day, my fighter group leader wanted to take off after this big bright object flying right in front of us about ten miles out. I had to threaten him with court-martial if he went after it. From what I just heard, you had a close-up encounter with this thing that prompted that neutrality policy. Sounds like I'd be dead if those fighters had attacked."

"I guess you could say that," JD replied, not wanting to give away too much.

"Well, thanks."

"You're welcome, Colonel. Now, about my mission . . . ."

"They're here on base, sir. They were supposed to be flown to Fort Worth tonight. I've been ordered to surrender them to your authority. General Ramey just relayed the order directly from General Eisenhower."

JD thought for a moment. "I'm assuming most of the men on base have a security clearance because of the nature of your training mission?"

"Yes sir."

"Do you have a way to sequester men without high level clearances, so they can't see out?"

"I can make that happen, yes sir."

"Thank you. May I use your phone again?"

"Of course, sir." Blanchard started to thaw a bit.

"Thanks." JD had the base operator call his parents' number. Bob answered.

"Tell them to come to Roswell Army Air Field one hour after they talk to you. Call me here at Roswell when they check in . . . hang on." JD covered the mouthpiece and looked at Blanchard. "What's the main number here?" Blanchard scribbled the number on a pad and handed it to JD, who read it to Bob. "Tell the operator to connect you to me in Colonel Blanchard's office. We'll be ready . . . sure, if they let you, but wear a uniform." JD hung up, then immediately called Admiral Nimitz again to inform him of the newest developments. As he placed the receiver back in its cradle, he puffed his cheeks out as he exhaled. "Now we prepare and we wait," he said to Blanchard.

"For what, if I may ask?"

"The commander of an alien ship will contact the man I just spoke with. He will be here one hour after that, at which time we will return the bodies to their ship to be taken home. I'll need you to sequester your men that don't have security clearances so they don't witness any of this."

"I'll call a drill for all personnel to shelter in the bunkers with the exception of eight men and my Flight Surgeon. He can bring the bodies from the morgue."

"You can shelter the entire base?" JD was impressed.

"You might as well know, we have several atomic bombs on site, sir. We're still not entirely sure what would happen if one of the warheads should start to leak radiation, or what might happen if their storage area were to be breached in an attack, so we have room for everybody to hunker down underground until my eight-man radiation response team can get the material contained. They obviously are highly credentialed."

"Obviously. Thanks for going to this trouble, Colonel. You'll understand my hurry and concern before long. I suppose you'd better let your base operators know that a Chief Warrant Officer Robert Jenkins will be calling for me soon."

"I'll let them know now. I'll also call my Flight Surgeon and let him know the plan."

"Before you do that, could you direct me to the can? Your tea is doing its job," JD grinned.

"Left at the office door and three doors on the right," Blanchard smiled back as he picked up the phone.

JD returned to the office, where he and Blanchard finally began a more relaxed conversation talking about their upbringing and careers. Blanchard impressed JD. He was intelligent, articulate, and had a vision for the new Strategic Air Command that put a new spin on air power in combat. With the official formation of the United States Air Force not far away, JD had the opinion that this man would have several stars before he retired.

Although they were beginning to get along, JD noticed that Blanchard never fully relaxed. He decided the tension was due to the fact that Blanchard knew something he had never experienced was going to happen soon, at a facility that he was responsible for, that just so happened to be housing atomic weapons. At 1730, chow call sounded. Blanchard called the officers' mess and requested two meals be brought to his office. He and JD were halfway through their meatloaf when Blanchard's phone buzzed.

"Yes," he answered, then handed the receiver to JD. "For you, sir."

"Admiral Roberts," JD answered.

"JD, it's me. We're leaving in five minutes," Bob said.

"We?"

"Yeah," Bob almost giggled with excitement.

"Very well. Thank you." JD hung up and looked at Blanchard. "You're up, Colonel. They'll be here in an hour."

"It's going to piss off my cooks, but oh well," Blanchard said as he picked up the phone. He dialed a number and waited a few seconds. "This is Colonel Blanchard. Execute a Radiation Containment Drill, Condition One immediately. I will give the all clear personally. Is that clear? Very well."

Alarms and sirens sounded a minute later, echoing all across the base. Buses and trucks suddenly appeared as if from the sky, pulling up in front of the mess hall, officers' mess, hangars, barracks and other predetermined rally points. Men began pouring out of buildings and boarding the vehicles in an organized stampede. Colonel Blanchard's staff car screeched to a halt in front of headquarters, where his two aides piled in and, after informing the driver that they were having a drill personally supervised by the CO, sped off. As they filled, the vehicles headed to a complex of bunkers on both sides of the runways of the base. MP's in jeeps began a final sweep of the buildings to make sure no slow pokes were left behind, then headed for the bunkers themselves, leaving a jeep parked in front of the headquarters building for Blanchard.

Blanchard called the Flight Surgeon's office and ordered the bodies, already loaded into an ambulance, to be driven to the hangar closest to headquarters.

"If you'll come with me, Admiral," Blanchard said as he rose.

The two walked out to the jeep, where Blanchard got in the driver's seat, moving a walkie-talkie from the seat to the dash, and headed to the hangar. They met the Flight Surgeon's ambulance on the hangar tarmac. Blanchard received word from his Chief of Security that personnel were assembling by units at the bunkers. Blanchard introduced JD to the Flight Surgeon, Major Steven Crawford. A few minutes later, Blanchard was informed all personnel were accounted for, except for Major Crawford, and were in shelters. Blanchard advised that the doctor was with him and repeated his order that everyone was to remain sheltered until his personal order cancelling the drill was given. Twenty-five minutes had passed since the alarm sounded. Twenty-five more minutes passed before JD looked up at the northern sky.

"There they are," he said calmly.

"Where?" Blanchard was trying to maintain his military bearing, but his excitement was obvious.

"Bearing about two-five, forty-five degrees above the horizon," JD answered.

The single bright light continued moving southwesterly towards the base at a high altitude. It slowed and passed over the base, then circled slowly to the west and began a gradual descent.

"Holy God," Blanchard breathed, "how big is that thing?"

"About three hundred feet long, one hundred feet wide," JD replied.

The craft continued its slow descent until finally it hovered ten feet off the concrete, fifty feet from the men. The doors on the front of the craft began opening until six feet separated the two doors. A few seconds later a man wearing the uniform of a Chief Warrant Officer in the United States Navy was visible in the doorway. He slowly floated out the door and down to the tarmac surface. After getting his balance, he strode towards the men, stopping a few feet away and saluting.

"Welcome to Roswell, Chief Warrant Jenkins," JD smiled. "Colonel Blanchard, Major Crawford, this is Chief

Warrant Officer Robert Jenkins."

"Just checking," Blanchard said as he returned Bob's salute. "You two *are* humans, right?"

"Very much so, Colonel," JD chuckled, then turning to Bob asked, "are they ready?"

"Yes sir, Admiral," Bob replied, "they would like four of us to support the coffins while they're carried aboard."

"Very well," JD said, "Major, I'll help you with the bodies, if you don't mind."

"Of course," Crawford said, his eyes still glued to the craft.

JD gently guided the shocked doctor to the back of the ambulance, where they unloaded a folding gurney and placed one of the undersized coffins on it, then rolled it to where Colonel Blanchard and Bob stood waiting. The four men hoisted the coffin off the gurney and JD looked up at the ship.

"We're ready, Captain," JD said.

Blanchard shot a curious look at JD that was immediately replaced with one of total surprise as the four men were gently lifted off the ground. A few seconds later, they stood in the bay of the craft. JD and Bob, having been in this area before, directed the other two men to set the coffin down. They were then sent back to the tarmac, where the second coffin was retrieved from the ambulance and the process was repeated. Once again back on the ground, the men saw a small figure standing in the doorway.

"*James, Robert, we are very grateful for your help today. The families of my crew will be grateful as well. We will depart for home now. Our mission was nearly complete when this accident occurred.*"

"We were happy to help. These men with me deserve your thanks as well," JD said aloud.

"*Please relay my gratitude.*"

"Will we see you again?" Bob asked.

"As for me and my crew, no, Robert. Another mission may return in the future, but not for some time."

"Then farewell, Captain," JD said. He saluted the figure, Bob, Blanchard and Crawford following his lead.

"Farewell, Admiral."

It was the only time JD had ever been addressed by rank by the being. He raised a hand and stepped away from the door as it closed. The craft slowly backed away from the men and rose several hundred feet, then shot into the early evening sky and disappeared.

"What the hell did I just see, Admiral?" Blanchard was shaken.

"A scientific research ship," JD answered, "minimally defended and armed, according to the commander of the craft."

"And that's what killed all those Japanese ships?"

"It did." JD realized Eisenhower had finally gotten the whole story to Ramey. "Now I hope you understand my urgency when I arrived."

"I do indeed. I hope you'll forgive any disrespect, sir. My initial orders from General Ramey were quite clear."

"Completely understandable. The captain of the ship asked me to relay his thanks, by the way. Now, we'd better get your men back to their chow."

"Oh, yes. I suppose so," Blanchard said, coming back to reality, "I'll have the mess send over more food to HQ, if you'd care to stay. Chief Warrant, can I get you anything?"

"No thank you, sir," Bob answered.

"I've been quite enough trouble to you, Colonel," JD said. "We'd best be on our way. I do need to call Admiral Nimitz before we leave, however."

"Of course," Blanchard said as he turned to Crawford. "Doc, are you okay to drive?"

"Yes sir, I think so," the major replied.

"Very good. Meet me in my office tomorrow at 0800. In the meantime, be aware that this incident never happened. Dismiss, Major."

"Yes sir."

The Flight Surgeon got in the ambulance and slowly drove off as Blanchard radioed the all clear to his security forces and ordered the radiation response team to headquarters for debriefing. Bob jumped in the back of the jeep and the three men drove back to headquarters. The first buses began arriving back not long after the three men entered the building. JD had to wait for the telephone operators to man their posts before he could call the Navy Department. Soon JD was connected to Dougherty. It occurred to JD that his old Gunnery Officer was putting in some overtime. It was 2130 in Washington.

"What the heck is going on, Skipper? The President himself just called the Old Man!"

"Sorry, Thom. This is above even your clearance. Can't say."

"Understood. Do you want to wait or should I have the boss call you when he's finished with Truman?"

"I'd better wait."

"That's fine, but Eisenhower is in line ahead of you."

"Trust me when I tell you he'll want to talk to me first."

"Well, the President just hung up. Let's find out." There was a short pause before Dougherty came back online with, "I'll be danged. You were right."

"Thanks, Thom. I'll give you a call soon," JD said before being transferred to Admiral Nimitz.

"The bodies have been delivered back to their ship, sir. They're headed home."

"Very well, Admiral. I'll relay the news to Ike and the

President," Nimitz said. "As you can well imagine, you'll be debriefed by ONI soon. In the meantime, you know that mum's the word."

"Absolutely, sir."

"Well done and thank you, Admiral. Ike sends his thanks as well."

"My privilege, sir," JD said as he hung up. He turned to Blanchard and extended his hand. "Colonel, we got off to a rough start, but I want to thank you very much for your assistance today."

"Good to meet you, sir. Safe travels," Blanchard said as he shook JD's hand.

"I do have one request of you, Colonel. Just as you told the major that this never happened, when you and I are debriefed, I don't think that Chief Warrant Officer Jenkins needs to be in the narrative."

"I have no idea who you're talking about, sir. You arrived alone and left alone. My sentries and Flight Surgeon will confirm that."

"And I have no idea what you keep in those bunkers. Chief Warrant, shall we?"

"By your leave, Admiral." Bob stood and walked to the door, where he turned and saluted Blanchard. "Colonel, I thank you sir."

JD saluted as well.

"Chief Warrant, Admiral," Blanchard replied as he returned the salute.

The brothers walked out to JD's car. Bob remembered protocol and opened the rear passenger door for his superior officer. JD grinned, thankful Bob remembered. He certainly had not. They drove back into Roswell and Bob parked in front of a diner on Main Street. His refusal of dinner to the Colonel was to avoid eating warmed up Army food. Actually, he was starving. They ordered hamburgers and French fries to go, and refilled the thermoses with coffee for the drive home.

When they returned to the car, JD got behind the wheel. They drove to a gas station that was still open to top off the tank, and JD called Jeanne and Alice from a pay phone to let them know he and Bob were on their way home. He told them that should anyone call for Bob, they were to say he was fishing up near Angel Fire and would be home late that night. Back in the car, they drove in silence for several miles, eating their dinner as night settled in on the highway.

"That was quick thinking back there, JD. I should have stayed home," Bob said apologetically.

"You were fishing. What are you talking about?" JD smiled.

"The Captain let me on his bridge," Bob said after a pause.

"Really?" JD perked up immediately. "What's it like?"

"No helm, no seats, just a big bank of screens, kind of like radar, but completely flat and different colors. They just touched different parts of the screens to control the ship. We left the atmosphere for a while."

"You were in *space?* You lucky dog!"

"Yeah. I don't know how high we were, but I could see the Pacific and the Gulf of Mexico at the same time. It was quite the flight."

"Then it was absolutely worth you coming along. I envy you, brother."

"Envy me for what? I didn't catch a single fish. Just ask Dad and Momma."

They drove in silence again as they finished their meals. Bob put the wrappers back in the bags and refilled JD's coffee before he spoke again.

"You won't believe this, but Momma cried when she

found out they were going home."

"You're kidding me, right?" JD said as he cast a sideways glance.

"Nope. She said they know more than her doctor and now that she's getting old, they up and leave her," Bob said with a laugh. "I asked her if she wanted to come with me, but she said she'd been on the ship enough times to suit her."

"That's our Momma," JD smiled.

"Did Jeanne tell you Little Phil called?"

"No. I guess I didn't give her much of a chance to talk."

"Then I guess I ruined the surprise. He'll be home on leave next week."

"Hot damn and hoorah! That's great news!" JD exclaimed.

"I thought you'd like to hear that. Momma's tickled to death."

"I bet she is. I've really missed that boy!" JD's smile shined in the light from the dashboard.

He was about to ask another question when a jackrabbit darted out in front of the car, flashing in the headlights. A split-second later, a larger animal ran onto the road in pursuit of the jackrabbit. JD tried to slam on the brakes, but the sound of the bumper striking the animal and the bump of the passenger side tires going over it shook the car. JD had to fight to keep control, but was able to stop the Ford without leaving the road.

"What the hell was *that?*" JD exclaimed.

"I'm not sure," Bob said, shaken, "turn around and let's find out."

JD made a U-turn in the empty highway and started back. Seventy-five yards ahead, the figure of an animal came into the headlight beams, lying motionless on the pavement. JD slowly drove past then turned around again, stopping with the beams of the headlights squarely on the animal. The brothers got out and stared at the creature. It looked something like a dog: the body was about the size of a coyote, but it had slightly shorter legs, a lower jaw that appeared a little too short for the face, and was hairless. The two were silent for several seconds before Bob began snickering, then lost control as the snicker escalated into uncontrollable laughter.

"No way. No damned way," he guffawed. "Only us. I swear, crap like this could only happen to us. Not even Dad and Momma will believe this!" He couldn't talk any more for laughing.

"It can't be," JD said, starting to laugh as well. "This simply can't be what I think it is. They're not real." His laughter increased at the absurdity of the situation.

"Oh yeah? Neither are spacemen!" Bob said, trying to catch his breath, and then collapsed against a fender laughing again. "They ain't real either!"

"Thank God you weren't here to see it!" JD said, sending both of them into another round of hysterical, fender-pounding laughter. Finally catching his breath, JD reached down and took the animal by the tail, dragging it to the shoulder. "We better get moving before somebody comes along," he said.

Bob had regained a little composure, but cracked up again as he got back in the car.

"What now?" JD grinned as he closed the door and dropped the car in gear.

"It would be just our luck . . . for a game warden to show up," Bob gasped between more paroxysms of laughter, "and write you . . . write you a ticket . . . for killing a Chupacabra out of season!"

JD was able to keep driving but just barely. Finally, the two were simply not able to laugh any more.

"Oh Lord, JD," Bob said, wiping his eyes, "when the hell will we ever have a normal life?"

"Damned if I know little brother," JD chuckled as he shook his head incredulously. "Maybe someday."

Acknowledgements

This book was inspired by memories shared by my father. I felt I owed it to him to mention him in a couple of places.

Men like Charles Reordan, Chester Nimitz, Frank Jack Fletcher, Raymond Spruance, and William Halsey were my heroes as a boy and still are today. The responsibility borne by these men was beyond what most people could comprehend, let alone cope with, and I have strived to reasonably divine their responses to the incredible events that I presented to them. I hope I have honored their memory. All references to them and other historical figures in this story are, however, purely fictional.

Whenever possible, I have tried to place my characters in places and on ships that actually existed and actually went on the missions portrayed. Within that historical context, however, all the events of this story are also fiction.

About the Author

K. W. NEWENS grew up in southeastern Colorado, where he spent nearly all his time, outside of school, working for and with his two uncles, farming and feeding cattle. His father, a Navy veteran, worked for the Department of the Army. His father's service memories, coupled with travelling to veteran-related reunions and meetings, sparked K. W.'s lifelong interest in military history and hardware.

He graduated from Colorado State University as a Doctor of Veterinary Medicine and returned to southeastern Colorado to practice mostly large animal medicine. A small-scale stockman and animal lover, he has had to feed at least one animal (and sometimes dozens) of some kind every day of his life from age six on.

The odd man out in his family, his wife, daughter, and son are all teachers. Both he and his wife are enthusiastic trout fishers, and spend as much time on the waters of Colorado as they can.

www.ingramcontent.com/pod-product-compliance
Lightning Source LLC
Chambersburg PA
CBHW051559100726
47898CB00001B/156